NAUTICAL
CONTRABAND

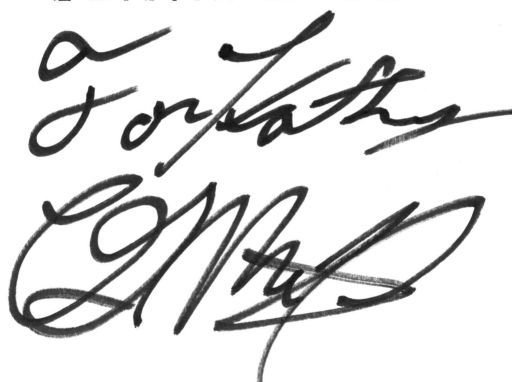

Books by
C. G. McDaniel

DEUMBRA
NAUTICAL CONTRABAND

Upcoming
RHUMB LINE BEND

NAUTICAL CONTRABAND

A Krewe of Jupiter Novel

C. G. McDaniel

iUniverse, Inc.

New York Lincoln Shanghai

NAUTICAL CONTRABAND
A Krewe of Jupiter Novel

iUniverse, Inc.

For information address:
iUniverse, Inc.
2021 Pine Lake Road, Suite 100
Lincoln, NE 68512
www.iuniverse.com

ISBN: 0-595-32339-1 (pbk)
ISBN: 0-595-66532-2 (cloth)

Printed in the United States of America

For more information on the Krewe of Jupiter series of novels by C. G. McDaniel, visit www.Krewe-of-Jupiter.com on the World Wide Web.

For My Wonderful Cecelia,
without your love and support,
this and all my other dreams would be without meaning.

PROLOGUE

▼

September 1983

There *are* few things more beautiful than a straight flush: the ripples of silvery moonlight on brackish water beneath cane fishing poles; the far-off moan of a midnight freight train calling not once, but twice; or the bare silhouette of the girl next door at her second-floor bedroom window.

However, at this moment, I couldn't seem to recall those visions as I laid out the cards in front of me.

"Gawdamn," my friend Buddy sputtered. "Will you look at that?" He grinned, slapping me on the back of my uniform so hard my teeth clattered together. Anthony Phillips, or "Buddy Bear" as he is known around the Citadel campus, is a big guy. He's six foot two and weighs in at about two-eighty.

If you saw him walking across the commons, you'd wonder how the Citadel ever admitted such a slob. Buddy seldom wore his uniform cap over his too-long-for-regulations dirty blond hair. He always had the collar of his uniform unbuttoned because his huge neck was so huge. Usually one or two other buttons had escaped their tenuous holes, and patches of white T-shirt were always peeking through.

It would be easy to dismiss Buddy Bear, but that would be a mistake. He came from Savannah, and everyone knows how well Savannah keeps secrets. Charleston has always been the outgoing princess of the South, and Savannah has always been the not-as-popular stepsister. Folks from Savannah know how to present the public face that everyone expects, and how to savor and keep their true presence to themselves like a long steaming pot of low-country boil.

Buddy was like that bubbling pot. With the lid on, he presented just the face that everyone expected from him. If he over-boiled—Well, let's just say that it takes all kinds of crustaceans and hot spices to make a low-country boil.

This time, we were in way over our heads. As seniors at the Citadel, we thought that we were big men on campus. We got weekend passes to chase the fair ladies and indulgences of Charleston almost every weekend.

Buddy and I had been roommates since our first year as knobs. I was a computer science major, and he was big into the military sciences. His old man had won all kinds of ribbons in battles mostly forgotten, and he had bred Buddy from an infant to be a military man. His dad was totally dismayed over his son's flabby exterior, but behind that shell Buddy had one of the best military minds I had ever known.

We were tired of going to the same clubs down by the old market every weekend. We were seniors and wanted some new action. I had heard about a weekly poker game that was held in the backroom of a little bar off Shem Creek.

Charleston is a peninsula, bordered by the Ashley and Cooper rivers that form Charleston Harbor before flowing out to sea. The surrounding area is dotted with barrier islands that shield the surrounding coast from the cruel slap of Lady Atlantic. Small tidal creeks and marshy rivers crisscross the surrounding areas.

Shem Creek was just such a tidal creek. You took the Cooper River Bridge from Charleston over to Mt. Pleasant. Shem Creek dissected Mt. Pleasant about a mile before you got to the rotating bridge that led to Sullivan's Island.

Shem Creek was shrimper's territory. The big shrimp boats lined the dock on either side of the tidal creek to rest for the night and dump their catch before heading back to sea at dawn. Restaurants and bars lined the docks for the fresh catch coming off the boats. Large fresh shrimp and crabs were hauled off the boats and onto the plates of Shem Creek patrons within minutes.

Shem Creek's establishments were reputed to have the best seafood in the low country, but there was always an air of seediness mixing in with the aroma of Old Bay seasonings. The weathered gray restaurants and bars all sported huge flashing neon signs that alternately advertised their names and their wares. An oyster-shell driveway led from the main road past each juke joint.

We felt as out of place as a priest in a whorehouse when we pulled my convertible '67 Jag E-type in front of Donnie's Shrimp-n-Beer. Our light-blue cadet uniforms fairly glowed among the drab workday attire of the shrimpers and locals.

That was okay. We weren't there for shrimp and beer. We were there for high-stakes poker. The backroom of Donnie's was rumored to be the place for some illegal poker action. In fact, it was near legendary how Donnie Rhodes had won ownership of several of the seedy establishments up and down Shem Creek through these very poker games.

Buddy and I walked into Donnie's place. It was salt-weathered gray clapboard on the inside as well as the outside. Yellowed pictures of trawlers and sloops hung on the walls. Fishing nets and glass floats hung from the exposed truss tin roof. The floor crunched with each step we took over the generations of peanut shells on the floor.

"How does this place ever pass health inspection?" I whispered. "Half the health inspectors in Charleston County owe Donny Rhodes money," Buddy whispered a little too loudly. Buddy had never perfected the fine art of whispering.

A large bar dominated the middle of the main room. We sidled up to it. The dim room was almost three-quarters full, and filling up fast. About twenty small round tables were set up around the perimeter. Patrons were getting down to business on big pots of peel-and-eat shrimp that were literally being dumped onto their tables; a few meaty red potatoes were mixed in for good measure. Waitresses in cut-offs and tube-tops, who were way too old to be wearing cut-offs and tube-tops, delivered the beer. The smell of shrimp, beer, and old peanuts was overpowering.

"I'll have a Heineken," I raised my finger to the bartender. He smirked, "We don't got none of that foreign crap. We got Bud and Miller on draft."

"Give me a Miller," I grimaced.

"Make that two," Buddy added. Buddy isn't quite as discriminate a beer drinker as I am.

As the bartender pulled the tap, I ventured, "Say, I hear there is some backroom action here?"

"I don't think there is anything here you college boys would be interested in," the bartender sneered. He was skinny with shoulder-length hair and mustache and cheek fuzz that never filled in.

I dropped a wad of bills, held together with a rubber band, onto the bar. The first three bills were fifties, with a hundred ones hidden underneath for padding. "Look, I've got the bucks to play."

The bartender snickered, "I know you Citadel boys think you are God's gift to Charleston, but I got news for you: Donnie Rhodes wipes his ass on more money than that."

"Okay then, how about this?" I laid the pink slip of the Jag on the bar.

Buddy grabbed my elbow, "Kris, are you sure about that? You've been restoring that car since you were fourteen."

"Yeah, I'm sure. I know we can beat these guys."

The bartender looked out the screen door to the parking area. "Is that a Sixty-seven?"

"Yep," I replied.

"Fully restored, mint condition?"

"Absolutely."

"Wait here." The bartender turned without waiting for a reply and entered a plain wooden door at the back of the bar. I heard the lock click behind him.

A couple of minutes later, I heard the lock click again and the bartender motioned us over. He ushered us into the room, then stepped out behind us. I heard the key slide into the lock, barring the door from the outside.

I had thought the main bar area was dark, but it took my eyes a minute to adjust to this new gloom. I felt Buddy take one step in front of me, always the protector.

There were four men sitting at an old foldout card table, a single, bare light bulb hung from the ceiling. This had probably been a storage shed at some point.

An older, white-haired man in a rumpled, tan three-piece suit chewed on a cheap cigar. The smell mingled with the odor of shrimp made me want to gag.

"Aw shit, Donnie! What are we running here, a daycare center?" This from a short, bald tubby guy with a '70s tie. Baldy was directing his comments toward a man with his back to us. A man I immediately knew was Donnie Rhodes.

Most surprising, however, was that sitting across from Donnie Rhodes was another Citadel cadet, uniform jacket hanging on the side of his chair.

"I mean, it's bad enough we have to let Bonnet in the game, but these two as well? Is this a card game or a fucking Citadel marching parade?" Baldy grimaced.

Donnie Rhodes turned in his chair to look at us, but directed his comments to Baldy, "Shut up, Livingston, they got a Sixty-seven Jag to put on the table; that's good enough for me. Pull up a chair, boys."

Rhodes was tailored, making his compatriots look even more dated. His shoulders were broad and his skin dark. He looked like a man who spent his days on his yacht and his nights in a pool hall. He even had a worn, blue wool captain's hat sitting on the table in front of him.

Tan-Suit pulled the stogie out of his mouth, "You want a Jag, Donnie; I can get you a Jag. I probably have one on my lot west of the Ashley, or I can get you one at the auction."

"Yeah," Rhodes grinned darkly, "but it's much more fun to take it from these boys than to buy it, Clyde."

As we pulled up chairs, I looked closely at the cadet. I vaguely recognized his face. I think he was a junior. He had that native Charleston blue blood look. He probably had a home address south of Broad Street.

I came from up-country South Carolina. If Savannah was considered Charleston's stepsister, we up-country Carolinians were definitely considered the bastard cousins twice removed.

The cadet nodded, "Evening, gentlemen, my name's Jason Bonnet. Take these seats beside me." His accent had unmistakable Geechee and Gullah undertones, definitely an old-blood Charlestonian. "Don't pay any mind to these old men. I'm going to take all their money anyway."

Livingston grumbled under his breath.

"Don't get too uppity there, Bonnet," Donnie Rhodes looked as though he smelled something putrid. "The only reason I let you in this game is because I know if I can't beat the money out of you, I can get it directly from your aunt Edna." When Rhodes said *directly,* it sounded thick and oily.

Jason Bonnet's eyes flashed for a second, and the corner of his mouth twitched slightly. Then his smile broadened over teeth that were far too white. "Oh, I don't think that will be necessary Mr. Rhodes."

This time it was Donnie Rhodes's turn to flinch, "Are we here to talk or to play cards?"

They gave me three grand in chips for the Jag; I knew it was easily worth four times as much. I gave Buddy the two-fifty in cash I had. He was out by the third hand.

This was definitely high stakes: one-hundred-dollar ante and no ceiling on bets. The pot for each hand was at least a grand.

After three hours of play, I was doing well, up by six grand, nine counting my original three. Livingston and Clyde were looking pissed. They were down to a couple of grand each. Bonnet was just behind me with five grand in chips. Rhodes, however, was steaming. This was a man who wasn't use to losing, and he was down to fifteen hundred in chips.

Livingston and Clyde folded. Now it was just Rhodes, Bonnet, and I. The pot was up to Rhodes's limit, and he called me. I had just laid down my beautiful straight flush.

Buddy got up to stretch his legs. Without thinking, he walked behind Rhodes. Livingston went off like the Citadel curfew alarm, "Cheat, cheat, the goddamn cadets are cheating!"

Buddy didn't even realize they were talking about him. Livingston and Clyde were out of their seats and had him pinned to the wall before he knew what hit him.

Rhodes drew a gun from beneath the captain's hat; it was a cheap, ugly .38 with a faux wooden handle.

He pointed it at Bonnet, "I know you're the ring leader here. Show your cards." Bonnet's gaze didn't stray from the gun. He turned his cards over slowly.

"A pair of twos," Rhodes foamed, "you punks were driving up the pot, so that your friend there"—gesturing toward Buddy—"could pass my hand to you."

Bonnet's eyes sparkled. "It's called bluffing, you schmuck, and my cadet friend there didn't get up until after you had already called the hand."

Rhodes was furious. "You calling me a liar, boy?"

"No, sir." Bonnet slipped me a look. "I'm just trying to show you the light."

And with that Bonnet heaved the card table over onto Rhodes. Taking Bonnet's cue, I went after the hanging bulb, ripping it from the ceiling in a shower of sparks. As Rhodes's chair tumbled backward, the gun went off with a flash and a report that nearly deafened me in the small tin-roofed room.

Before the light went out, I saw Buddy come to his senses and bang the heads of the two older men together. They slumped to the floor.

The door was right behind Buddy, and the flimsy lock was no match for his meaty shoulder. We spilled out into the bar and headed for the front door.

In the parking lot, we ran for my car. Looking furtively back at the bar door, Bonnet grabbed me by the shoulder. "Hey, can I hitch a ride with you guys?"

"Sure," I replied, as we hastily jumped into the Jag, "but don't you have a car here?"

"No," he grinned, "I rode in with my uncle."

"Your uncle?" I tilted my head, as we threw oyster shells everywhere pulling onto the main road.

"Yeah," Bonnet laughed, "Donnie Rhodes is my aunt Edna's soon-to-be ex-husband number four!"

As we jockeyed for space in the two-seater, we sped through Mt. Pleasant and into the massive open arms and multiple spans of the Cooper River Bridge.

Buddy looked at Bonnet in awe. "You mean your own uncle would pull a pistol on you and accuse you of cheating?"

Bonnet grinned again, showing that full set of too-white teeth, his dark hair blowing in the wind, green eyes snapping. "Well, it's not the first time, and I was cheating!" He turned his cadet cap over to show several cards peeking from the lining. "I've been feeding Kris and me the good cards every time I dealt!"

We all broke into laughter that echoed off the pillars of the mighty bridge and into Charleston.

"One last thing," Bonnet grimaced, "could you take me to the infirmary, I think I'm shot!"

For the rest of our days at the Citadel, we three were roommates. Then Buddy and I graduated and left Jason to finish his final year. We wouldn't see Bonnet again for another twenty years.

CHAPTER 1

▼

Donnie Rhodes dragged the drenched Mirasel from the deep-water tunnel into the shallower water of the cathedral-like cavern. Their guide, Remy, scampered out behind them, while a bellowing Jones Jenkins brought up the rear.

"What the hell was that, Remy?" Jones screamed, firing his pistol back into the tunnel! The shot produced an echo that seemed to shake the rock walls of the cavern.

"It must be the temple guardian!" Remy replied, frozen in fear, "But I thought those were tales told to scare small children on dark nights."

Donnie Rhodes grimaced, pulling his blue-wool captain's hat over his ears. "Well, whatever the hell it is, it's going to be making another go at us soon. That peashooter of Jenkins's just distracted it."

"We have to open the temple gate." Mirasel managed to look radiant even with her thick auburn hair plastered wetly to her pretty face. "The map made reference to opening the gate and trapping the guardian."

Jenkins raised his arm to backhand Mirasel. "Then open the fucking gate, bitch, before it's too late!"

Rhodes stepped in between them. "Touch her, you red-faced bastard, and I will personally feed your ass to those things!"

Remy nodded, "Yes, yes, the legend says you need to use the *zemís* as the key to open the gate."

They all ran to the center of the chamber where a gnarled, blackened tree stump jutted from the shallow water.

Pulling an ugly dark statue from her pack, Mirasel placed it gingerly in a carved alcove in the side of the stump. Immediately the alcove closed over her hand, and a great groaning of ancient machinery emanated from all around them.

The floor of the great cavern began to tilt from the center outward. Rhodes, Jenkins, and Remy fell to their knees in the shallow water. The chamber was turning into a great inverted funnel. The water ran off in all directions toward the outside edges of the cavern.

Remy was the first to understand what was happening, and he yelled above the din, "The guardian is too large to move out of the water. It will be trapped in the deep water of the access tunnel and will not be able to follow us."

Then the floor opened up around the ancient black stump, leaving Mirasel dangling from her trapped hand. She gave a little yelp and quickly found her footing on stairs that had appeared at the base of the tree and seemed to descend into darkness.

"The temple entrance!" Rhodes yelled.

"Out of my way, darkie! Some goddamn guide you are." Jenkins shoved Remy to the ground, made his way to the stairs, and started down two at a time.

Donnie Rhodes paused to give Remy a hand. "I'm sorry, Remy, you didn't deserve that."

"No problem, Mr. Rhodes, I've seen it from his type before."

The alcove opened and Mirasel pulled her hand free. She rubbed her wrist, eyes wide. "Look at the runes!"

Indeed, great symbols were carved into the tilted floor in a huge spiral that circled the temple entrance until it ended at the stairway.

"We have to translate this before we go any farther, Donnie," Mirasel pleaded. "It's not safe to go into that temple uneducated."

Donnie Rhodes grimaced. "I'm sorry, Mirasel, you know I like you, but I'm here for the ruby horde, and the other two treasures as well. The ancient guardian is trapped, and that so-called partner of ours is already ransacking the temple looking for those rubies. Stay up here and translate all you want, but I am going after those gems before that thieving Jenkins gets his hands on them."

Rhodes disappeared down the dark winding stairs.

"I'll stay with you, Ms. Mirasel," Remy smiled crookedly. They began at the far end of the cavern and the long spiral of runes.

✳   ✳   ✳   ✳

Rhodes entered the dimly lit subterranean floor of the temple. Thick dust filled the air.

Jenkins had already destroyed much of the chamber. It had once been an ornately carved room filled with statues and a huge altar to a long-forgotten religion. Now it was rubble. Taking an iron spear from one of the warrior statues, Jenkins had already obliterated each and every carving, hoping to find the rubies hidden inside.

There had to have been at least thirty priceless works of art in this room. They had no doubt taken decades for the skilled artisans to carve, and Jenkins had destroyed them in fifteen minutes.

"Where the fuck are the rubies?" he coughed in Rhodes's general direction.

Donnie Rhodes shook his head, "I don't know, but you are about as subtle as a goddamned grenade launcher."

"Screw you, Rhodes!" Jenkins sneered. "Do you want to find the rubies or not?"

"You know I do."

"Then stop your preaching and come over here and help me tear this altar apart."

Rhodes followed reluctantly.

✳   ✳   ✳   ✳

No rubies were found on the first level, but on the next level, they hit the jackpot. This level must have been some type of storehouse. Row after row of storage bins stood at least twenty feet high. And each bin held a single, perfectly cut ruby.

"That goddamned pirate!" Jenkins bellowed. "Why the hell did he have to put one ruby in each bin? It's gonna take us an hour to gather them all."

Rhodes shrugged, picking rubies as if they were oranges. "I don't know. Mirasel is the expert on all this. She could tell us for sure."

"Yeah, where the hell are Mirasel and our clueless guide?"

"I left them upstairs translating the runes on the cavern floor."

"Fucking waste of time."

"That's what I thought, too, but Mirasel isn't interested in the treasure. She wants the book that is in the last temple."

"Fine with me," Jenkins grumbled. "They don't help gather the rubies; they don't get a share."

Steely-eyed, Rhodes turned to Jenkins. "That's not the deal, and you know it!"

"I don't give a goddamn about the deal," Jenkins sneered, "In fact, I think I'll be taking all the rubies!"

Then he whipped out his pistol and pointed the ugly black barrel at Rhodes. "I think we have about all the rubies, so why don't you just pass your bag over to me and march your ass back up the stairs to join the rest of the gang."

"You're making a big mistake." Rhodes warned.

"Am I?" Jenkins snickered. "My only mistake was thinking I needed you morons to find the treasure. Now get up the friggin' stairs before I give you lead poisoning."

As Rhodes and Jenkins rounded the stairs back up to the temple level, Mirasel and Remy were just coming down from the cavern.

Rhodes ushered them all into a tight pack with a wave of his nasty little pistol.

Remy wailed, "What have you done to the temple? My ancestors will never forgive me for leading you here!"

"Shut up, you sniveling piece of shit!" Jenkins hit Remy across the cheek with the butt of the pistol. Remy folded onto the floor.

"Remy!" Mirasel screamed, covering her face with shaking hands.

Donnie Rhodes growled, "You really are an asshole, Jenkins."

"Yeah, well now I'm a rich asshole, and you three are deceased! But first, hand over the map so I can get to the next temple."

"Fuck you, Jenkins. I told you I burned the map. Now it's all in my head."

"Well, that's pretty interesting since I saw you studying it at Eden Rock last night, and I also saw where you hid it! Would you have one of your famous cigars on you, Donnie boy?" Jenkins sneered.

"I gave them up," Donnie mumbled, "They're bad for your health, you know."

"Ah, always the jokester, Mr. Rhodes. Let me rephrase it so you understand. Give me the cigar out of your left jacket pocket, or I will be forced to shoot sweet Mirasel in the head."

"Okay, okay!" Donnie held up his hands. He reached into his jacket pocket and pulled out the sterling silver cigar holder he carried. Then he carefully unscrewed the cap, pulled out the Cuban, and stuck it into his mouth. He tapped on the bottom of the case, and out popped a roll of yellowed paper.

"That would be what I am looking for, Mr. Rhodes." Jenkins smirked grimly. "Please have Mirasel pass it to me."

Mirasel took the map from Rhodes and handed it to Jenkins.

"Got a light?" Rhodes quipped, around his cigar.

Jenkins started backing up the stairs, pistol still trained on Rhodes and Mirasel. "Oh, I don't think you or your compatriots are ever going to see light again!"

When he got to the top of the stairs, Jenkins grabbed the *zemís* key from its alcove in the tree stump. The entrance to the temple snapped shut, and the inverted funnel of the cavern floor once creaked back to a level position. The water in the tunnel came pouring back into the cavern.

Jenkins crowed in triumph in the empty cavern as the water rose to knee level. He had that god-forsaken pirate's map to the other temples and he had the ruby horde. Now he just had to get past the ancient guardian. As good as he felt right now, nothing was going to stop him.

✳   ✳   ✳   ✳

Back in the temple, Mirasel sobbed in the near-total darkness. She had managed to find Remy and to support his head. He was alive but still out cold.

Donnie Rhodes chuckled. Pulling a match from his pocket and lighting it with the same movement, he encouraged the end of the cigar to glow.

"What's so funny?" Mirasel snapped. "Remy is hurt and we are buried alive!"

"My dear Mirasel, I love irony. This cigar is a Cuban, the genuine article, but that map I just gave our friend Jonesy was as fake as a three-dollar bill!"

"Then you really did burn the map?"

"Yes, ma'am, I did. I didn't want Jenkins or your family getting hold of it. I do, however, have a backup plan hidden safely in my room at Eden Rock."

"So what did you give Jenkins?"

"If he follows that map, he is going to be taking a prolonged tour of the Turks and Caicos, which is about as far from the next temple as he could possibly get."

Remy gave a groan and managed to sit up.

"Ah, it sounds like our friend is coming around. How's the head, Remy?"

Remy groaned, "My head isn't what I am worried about. I will be shunned by everyone on this island for what I allowed to happen here."

Mirasel frowned. "I don't think you have to worry about it, Remy. Jenkins has entombed us down here."

Remy pulled himself to standing. "One good thing, even if Jenkins does manage to find the next temple, he will never get in."

"What's he talking about?" Rhodes queried.

"The runes!" Mirasel exclaimed. "When I translated the symbols on the floor of the cavern, they revealed that we have to have another *zemis* key, which is hidden in this temple, to open the next one."

"Ah!" Rhodes took a deep pull on the cigar, "It's too bad we don't have the *zemis* that opened this temple gate. We could have used it!"

"Each key is specific to each temple," Mirasel explained, "but we do still have the original key. I'm a scientist, and I know better than to bring a priceless artifact like that into the elements. I made a plaster of Paris cast of the *zemis* and left the original at Eden Rock. The key we used upstairs was a fake; it will eventually melt away in the flooded room."

"Very good, Mirasel!" Rhodes fairly crowed. "But unfortunately neither the hidden key nor the one at the hotel does us any good right now."

"I think I can help with that." Remy grimaced. "There is another way out, but it's treacherous. We have to pass through the ancient guardian's nesting chamber. I hope the guardian is busy with Jenkins, and if we are lucky, it isn't hatchling season."

"Hatchling season?" Mirasel asked shrilly.

Remy sighed. "For thousands of generations, the ancient guardians have given birth, lived, and died."

Donnie Rhodes tipped his captain's hat in Remy's direction. "Sounds like fun. After you, kind sir!"

Remy led Donnie Rhodes and Mirasel into a darkness that would last for twenty years.

CHAPTER 2

▼

I should have known by the thickness of the salt breeze, and the way the fox tail palms were showing the backs of their fans, that a trouble storm was brewing. A little better than ten miles from the Jupiter Inlet, we rarely smell the sweet breath of Lady Atlantic so strongly.

The horses had been acting spooky for the last hour. My friend Anthony Phillips, affectionately known as Buddy Bear, and I had been watching their antics from the raised front porch of my barn at La Vie Dansante.

My name is Saint Kristopher Grant, and La Vie Dansante is my home. I guess my parents always knew I was a wanderer, and named me after the patron saint of travelers. My home's name comes from an old Jimmy Buffett song, and is French for "The Dancing Life." The name is quite appropriate for my Jupiter, Florida, spread. My wife, Lillian, competes on the dressage circuit. Under her knowing hand, her horses fairly dance across thin air.

We sat, watched, and rocked as the horses fled, and the big dark boomers came rolling in over the trees from the ocean. Soundless heat lightning flickered to the north and south as the approaching storm bulldozed the air in front of it.

I heard a low rumbling sound that I thought was the first peals of the approaching storm. But then I realized it was coming down the road that fronted La Vie Dansante. I could only see a gray outline at first—some kind of low-slung sports car approaching with no lights in the evening shade. The motor was a big American V-8, no confusing that music with the sound of the so-called modern wind-up boxes of today.

We stood, simultaneously shielding our eyes, squinting for a better look. Buddy has eyes like a damn cat, and he made it out first. "It's a Vette, pre-Stingray, I think."

And then I could see it clearly, too. "It's a Vette, all right," I whistled, "a nice one, too, a Fifty-nine or a Sixty; see the double headlights?"

"Yep." Buddy grinned. "Sexiest ass the General ever put on a car was on the Sixty Vette."

I started to agree but was surprised when the Vette turned into the drive in front of my barn gate. We walked up to the gate through the pasture grass to greet the stranger. It was a good fifty yards, and night had truly fallen now. The velvety bowl that made up the Florida night sky let few stars through in the stormy darkness.

We had to get within five feet of the gate before the stranger turned off the rumbling old Vette and got out. As he turned to face us, I would have known that smile over far-too-white teeth anywhere.

"Jason Bonnet," I exclaimed, "I thought for sure you were dead by now!"

Bonnet beamed, "As Mr. Clemson would have said, 'Reports of my denial have been exaggerated!'"

That was a typical Jason Bonnet misquote. Jason hadn't changed a bit. He still had that same Charleston blue-blood air; dark hair, snapping eyes, carved-out-of-stone profile that made the women melt.

Jason walked through the open gate and slapped Buddy on the back. "Buddy Bear, as I live and breathe, I knew old Grantford over there was here, but I didn't know you were in this neck of the woods, too!"

Grantford. I hadn't heard that nickname in twenty years. Bonnet had been the only one ever to call me that. We had all been roommates during Buddy's and my senior year at the Citadel.

Jason Bonnet was the consummate con artist. He thrilled at wooing the ladies; it was sport to him. He usually had several shady schemes going on at any single time. We were constantly bailing his ass out of trouble, but you couldn't dislike Jason; no one did. He was a charmer. He was good at it, and he knew it.

Once twenty years ago, on a late night in our dorm room, lying awake in our bunks, he had given us some insight into his personality. He said it was all in his genes.

I remembered his hoarse whisper in the dark, "I'm descended from the notorious pirate Stede Bonnet. I'm the great-great—great-grandson of the Gentleman Pirate who was hung at the Charleston Battery, and buried with all his men below the low tide mark."

Going to school in Charleston, we knew the legend of Stede Bonnet. Everyone did. Stede Bonnet was rumored to have talked himself out of jail, into the bed of Charleston's blue-blood ladies, and almost out of hanging. The women of Charleston were said to have mourned at the gallows at his passing.

Gentleman Pirate was definitely a term that also applied to Jason Bonnet. You never knew what was a lie and what was the truth. Twenty years later, I still had no problem believing his ancestors had been rovers on the high seas.

Bonnet shook my hand. "It's good to see you again, Grantford. I'm down here on special business and wanted to look you up."

"Plus"—he gave us a way-too-familiar look—"I need y'alls help with something."

I looked at Buddy, and he looked at me. The sense of déjà vu was overwhelming. How many times had Jason Bonnet gotten us into trouble in the past with those very same words?

With that, the sky finally opened up. When it rains in Florida, it doesn't last very long, but God will do his damnedest to drown you in the short period he has.

Huge pelting raindrops hammered us. The top was down on the Vette. "Jason, put your top up," I screamed over the torrential roar.

"I can't." He grinned crookedly. "I just stole it and I don't know how!"

I rolled my eyes at Buddy. I couldn't let this beautiful car get ruined. "Open the gate wide, Buddy!"

He ran and opened the gate. I grabbed the keys from Jason and jumped into the Vette. I fired it up and, as quickly as possible, pulled the car into the dry center concrete hallway of the barn.

I motioned to Jason and Buddy, and we made a break for the main house. The storm was upon us.

CHAPTER 3

▼

We crossed the three hundred yards from the barn to the house in record time, but we were still soaked to the bone. We stomped and shook the rain from our hair as we made our way around the circular porch toward the front door.

Jupiter, Florida, is really divided into three main areas.

Jupiter Island is the barrier island on the east side of the great Intracoastal Waterway. You can't see the twenty-thousand-square-foot mansions from the road because that is considered the backside of the house. Take a trip up the Intracoastal by boat for a jaw-dropping view of where you live when money is only a way of keeping score.

The second area of Jupiter is where the regular folks live. The heart of Jupiter is a big melting pot that runs from the west side of the Intracoastal to I-95. It's about ten miles wide.

Planned subdivisions and supermarkets, sidewalks and inline skaters are slowly encroaching on the heart of Jupiter. It's a constant struggle to keep that old Florida feel while still having a pizza delivered in fifteen minutes or less. I fear it's a losing battle.

Then there is west of Jupiter, known by the locals as Jupiter Farms. West of I-95, it's still only ten minutes to the sea. Cow pastures go on for as far as the eye can see. There are generations of families living on their land. There are estate homes, citrus groves, and equestrian farms.

The lawns are a little less manicured, as a kind of homage to the Florida swamps and jungle that were here before the homes were built. Huge trees dripping with moss form a canopy over dirt roads. Tropical birds, the second and third generations of pets that escaped long ago, flit from tree to tree. The Loxahatchee River crosses the land on its way to the sea, and it's filled to the brim with snook, tarpon, and green shrimp. It isn't uncommon to see people on horseback riding the canals and back roads.

That is why Lil and I love this land. Jupiter Island has given up the ghost to the new Florida. The heart of Jupiter fights the demon daily, but Jupiter Farms is still old Florida through and through.

I didn't even get my hand on the door handle before it opened. There stood Lil, hands on hips, all five foot six inches of her. Lil's brown eyes were snapping, and I could tell by the tilt of that blond head that we were in trouble.

"No way, guys." She tapped her foot. "There is no way you are setting foot in my house looking like that."

I looked down at our dripping clothes and mud-spattered shoes and grinned.

Buddy stammered, "No problem, Lil, we were planning on staying on the porch anyway."

I caught the slight twinkle in Lil's eyes as she regarded Buddy like a mischievous child. "I know Kris doesn't know any better, he has those up-country Carolina manners, but I expect more from you, Buddy!"

I grinned at Lil as Buddy examined his shoes and mumbled, "Yes, ma'am." Buddy has always had a little bit of a crush on Lil. She and I both knew it. It was innocent enough. But she loved to push his buttons when she got the chance.

Jason had been hanging back a little, but now he stepped forward, thrust out his hand, and beamed that smile at Lil. "Pleasure to meet you, ma'am"—he lifted her hand to kiss it—"My name's Jason Bonnet."

Lil yanked her hand back as if she'd been bitten by a snake. "Oh, I know exactly who you are, Mr. Bonnet." She took a half step backward, "My daddy told me all about you. I sure hope you have grown up and lost some of your family ways."

With that, Lil turned her attention back to me. "Why don't you guys stay out on the porch till you dry?" She gave me that wife-to-husband look. "I'll have one of the twins bring you some Rolling Rocks." And she shut the door.

We made our way to several cane-bottom chairs sitting on the round porch. Jason looked at me quizzically, "What did she mean that her daddy warned her about me?"

I grinned, "Remember the old guy who hung around with your uncle, the one who owned all those car lots and convenience stores?"

"Yeah." His brow furrowed. "What was his name, Clyde?"

"Yep." I smiled, taking a beer that my daughter, Sarah, brought out. "I married Clyde's daughter!"

"You're shitting me!" Jason hooted.

"Jason," Buddy hissed motioning toward Sarah, "We got a kid here."

"Oops, sorry," he grinned, beeping Sarah on the nose. She handed out the other beers and went skipping back into the house.

"It's interesting to hear Clyde's name again, since the matter I need help with has to do with dear old uncle Donnie," he lowered his voice a notch.

Buddy grimaced, "I don't know if I want to know. You've been here twenty minutes and you already have us hiding stolen property for you." He gestured toward the barn.

"Yeah, why don't you tell us about the stolen Vette before you start dragging us into the seedy life of Donnie Rhodes?"

Jason held up both palms. "Okay, okay, I guess the Vette isn't really stolen. I just kind of borrowed it without permission."

I let out a long sigh as Jason began his tale.

CHAPTER 4

▼

Jason grinned a crooked smile. "The Vette is actually kind of Aunt Edna's once removed."

"Whatever that means," Buddy huffed.

Jason playfully punched him on the arm but hard enough to leave a bruise. If anyone else had done that to Buddy, there would have been nothing but table scraps left. I saw his eyes flare and then the anger dissolved into mirth. It was just damn near impossible to stay mad at Jason.

"How's Aunt Edna doing anyway?" I remembered her as pretty old when we were in college; she must be ancient now.

"Oh, she is as feisty as ever. She just put husband number six in the grave. She has outlived all of them but Uncle Donnie." He recalled fondly.

"She's still on me all the time about making something out of my life. She says it's a disgrace for a Citadel graduate and a man of my age to still be living with his widowed aunt."

Buddy and I exchanged looks out of the corners of our eyes.

"But I keep busy," he defended himself, "I opened myself up a little business, kind of a proactive detective service.

"Charleston businessmen come to me when they think their wives have been or might be cheating on them. Instead of skulking around in bushes with a disposable camera, waiting for the lovely lady to slip up, I seduce them."

"A little wine, some low-country Bonnet charm, and you would be surprised at how many of them agree to join me in a night of frolicking at the old Planter's Inn downtown.

"Course when we walk in the door of the hotel room all lovey-dovey, they have no clue that their steaming hubby is right there to catch them in the act."

"Isn't that entrapment?" I asked incredulously.

"Of course it is, but you know how tight-assed and old-fashioned the courts of Charleston are."

He leaned in conspiratorially. "You know what else," he whispered. "Those women are really hot. You'd be surprised at how many of them welcome a post-divorce visit from ol' Jason Bonnet to help soothe what ails them."

We had been hypnotized into leaning inward toward Jason, but now we both jumped back like hot coffee had been thrown in our faces.

"You are the lowest of low," Buddy stammered, red-faced.

I felt for Buddy, knowing that he was transferring his own woes with to Jason's tale.

Buddy runs security for the world-famous Celestion Hotel and Resort on Jupiter Island. At close to a thousand dollars a night for some rooms, the Celestion has a renown clientele.

Buddy's wife had run off and left him about six months earlier. He was served with divorce papers at the Celestion. He almost put the server in traction when he tried to sneak over the sea wall. Not only was Lisa divorcing him, she also had an injunction preventing him from entering his own house. Even though she was on a yacht with her new billionaire boyfriend somewhere near Eleuthera.

Buddy had always made poor choices with women. I knew Lisa was a gold digger the first time I saw her. She had only wanted him for one thing, access to the Celestion's clientele. As VP of security, Buddy and his guests had free reign of the place. All it had taken was a little attention from the tight little blonde with the heavy breasts, and he was a goner.

They were married in less than a month, and she left him for a rich man twice his age in less than six months. The Big Guy had done everything he could for her, had treated her like a princess. She had used him and thrown him away like last year's Worth Avenue handbag. Buddy had been heartbroken and homeless for the first time in his life.

I offered the furnished apartment above my garage/workshop until he could get his life put back together.

"Oh come on, Big Guy." Jason punched him again. "I don't do anything with these women that they're not already doing anyway.

"Isn't it better that the poor sap who is married to her finds out before he gets hurt?" Bonnet gazed deeply into Buddy's eyes, connecting somewhere inside where the pain was still profound and raw.

Buddy hung his head. "Yeah, I guess you're right."

I shook my head. There was no way that Jason Bonnet had any idea what Buddy had gone through in the past year, yet he found that soft spot every time.

Jason was fully capable of using this power for his own gain—I was more than aware of that—but he and Buddy were old friends, and he'd used it to help heal his wounds just a little.

He drew back to punch him again on the arm.

Buddy grinned, "You rabbit-punch me again, Bonnet, and you are going to wake up on a gurney in the emergency room."

Jason faked fear and gave him a light tap instead. Buddy gave a faux growl and grabbed Jason in a huge bear hug. Both chairs went flying.

"Let me go, you behemoth," he squealed. And then it was twenty years ago, and we were all laughing, best friends again.

It's amazing how that happens. Friends wander in and out of your life like animals in a jungle clearing, close for a while and then forgotten. But there are a very few, who, no matter how long they've been gone, are always in your heart. You think about them daily, even though you don't even realize it. And when they return, they are your family, your compatriots, your partners; it's like they never left. That's the way we were, bonded by the Carolina waters and the marshes, and the Citadel rings on our fingers, forever brothers in a moment in time.

We set our chairs back up on their legs and clinked our emerald green Rolling Rock bottles. We were now totally focused on what Jason had to say.

"Well, as I was saying," he continued, "Aunt Edna just buried husband number six. It's been a rough few months for her, as Paw Bonnet just passed away last month as well."

I had only met Jason's grandfather once. He had been in his eighties back when we were in school.

I must have looked shocked because Jason said, "Yeah I know the old guy was a hundred and four when he died, and still had three girlfriends half his age."

"We Bonnets have always had very long constitutions." He grinned at his own innuendo.

"Anyway, when Paw passed, he left his entire estate to Aunt Edna."

"You remember Otis?" He queried.

"Sure." Otis had been Aunt Edna's butler, cum chauffeur, cum jack-of-all-trades for years. He'd come over from Barbados in the late fifties. I remembered him as a tall man, strong, dark, and noble. Fiercely loyal to Aunt Edna and her protector, he shared her dismay in Jason's lack of initiative. Aunt Edna's frustrations with young Master Bonnet were tempered with love. Otis just wanted to take Jason out behind the woodshed and introduce him to some hickory tea. Of course, Aunt Edna wouldn't hear of that. Jason had known this and had always taken great glee in pushing Otis's buttons whenever he had the opportunity.

"Paw had that great big house out on Sullivan's Island. Aunt Edna put together a list of all the art items she wanted brought back to her home on the Battery and sent Otis out to inventory the estate."

"Well, you know Otis; he is so damn thorough. He went through everything and realized that one painting was missing. It was a portrait of my great-great-great-grandfather himself, Stede Bonnet, the Gentleman Pirate.

"So Otis started tearing the house apart from top to bottom, looking for the portrait. He found a hidden panel at the top of the double circular stairway in the foyer. He located the secret trigger, and lo and behold, there was the framed missing portrait.

"So Otis was ecstatic, right? Then he slid the painting out and saw that it has been slit open from top to bottom. It happened so quickly that the defacer left his tool behind. Lying on the bottom of the compartment under a thick layer of dust was an old Bowie knife, with an ornately carved black wooden handle. And there was a tarnished silver medallion embedded in the wood. Otis blew off the dust and saw that the medallion bore the initials DR.

"So he brought the knife and the painting back to Aunt Edna. She and I were having tea on her piazza. Aunt Edna was sadly clucking over her ruined ancestor, when Otis showed her the knife. She recognized it immediately. She was so startled that I had to catch the painting before it hit the ground.

"She reached for the knife, and Otis carefully handed it to her. She gently stroked the black wooden handle with the ornately carved panther head on the hilt, careful not to touch its sharp fangs.

"Then she looked up at Otis with tears in her eyes. 'Do you know what this is, Otis? This was the wedding present that I gave my fourth husband on our marriage night.'

"Otis and I quickly counted backward and said in unison, 'Donnie Rhodes!'

"'Yes, dear Donnie, the rotten scoundrel,' she said, with a twinkle in her eye. 'Most of my dear departed husbands married me for my money, never planning to work another lick in their life. Donnie, on the other hand, was quite the entrepreneur and owned several disreputable businesses. Oh, he wanted my money, too; he just liked to put it to use in numerous shady deals.'

"'He was the only one of my six husbands I divorced; the rest passed on. Donnie had so many back-alley deals going in Charleston that he had to leave town or face arrest.

"'I set him up as part-owner of some little motel I had picked up down in Florida. Sent him away in the middle of the night with his clothes in a paper sack thrown into the passenger seat of that old yellow sports car of his.'"

"The Vette?" I interrupted.

"Shhh," Buddy hissed.

"Aunt Edna started the divorce process the next morning," Jason continued.

"So all that time, I'm holding this painting that I had caught, face-down. I happened to notice that there was something on the back of the canvas. I took a closer look. There was an ink stain from some kind of diagram."

"Like the shroud of Turin?" Buddy whispered, wide-eyed.

"Something like that," Jason murmured, "Anyway Otis being Otis doesn't think I'm capable of figuring it out so he got his magnifying glass out and started examining the thing.

"Aunt Edna has built Otis a little lab in her house. Otis told her some years ago that he was disappointed that he had never gone to college. Aunt Edna being the kind soul that she is promptly insisted that he start attending school at night at her cost. Well, that was twenty years ago and she would never let the man quit. He has masters' degrees in architecture, mathematics, and finance, and doctorates in chemistry and biology."

"You mean to tell me," I hooted, "that you have to call him Doctor Otis now?"

"Nope"—a sly grin crossed Jason's face—"I specifically still call him the Big O just like I always did, which continues to drive him crazy."

Jason's grin warmed into a fond smile. "I have to hand it to him. With all his degrees, he could have done anything, but he is loyal to Aunt Edna just as he always was. He keeps his skills sharp by working on consulting projects at night. He is actually well respected around the world for his abilities.

"So Otis disappeared into his lab for an hour and came back, with a solemn look on his face."

With his best Barbados accent, he imitated Otis, "Ms. Edna, it appears that there was once some sort of map hidden beneath this painting. Over the years, the sun's rays heated the canvas and the map's parchment and caused a partial ink transference. It's very faint, and all I can really tell you is that whatever the map leads to appears to be in the general direction of the Caribbean."

Lapsing back into his regular voice, Jason continued, "There was another spark of recognition in Aunt Edna's eyes, but she said nothing. Otis added, 'Ms. Edna, I also need to tell you, that I was able to get enough of an ink sample from the canvas to date the map. It appears to be somewhere between two hundred fifty and three hundred years old.'

"Aunt Edna started to cry. You guys know me; I can't stand for Aunt E to cry. I tried to comfort her, but she suddenly stood up and looked Otis and me in the eyes. 'I would trust the two of you with my life,' she said. 'You must both go to Jupiter Island, Florida, to the Gator Tail Inn. Find Donnie Rhodes, and find the missing map. That good-for-nothing carpetbagger took it; I'm sure he did.

"'In fact, Donnie disappeared only six months after leaving Charleston, and he left the Gator Tail to fall into ruins. I don't know what's left of the place, but if there are any clues as to what happened to that map, they will be there.'"

We let out a collective breath. Buddy whistled, "So you mean that Donnie Rhodes and that map might be right here in Jupiter?"

"Well, after being to the Gator Tail, I kind of doubt it," he smirked.

"Otis and I got down here this morning. We fought like cats and dogs all the way from Charleston, in that big Caddy that Aunt Edna owns. I figured he and I would give the place a quick once over, I would come out here and see Grantford, and then we would be gone.

"The Gator Tail Inn isn't quite what we expected."

"I bet," I smirked. "I've never heard of it and I can't picture big-money Jupiter Island having a place called the Gator Tail Inn."

"Well, they haven't in at least fifteen years. The place is an eyesore. It sits just off the bridge, on the Intracoastal, kind of tucked back into a corner where it isn't obvious. Seriously prime real estate. I think Aunt Edna's lawyers have been approached multiple times about selling it, but she wouldn't budge. I guess she kind of kept it for sentimental reasons and all.

"So Otis and I finally found the place, and it was a good thing because another ten minutes in that car and one of us would have killed the other.

"The big surprise is that Uncle Donnie had worked his entrepreneurial magic on the Gator Tail. He had turned her into a topless bar and associated cheap-ass motel."

"Man, oh man," Buddy muttered, "I bet the founding bigwigs of Jupiter Island loved that."

"Well," Jason said, "they haven't had to worry about that house of ill repute for some time. Now they just have to worry about it falling in on itself and trapping some misguided wino, or maybe Otis.

"The place is in horrible shape. Big alligator neon sign with a come-hither look on its face. Used to actually move its tail, but the neon tubes are all busted and the motors are frozen up. It's all early Fifties Florida Howard Johnson style buildings, ceiling tiles sagging from rain leaking inside and a plywood stage leaning and collapsing. There's a not-so-discrete door in the bar leading to the motel check-in area. You could probably get a lap dance and a room as a package deal in those days.

"I could just see Uncle Donnie, huge cigar hanging from his teeth, sitting in a dark booth in the corner, leering at the girls on stage, leering more at his patrons and their rolls of twenties.

"It should have been condemned years ago. The only thing it has going for it is a beautiful waterfront dock area on the Intracoastal. The Gator Tail itself would cost more to knock down than it's worth. The land is probably worth a cool million."

"Try four or five million," I stated flatly, "Jupiter Island is the most expensive real estate in the U.S."

"So Otis and I were going room to room sorting through all this rubbish. I admit I was trying to get his goat, telling him since he was the hired help, I should be supervising his work, while sitting back drinking a piña colada. Well, he, of course, didn't appreciate that one bit. So he was getting angrier and angrier, and once I find the right button with him, I can't help but jump up and down on it."

I rolled my eyes. How many times had I seen that happen?

"So he was really about to blow his stack when we entered a room that must have been like Uncle Donnie's private garage. There was a big lump in the middle of the room covered by a dusty old tarp. I figured it was just more rubbish, so I jerked the tarp off with one quick move. Well, that move filled the room with dust and crap, and Otis was cursing and coughing at me in one of the two or three languages he knows.

"When the dust settled, we just stood there in silence. There up on blocks was Uncle Donnie old 1960 fuel-injected Corvette, golden yellow with white coves. She was beautiful.

"After a couple of minutes of eyeballing, Otis went back to sorting through trash. 'Are you crazy?' I asked him. 'This baby is a classic; we have to try to get her running.'

"That was it for Otis, I guess. He jumped up on his soap box and lectured me for the next hour about responsibility, my immaturity, and what we were down here to do for Aunt Edna, *blah, blah, blah.*

"We didn't speak much after that. He kept searching through the trash, and I started looking for the tires for the Vette.

"I found them, stacked properly so the moisture wouldn't rot them. It took me about an hour, but I got the Vette back on her own four feet.

"All that time working with you on your Jag years ago, Grantford, really paid off. By late afternoon, I was ready to put gas in her.

"Damn Otis wouldn't give me the Caddy's keys so I could go get some gas, so I walked. Do you know that island doesn't have a gas station on it?"

"Why build a gas station when you can build a twenty-million-dollar mansion on a lot?" Buddy questioned ironically.

"I see your point. Anyway, I had to walk all the way across the bridge, get a can of gas, and bring it back to the Gator Tail.

"By this time the sun was really getting low, and I wanted to get out here to see you. I was so mad at Otis that I poured the gas into the Vette, and she cranked on the first try. I eased out across the broken glass of the missing garage bay door, and around the grass to the front of the Gator Tail. I thought about asking Otis to come along, but I could see him shaking his fist and yelling as he climbed toward me from the trash heaps.

"Screw it, I thought, and left long black marks from the base of the Jupiter Island Bridge to where the metal grating of the draw starts.

"And here I am. I got your address from one of your old Christmas cards to Aunt Edna!"

Jason Bonnet grinned widely, obviously happy with himself.

✳   ✳   ✳   ✳

We let out a collective sigh.

"So what do you think the map leads?" Buddy asked.

"Well, I can't say for sure," he grinned, leaning back in his chair, "But I would probably imagine it's riches beyond your wildest dreams, Buddy Bear."

"I mean, it's gotta be a map to ol' granddad Stede Bonnet's pirate treasure. The dating of the ink that Otis did puts it in the right timeframe, and after all it was hidden behind the portrait of the man. It's got be his treasure." Jason's eyes snapped.

"I don't know," I murmured, "I remember a lot about kidnapping, wooing, and conning the Charleston elite, and an ultimate hanging, but I don't remember any references to treasure from my history lessons."

"Com' on you guys," Jason sighed audibly, "You know the history of Stede Bonnet. He marauded the eastern coasts from North Carolina all the way to Florida. He was the banished apprentice of Blackbeard. There has to be treasure."

"I thought the apprentice part was just a legend?" I commented.

"Well, there is a lot of stuff that doesn't get printed in the history books, Grantford," he said wistfully. "There is another whole story that's been passed down for generations in my family."

Buddy looked perplexed. "I must have slept through that class, Jason, how 'bout you refresh my memory."

Buddy had never slept through a class in his life. He was just trying to get Jason to give his spiel so his military mind could sort the facts from the fiction.

Twenty years ago, he would never have fallen for Buddy's act. We knew each other too well, but time and excitement had clouded Jason's perception, and he took the bait, hook, line, and sinker.

"I can tell you the real story, the one Aunt E shared with me, the one my family only tells with the shades drawn and the lights dimmed." A far-away look came into his eyes as he began to relate the story he knew so well.

"When Stede Bonnet was nineteen or so, he ran away to sea in a one-man boat. He planned to get filthy rich as a pirate and retire by the time he was twenty-five. Blackbeard, who's real name was Edward Teach, picked him up his second day out. Teach wanted to gut him like a fish, but Stede was a quick talker like all us Bonnets have always been. He convinced Teach that he had come looking to join up with him. Teach put him to work swabbing decks.

"Blackbeard was on this mind trip, see; he felt that he was on a mission from God. There was this heavy-duty Cherokee chief, a close friend of Teach's, who'd told him of a mystical medicine woman on some great island beyond the West Indies. The chief said that this old medicine woman could give Blackbeard a ship that was swifter than the wind and stronger than any storm.

"Teach was obsessed. Unfortunately, his archenemy Colonel William Rhett, the great pirate hunter, had almost caught him twice. Blackbeard was sailing the *Queen Ann's Revenge*, the fastest damn ship around back then. Teach immediately set course from Plymouth to the Caribbean and picked up Bonnet along the way."

Totally enthralled, I interrupted, "Which island was it? That could be what the map leads to."

"Shhh!" Jason eyes narrowed. "Don't you think I've thought of that? I've never been able to talk Aunt E into spilling the name; I'm not sure she really knows.

"Anyway," he started again, "Bonnet did the dirty work and swabbed the decks. But whenever Blackbeard attacked another ship as they hauled ass down the coast, Bonnet fought more fiercely and bravely than ten of Teach's men combined. Within weeks, Blackbeard made Bonnet his first mate.

"They finally arrived at the nameless island on a bright tropical day. Teach, Bonnet, and a bunch of the crew made their way to shore. Blackbeard's eyes were all wild, like he was possessed or something. He began hacking madly through the jungle with his cutlass. Bonnet and the crew followed, straggling behind Teach as he was pulled toward some mysterious destination.

"Two hours later, they wound up on the edge of this huge river. The currents were crazy, but somehow they made it to the small island that split the waters but was hidden from view."

"What the hell does that mean?" Buddy murmured.

Jason grimaced. "I'm just telling it the way Aunt E told me.

"Apparently there was a huge steaming tar pit in the center of a small clearing on the island. The mist rising out of the pit made their heads feel funny and woozy. But what really caught their attention was the huge black tree growing out of the far edge of the tar. The tree was as black as a Charleston lawyer's heart. It would have taken thirty guys holding hands to stretch around it. It flew so high into the island sky that it seemed to reach heaven.

"Fifteen feet above the base of the tree, there was an open doorway carved like the mouth of a roaring panther head. Teach made his way around the tar pit. Bonnet followed on his heels, now curious himself. The sailors looked nervously at one another and trailed after Bonnet.

"They drunkenly edged around the tar pit and then began climbing up the sloping trunk toward the ferocious-looking doorway. Teach scrambled, like an excited kid, down the beast's throat. Bonnet was much more careful getting around the razor-sharp, carved wooden fangs, and so he was a few seconds later than Blackbeard entering the jaws.

"It took him a few seconds to get used to the flickering light of the single torch burning on the wall. He had to shake his head a couple of times, whatever gas was coming out of the tar pit was making his vision shift and ripple. There seemed to be hundreds of clay pots and jugs lining the walls. A woven grass mat lay in one corner.

"In the center of the chamber sat a thin, shrunken old black woman with wispy traces of white hair. She sat Indian-style on the floor with Teach sitting awkwardly in front of her. The old woman was holding the big pirate's hands and talking. Teach was grinning oddly, his head tilted to one side.

"The old woman's toothless mouth was moving in an ancient language that Bonnet didn't know, yet he understood every word in his head.

"'The great Cherokee chief sent me to you,' Teach said.

"'Yes I know,' the old woman murmured.

"'He said that you could give me a ship that was faster than the wind and stronger than any storm,' Teach's voice whistled.

"'Yes, yes, a ship of night, not seen to sight.'

"'Please, yes,' Teach stammered, 'I'll give you anything you want.'

"'I have all I need'—the old woman squeezed Teach's hands—'but I can not give it, I can only grant it.'"

He grimaced. "My great-great-great-grandfather had no patience for that kind of crap.

"'Tell me what I must do,' Teach squeezed the old woman's hands.

"Her pale green eyes had glowed warmly. 'You must never use it for evil, and you must turn away from your treacherous ways.'

"Stede jumped forward. He had had enough of this bullshit. They were marauders, goddamn it. They took what they wanted, instead of sitting around holding some relic's hands. Bonnet drew his sword and ran the old woman through where she sat.

"Blood gushed from the open wound as the old woman stood and staggered toward the doorway. The others stared after her, stunned. At the edge of the doorway she turned and faced Bonnet. She raised one crooked bloody finger, pointed it at my grandfather, and grinned garishly at him. She then leaped backward from the mouth of the cave. Her old wrinkled hands caught on the sharp wooden fangs. She hung there for a split second and then burst into flames. Within seconds, only her ashes were left to sink into the tar pit below. The pit enveloped her into its ever-folding arms with a deep belch. The noxious tar gases seemed to clear, and it was as if she had never even been there.

"They all turned to look at my ancestor. 'You fool,' Blackbeard screamed, slapping Bonnet across the face with the back of his sword. Bonnet tumbled to the ground. 'Now how am I supposed to find out how to get the ship?'

"My grandfather saw red. He put his hand on the hilt of his sword. All ten crewmen drew their swords in response. Bonnet relaxed his hold. 'I don't want to see your face on my ship again,' Blackbeard cursed. 'You can rot in this jungle for all I care.'

"My grandfather decided that a submissive posture was more likely to save his life at that point, so he slunk back into a dark corner of the cave.

"'Coward,' Teach spat and turned his attention to his surroundings. He looked around at the inside of the imposing tree. 'Men,' he commanded, 'we will go back to the ship and bring back all able-bodied seamen. We'll build our ship out of this tree!'

"They stalked out of the cave, leaving Bonnet alone in the darkness. There was something hard against his back. He grabbed the object and made his way out of the cave. In the sunlight, he saw he was holding a book with pages made of dried grass paper. The covers were made of the same hard black wood as the great tree. The title was carved into the cover in strange symbols. Once again, he realized that he could understand the old woman's secret language. The cover said, 'Legacy and Destiny.' Bonnet grinned. He knew he had discovered something very powerful. He slipped silently into the jungle.

"It took thirty men a week to cut down the great tree, but it finally fell with a saddening crash. It took three months to cut up the tree, drag it to the beach, and build the mighty ship.

"As the ship grew nearer to completion, Teach gave in and allowed Stede Bonnet back in his company. By the time Blackbeard christened the huge black ship the *Royal James*, Bonnet had once again talked himself into Teach's good graces and his first mate post.

"They sailed from the island and devastated America's coast for six months. Colonel William Rhett couldn't even get close to the black ship.

"My grandfather once again held his old post and did his job well, but Blackbeard no longer trusted him. Teach watched Bonnet's flickering quarter's lantern flame until the early-morning hours. Bonnet seemed to relish any excuse to retire to his quarters. Teach didn't like it one bit. One night he took a peek into Bonnet's quarters and what he saw made every hair on his beard stand up and tingle. Bonnet sat within a silver-encircled star on the floor with an open book in his lap while small red demons danced and sang silently around the circle. The next morning Teach called his whole crew together. Hypocritically waving a tattered Bible around, Blackbeard damned Bonnet for dabbling in black magic. One of the demons had whispered to Bonnet what to expect, and he had hidden the book beneath his clothes. Blackbeard tied him up and set him adrift in a rowboat with no oars.

"Two days later the British Royal Navy picked him up. Bonnet's reputation as a pirate was already well known in England, so he was tried as a marauder. Once again the Bonnet tongue allowed him to talk his way out of a jam. The king granted him a full pardon, as long as he agreed to quit being a pirate. Bonnet promised and thanked the king graciously before heading out in search of Teach.

"After a month, he finally found the small lagoon that Blackbeard was using as his new lair. It was close to Charleston for easy marauding.

"In the middle of the night, Stede sneaked aboard the dark ship. Teach was drunk and asleep in the huge chair his men had built him on deck. With one mighty thrust, Bonnet shoved his sword through Teach's scalp and out his lower jaw. Blackbeard grabbed at the bloody sword before he fell forward dead. Bonnet severed the head as a keepsake and tossed the body overboard."

"And I bet I know the rest from my studies," I stated.

"Go ahead…"

"Bonnet took over the black ship and her crew, and rechristened it. Then, he started a huge marauding spree up and down the coast, from the lair near Charleston."

"If I remember correctly," Buddy began, "he captured a ship called the *Eagle* and held her passengers for ransom. Someone important—the governor's daughter, I believe—was on board the *Eagle*."

"I thought you didn't remember the story?" Jason chided.

Buddy grinned sheepishly.

"Yes," Jason continued, "he tried to hold the governor's daughter for ransom, but the great pirate fighter, Colonel William Rhett, outsmarted him and captured him.

"There was a huge trial, considered to be the trial of the century, and my grandfather and twenty-nine of his men were found guilty and ordered hanged.

"Even then, my ancestor talked his way out of prison.

"Aunt E says the main reason he escaped was that he was tormented by the old woman he killed and wanted to make retribution. He was caught again after a great chase by Colonel Rhett."

His eyes once again clouded over. "The gallows waited. My grandfather maintained his composure and silently straightened his shoulders. His remaining twenty-nine men were already assembled outside with eight other guards. The guards marched them down the streets of Charleston toward White Point Shoals.

"As they approached the shoals, a jeering crowd cursed and threw rocks at them. The guards marched the men up the gallows stairs and lined each one up in front of a noose. Bonnet took his rightful place nearest the hooded executioner. The guards placed and tightened the nooses around each man's neck.

"Colonel Rhett commanded the guard to loosen Bonnet's gag, stating that every man deserves a last word.

"The guards obliged. The jeering crowd fell silent. Thunder rumbled and lightning struck the harbor behind them, but all ears were on the Gentleman Pirate.

"Bonnet grinned widely at the crowd.

"'Pray then, ye learned ghost, do show, where can this fearsome brute now go,' Bonnet boomed, 'whose life is one continuous evil, striving to cheat God, Man, and Devil?'

"Bonnet turned from the crowd to Colonel Rhett. 'You should have known, Rhett; no mere man could kill the great Stede Bonnet.'

"Bonnet raised his boot and kicked the gallows trip handle. With a sudden sickening snap, thirty men fell and thirty necks broke simultaneously.

"The sky opened up with peal after peal of thunder. Rain fell in unending waves. The wind blew, sucking at the gray hanging bodies as if trying to pull them back to sea. The crowd ran, falling and tripping over themselves."

I chimed in, "The history books say a third of Charleston drowned that night in the sudden hurricane! The entire town was flooded for a week. By the time anyone could make it back down to the gallows, there wasn't much left of the storm-battered bodies to bury."

Jason bit his lip, "Yep, they say noosed bodies were found as much as a mile away. Bonnet's was the only one still hanging from the gallows. They were all buried in the marsh during low tide, just beyond the low-water mark. There were too many reputable citizens to bury to worry about some worthless marauders." Jason choked back tears.

Buddy finished the story. "Leaving Charleston to lick its wounds and immortalize their brief encounter with Stede Bonnet, the Gentleman Pirate."

"That is such a load of bullshit," I huffed. "Dark books and mystic ships, give me a break."

"You shut-up, Grantford." He jumped from his chair, shaking his finger in my face. "Aunt E doesn't lie, and that's my family you are talking about."

I think this was the only time I had ever seen Jason Bonnet actually angry. Sure he would put on the right face when it was required; it was one of many he could conjure up on a whim. But this was real, I saw it, and I could tell by his surprised look that Buddy saw it, too.

Buddy put both of his big meaty hands on Jason's shoulders. He could have cracked him like a low-country blue crab claw if he had wanted. "It's okay, Jason, we believe you," he stated quietly.

The fire faded slowly from his eyes. He backed away from me and sat down.

There was an awkward silence. It was a rare thing.

Finally, Buddy cleared his throat. "Okay, Jason, so we have some insight into your great-great-great-grandfather, but what makes you think the missing map leads to his treasure?"

"What else could it be?" Jason queried.

"Maybe it leads to that book that he stole," Buddy stated.

Jason's eyes flashed.

"Um, borrowed," Buddy amended.

"Either way," I jumped in, "we are talking about something of immense value that would no doubt attract Donnie Rhodes like Carolina skeeters to a porch light."

"So will you guys help me?" His voice almost pleaded. "Otis and I cannot find this thing alone, and I don't know if we can stand each other much longer without someone to referee."

I looked at Buddy, and he looked at me, "Tomorrow's Saturday. We can at least go out and help you sort through the debris at the Gator Tail."

"But you and Otis," Buddy chimed in, "are going to have to baby-sit yourselves."

"It's a deal!" Jason beamed.

"It's pretty dark," I said. "If it's okay with Buddy, you can bunk with him here tonight."

"As long as I get to reserve the right to poke a potato down his pie-hole if he starts snoring," Buddy grinned.

Jason feigned shock at his brutish behavior.

"But first," I stated, looking out at the night sky, "it looks like the storm has passed. I want to go back to the barn and put up the top on that beautiful Vette before Lil's damn horses fill it with shit."

"Speaking of cars," he asked. "Whatever happened to that great old Sixty-seven Jag you had?"

"He traded it in about a year ago," Buddy grumped.

"How could you possibly trade in something that beautiful, that you had loved for so long?" Jason's eyebrows rose.

"Simple, I got something better."

"Want to see?" I stood carefully, kicking Buddy in the calf when he rolled his eyes.

"Sure," he said carefully, looking from me to Buddy, then back again.

CHAPTER 5

▼

We walked together toward my two-story garage that is separate from the main house. A little stairway on the right side leads to the second floor and my karate dojo, which Buddy has taken over with all of his boxes. At the far end of the dojo is the little efficiency apartment that he has been using.

Jason walked up to the door leading to the garage area, but I said, "No, it's around back; it will not fit in the garage."

"What kind of car did you get anyway, Grantford?" He puzzled.

Buddy just shook his head.

I walked around the far corner of the garage and felt along the outside wall in the now clouded darkness. I found the toggle and, with a quick flip, illuminated the outside area to the left of the garage, with the powerful stadium lamps that I had installed on high poles so I could work after dark. I heard Lil's horses grumble disapprovingly out by the barn. Buddy made a similar sound as he shielded his eyes, waiting for them to dilate.

Jason never flinched. "What the hell is that piece of shit!"

I grimaced. "That isn't a piece of shit; that is a PBY-5A Catalina."

"She was the best all-purpose flying boat built during the World War II era. Out of the thousands built for the war, only about fifty-nine PBY-5As were built by the Consolidated Aircraft Corporation at its New Orleans plant at Lake Pontchartrain."

"You were right the first time." Buddy frowned. "It's a piece of shit."

I glared at him. "This baby was the last of the flying boats to be built in New Orleans."

Jason was giving Buddy a look that was all too familiar. I saw it all the time from both Buddy and Lil. It was the look that said I was friggin' nuts.

I guess I could understand. The old girl wasn't in the best of shape. Her massive wing was ripped off and was leaning against the far side of the garage. Both engines were missing from the wing. Her front landing gear was crumpled and her back two tires were rotted away. Her once-beautiful body was patched and rusted. There wasn't a piece of glass in any of her windshields or gun turrets. The old girl had seen better days. Built in 1944 for duty in the Pacific during the war, she had been turned into a Coast Guard rescue plan in the early fifties, up around Pensacola. The Coasties had inadvertently ditched her in a remote freshwater swamp up in the panhandle in 1956. It had been deemed too costly to try to pull her out of the bog. So they left her in a watery grave for the next forty-six years.

The Coasties didn't think there was anything left of her, so I had no problem purchasing her remains for five hundred dollars. The real cost came in getting her out of the bog and transported to Jupiter. For that, I traded my old Jag to a little, fat sweaty man who owned Jupiter Marine Salvage. His name was Orin Lawson, and his piggy eyes fairly burst from his face at the opportunity.

I had gone up to the North Florida swamp to watch them pull her out. Buddy and Lil might have thought she was a piece of shit, but I had been totally amazed at how well preserved she was. If she had been in salt water, there would have been nothing left. The rich black bog water had eaten away her paint but left most of her metal undamaged. You could still see the vestiges of her Coast Guard orange stripes on her wingtips and tail. Elsewhere, in place of paint, she wore a coating of brown and green swamp gunk. Ironically enough, all the rust that she now wore had appeared in the year since she had been resurrected from her watery grave. Wherever the Florida rain had washed off the swamp gunk, surface rust appeared. She was a brown, green, and rust mottled mess, but thankfully all of that would sand off easily.

Her avionics were ruined, and her wing had been ripped from the fuselage in the crash, but she was still beautiful to me. I removed and trashed both of her tired old engines, and I ordered twin 1700hp Wright Cyclone R-2600s that were due to arrive any day.

I looked down her long flank, imagining how she had once been. The PBY-5A Catalina is a beautiful plane in the air and sea, albeit rather awkward looking on land. The wing and engines sit high up on a tower that soars ten feet above the cockpit. Her elegant wings have retractable floats for water landings. She has a gun turret below the cockpit windshield and twin blisters on her tail for gunners as well. At more than sixty-three feet long, she can hold twenty men cramped or a dozen in comfort. The US of A never contracted for a more competent and trust-worthy flying boat.

I had spent the last year restoring her. She was much closer to finished than a first glance would lead one to believe. I started restoring on the inside. She had all new avionics and controls. Almost everything internal had been replaced. New engines were on their way, and I had been able to find an original front gear from a donor plane at an old airplane bone yard near the original factory in New Orleans. The hard part would be getting the new engines on the old wing and getting the wing reattached to the fuselage. That was a job that was beyond my ability to do alone out of my workshop.

Jason repeated himself, "Look at that shit!"

"Hey, she's not that bad," I started, but then I noticed that he wasn't looking at the plane as a whole, but her nose art.

"The plane is great, Grantford, but you have got to explain the meaning of this," he said, gesturing at the nose of the Catalina.

Buddy lumbered over, clucking to himself. "You mean you like this piece of crap, too?"

"Sure, she's beautiful," he remarked breathlessly.

I grinned at Buddy, who just shook his head in bewilderment.

"But tell me about her." Jason gestured again at the Catalina's nose. "I've never been so aroused and disgusted at the same time in my life!"

I laughed, turning an appraising eye to the nose art. "Well, I guess she is the embodiment of this old girl.

"She was built in New Orleans; that's why her affectionate crew christened her the Lady Orleans."

"I'm assuming that's also the reason for the freaky combo of parts we have here?" He pointed.

On the side of the PBY-5A was the faded body of the most gorgeous naked female you could ever lay eyes on. Long slender legs, one bent at the knee, a flat stomach and full perky breasts that were at full side-shooter salute. A purple cape across her lap lent a minor amount of modesty. She was gorgeous all right, till you got past that beautiful bosom, for there atop her shoulders wasn't the sultry smile on a redhead or blonde—no, not for the quirky crew of the Lady Orleans—atop her shoulders was the gross, tentacled reddish-brown head of a genuine Mississippi Delta mud bug. I had to agree with Jason; it was both stimulating and repulsive time to see that beautiful body attached to the head of a crawfish.

"Yes," I grinned, "it's funny how way back then they could have known to use Lil as the model for the body, and Buddy for the head."

Jason fairly cackled. Buddy's red anger turned into a blush as he quickly went from being pissed at my ribbing, to being embarrassed about thinking of Lil naked.

I slapped him on the back good-naturedly, and he grinned sheepishly.

"So what's that gold emblem on her cape?" Jason queried.

"I had to put a little research into that one. In fact, I just found out today. It turns out that it's the emblem of a long-defunct New Orleans secret society called the Krewe of Jupiter."

Their mouths dropped open simultaneously. "You're kidding," Buddy whistled, "How is that for coincidence?"

"Do you understand what this means?" Jason beamed. "This is fate, we were all meant to be here and now, together in Jupiter, finding this map."

"There is no such thing as fate. You make your own fate."

"You don't actually mean…," Buddy stammered.

"Damn straight," Jason chuckled. "We are the Krewe of Jupiter."

CHAPTER 6

▼

Buddy and Jason headed up to the efficiency apartment above the garage. We had been laughing and joking for two hours as I showed them the lady's every nook and cranny. Buddy kept up his 'This is a piece of shit' attitude, but I occasionally caught the gleam of admiration in his eyes at my restoration work. Jason, on the other hand, was like a kid in a candy shop.

I could have talked all night about the beautiful Catalina, but I noticed Jason stifling a yawn.

"Why don't you guys catch some shuteye? I'll go out to the barn and take care of the Vette."

Jason yawned again, "If you can name your airplane, I want to name my car."

"You could call her the Five Finger Discount, since you stole her."

"Very funny, Buddy Bear, but since Aunt E gave the car to Uncle Donnie, and he is nowhere to be found, I consider it not to be stolen, just my early inheritance."

Buddy rolled his eyes. "Whatever you say, Jason."

His face broke into a beaming smile. "I know, since this was Uncle Donnie Rhodes's baby originally, I'll name it in his honor."

"You're gonna name it Donnie?" I asked incredulously.

"No, Grantford. Rhodes, Rocky Rhodes to be exact."

"Good God, like the ice cream," Buddy said. "You won't find me naming my Harley nothin'."

It was settled. We both knew better than to argue with Jason when his mind was made up.

With that they headed for the apartment stairs, and I headed for the barn. Over my shoulder, I could hear Buddy already recounting his recent marital woes to Jason, who was clucking comfortingly. It would be good for him to cry on Jason's shoulder a little.

Buddy and I have discussed his troubles at length, but I'm the analytical type. I guess it comes with the territory, being in the computer field.

It's kind of a safety net for me. No fate for Mrs. Grant's son. He controls his own universe. No wishes, no fate, no magic; black and white, right and wrong, reality not fantasy. Good old safe, secure reality; too bad it hadn't worked out worth a shit so far.

But in my heart, I knew Buddy needed more. He needed more than someone to analyze and propose solutions. He needed someone to commiserate, to cry in his beer with him. I wanted to be there for him. Hell, he was my best friend in the whole world, but every time I tried, I got this knot in my throat, and the comfort turned into solutions. I guess that kind of thing just comes easier for some folks, folks like Jason.

Tonight would be good for Buddy. He and Jason would down a few beers, fry up some ham and eggs on the little efficiency apartment's stove, and the story would come flooding out of Buddy. Jason would listen and say the right things. He always has, and Buddy Bear would finally be on the road to healing.

As I approached the Vette through the large center hall, I held my breath. It would be a crying shame if Pharaoh or one of his cronies had soiled the interior of the Vette. I grinned to myself; Rocky Rhodes was one beautiful piece of machinery. She had a custom flake metallic yellow paint job with white coves that was definitely not the original laid on by the factory.

Looking over and into the interior of the roadster with foreboding, I walked up to the driver's door. There was a sickening squish, followed by the faintly sweet aroma of fresh manure, as my shoe sank into the fresh pile up to my ankle.

"Damn it, Pharaoh!" I cursed loudly. There was a soft snickering from the dark corners of the biggest stall. Pharaoh hadn't done his business in the Vette; he had dropped a steaming load right outside the driver's door where he knew I was sure to step.

I grumbled and cussed my way over to the barn's wash area where I could hose my foot off.

Bending over to wash the last of the crap off of my shoe, I caused myself to start when rising. I had caught my reflection in the old cracked hand mirror attached to the barn post.

Who was that old stranger staring back at me? When I was younger, I'd hated my boyish looks. But suddenly, I thought, rubbing the salt-and-pepper stubble on my cheeks, that wasn't a problem.

It didn't seem quite fair the way it had happened. I went from looking ten years younger than I was to looking ten years older. The thoughts and emotions of the past started to knock on the door of my mind, but I quickly barred the latch; all that was behind me now.

Even so, I still hadn't gotten over the shock of the physical changes. Lil pretended not to notice, but how could she miss it?

Oh sure, those same piercing brown eyes still gazed back at me from the mirror, but they were colder now. The frown lines and crow's feet were new. Most notably, the shock of almost black hair on my head was now completely white at the temples, and the gray was snaking its way though the rest of my hair as well. At this rate, in another twelve months I would be completely gray. It's strange how I had put on twenty pounds, but my face still looked gaunt and sad.

I turned away quickly. I was okay now. Things were fine. I had a great life, great wife, great friends, great job. But there was still a hole; a hole that had been there for five years now. Lil had filled in her hole, with friends, family, and professional therapy.

Analytic bastard that I am, I refused to allow my hole to be covered up. I don't want it filled in; I want it removed. I want the hole never to have existed. I want to change history; I want to do what I should have done then.

"I want my son back!" I screamed aloud into the Florida darkness. I felt a nudge at my back as I wiped away the stinging tears with back of my hand.

It was Jazmine, motherly horse that she was. I stroked her nose. "You know what it's like, don't you, old girl," I whispered as I searched in my pocket for a carrot stub. Jazz nickered softly and looked deep into my eyes with her indigo ink eyes.

"Don't go telling Lil about this now," I smiled aloud, "you'll totally ruin my reputation as a horse hater."

"Don't go telling Mom what?" A sweet little voice floated from behind me.

I jumped about ten feet in the air. "Geez, Savannah, you scared me half to death!"

Savannah giggled. She and Sarah are fraternal twins, as different as night and day.

"What are you doing out here this time of night, young lady?" I questioned with false sternness.

"Mom sent me out to get you and says she isn't going to keep supper warm for you any longer if you don't get in the house," she quoted sternly. "Besides, Spooner wanted to go for a walk," she beamed sweetly.

As if on queue, the beagle at her feet barked, wagging his tail in my direction.

I grinned despite myself. I profess not to be an emotional animal person, but it's hard not to like a beagle.

"Okay, Stinky Cheese"—I tousled Savannah's thick hair that reflected the color mine used to be—"let me put the top up on this car and we will be back to the house."

The power motors on Rocky Rhodes hummed warmly as the forty-three-year-old top clicked into place like well-oiled clockwork.

I shut the stall doors for each horse, keeping a wary eye on Pharaoh, who had his back haunches pointed in my direction.

Holding hands, Savannah and I walked to the front of the barn. I checked to make sure Spooner was at her side and that I hadn't inadvertently locked him in a horse stall.

With a flick of a finger, I hit the master switch and turned off all the barn lights.

The darkness was instant and all encompassing. All three of us waited a few seconds for our eyes to adjust. Then suddenly like the raising of a velvet curtain, the beautiful star-splashed moonless Florida sky was above us, the storm clouds had flown westward searching for new lands to soak.

A soft wind blew, and I felt Savannah's long hair tickle my arm. The golden yellow light of La Vie Dansante beckoned from across the pasture.

Suddenly a shooting star flashed overhead. "Oh, look," Savannah whispered, "he blew us a kiss."

"What?" I asked confused.

"Skylar." She smiled in the darkness. "Mommy says whenever we see a shooting star it's Skylar blowing us a kiss from heaven."

And suddenly I could say nothing. My body shuddered with silent sobs, as the tears rolled down my face. Savannah hugged me in the darkness, and we cried together for my first-born son, and her older brother, now five years gone from leukemia.

CHAPTER 7

▼

A myriad of stars winked and called in the night sky, but no more blew kisses. Savannah and I made our way from the pasture to the front door.

Lil met us at the door and shooed Savannah off to bed to join her twin sister's dreams. She playfully swatted me on the rump for making her keep supper warm and herded me off to the kitchen to eat.

She then went up the great curving stairway in the atrium to the game room to play a quick round of pool with Jessica, my twenty-year-old stepdaughter from Lil's previous life in Charleston. Jessica goes to Palm Beach Community College, and even though she is pretty independent, she and her mom still have a close bond.

I pulled the still-steaming plate from the stove, and fixed myself a cold Diet Mountain Dew, the technology guy's universal beverage of choice.

I forked at the beef stroganoff absently. It had been five long years since Skylar had passed, but it still felt like yesterday.

I remember his last few minutes, and the rage that coursed through my veins. He had thankfully been in a coma for the last several days; the morphine could no longer ease the pain that wracked his frail twelve-year-old form. He was thin and gaunt, a photographic negative of the bike-riding, fence-climbing, freckle-faced boy he had been before.

Sweet Lil sat by his bed and sang him the songs that we lulled him to sleep with as a baby. Skylar knew all the lyrics to Loggins and Messina, James Taylor, and Jimmy Buffett, before he knew the words to Old McDonald.

As he slipped away from us, Lil sang his favorite, House At Pooh Corner, as the huge tears rolled down her face.

He caught two quick successive wheezing breaths, and then he sank deep and forever into the oceans of white linen that would soon be pulled up over his beautiful face, by anxious nurses who were already running into the hospital room as alarms wailed, and so did I.

Why this boy, why this life, so fragile and new and fresh? There couldn't be a God, because if there were, he would reach down and caress my boy's poor worn face and make him whole again. Where was the miracle? Where was the fate?

Lil's head was buried in my chest, the tears drenching my shirt, as the boxes and wires and needles and a half-dozen sets of skilled hands tried to bring him back. It was no use. I knew it before they started.

My son had taken more than his allotment of pain and suffering. He'd borne his burden with courage until the end. But now he was gone.

My wail turned into a scream of anguish, rage, and guilt. The louder I screamed the tighter Lil held me to her. She cried silently as I screamed for revenge. Then there had been a bee sting, a slight prick on the arm as the kindly nurse put me out of my misery. Unfortunately, she could help for only a few hours; there was nothing she could do about the rest of my life.

I looked down at my plate, as usual Lil had done a great job with supper, but I had no appetite. I whistled for Spooner, and the eager beagle came bounding around the corner. I sat the plate down on the kitchen floor for him. He slurped and gobbled and generally made a big mess as his tail whipped back and forth at a frantic pace.

"Slow down, old friend." I patted his head. "You eat like there is no tomorrow." I fought the sting of tears in my eyes, as I recognized my own faux pas.

Jessica stuck her head in the kitchen door to say good-bye as she headed out the door to go to the movies with friends.

"You okay, Kris?" She peered at me worriedly.

"Yeah, I'm fine." I forced a stiff smile to my face. "Just a lot of ghosts about tonight."

She nodded sadly and shut the door behind her, knowing that she too would be haunted tonight by the ghost of the stepbrother who had been just three years younger than she when he'd died.

I leaned down and picked up the empty plate before Spooner licked a hole right through it, and absently dropped it into the sink.

I made my way up the back kitchen stairs. Lil had already turned out the lights in the game room, and a soft glow emanated from under our bedroom door.

I opened the door with a click, causing Lil to give a little squeal as I startled her. I grinned a crooked grin. She was just putting her nightgown on for bed and had just slipped it over her head, to let it flow down her wonderful curves.

I never tired of the sight. Nearly eighteen years ago, Lil was the most beautiful woman I had ever met, and she still is. At forty-five she has the clear skin and supple figure of a thirty-two-year-old.

It is amazing that she has borne four children. You would never know it. The swell of her breasts under the nightgown were still firm and high, with rounded points of excitement to catch a man's eye. Her trim thighs and sweet little behind were tight as a drum from hours of competitive posting on horseback.

She tossed her blond hair back and gave me that sly look: chin down, head tilted, red lips parted—the tigress ready to pounce.

I sighed weakly. Then she noticed the redness around my eyes and understood in an instant.

She pulled me close and we slipped into the soft familiar smell of our marital bed. I lay my head on her chest and she stroked my hair. No words were required; we loved, we shared.

Is it possible to love someone so much that you burst? I certainly hope not, because I loved her with all the love in the universe when I first saw her, and amazingly that love has doubled every day since.

She is warm, and genuine, and honest. She is the smartest woman I know. We joust and fight with the same vigor that we make love. She is my friend, my confidante, my lover. She is my Lil. I breathed in the wondrous familiar scent of her.

Slowly, every so slowly, my hand found the trail to her tight little tummy. I explored farther and was rewarded with a sultry little moan. Her hands began to wander as well. The familiar ritual that is no longer you and me, but we, began.

And when it was done, I murmured, "I love you, my Lil, with all of my heart."

She tilted her velvet brown eyes up to me and smiled. "I love you too, baby, as long as we have each other, everything will always be all right."

I reached over and turned off the lamp. The Florida moonlight shone through the huge arched windows that ran along the second-floor tower that held the master bedroom sitting room. Long dark shadows reached for the bed, but I had no fear, because I knew my Lil was right.

CHAPTER 8

▼

I awoke the next morning to sounds of heavy machinery, followed by loud yelling, and frantic cries for help. I rushed to my window that faces the garage.

"Oh, good God," I mumbled, quickly throwing on the official Florida weekender uniform of khaki shorts and loud tropical luau shirt. "What is it?" Lil murmured sleepily, hugging her pillow. I ran my finger lightly across her exposed thigh as I made for the door. "Buddy is choking the life out of Jack Mason," I called over my shoulder as I took the stairs two at a time.

By the time I got outside, Buddy had Jack Mason backed up against his flatbed truck. The former MP's meaty ham fists were around poor Jack's throat, and Jack's feet were dangling a good five inches above the ground. Jason was holding two confused looking Guatemalans at bay with a large palm frond. Buddy was in an old robe of Lil's and Jason was in nothing but his boxers.

"What the hell do you two think you are doing?" I demanded.

Jason poked the palm frond menacingly at his prisoners, "These guys and their boss over there was trying to steal the Lady Orleans.

"They thought they could sneak in here while everyone was still asleep and make off with her," he snarled. "But you gotta get up pretty early indeed to get past us."

I grabbed the frond from Jason snapping it over my knee, "Give me that before you put your eye out."

"Buddy," I barked, "Put Jack down, he's turning blue!"

He dropped the man instantly.

Jack Mason crumpled to the ground, wheezing and holding his throat.

"Are you okay, Jack?" I bent over the thin man who was now hyperventilating. He accepted my hand and slowly struggled to his feet. Jack Mason looked like an old seadog from the greasy ball cap pulled tight on his head, to the scraggly three days of gray beard that followed the salt lines on his face.

"I think so, Saint Kristopher, but you really need to get your attack dogs under control," he coughed, sucking in one great lungful of air after another.

I turned to Buddy and Jason, "You guys owe Jack and his crew an apology."

"But Grantford," Jason whined, "They came in with this flatbed truck with the crane attached to the back, at six on a Saturday morning. We thought he was out to steal the Orleans."

I frowned at Buddy, "You should know better than to overreact like that."

He grinned sheepishly, "Sorry, Kris, Jason shook me awake screaming about airplane thieves, and I guess I just kind of got caught up in the moment."

"Sorry, mister," Buddy stuck his big paw out to Jack, who cautiously shook it. He grinned and slapped Jack on the back good-heartedly. Unfortunately this caused him to go into another coughing fit. Buddy looked both concerned and embarrassed.

I turned to chastise Jason, but he was already speaking thoughtfully in Spanish to the two Guatemalans. Unfortunately, Jason slept through most of his Spanish courses, so instead of saying he was sorry; it inadvertently came out as a vague comparison of their sister to a cow. They weren't amused, but decided to keep their distance from the strange man who waved sticks while running around in his underwear.

Jack finally pulled himself together. I grasped his hand, "I am truly sorry for this rude treatment, old friend. Please forgive the enthusiasm of my house guests."

Jack harrumphed, but I could see the traces of a grin at the corners of his mouth.

"Jack, I would like you to meet two old college buddies of mine, Anthony and Jason. Guys, this is Jack Mason, world famous chief mechanic at Calypso Island Airways in Miami."

"Pleased to meet you," Jason rambled over, extending his hand, and turning on that thousand-watt Bonnet smile. It would have been more effective if he had been dressed in something more than white boxers with huge red lobsters printed all over them.

Gratefully, Buddy didn't even try to shake the poor man's hand again, as he tried to look solemn in Lil's old pink terrycloth robe with Hello Kitty all over it. "Just call me Buddy, everyone else does."

"Son," Jack grinned, "as intimate as you and I just got. How could I possibly call you anything else?"

Everyone laughed, thank goodness, as the tension melted away.

"What is Calypso Island Airways?" Jason queried. "I've never heard of it."

"You don't get out of Charleston enough," I grinned sardonically. "Calypso is the longest continuously operating island transport in the U.S."

"Yeah, I've heard of you guys," Buddy ventured. "Your entire fleet is made of seaplanes, right?"

"As Kris mentioned Calypso Island Airways is the oldest of its kind. In fact, our early years were during Prohibition when the smuggling of liquor between the Bahamas and the U.S. was in full swing. Rum running was one of our biggest money-makers. We didn't discriminate among passengers; we carried the smugglers, but also the lawmen who chased them."

"Pirates and smugglers." Jason pretended to swoon. "My kind of folks!"

"And best of all," I beamed, "Calypso has the largest inventory of seaplane parts in North America. If Jack doesn't have it in his warehouse, then it probably doesn't exist."

Jack looked slightly embarrassed. "Yes, but the question is can I find it in my warehouse?"

I laughed. "Old Jack here has been a mechanic at Calypso's for what, thirty years now, Jack?"

"You're showing my age now, Kris," he chuckled, "more like thirty-five years. I started as an apprentice mechanic when I was only sixteen."

"There is no one on God's green earth who knows more about restoring and maintaining flying boats," I stated truthfully.

Jack reddened slightly but didn't dispute my claim.

"So does that mean that you are selling the Lady Orleans to Calypso?" Jason's face sank.

"No, no." I shook my head vigorously. "Jack is just helping me finish her off. I've done everything I can on her. Jack has the skills and the parts that I don't have, to get her in flying shape."

"Aye," Jack grinned, "and I've also got two brand-new seventeen-hundred horse power Wright Cyclone R-2600 engines that just came in yesterday with your name on them."

I felt my face light up like a kid at Christmas. "So what do you think, Jack? How long before you'll have her ready to fly?"

Jack rubbed his whiskered face. "Well, before your large friend set about throttling me, I did get about ten minutes to look her over."

He paused, "In my professional opinion, she's a pig."

Buddy hooted, "See, I told you!"

I glared in his direction. "Yes, but you can fix her, right, Jack?"

Jack looked shrewdly at the Orleans, sitting forlorn and rusty in the shadow of the garage.

"Well, it's going to take some work, son, but I never said it couldn't be done."

Buddy mumbled, "Putting lipstick on a pig don't do a thing but piss off the pig."

Jason punched him in the arm for the umpteenth time in the last two days, "Let the man tell us what he can do, Mr. Cynical." Buddy rubbed his arm but said nothing.

"Well, Kris," Jack began, "first of all, we've got to attach the wing and get those new engines mounted. That's going to take two or three days if the Betancur brothers"—Mason gestured at the two Guatemalans "and I work round the clock."

"I've got to install that landing gear you salvaged"—he pointed to the crumpled nose gear—"that will take two days. I've got plenty of tires in the warehouse, so that shouldn't be a problem. Assuming you have all the avionics and wiring right, we need another week to test out all the hydraulics and various systems.

"After that, everything else is cosmetic." He frowned. "Unfortunately that is going to take a while. All the missing or broken glass in her airframe is going to have to be custom cut for her windshield, portals, and gun turrets.

"That is going to take at least a month. All that surface rust and hardened gunk is going to need to be sanded off, and then she will need a new coat of paint, maybe two to cover up that hideous nose art."

"No way!" Buddy and Jason fairly shouted in unison.

I looked at Buddy. Was that a sign of affection? He pretended to look the other way.

"You can't paint over Lady Orleans," Jason begged "That's her heart and soul!"

"What do you say, Jack?" I queried. "Can the nose art be saved?"

Jack looked skeptical, "Well I don't know why you would want to, but yeah, I guess she could be salvaged. In fact, I've got a kid who does air-brush work for me who can probably make her look good as new."

I grinned. Jason beamed. Buddy just looked relieved.

"Sounds like you are saying two months to get her in shape, Jack?"

"At a minimum," Jack hedged. "The Catalinas were the best of a breed, but this old girl has been sitting on the bottom of a bog for a long time. There are a lot of bug-a-boos and gremlins lurking just beneath her skin."

Jack contemplated, "I wouldn't bet on her being completely finished for three months."

"Geez, that sounds like forever, but you're the expert, Jack, whatever you think needs to be done, let's do it!"

"Good man." Jack patted me on the shoulder. "We will do her proud."

Jack spoke several words of Spanish to the Betancur brothers, and they went scurrying to secure the lifting chains around the fuselage and the wing.

I hustled Buddy and Jason back upstairs to the apartment to get dressed, before Lil or the twins came out and saw them in their sorry state of affairs.

Jack and the Betancurs made short work of loading the lovely Lady. They had been salvaging abandoned seaplanes and restoring them for Calypso's service for years; they had it down to an art form.

Jack expertly worked the mini-crane attached to the back of the long flatbed truck. In less than five minutes, the wing was lashed down securely. It took a little more maneuvering, and lots of shouting in Spanish, but in less than fifteen minutes the great fuselage was resting comfortably on the flatbed as well.

Buddy and Jason came back down just in time to see that spectacular show of logistics.

I shook Jack Mason's hand.

"We'll take good care of her, Kris. Don't you worry about that."

"I know." I sighed tight-lipped, running my finger along her wing. "Be safe, old girl."

With that Jack and the Betancurs hopped in the truck, made a wide circle, and headed for the pasture gate. Then they were gone, rumbling up the road, and turning back toward Miami.

I felt a dull ache as they turned the corner and disappeared. Buddy placed his hand on my shoulder as Jason uttered a sigh.

CHAPTER 9

▼

I sat in the passenger seat of the newly dubbed Rocky Rhodes and wondered what in the world I was getting myself into. Jason was as happy as a cottonmouth on a low hanging branch when he was behind the wheel of the Vette. He kept speeding up and zooming in and out of traffic in a vain attempt to ruffle Buddy's feathers.

It was a lost cause, the Big Guy rumbled behind us on his Harley, hair flapping in the wind, happily oblivious to what Jason was doing.

On our drive toward the Gator Tail, we were just leaving Jupiter Farms. The horse pastures, palm farms, and crisscrossing flood canals gave way to the massive concrete spaghetti bowl that was the Florida Turnpike and I-95 junctions.

Rocky Rhodes burbled along through the residential heart of Jupiter; past everyone doing Saturday morning things. Kids played ball in the parks. Little old ladies walked their dogs. Adventurous inline skaters whizzed by a mother who was teaching her five-year-old how to ride a bike. Kids on silver scooters were everywhere.

The subdivisions dwindled and we merged into the heavier marina district traffic on A-1-A.

Traffic came to a stop ahead as the big drawbridge over the Intracoastal yawned to let a sailboat pass.

With the Vette's top down, we could look down the embankment that sloped from both sides of the ramp leading to the bridge.

I looked up and down the winding waterway in both directions. Jupiter really was the most beautiful spot on earth. The sparkling water in the Intracoastal was filled with every imaginable watercraft, from Jet Skis, to sailboats, to massive yachts of eighty feet or more.

From behind me I heard Buddy whooping from the saddle of the Harley. I turned and saw him waving and yelling furiously at several young and curvy, bikinied ladies on the deck of the sailboat passing under the bridge. They squealed back, laughing and waving. He grinned a big shit-eating grin and shouted above the low idle of the Harley to me, "Damn, I wish I were sixteen again!"

I shook my head, rolling my eyes to Jason. Jason flashed a smile. "We definitely gotta get him a woman." The smile faltered, "Just a hell of a better one than he had last time."

I grunted my agreement. The bridge had closed and traffic started to move. Jason focused intently on the car in front of us. "I'm not going to let any more selfish bitches bust down our Buddy Bear."

I smiled inwardly. Jason had indeed worked his magic on Buddy's psyche last night.

Topping the bridge, we had a beautiful view of Jupiter's most famous landmark to our right. The Jupiter Lighthouse has been a beacon for seafarers since 1860. The one-hundred five foot red-block tower is topped with a black lantern house. The elegant old girl still makes my heart soar every time I see her.

Just past Lighthouse Park, we turned right and headed back over the small drawbridge that leads to Jupiter Island.

"Almost there," he stated absently.

"Yeah, I'm surprised that they haven't turned the entire island into one big gated community," I ventured as we rumbled over the bridge.

Jason made a hard pull to the left and took Rocky Rhodes down a steep overgrown drive that looked like it was going to double back under the bridge. I grabbed the doorframe tightly, for a second there I thought Jason had thrown us over the side of the bridge ramp. The old drive was almost completely undetectable from the road.

Buddy must have thought the same thing, as I heard the big Harley's brakes squeal to a stop behind us. I looked back and saw him gingerly coaxing the big hog down the steep drive.

We came around a little bend and there she was, the Gator Tail. She really did look like a 1950's Howard Johnson's rip-off, complete with a sagging orange-roofed A-frame with a tattered white steeple on top. I could see the ramshackle flat roofed motel rooms meandering out back behind the A.

What really caught you're eye though was the Gator. I was about to comment when Buddy cut his engine and exclaimed, "Holy shit, will you look at that!"

The neon namesake of Donnie Rhodes's monstrosity was at least thirty-five feet tall. She must have been quite the sight when all of her neon was working. Covered in green neon scales, she had big red lips that flashed from smiling to a pucker. She had big blue neon eyes with long lashes whose flashing would have caused her to look like she was winking. It was also obvious that at one point her motorized tail had fanned up and down over the entrance to the topless bar.

Much of the lower neon was broken now, probably from the weather and bored local kids throwing rocks.

"Isn't she a beauty?" Jason whispered, getting out of the car. "I can't wait to get her back in working condition."

I've never been able to raise one eyebrow, but if I could have, I would have. "And you guys think I'm crazy for wanting to restore the Lady Orleans!"

Buddy was just about to make a smart-ass comment when we heard thrashing about behind one of the nearby huge mounds of debris.

We cautiously crept toward the ten-foot trash pile of discarded moldy mattresses and rotted fiberboard furniture. No one said it, but based on the condition of this place we were all expecting a very large rat.

We all felt the blood rush from our faces as a flurry of trash exploded from the top of the pile.

I froze. Buddy rooted himself for a fight with an audible grunt. Jason grabbed Buddy and gave a terrified squeal.

Otis's head popped up from the trash heap. We all blew out a sigh of relief, and Jason tried to fake that he had stepped on a piece of glass.

Otis looked and sounded like the disembodied Great Oz from the Emerald City.

"You," he thundered at Jason. "Where have you been? Do your aunt's wishes mean nothing to you?"

"Big O, how's it hanging, dude?"

"Don't call me that, you lazy, free-loading blue blood," Otis snarled as he extricated himself from the trash heap and came stomping down the side. The angrier Otis got, the stronger his Barbados accent came into play.

I smirked in Buddy's direction, "Isn't it nice to have the whole family together again?"

Otis squinted, pulling his spectacles out of his pocket. "My God, after all these years, it can't be."

"In the flesh," Buddy beamed.

"Master Saint Kristopher and Master Anthony, how are you?" Otis grabbed us both by the hands.

"Not eighteen any more, old friend. Just call us Kris and Buddy."

"Ah yes," Otis laughed, "the old Charlestonian habits die hard."

"Except for this one"—Otis curled his lip toward Jason—"I would rather have flaming Barbados sugar cane shoots stuck under my fingernails than to call that one Master."

"Awww, I love you too, Big O."

"I assume this jackal in playboy's clothing has shared with you why we are here in this God-forsaken trash pile?"

"Yes, we told Jason we would come out and help him search for the map today."

Otis beamed, "That will not be necessary."

"You found it?" Buddy exclaimed.

"Not exactly," Otis' eyes narrowed, "I found something even better!"

CHAPTER 10

▼

I had to admit, it was good to see old Otis again. As a wet-behind-the-ears college student, his advice had helped me more than once. Buddy had always thought of Otis as his surrogate father, since his real father had given him little support. There had been many a night long ago when we had lost track of time at Aunt E's and missed our curfew. Otis always managed to sneak us back on campus without anyone being the wiser.

Otis had aged well. The strong Caribbean face held a wide blunt nose and piercing chestnut eyes. His strong white teeth were still easy to smile. He wasn't as tall as I remembered—maybe five foot nine. But he had a wide muscular chest and was well grounded with stout legs. His olive-brown face was still free of age spots with just a few laugh lines and crow's feet. The only betrayal of Otis's age was his brilliant silver crew cut.

I laughed to myself; the widows of Charleston must be falling all over themselves for a date with the stately Dr. Otis.

"So what did you find, Big O?"

Otis sighed, but was too happy at seeing us to fight with Jason. Although they fought like an old married couple, I knew that they would lay down their lives for each other if necessary. "Come on," Otis beckoned, "I'll show you."

We followed him around the side of the Gator Tail, past the faceless motel room doors with their seedy secrets.

I swallowed a gasp. I knew that the Gator Tail was on the water, but I had no idea that she had this kind of water frontage. In front of us, the Intracoastal opened up across at least four hundred feet of deep-water dockage. Because of the nearby bridge, the waterway was much wider than normal here. It was probably seven or eight hundred feet to the other side. A trawler yacht, a forty-plus footer, lay anchored across the far side of the channel. Even at its size, it posed no barrier to boat traffic passing under the bridge.

"Holy cow, Jason." I gestured across the breadth of the water frontage. "Did I say this place would be worth five million? Try more like ten!"

Buddy agreed, but Otis was already heading down the inside wall of the line of motel rooms. We hurried to catch up.

As we got to the last room that backed up to the huge A frame, we noticed that it was a double suite.

"Uncle Donnie's lair?"

"Why the hell are you whispering, Jason?" Buddy ribbed. "I doubt very sincerely he is in there sleeping."

"Don't be so sure," Otis hissed flatly. "Some nightmares never go away."

I felt the little hairs on the back of my neck stand at attention as Otis turned the doorknob and entered the dark hole. Buddy threw out his chest and followed Otis unabashed. I dragged Jason in with me.

It took a second for our eyes to adjust to the gloom. I'm not sure what we expected, but based on the rest of the Gator Tail, it was sure to be a pit.

We couldn't have been more wrong. Sure the room was musty and bore that unmistakable smell of old quickie sex and urine-soiled carpet that seems to cling to all cheap hotels, but the room itself was pristine—1970's pristine, but pristine.

A big round bed filled the middle of the suite. I noticed the rusty, coin-fed Vibe-O-Matic attached to the headboard. The bright orange linens were turned back, as if waiting for Donnie Rhodes to return with one of the Gator Tail's dancers. It was eerie. I almost expected to see mints on the pillow, even though Donnie Rhodes hadn't slept in this bed in two decades.

"Look at that!" Buddy exclaimed.

At first I thought he meant the tiled mirrors on the ceiling, but on closer inspection I saw that the Big Guy was pointing to the rolled-up trapeze that was attached to the ceiling.

"Hoo-wee," Jason whistled. "Uncle Donnie was a hell-cat!"

"I don't even want to think of that nasty bastard being married to Miss Edna," Otis spat.

There was an old leather bar in one corner of the room; bottles of forgotten inhibitions sat in dusty silence. A fake zebra-skin rug lolled in front of an old TV with a cracked screen. A dilapidated fiberboard chest of drawers clung to a corner. That was about it.

"So what are we here to see, Otis?" Buddy's brow furrowed.

"Well, let me show you what led me to what I found." Otis walked through the bathroom doorway.

We all crowded into the small motel bath. Donnie Rhodes may have knocked down a wall to give himself a double room, but the bath was the same minuscule size found in cheap motels around the world. The bathroom hadn't fared as well over the years as the bedroom. Greenish black mold covered everything. We huddled in the middle of the room in fear of contracting instant ptomaine or hepatitis poisoning if we touched anything.

Otis yanked the rat-gnawed shower curtain open. I felt the bile rise in my throat as a half dozen two-inch-long roaches scattered down the tub drain.

"Is this supposed to get fun anytime soon, Big O?" Jason muttered grimly.

"Patience, Jason," Otis hissed.

He reached down and flipped the little corroded lever that closed the drain. There was a creaking sound, and the spring-loaded back panel of the shower slid away, revealing a large glass window.

"Damn," Buddy exclaimed, "is that what I think it is?"

"Yes"—Otis drummed his fingers on the glass—"a one-way mirror. See-through on this side, reflective on the other."

"So what does it look into?" I squinted, trying to see through a decade of film and scum.

"It's the dancers' dressing room," Otis grimaced.

"Boy, oh boy, Uncle Donnie was a serious perv."

Jason had an uncanny knack for stating the obvious.

"I started thinking"—Otis rubbed his chin. "It was plain that Mr. Rhodes had an alternative lifestyle, and a passion for secret doors. So where would he hide the map?"

"I got it," Buddy snapped his fingers. With one motion of his big burly arm, he swept us all back into the bedroom.

Then he walked over to the bed and pointed at the ceiling. "It's the trapeze. Isn't it, Otis?"

"Smart boy." Otis walked to his side. "Unsnap that little latch and the trapeze will unroll."

Buddy didn't even have to stand on his toes to reach up and unsnap the lock. The trapeze unrolled with a ring. It was the triangle-shaped variety, hooked to the ceiling with a stout chain.

He gave the chain a tug. Nothing. He tugged again, harder. Still nothing.

Jason poked him in the ribs, "Hop on it and hang there Buddy Bear, that will do the trick for sure."

Buddy was too caught up in thought to pay attention to Jason. "I don't get it, Otis. What am I missing?"

"It took me a while to figure it out, too. "I had to start thinking like Donnie Rhodes." He wrinkled his nose.

"Rhodes wouldn't have had the trapeze just for show," Otis blanched. "He would have wanted to use it: bedroom toy by night, secret hiding place by day. But he couldn't afford for one of his floozies to spring it accidentally during their high-wire act, so he made the compartment trigger a two-step process."

Otis walked over to the headboard. He dug around in his pocket until he found a quarter, holding it up in front of the Vibe-O-Matic.

"Uh, Otis, Mr. Doctor Professor," Jason teased. "This place hasn't had electricity in years."

"It never worked," Otis smirked. "It's the first-stage mechanical trigger for the secret compartment.

"Quite ingenious actually. If you didn't know the process, and just dropped in a quarter, you would think the vibrator was broken.

"If you pulled on the trapeze alone, just as Buddy did, you would think it was just a sick bedroom toy.

"However—" Otis dropped the coin in the slot of the Vibe-O-Matic. There was an audible click. "When you do them in sequence"—he motioned to Buddy, who pulled on the trapeze. "Open sesame."

There was the mechanical sound of rope weights dropping and gears grinding. A three-by-five-foot panel of mirrored ceiling above the trapeze slowly dropped to the bed on complaining ropes. Sitting on top of the ceiling panel was an old-fashioned iron safe.

"Luckily"—Otis gestured at the strong box—"I brought my stethoscope. It took me about an hour, but I got it open."

Jason reached and pressed down the lock actuator arm. The door opened with a rusty screech.

We all peered in intently. There was a snub-nosed .38 with a faux wood handle and an old notebook sitting in the safe. Jason pulled the binder out. Buddy gingerly took the pistol and tucked it into the back of his belt.

Jason's face fell, "Unless Granddad Bonnet invented spiral notebooks, this doesn't look like the map to me."

"It's not," Otis stated matter-of-factly. "It's Donnie Rhodes's business journal. It appears that for 'insurance purposes' he kept track of all his shady business deals and sexual exploits in that notebook."

"*Eww!*" Jason held the notebook with two fingers at the thought.

"I'll be taking that," a voice drawled from the motel doorway.

We all jumped at the stranger's interruption. He had a deep, old Florida, cracker accent. He was young, no more than twenty-five, and skeletally thin. He had painted-on faded jeans with a huge silver and brass belt buckle, and a pearl-buttoned shirt, with an elaborately embroidered yolk. To top it all off, his ten-gallon cowboy hat looked about two sizes too big.

Any other time, we would have broken up laughing at this dime-store cowboy, but it's funny how a double-barreled twelve-gauge shotgun pointed at your chest just seems to take the humor out of everything.

CHAPTER 11

▼

"You boys should never have come here," the Dime-Store Cowboy drawled. "At least you found the journal though, I been searching through this trash heap for three weeks. Now hand it over!"

We were stunned. Hell, I work behind a desk every day; I haven't had a real gun pointed at me since boot camp. Buddy, on the other hand, was in the Military Police. Out of the corner of my eye, I saw him subtly shift to a different angle to the rodeo reject. Otis was taking Buddy's cue and angling to the strangers' flank.

Jason just looked pissed. I knew he wasn't used to anyone taking anything away from him. A sparkling smile spread across his face. "Sure, friend, you want it; you got it."

With that, Jason flung the spiral notebook directly at Dime Store's head. The notebook sailed like a ninja throwing star, end-over-end, before fluttering open at the last second right in the guy's face.

The startled cowboy's instinct was to throw his hands up to protect himself. Unfortunately, that caused the shotgun to swing upward. Jason and I hit the deck just in time as Dime Store's tense fingers reflexively pulled both triggers.

The noise in the small room was instantaneous and deafening. The ugly nostrils were pointed toward the ceiling when they belched their buckshot, but a shotgun isn't called a scattergun for nothing. I felt the hot wind as the pellets whizzed just above me, like a sandstorm in the desert.

Buddy and Otis had flanked the stranger and were well outside of the shot pattern. Unfortunately, the mirrored ceiling wasn't so lucky. It shattered into a million pieces that rained down on us like shards of silver lightning. The ropes holding the platform sheared through, with four twangs, like guitar strings tuned past their limits. Jason and I covered our heads, and held our breath; it was about all we could do.

Dime Store tried to juggle the shotgun and the fluttering notebook. But something had to give. Greed won out over self-preservation and the shotgun clattered to the floor.

Buddy pulled Donnie Rhodes's .38 out of his belt and pointed it at the stranger.

Otis was prepared to spring.

Dime Store immediately reassessed his position, turned tail, and ran. Buddy was hot on his heels.

"Are you guys okay?" Otis paused.

"Yes, yes," Jason bellowed. "We have to get that notebook back!"

Otis sprang out the door after Buddy.

Jason and I shook the shards of glass out of our hair and were right behind him.

When our eyes adjusted to the bright Florida daylight, we could see that Buddy had Dime Store cornered down by the waterfront.

He pointed the pistol at the cowboy while Otis had his flank. The wide Intracoastal blocked the stranger's retreat. Jason and I came trotting up.

Buddy was talking slowly and softly. The cowboy had that same crazed look that jumpers have right before they leap from the tenth-floor ledge.

"It's okay, man," he soothed. "No hard feelings, no harm done; just give us back the journal."

"Get away from me. I shouldn't be out in the open like this; it's not safe."

I suddenly realized that the cowboy wasn't shaking because he was afraid of us.

I looked around, but everything looked the same as it had just a few minutes ago.

"You want to tell us why that journal is important enough to blow holes in someone for?" Jason demanded.

"She almost found it once." Dime Store was sweating profusely, big yellow stains spreading in the armpits of his rodeo shirt. "She has to be warned before they find it."

"She who?" I asked. "And find what?"

He opened his mouth to answer, but his face twisted into contortions that reminded me of the Edward Munch painting, *The Scream*.

Like the painting, no sound came from the cowboy's tortured mouth, but unlike the painting there was a two-foot pointed metal rod protruding from his chest.

Dime Store fell forward onto his face, forcing the rod out through his back. In South Florida we dive a lot, so I immediately recognized it as a spear from a JBL mini-carbine spear gun.

The journal fluttered to the ground.

By the looks on everyone else's faces, I knew that they hadn't realized what had happened. Buddy was afraid of the water, and the sea off Charleston was too murky for either Jason or Otis to have done much diving.

"Get down," I yelled. "Everybody flat on the ground, somebody out there has a spear gun."

Everyone dropped. I scanned the water; the JBL has a nine-foot accuracy range, so whoever did this was close, very close. I also knew that, in the hands of a professional, it takes about thirty seconds to reload a spear gun in the water. I didn't want to provide any easy targets.

It was then I saw the bubbles heading away from the seawall across the Intracoastal.

"There"—I pointed the bubbles out to my confused friends. "It's a diver, just one by the looks of it."

We got slowly to our feet. It was obvious the diver was making a getaway, rather than preparing for another round. The bubbles trailed in toward the big trawler yacht that was anchored on the far side of the waterway.

We watched in fascination as the bubbles stopped and a head broke the surface by the big boat's dive platform. A figure in a flat, black wet suit climbed aboard and tossed a scuba tank to the side. Almost instantly we heard the clank of the anchor chain rising, and the burble of the engines growling to life.

The figure removed a mask, unzipped a wet suit, and stepped gingerly out of it. We all gasped, as it was instantly obvious that the assassin was female; she wasn't wearing anything under the wet suit. She shook out her blond wet hair and grinned in our direction, hands on gorgeous hips. The captain of the boat pushed the throttles forward, and the luxury trawler began sliding north, away from the bridge. The beautiful assassin gave a slight bow, blew us a kiss, and disappeared into the ship's salon.

As the boat slipped away, I could just make out her name: *The Nefarious*, registered out of St. Barts.

We gathered our wits and hurried over to the cowboy. Otis rolled him over gently. Florida sugar sand had coagulated with the blood coming from his nose and mouth. A small lake of the red stuff pooled on the ground where his chest had been.

As gently as I could, I ripped the back of his shirt away and pulled the spear the rest of the way from his back. He let out a shuddering moan, and I felt bad for the move.

He had an intricate tattoo running from the base of his spine to between his shoulder blades. It was a wandering rose, with a huge white flower at its apex.

His hat had tumbled off during his fall, and I could see rolled up newspapers in the brim, his vain attempt to size it for himself.

Otis held the man's head on his lap as his life spilled away. "You have to find her," he burbled, great bubbles of blood forming at his nose on each word.

"Find whom?" Jason demanded sharply. "The chick with the spear gun?"

"Gentle, Jason, the man is dying," Otis reprimanded.

He softened, "The woman with the spear gun?"

"No," Dime Store gurgled, "My Rose, the lady with the white rose tattoo." The young cowboy went through a series of convulsive shudders, and then he was gone.

Otis laid the man's head in the sand, and covered his face with his too-large hat.

We all stood around, not knowing what to do next. Buddy opened the .38 and looked into the cylinder. "Figures no ammo." He clicked it shut with a flick of his big wrist. "Well, I guess we need to call the cops, but they don't need to see me with this." He gently slid it deep into the pocket of his pants. "I'll drop it in my saddle bags before the police get here."

Jason picked up the journal, "There is also no need to have the cops confiscate this." He stuck the journal into the back of his pants.

Otis grimaced, "Any other evidence you boys want to hide."

"Lighten up, Otis," Jason barked. "None of us know what just happened here, but we sure as hell don't need to spill our guts to Jupiter Island's finest about Aunt E's map. Do you really want to pull her into all of this?"

"No, you're right, but I'm a scientist and devoted to your aunt. It's not like I see cowboys speared on a daily basis."

Jason patted Otis on the shoulder. "None of us do, old man, but we have to be smart about how we handle this. After all, do you really think the cops are going to believe that we were hunting for a secret treasure map, found a hidden safe, got its contents hijacked by this cowboy who was assassinated before our eyes by a spear gun-waving, naked blonde? I mean, come on!"

Buddy was wide-eyed. "He's got a point. Unless we come up with a good story quick, we all may wind up in the county lockup."

I sighed grimly, "Okay, try this on for size. We had hired Dime Store here to help us clean out the Gator Tail so it could be sold. A friend of a friend recommended him, so we didn't know him that well. We were in another part of the Gator Tail, when we heard him cry out. We came running and found him lying here with the spear in him, and that boat pulling off from the dock."

"That could work," Buddy agreed. "It will look like it was maybe a drug sell gone wrong; no lack of them in South Florida."

"Yeah, and we were just innocent bystanders who were completely unaware that Dime Store here was into some dirty business," Jason commented.

"Okay, is everyone agreeable to that?"

We all nodded.

"Miss Edna isn't going to like this one bit," Otis frowned.

"What Aunt E doesn't know will not hurt us," Jason deadpanned in Otis's direction.

Otis grumbled but said nothing more.

I flipped open my cell phone and dialed 911. Within twenty minutes, the Jupiter Island's entire force—three police cars—came blaring down the Gator Tail's drive, lights flashing.

There was seldom ever any crime on Jupiter Island more shocking than trespassing or a drunken domestic disturbance, with spouses throwing martini glasses at each other. A murder was unheard of.

The Jupiter Island police force took hundreds of pictures, questioned us for hours, and ransacked the Gator Tail, as if that were possible. We had had just enough time to reattach the platform's ropes and get the safe back into the ceiling before we were overwhelmed with blue uniforms. We stuck the cowboys' shotgun up there, too. Thankfully, the cops assumed the broken mirrors were just part of the general dilapidation of the Gator Tail.

Five hours later, we stood outside the front of the Gator Tail, exhausted. The police and coroner were finally gone, and we were alone with our thoughts.

Jason broke the silence, and we all jumped. "One thing I don't understand, Otis?"

"He only doesn't understand one thing?" Buddy asked me sardonically.

I shrugged.

Jason ignored us, "If you already knew where the journal was, why were you digging in this front pile of rubbish when we came up?"

Otis beamed. "Because I had already had the chance to review the journal, and I knew there was something we would need in there."

"What?" I questioned. "A grimy old mattress?"

"No, Saint Kristopher," Otis inadvertently slipped back into his formal manner, "Donnie Rhodes's desk."

"What's in his desk?" Buddy tilted his head.

"This," Otis pulled a crumpled piece of paper out of his pocket, handing it to me.

"It's the registration for an airplane, and a really nice one too!"

"What kind of plane, Grantford?" Jason peered over my shoulder.

"A modified Lake Amphibian," I enthused.

"I've heard of them," Otis ventured. "They're the little seaplanes with the engine on top, right?"

"Yes, but there is something about Donnie Rhodes's Lake that sets it apart from the garden variety. It's a Seawolf."

"A Seawolf. What does that mean?"

"Well, I don't know how Donnie Rhodes managed to get his hands on one, but the Seawolf is a specially made Lake that is modified at the factory for military use.

"The Seawolf has a fifteen-hundred-mile range and fourteen-hour endurance.

"And," I added, "it's not sold to the general public"

"So what was Uncle Donnie doing with a souped-up contraband seaplane like that?" Jason looked at Otis.

"I don't know yet," Otis confessed. "I haven't gotten that far in the journal. We need to analyze its contents."

Buddy rubbed his ample stomach, "Well, I am analyzing my contents, and they are empty. In all the excitement today, we missed breakfast and lunch."

I beamed, "Yeah, who's up for the Dune Dog? We can grab a bite and start delving into the journal."

"What's the Dune Dog?" Jason wrinkled his brow.

"What's the Dune Dog?" Buddy sighed reverently. "Only about the best open-air chili dog and rock lobster emporium in all of South Florida!"

"Chili dogs and lobster?" Otis shuddered apprehensively.

"Trust us," I grinned, "You are in for a delectable delight."

We made our way to our vehicles.

"Want to drive Rocky Rhodes?" Jason jingled the keys under my nose.

"I thought you would never ask." I snatched the keys from him.

I slipped into the Vette's seat, and almost cut myself in half with the steering wheel. I held my breath and slid the seat back. I had forgotten that Jason is several inches shorter than me. I moved the side mirror slightly and then reached up to adjust the rearview mirror.

My hand froze in midair.

Jason must have seen the shocked look on my face, and noticing that I was looking in the rearview mirror, he turned in his seat to see what was causing my face to drain of all color. Behind us Buddy was casually putting up his kickstand, and Otis was disappearing behind the wheel of the big black Caddy.

He turned back to me perplexed, but sudden understanding appeared on his face as I moved the rearview mirror so that he could look into it.

On the face of the mirror in red lipstick were the words: *GIVE IT BACK, OR ELSE!*

CHAPTER 12

▼

We crunched into the Dune Dog's gravel lot. It's really little more than a large thatched-roof hut. The outside tiki lamps had already been lit for the evening, even though it was only three o'clock.

The only enclosed portion was the central hub where the kitchen area was located. Gray, weathered picnic tables ringed the hub. Clear plastic roll-down windows were attached to the eves to repel the afternoon storms, but they were rarely down for more than fifteen minutes.

The appeal of the Dune Dog was open-air eating. We were only a stone's throw from the Intracoastal and Lady Atlantic, and the salty breeze was heavy and warm.

As we piled out of our vehicles, Jason grinned, "Did you see the name on the stern of the trawler yacht at the Gator Tail?"

"Yeah, the *Nefarious*, registered out of St. Barts, why?"

He sucked a long breath of fresh sea air. "The *Nefarious* was what Stede Bonnet rechristened the *Royal James* when he stole it from Blackbeard. It's the same name as the original ship that was created from the great black tree."

I shivered, even though it had to be at least eighty degrees outside.

Our troubles evaporated as our stomachs took over. The smell of thick, heavy chili and boiling shrimp and lobster grabbed our empty stomachs and shook them hard.

I could tell that Otis's and Jason's concerns over the place had evaporated.

We squeezed into a picnic table toward the back: Buddy and Otis on one side, Jason and I on the other.

"The trick," Buddy stated authoritatively, "with the Dune Dog is to mix the tastes. You cannot eat just chili dogs, and you cannot eat just lobster. They must be mixed and savored; as they complement one another like a fine wine does excellent veal."

Jason rolled his eyes, "You have got to be kidding?"

Otis wrinkled his nose. "Not the kind of place where I would normally order lobster."

I shook my head in faux disappointment. "You two have been dining in those vanilla five-star restaurants in Charleston for way too long. It's time to open up your senses. I wouldn't go so far as to recommend the Buddy Bear special, but the ten-dollar rock lobster can't be beat."

"Hey, your loss," Buddy shrugged.

Jason looked skeptical, "What kind of lobster can you get for ten dollars? Are you sure it isn't one large shrimp?"

"Trust me," I grinned.

A dark-haired Latin lovely suddenly dropped onto Buddy's lap and threw her arms around his big neck.

"My Butty Bear, how are chu?" She trilled with a thick Cuban accent.

He blushed at the embrace that put her copper brown breast within inches of his nose.

Jason leaned over to me, "Did I say we needed to get Buddy a woman? I think he needs to get me one!"

I grinned, "Hi, Violet, these are our friends, Jason and Otis."

"Veddy nice to meets you." Violet hopped up from Buddy's lap and whipped out her pad. "How is the Lil and her ponies?"

"Everyone is great," I beamed.

She eyed Jason up and down. "And what can I get for you, Mr. Male Model Romance Novel Man?"

Jason actually stammered; I had seldom seen him flustered. "I'll have the lobster deal and a Rolling Rock, if you have it?"

"Of course, we having it," she jotted on her pad.

"And you, Mr. Long John Silver Hair?" she questioned Otis.

Otis politely ordered the lobster special as well.

Violet turned to me, "Mr. Kristopher, will you be ordering Mr. Buddy Bear's special tonight?"

"Oh no," I groaned, "I would be up half the night if I ate six chili dogs and two rock lobsters. I'll have the lobster special and a Rolling Rock as well."

"Suits yourself," she turned to Buddy. "So, Mr. Smoky the Bear, you aren't going to disappoint Miss Violet, are you?"

"No, ma'am," he had finally regained his voice. "I'll have the usual."

"Very good!" She twirled away making sure to give us a clear view of her swaying rear as she entered the kitchen door.

"*Whew*," Jason exhaled enthusiastically.

"Gentlemen," I announced, "welcome to South Florida."

Less than five minutes later, Violet had us loaded up with Rolling Rocks all the way around.

Jason shared the history of the mysterious boat's name with everyone, and I described the lipstick message. It was obvious that the journal was very important to someone.

As we waited for our food, Jason pulled out the notebook and laid it in the middle of the table.

There was nothing spectacular looking about it. It was a standard spiral notebook with a red cardboard cover. On the inside front cover was Donnie Rhodes's name and the Gator Tail's address. The contents were in spectacularly neat order. It was in a transaction layout with dates, dollar figures, names, and subject matter all placed into careful columns.

The first entry was dated just after Donnie Rhodes had arrived in Jupiter. It was for fifty thousand dollars. Rhodes had itemized nearly a hundred different items he had bought from Sea Breeze Restaurant & Lounge Supply. Everything from a $10,000 mahogany bar to three chrome dancer poles for $500. It appears that Donnie Rhodes had planned on turning the Gator Tail into a strip club right from the beginning. There was another transaction the next day to Island Liquors for $10,000.

"Looks like Uncle Donnie started interviewing employees right away," Jason pointed to a transaction.

He was right. Rhodes detailed the time, date, and acts performed on him by each of the strippers he hired. He apparently even had a pay scale associated with the "quality" of the acts performed.

"This man was one sick individual," Buddy commented.

"You're telling me," Jason stated flatly.

We flipped through page after page of stripper reviews and Gator Tail start-up costs. Apparently Rhodes was very picky about his employees; he only hired about twenty-five percent of the strippers he had sex with.

"There's a familiar name," Buddy pointed to a transaction.

I scanned the page. "Yes, several familiar names, it looks like Rhodes was paying off some pretty high-level Palm Beach County officials to get the Gator Tail in business."

"He would have to be." Buddy agreed. "There had to be some serious palm greasing to get a place like the Gator Tail opened up on Jupiter Island."

"Oh my God, Buddy, look at that name," I gasped.

"Jones Jenkins," he read. "Hey, wasn't that the zoning board chairman who embezzled ten million dollars, and disappeared down to the islands?"

"Exactly," I recalled. "That had already happened by the time we moved to Jupiter, but it was one of the biggest things to ever hit these parts."

"There were all kinds of conspiracy theories floating around," Buddy remembered.

"Well, it appears that at least one of them was true," I ventured. "The twenty-five grand payment listed here isn't to Jones Jenkins, but to a Uilleam Urbay for the 'Termination' of Jones Jenkins. The notes column says, *Elimination of Zoning Problems*."

We all fell silent.

"Man," Jason's voice wavered, "I knew Uncle Donnie was a crook, but I didn't think he was capable of murder."

"It's becoming more and more apparent why this journal would be important to a lot of people around here," Otis ventured.

"Where is the part about the Lake Seawolf?" I asked Otis.

"The page has a picture attached; that's what made me flip to it. Probably about three quarters of the way through."

I flipped through the pages until I got to the heavier one with the Polaroid attached. I pulled the picture loose from the double-sided tape that was holding it to the page. There was a grinning Donnie Rhodes standing next to the wildest looking airplane I had ever seen. The plane was sitting in the water with its cockpit open. Rhodes was standing beside it on the dock, as if about to get in. The plane was white, with red and green stripes running down the fuselage, floats, engine cowl, and tail. As the stripes got closer to the nose, they wavered, crossed, and flowed together, turning into an elaborate rendering of flowing feathers that ended at the nose of the plane with the head and beak of a fierce-looking parrot. Above the stripes on the engine cowl was the word *Jaega*.

I handed the picture to Buddy, "Recognize the name of the plane?"

"Jaega, Jaega," he pondered aloud. "Oh yeah, the Indians, right?"

"You got it," I grinned.

"What are you talking about Indians?" Jason wrinkled his brow.

"When the Spanish first came here, they found the Jaega Indians living along the Loxahatchee River and what would become Jupiter Inlet. The Indians called the Loxahatchee, which intertwines through Jupiter and feeds the inlet, the Jobe River. Later, when English settlers found the area around 1763, Jobe sounded to them like the mythological god Jove, or Jupiter, and the name Jupiter has remained ever since."

"If I recall correctly," Buddy added, "the Jaegas were fierce shipwreck salvagers."

"Well, that sounds pretty appropriate for Uncle Donnie so far," Jason deadpanned.

I started reading the Jaega's journal entry while the guys passed around the picture.

"It looks like Rhodes bought the plane illegally from Jupiter Marine Salvage."

"That's the guy you traded your Jag to for salvaging the Lady Orleans, right, Kris?"

"The one and only," I grimaced, "I knew that piggy-eyed bastard was bad news."

"There is a *Palm Beach Post* article here. It says," I paraphrased, "that the Coast Guard Lake Seawolf sank while taxiing during rough seas on a training maneuver in the Jupiter Inlet, and her two crewmen drowned.

"A Mr. Orin Lawson, owner and proprietor of Jupiter Marine Salvage, rushed to the scene with his salvage boat, the *Sweet Revenge*, and raised the plane that was sitting in twenty feet of water.

"A Coast Guard cutter arrived just as Mr. Lawson broke the surface with the Seawolf. Mr. Lawson refused to turn the Seawolf over to the Coast Guard, claiming ownership under international salvage laws.

"The Coast Guard demanded that he at least turn over their dead crewmen to them. The infuriated Captain James of the cutter reported that Lawson stated, 'You want them, go get them', and unceremoniously dumped the bodies of the crewmen into the sea."

"Geez, nice guy," Jason scowled.

I continued, "The Coast Guard jumped to recover the bodies. By the time the grizzly chore was done, Orin Lawson and the *Sweet Revenge* had steamed away.

"The Coast Guard filed suit against Jupiter Marine Salvage the next day for the return of their plane. The judge quickly awarded in the Coast Guard's favor, and more than happily issued a search warrant for Lawson. But when they got to the big warehouse of Jupiter Marine Salvage, the plane was nowhere to be found.

Orin Lawson was quoted as saying the plane fell overboard on his way back to port, and he didn't recall exactly where it sank."

"Wow," Buddy commented, "I guess naming the plane after marauding Indian ship salvagers was appropriate."

"Uncle Donnie's little joke," Jason added grimly.

Otis spoke up, "So that's why the loud paint job. What could be more opposite of the traditional subdued Coast Guard orange and white than that wild killer parrot paint job?"

"Exactly," Buddy commented, "Hide in 'plane site,' pardon the pun."

"So what else is in there about the Jaega?" Otis quizzed.

"Well, let's see," I scanned the journal page. "Looks like Rhodes stored her in an old warehouse north of here in Port St. Lucie. Numerous bills for parts and labor to fix the water damage; looks like it took him about a hundred grand to get her into flying condition again."

I flipped a couple of pages ahead. "Donnie Rhodes was doing all kinds of illegal things with the Jaega; everything from drug runs to Jamaica to smuggling rich illegal aliens out of Cuba who had pissed Castro off."

Otis looked perplexed. "Are you saying that Rhodes did all the flying himself? Seems a man like him wouldn't want to get his hands dirty?"

Jason commented, "Uncle Donnie was a schemer. He was always looking for a new angle to make money; he got off on it."

"So you think he would have gotten off on smuggling?" I asked him.

"Of course, what do you think attracted him to Aunt E and the Bonnet family in the first place?"

CHAPTER 13

▼

Violet carried tray after steaming tray to our table. She set up a little side table for Buddy's six foot-long chili dogs and two lobsters. I saw the surprise in Jason's and Otis's eyes at the amount of food they had.

"This lobster is at least four pounds." Otis drew a deep breath. "How do they sell it for only ten dollars?"

"Yeah." Jason licked his lips. "I'm going to have to send mine back, the claws are missing."

Buddy rolled his eyes good-naturedly. "Jason, you dumb ass, that's a Florida lobster, not a Maine lobster. They don't have claws."

"Oh, okay," Jason dug in without another thought.

"We have a little something down here called lobster mini-season a couple of times a year," I commented while passing Buddy the Doc Ford's Green Flash hot sauce that I knew he was about to ask for.

"It's a crazy free-for-all when everyone can legally dive for their maximum limit over a two-day period. Mark, the owner and head chef of this place, shuts the place down during lobster mini-season and takes all of his employees and as many friends as he can squeeze onto his boat to dive for their maximum.

"If they are lucky, they can get enough lobsters to keep us in ten-dollar specials until the next mini-season."

"You don't want to be on the water during lobster mini-season," Buddy commented with his mouth full. "The waters all around Jupiter are chock-full of drunken divers on overcrowded boats; it's one big party."

"Sounds like your kind of scene to me," Jason grinned.

"Not me." Buddy shook his shell cracker at Jason. "I hate the water. You will not catch me diving, sailing, or"—he gave me a sideways glance—"landing on the wet stuff."

I shook my head with a sigh. "You can tell how bad Buddy hates the water. Hell, Lil has to hose him down when she gives the horses a bath, just so he will take a shower!"

Buddy growled playfully at me between bites as everyone laughed.

After that, for the next forty-five minutes, the only sound was the cracking of lobster shells and the clinking of Rolling Rock bottles. On top of the lobsters, Violet showered us with red potatoes, hot corn on the cob, and hush puppies.

Before it was all over, Jason had nabbed two of Buddy's chili dogs and converted to the Church of the Buddy Bear Special.

Violet passed around hot lemon-scented washcloths to everyone, as we lolled about our chairs like chunky sea buoys.

"So," she simmered, "did Violet make chu boyz happy?"

We all groaned an affirmative.

She abruptly gave Buddy a slap on the back of the head, "Good, then you boyz give Violet a better tip than you did last time."

When Buddy's eyes stopped rattling in his head, he swiftly stammered, "Yes, ma'am."

"You, Mr. Kristopher." She raised her finger to me. I cowered behind Jason, who tried to scamper underneath the table.

"You need to teach him better." She patted his head with the hand she had just used to slap him. "After all, the Buddy Bear, he just a big dumb animal."

"Yes, ma'am," I squeaked, grinning. "I'll make sure he tips double tonight."

"Hey," Buddy exclaimed.

Violet stopped rubbing his head and gave him a cross look.

"Okay, okay, double it is," he grinned from ear to ear.

"Good, then I'll go get your check," she smoldered off toward the cash register.

"This place is dangerous." Jason peeked at Violet's rump at the register, as it bounced to the steel drums blasting over the speaker system. "I like danger."

"Speaking of danger," Otis turned serious. "There is enough in that journal to take weeks to decipher to get the big picture. In the meantime, why don't we skip to the last few pages to see if that can give us some kind of clue as to what happened to the infamous Donnie Rhodes?"

I turned the journal to the last three pages, as we all squinted to see it in the remaining rays of the day. Soon Violet would be turning on the Dune Dog's buzzing ancient fluorescent lights.

The last few pages seemed to be about Rhodes getting the Jaega ready for a long flight to the islands. He had a couple of paying passengers who were looking for something that was lost and he had the map to find it.

It was the first real evidence that Rhodes actually had the map; we all felt vindicated.

"Well, that settles it," Jason commented. "We just hop a jet down to St. Barts and pick up the trail there."

"I'm not hopping a jet anywhere," I stated flatly. "You may be free to island hop, but Buddy and I have real nine-to-five jobs here in paradise."

Buddy shook his head, "I'll help you as much as I can tomorrow, and after work next week, but it's 'The Season' at the Celestion, and I have to stick close."

"The Season" in South Florida is that time of year when the rich and/or retired snowbirds flock to South Florida, to tie up our golf courses, idle their Bentleys in the fast lane, and generally cause you to have to wait two hours to get into any restaurant.

Jason looked deflated, "But I can't do this without you guys. We're the Krewe of Jupiter, remember?"

"I'm sorry, Jason, we're not nineteen anymore. We can't just go running after every treasure that floats over the horizon."

"But how do you ever get the treasure if you don't venture over the horizon?" he asked meekly.

"Kris is right," Otis interceded. "We don't have enough evidence to go flying down to the islands half-cocked. In fact, tomorrow morning I am going to drive back to Charleston to do some in-depth study of this journal. After a few weeks of meticulous due diligence on the document in my lab, I am sure I can come up with a sound plan for us to follow."

"I can't believe you guys are deserting me like this," Jason appealed to Buddy.

"We aren't abandoning you, pal," Buddy soothed, "Things are just a lot more complicated than they used to be."

Jason sighed dejectedly.

"Look, Jason, we still have some leads we can follow. Jones Jenkins was a very sly and dirty politician when he was chairman of the zoning board. Even before the embezzlement story and his subsequent disappearance, there were numerous hints and allegations of payoffs and bribes. Jenkins's wife is still around, the now-scorned socialite Biddy Jenkins. She could be one point of attack."

Buddy rubbed his ample upper lip, "Orin Lawson and Jupiter Marine Salvage could be the second prong."

"And last," I added, "trying to find out more about the mysterious *Nefarious* and her deadly diver would be the third route; a boat like the *Nefarious doesn't* go unnoticed, even in South Florida."

Jason agreed but not without being obstinate. He insisted on handling one of the three avenues by himself. We were highly skeptical. Jason tended to get himself into trouble when unchaperoned. He kept arguing and finally wore us down with his insistence that since we only had one day to devote to him, it made sense for us to split up to cover as much ground as possible. Jason was the master of the guilt trip.

We all finally agreed on our directions. Since Orin Lawson already knew Buddy and me from the salvaging of the Lady Orleans, Jason would hit Jupiter Marine Salvage. Buddy would utilize his Celestion credentials to get an audience with the Widow Jenkins. With my computer background and connections, I would focus on researching the *Nefarious* and her relationship to this sordid affair.

We piled out into the Florida evening. We shook hands.

Otis slipped into the Cadillac, promising to let us know something one way or another in a few days. He headed south on US-1 where he could eventually intersect with I-95 North toward Charleston.

Jason and I climbed into Rocky Rhodes, and Buddy got on his Harley. I was sullen and quiet; I wasn't thrilled with Jason going it alone to Jupiter Marine Salvage. Jason was suave with his lines and quick with his wits, but Orin Lawson was dirt-mean and greedy. He usually had a few goons hanging around his salvage yard to do the heavy lifting. I had a bad feeling about this.

Buddy was lost in his thoughts behind us, no doubt formulating an intricate plan for getting in to see the widow. Jason was a bundle of energy bouncing behind the steering wheel as we plowed through the muggy night

We drove back to La Vie Dansante in our own separate orbits, numbly agreeing when we arrived to start out on our separate journeys in the morning. Why did I have this overwhelming feeling of dread that it wasn't going to be that simple?

CHAPTER 14

▼

Morning came way too soon, and I found myself sitting in my library at La Vie Dansante, staring intently at my computer monitor. I checked the Coast Guard's News Bulletin Page to see if there had been any unusual activity lately; there was none. The Town of Jupiter police news blotter page only mentioned the shooting at the Gator Tail in passing, with a vague reference to an unknown trawler yacht leaving the scene. No other mention of the *Nefarious* was listed.

In desperation I did a search on *boat registrations* on the official Web site of the Government of St. Barts. I should have known better. There were nothing but harbor regulations, and airport hazard warnings, along with a few tourist tax hike notifications and visa requirements. They probably still kept their damn boat registrations on three-part forms, locked away in some damp island basement.

But of course that was exactly why people register their boats in places like St. Barts. No taxes, no questions; just pay the registration and all the evidence disappears.

The only other place I could think of that might have info was U.S. Customs. However, one look at their vault-like Web site and I knew they would never willingly cough up anything.

Now, I am a pretty technical guy. That being said, I don't claim to be a hacker. However, I do have acquaintances that exist on the opposite end of the spectrum from me. They make their money online in ways that are best not questioned. They have no visible means of support. They are pale and pasty, and their pupils are permanently dilated. They are the professional hit men of the cyber underworld, taking care of any problem you have for a favor or a fee. I happen to know one right here in Palm Beach County.

I pointed the nose of my BMW M3 convertible toward Jupiter Marina. Once there, I paid the inflated fee to an overly cheery ferry clerk and sat back for the short ride to Peanut Island, south of Jupiter in Lake Worth.

Although Peanut Island appears to be a well-forested natural island, it's in fact the dump for dredged material from the inland waterway, covered with Australian pines. The Lake Worth portion of the waterway was actually a freshwater lake until Henry Flagler opened it to the ocean. When Flagler finally reached Palm Beach with his East Coast Railroad, he built White Hall, his Lake Worth mansion, which is now a museum. Back in the freewheeling days of railroad building, Flagler had decided that he would prefer salt water in his backyard and simply opened the lake to the ocean. Peanut Island is the result of this dredging.

As the little ferry made its final run toward the Peanut Island dock, I could see the peeling old Coast Guard station and boathouse through the trees, an expansive white colonial building with red-tin roof that opened in 1936 and shut in 1996.

I wasn't here to see the abandoned Coast Guard station. I was here to visit a bomb shelter, and an ex-Seabee who had gotten lost in time.

The shelter is a stark reminder of how close the world had come to nuclear war: a bomb shelter, buried twenty-five feet below this island's surface and coated with lead, built for President John F. Kennedy in late 1961 as tensions heightened between the United States and the Soviet Union. It's tucked away behind the old Coast Guard station.

I slipped away from the guided tour and made my way to the bunker.

The cover story in the 1960s was that it was a munitions depot; but you don't have bathrooms, a communications center, and air filtration equipment in a munitions depot.

In 1961, the Seabees were sent on the classified task of completing the construction of the bunker. One of those Seabees was Dan Hall, called Shrimper Dan by his friends because his daddy had manned a shrimp boat off Shem Creek in Charleston.

I got to the hidden entrance of the shelter and pushed aside the bushes and scrub brush that covered the tunnel door.

The descending hallway was of round corrugated metal, much like a big sewer pipe, leading to the heart of the shelter. The way looked treacherous and damp, but the second I stepped into the pipe I realized the air was filtered, clean, and sanitized. Old Dan must still keep the air filtration system going, still waiting for the coming Armageddon.

Shrimper Dan had met a lovely lady when he was first in South Florida. Her name was Jill Trundle, and she was one of the early free-spirited flower children. He loved her with a passion that enflamed his soul. She was the only thing that had ever distracted him from his duties.

Vietnam deflowered the hippies, and the call came for Dan to serve his country overseas. Jill argued with him and begged him to stay. They would run away to Mexico or Canada together. It was an emotional struggle for Dan, but ultimately his devotion to his Seabees unit won out. They made love in the bunker, the night before he was shipped out.

Shrimper Dan served three tours of duty with his unit in Vietnam, and then went on to serve in a secret elite force that took care of any other dirty little skirmishes the government wanted them to tackle. Dan was one of the few guys ever to make the jump from Seabees to Special Forces.

Dan only received one letter from Jill. She wrote to tell him that on that night in the bunker, they had conceived his child, which he would never see. She could no longer support a country or a man who could perform the atrocities that were occurring in the war-torn world. That was the last Dan ever heard from her.

One day, Dan realized he had killed more people than he had ever loved in his life. He walked away, just dropped his gun and gear and left.

The military had way too much training invested in the Seabee to let him go that easy. Dan was on the run for years. A brilliant man, as he moved from town to town, he would enroll in local colleges, cramming as much knowledge about computers and telecommunications into his head as he could, until the MPs picked up his trail again.

If you added up all the courses he had taken, he probably had a master's degree several times over. He never had the luxury of graduating from any of the dozen or so schools he covertly attended.

Finally, he purchased everything he needed to go underground, and he came back to Peanut Island to disappear permanently into the long-abandoned bomb shelter.

As I got to the bottom of the tunnel, it turned left. I was in a shower area that would have been used as a decontamination area for the president and his aides in the event of nuclear war. I felt the hairs rise on my arms. I could almost see the ghosts of frantic Secret Service agents hustling a defiant President Kennedy into the room.

From there I entered the main room. There was a giant presidential seal painted on the hard gray floor, and an oriental rug under a set of bunk beds. There were a few lockers and a hardwood desk flanked by faded flags.

The ceiling was thick with pipes for the air-filtration system. The bunks were made with military corners. I knew that Dan was still here, even though I hadn't spoken to him in person in almost two years.

I knew better than to call out. He hadn't escaped detection for this long by being stupid. I was sure he was in the hidden communications room in the bunker; his early warning systems would have given him notice that I was coming. He was being careful, making sure that I was really alone.

I walked over to the presidential desk and picked up the red phone. There was no keypad or dial on the phone, and no dial tone, just a soft electronic whisper waiting for my word.

Feeling somewhat silly, I spoke into the phone, "Castro wouldn't know a missile if it shot him in the ass." I put the receiver back on the hook, hoping that Dan hadn't changed the pass phrase.

There was a metallic grinding of well-oiled gears. The wall behind the desk spun on a pivot, opening a small crack for me to pass through.

I was in the old communications system room, but the only thing old was the room itself. Modern raised flooring covered the area, and there were racks and racks of computer hardware, taking up every wall. Sitting at a gray computer desk in front of a bank of ten monitors was Shrimper Dan.

He had changed little in the past two years. He still had that same hawk nose and square chin. The eyes were the same faded blue. The shoulder-length, receding hair was now completely gray and tied up in a ponytail. He was probably in his mid-fifties but looked older, with frown lines like deeply plowed furrows.

He glowered at me. "What the hell are you doing here, you son of a bitch? Didn't I tell you I never wanted to see you again?"

I sighed audibly, "Yeah, I missed you too, Dan."

CHAPTER 15

▼

Shrimper Dan leapt to his feet, knocking his chair over. For a second, I thought the old Seabee was going to come after me, but he just stood there, eyes flashing, clenching and unclenching his fists.

"I'm sorry, Dan. I wouldn't have come if I hadn't needed your help."

"My help, my help?" he hissed through clenched teeth. "How dare you ask for my help after what you did to me?"

"I honestly thought I was doing you a favor," I murmured.

I had stumbled across Shrimper Dan several years ago. Not by finding his lair, that was practically impossible. I actually found out about him through the death of his elderly mother in Charleston.

I had attended an auction in Charleston for the estate of the late Grace Hall. Shrimper had been there and had outbid everyone, for his mother's meager possessions.

If anyone even made a motion to bid against him, he would drive the price up two to three times the intrinsic value of the item.

By the time it got to the items I wanted; only Shrimper Dan and I still sat in the cold, steel auction chairs. The auctioneer started the bidding process, but I waved him off. "I'll not be bidding on anything else today," I announced. "Please give the courtesy of any other purchase options to my friend here." I had been sitting one row back from Shrimper. He turned and gave me a solemn nod.

The auctioneer huffed and threw his hands up in surrender. "The rest of the lot for an additional two-fifty to you, sir?"

Shrimper nodded.

"Sold," sighed the auctioneer.

Dan didn't move from his chair. He just sat there staring at the cold hard ground. For a few moments, I contemplated leaving but felt drawn to the strange affair.

I moved up to the chair beside him. "She was your mother?" I questioned.

"I didn't realize she was so in debt to the IRS. I tried to buy the entire estate from the damn Feds right from the beginning, but they insisted on the public auction."

I stuck my hand out. "Saint Kristopher Grant, but my friends call me Kris."

"Dan," he smiled vaguely. "Back when I had friends, they use to call me Shrimper Dan."

"My pop had a shrimp boat on Shem Creek," he offered by way of explanation.

"Well, Shrimper Dan," I grinned broadly, "I would like to buy you a drink at one of the fine establishments along Shem Creek, in honor of the spirit of your mother and father."

"That would be nice." Some of the air seemed to refill his lungs.

So we drank beer and ate shrimp late into the night. We exchanged encrypted emails for the next year, and over time I had learned more and more about my reclusive friend. It took him nearly six months to share with me his secret location, and I was quite surprised to discover that he had been in Palm Beach County the whole time we had been communicating. Dan is brilliant and was one of the most gifted hackers I ever met.

As I got to know Shrimper Dan, he even cautiously invited me to the hidden bunker on Peanut Island. The all-encompassing world he had built there was incredible. He spent every waking hour building tools and utilities that he gave away as open-source software on the Internet.

Outside of his huge investment in technology, Dan's means were modest. He took a few jobs on the Internet to keep himself stocked with provisions and his technology up-to-date. Most of the functions he performed involved getting stolen data back for big corporations, or performing white-hat hacking services for those same corporations to identify their security flaws so that their data wouldn't be stolen again.

As our friendship grew, I learned more about his lost love, Jill, and the child he never knew. The world's technology had really only matured enough in the last ten years for him to do a true global computer search for her. He searched in vain. It was as if she'd dried up and blown away in 1962. It was the only technology mission he had ever failed at, and the only one he'd ever really cared about.

I felt bad for Dan and decided to do a little research myself. If there were no computer records of her, that could mean only one thing. She had a true paper trail to wherever she was, rather than an electronic one.

It's really hard not to leave an electronic trail these days. Everyone has utility bills, driver's licenses, tax receipts, and credit card slips. All of these leave electronic trails.

Wherever she was, she was somewhere that shunned the modern world. Jill Trundle was a poor, unemployed flower child. She couldn't have gone that far. I checked the historical records in the basement vault of the Palm Beach County Library. In an old yellowed newspaper clipping, I found a lead. There was a short story about a tribe of slave descendants who lived on a fringe island in the Bahamas called Crooked Island.

The island existed in virtual obscurity until 1783, when American loyalists began to settle there. These former plantation owners brought slaves and money to start a short-lived cotton industry, which, by the beginning of the Nineteenth Century, had more than forty plantations employing twelve hundred slaves. The cotton trade collapsed, and the plantation owners went broke. They couldn't afford to move such a vast number of slaves back to the U.S. So they left them.

The island is very hard to reach, and has no tourist facilities. However, the article went on to say that the island was having a strange appeal to the so-called hippies who were flocking there to escape civilization.

Bingo, just the thing that would have appealed to Jill Trundle, and it was only a half day's boat ride away. I made some static-filled phone calls to the Crooked Island customs offices, and after being forwarded fifty times, finally got a clerk with a thick Bahamian accent who looked up Jill Trundle's name in one of their big gray file cabinets. Sure enough, they had an address on file for her.

I had just gotten my general aviation license at that time, and so I rented a small Cessna. I talked Shrimper Dan into making the flight to Crooked Island with me. He agreed reluctantly.

As we sighted land, much to Dan's relief, we could make out the curved shallow lagoon. Crooked Island is one of four islands forming an atoll that hugs the beautiful shallow waters of the Bight of Acklins. The island opened onto the Windward Passage, the dividing point between the Caribbean Sea and the Bahamas.

I landed the small plane on a dirt runway, which was a first for me. I didn't share that with Dan. After two hours of red tape, we finally had the address of Jill Trundle. Shrimper Dan was finally starting to trade his stress in for some old-fashioned excitement.

A beat-up cab took us to the address on Sugar Cane Lane. My heart fell. The shack that had once been there was nothing but a burned-out cinderblock foundation. Judging by the head-high weeds and scrub palms, it had been torched long ago. We got out, and I asked an old black woman cleaning fish under the shadow of a tree, if she knew Jill Trundle. She nodded and pointed toward the end of the road. I saw what rose above the trees there, but I wasn't ready to give up hope.

Dan and I trudged the quarter of a mile to the end of Sugar Cane Lane, and the weather-beaten gray church, wind-burned steeple rising above the trees.

We entered the little overgrown graveyard with its leaning picket fence beside the church. It took us less than five minutes to find it. The small marker said simply, "Jill Trundle, Died Giving Birth, November 9, 1963."

I tried to talk to Shrimper Dan, to comfort him in some way, but he was a stoic rock. He wouldn't speak or look at me. He just trudged back to the waiting cab, and we rode to the plane. He gave me the silent treatment all the way back to Palm Beach International Airport.

I turned the rented Cessna back in and went back to Dan where he was smoking on the tarmac.

"I'm really sorry, Dan. I didn't know."

"Shut the fuck up," he hissed. "Stay out of my life. I don't ever want to see you again." He stormed off toward the gate.

I gave him some time to cool down, and then shot him an email. No reply. I kept trying to contact him for a few months but finally gave up.

And after two years, here I was in his secret bunker being berated by him once again.

CHAPTER 16

▼

"Look, Dan," I stammered. "I'm sorry about Jill. I'm sorry I dragged you to Crooked Island. I'm sorry I didn't go over by myself first to confirm that she was still there and alive.

"I'm sorry about a lot of things, but I'm not sorry that I spent six months of my life trying to help a friend find the love he lost. I know what it's like to lose someone. I know what it's like to ache to hold someone who was torn from you. I suffered through three years of sorrow before I started looking for Jill for you. I just wanted to make the pain go away."

Dan took a deep breath. "Skylar?"

I shook my head as I struggled to keep the dam from bursting.

Dan bit his lower lip as his brow furrowed. It made him look even older and, for the first time, even frail.

"I know you have no interest in continuing our friendship." I set my jaw. "But based on the problem I am tackling, one person has been murdered already, and I'm afraid there will be even more trouble before it's all said and done."

"I need your help on this one, Shrimper."

He sighed the grief of a thousand years. "Okay, Kris, what do you need?"

I pulled up a chair beside his desk and quickly repeated the whole story to him. How I was trying to locate the *Nefarious*, but couldn't find anything about her through the normal channels of the Internet. I told him that I thought U.S. Customs might be a good source, since she was registered in St. Barts. She had to have passed through customs at some point.

"Whoa"—Dan held his hand up—"infiltrating anything in the U.S. government's realm isn't something to be entered into lightly anymore. Since the terrorist attacks, the Feds shoot first and ask questions later."

"But can it be done?"

"Hell, yeah, anything can be done. If it should be done is the question."

"Let's back up for a minute. You said you couldn't find anything on the boat's registration. How about its manufacturer?"

"I didn't think about that," I admitted. I gave Dan all the specs I could remember on the boat.

He hands flew across the keyboard, and in a few seconds a beautiful trawler yacht filled one of the ten screens.

"Is that your boat?" Dan gestured with a magician's flourish.

My mouth dropped open. It was the exact same model boat as the *Nefarious*. "That's it. What is it?"

"A Grand Banks forty-two-foot trawler yacht," he commented. "They're very popular."

"The problem with popularity," I grimaced, "is that there are probably hundreds built every year."

"Agreed," Dan cocked his head. "But how many are shipped to St. Barts for registration each year?"

"Good point, so can you get into their records?"

"I'm betting these guys have virtually no security. I mean who hacks into a boat builder's systems?"

He looked up their corporate address and phone number. "Looks like they are based out of Seattle, Washington."

"Now I will just run this daemon dialer program to ping all of the phone numbers in a range of five hundred from their corporate number. Most office phone systems number their lines sequentially. If we're lucky, we'll get a hit on a modem line they have connected to their system."

It took less than ten minutes to get a hit. We connected and were presented with an ID and password prompt.

Dan stared at the screen. "I'm guessing that these guys are a small shop from a technology standpoint. After all, their core competency is building boats. Probably just have a small office network with a couple of servers that were set up by the office manager, who doesn't know squat about computer security. And if that is the case, and this is a Microsoft network..."

Shrimper Dan typed *Admin* for the ID and *Admin* for the password. Suddenly we were presented with the page for the companies internal Intranet. "We're in!"

"Damn," I whistled. "They never even changed their default ID and password."

"Oldest trick in the book," Dan grinned. "You would be surprised at how often it still works."

We went down a couple of blind allies before we finally found what we were looking for—an income statement listing the cost, shipping/registration destination, serial number, and buyer of every custom yacht built in the past three years.

I scanned the report. "Only five were registered in St. Barts. Of the five, three of them were larger than forty-two feet. Of the two left, one buyer was listed as the St. Barts Rum Company, and the other was purchased by a Mr. J. J. and delivered to a Ms. Frances Blakely.

"I'm pretty sure the rum company isn't shooting people with spear guns," I stated flatly. "It has to be this Frances Blakely lady."

"Could that be the blonde on the boat?" Dan inquired.

"Sounds like a good guess to me. Okay, so we have an owner, what now?"

"Well," Dan speculated, "let's work two angles at once. It's going to take my full attention to crack the U.S. Customs, so I'll start an automated name search program that will scan all potential sources for the name Frances Blakely."

With a couple of keystrokes, the search program was spinning through thousands of open and secured sources on one of the monitors.

Shrimper Dan grinned crookedly, "I really perfected my name search utilities when I was looking for Jill."

"Anyway," I spoke quickly to redirect his train of thought, "what do we have to do to get into U.S. Customs?"

"Just for the record," Dan frowned, "I'm not thrilled with this."

I patted his shoulder as he went to work.

"First," he spoke quietly as his fingers blurred, "we have to hide our trail. The best way to do that is to spoof our IP address. That way they will not know who it is. But unfortunately, Uncle Sam has some pretty sophisticated hacker tools himself and can trace addresses very quickly. We will only be able to stay in the system for about five minutes before they trace us back. I will spoof five different addresses. Each fake one will lead to another fake one, until it gets to the last one, which I will ensure is registered somewhere in the Middle East and will put up a fight when scanned by their systems. They can still ultimately trace back to us, but we should be safe if we get out of their systems in less than thirty minutes."

"Let's' do it!"

"Not so fast," Dan frowned, "With that kind of limited time, we have to plan on how to break in, how to search for what we need, and how to get out."

"Okay, so what's your plan?"

"We'll run a denial of service attack. Depending on their firewall, we can keep hammering it until we overwhelm it with sheer volume. If we are lucky, it will give up the ghost and let us in. Once we are in, we need to locate their central data warehouse. When we find that, it should be a simple matter of a simple search."

"And how do we get out?" I questioned.

"We sloppily cover our tracks, knowing full well that they will know we have been there. Without revealing our identity, we lead them straight to the security hole that let us in, but before we leave, we open up a dozen other holes and set up backdoors to get back in if we need to. They'll close the obvious hole, and we are free and clear if we need to get back in again."

"Wow," I enthused, "you are something else, Shrimper Dan."

"This is wrong, Kris. I don't like doing this against my former employer, no matter how much I disagree with what the government does. These kinds of tactics should only be used against the bad guys, not the good guys. The only reason I am doing this is to help catch a murderer."

"I understand," I sighed.

Dan went to work. The spoofed IP addresses routed our path all over the world. U.S. Customs used firewalls that were easily overwhelmed by our denial of service attack in ten minutes. We had less than twenty minutes left before we were traced.

"Damn it," Dan said.

"What?"

"I got in but unbelievably they have an old Renegade bulletin board system running, instead of a modern Intranet. That's the government for you."

"So what does that mean?"

"That means we have an extra level of security to crack."

I glanced up on the wall; fifteen minutes left.

Dan glared at the screen. "Take this, you bastard."

Lines of computer code streamed up the monitor quicker than I could read.

He hit the final key. "Now we are really in."

I looked at the clock again, "Five minutes, Dan."

"Okay," he said. "Here is the central data warehouse. I'll type a quick query on the boat's serial number and…There we have it. Checked through the port of Miami Customs office two weeks ago at three in the afternoon, by a J. Jenkins. That name mean anything to you?"

I thought my jaw was going to hit the table. "Damn straight it does, but you better hurry, we have less than a minute left."

Shrimper Dan loosely covered our tracks and ran his automated program to open the security holes and set the backdoors. We ended our connection with mere seconds to spare.

"So what do you think?" I queried. "Did we make it?"

Dan smirked, "I'll know in a few hours if the FBI shows up."

I blew out in relief. "So now I know who was on the boat, and I know when they came through customs, but I still don't know where they are."

Dan grinned, "I happen to still have a few friends in the military who give me access to some of their toys."

He tapped away on the keyboard, and a few seconds later a satellite image of South Florida was up on the map for the day and time the *Nefarious* went through Miami Customs.

"Now watch this."

My stomach actually got queasy from the vertigo as he zoomed in on the Miami Customs dock to a range of two meters.

"Amazing," I cried, "I can actually see her name on her stern."

Dan zoomed back out to fifty feet. "Now, I push another few buttons, and the super computers attached to these satellites take a digital signature of the *Nefarious*. It will now search through all its images over the last two weeks and sequentially display all that involve the *Nefarious* and her signature."

I watched in disbelief as the super-speed image of the *Nefarious* went up and down the Intracoastal. Dan slowed it down when he got to yesterday. I saw the *Nefarious* anchor across from the Gator Tail. I could see the commotion as the cowboy was shot. I watched as the yacht calmly moved up the Intracoastal, anchoring at the Port St. Lucie Marina last night, and moving to tie up to a little restaurant and bar, as the progression caught up to real time.

I squinted at the screen, "Hey, I know that place. It's Captain Harry's Last Resort."

"You are awesome, Shrimper Dan," I shook his hand, and told him I would catch up with him when this died down. I made my way toward Port St. Lucie and Captain Harry's Last Resort, totally forgetting about the search utility Shrimper Dan was running on Ms. Frances Blakely.

CHAPTER 17

▼

Several hours had passed since I'd left Shrimper Dan's, and I was now hurriedly leaving Captain Harry's Last Resort. As I jumped into the car and sped away, the voice mail notification on my cell phone was whining incessantly. I couldn't wait to tell Buddy and Jason what I had found on the *Nefarious* at Captain Harry's. I dialed in and Buddy's recorded voice came on the line. I knew there was something wrong by his hushed tones.

I'm on my way to Jupiter Regional Medical Center. Jason has been in an accident. Come as quickly as possible.

That was all he said. I knew there was more to the story that Buddy wasn't comfortable sharing over the phone.

I rushed to the hospital. Luckily Jupiter Regional was only ten minutes away, so the M3 made quick work of it.

I skidded into the parking lot to the disdainful looks of several nurses on their shift switch. I hopped out of the car without putting the top up, regardless of the rolling black afternoon clouds.

Goddamn it. I knew I shouldn't have let that lunkhead go off by himself. I should have made him let Buddy or me go with him. He was always so freaking stubborn, always had to save the world on his own, always the one who had to rescue the damsel in distress. Jason would give you the shirt off his back, and he would spend the whole day listening to your troubles when you had them. He would get you laid when you needed it and drunk whether you wanted to or not. Everyone always claimed to be Jason's friend, but he always shared more with us than with anyone else he'd hung out with.

Buddy and I had been starving college students. There had been many dinners and lunches that Jason had picked up because he knew we didn't have the means.

If there was trouble in one of the local Charleston bars, Jason always took on the dragon to save his friends, and he did it with that too-white-smile that made the dragon feel bad for blowing smoke in the first place.

But damn it, that was a long time ago. College wasn't the real world. The castles were made of paper and the swords were made of broomsticks. The only real danger was growing up.

This was the fucking real world; a world where the too white smile gets crammed down your throat. A world where a blind charge into battle can get you maimed or killed. The swords were steel now, and the dragon's teeth were real. I just hoped that Jason would be around to realize that.

I was already choking back the tears as I entered the automatic opening doors of the emergency room. One look at Buddy's haggard face sitting in the drab waiting room filled with shallow magazines and deep worries convinced me that my worst fears were on the mark.

"What the hell happened?" I numbly balanced on the hard plastic chair beside my large friend.

He looked up from his hands with red eyes that I had thought were bloodshot from crying. Now I realized that he was so angry that the capillaries had burst in his eyes, turning them a pinkish red.

The Big Guy fairly roared, "Those sons of bitches tried to kill him!"

The ancient nurse with the frosted hair behind her frosted glass window gave us a harsh look.

"Come on, Buddy," I whispered. "Let's get you outside so you can walk this off before you have a goddamn stroke right here." I grabbed his arm and coaxed him toward the door. "I can't have both my best friends wind up on a gurney in the same day."

We made it outside into the fresh breeze being pushed before the coming afternoon storm. I made him walk circles around the parking lot to burn off some of his fury. I dared not even talk to the man as we walked. Buddy is the gentlest person on the face of the planet until someone tries to hurt him or his, and then get out of the way because the Phillips steamroller is going to flatten whatever gets in his path until he makes it right.

After a couple of laps, I felt like I could give it a shot. "So what the hell happened, Buddy?"

He let out a long heavy sigh that seemed to cause him to shrink by two sizes. Suddenly he was no longer the over-torqued machine, but the confused and hurt kid that I had befriended in college.

"I had just gotten finished with the Widow Jenkins"—Buddy gave me a funny, sheepish look—"when Jason called.

"He doesn't have a cell phone. I mean, who doesn't have a cell phone these days? Anyway he was calling from this pay phone down the street from Jupiter Marine Salvage. He's telling me that he got the inside track on a lead when he made a mock sales call on Orin Lawson earlier. He was supposed to be going back to seal the deal, but what he really hoped to do was flesh out the lead on Rhodes."

Buddy's face screwed up, "I told the bastard to wait on me; that I could back him up in case there was trouble. He just laughed and told me not to worry; that he had it all under control. He had that cocky slick tone of his going. You know the one I mean?"

I knew Jason's Errol Flynn-cum-used car salesman face well; the swagger of a pirate and the gold nugget jewelry of a Yugo peddler.

"Anyway, by the time he hung up the phone, I was already throwing up gravel. I was too late. When I got to Jupiter Marine Salvage, the *Sweet Revenge* was already chugging away from her dock and out toward the inlet. I could see Orin Lawson at the wheel, and some huge redheaded monster making the ropes sound on deck. By the time I got to the dock, they were already a good hundred yards out.

"Then that I heard what sounded like gargling or maybe an outboard engine being flooded. It was such a strange sound that it took me a second to realize that it was human. It didn't take me long to find him."

Buddy gulped physically.

"He was just hanging there, Kris, left like a damn side of beef on a meat hook. They hung him from the flying prow of an old, rusted-out fishing boat. His feet were dangling a good two feet above the water. They'd made a noose out of the boat's old anchor chain and just hung him there to die. His eyes were bulging out, and he was turning blue when I found him, but he was still conscious and kind of twitching. By the time I figured out how to get him down, he wasn't moving at all. He was barely breathing, Kris—"

He broke down and the tears flowed from the Big Guy's eyes. I had to stretch up, but I put my arm around my old friend's shoulders and guided him over to a nearby bench.

He sniffed and snorted and pulled himself together. "I got him on the dock and used my cell to call 911. He was in bad shape, Kris. They had beaten him half to death before hanging him. His arm was broken. I could see the white bone end sticking through his friggin' arm. His face and head were covered in bruises; his head was swelling into a big black pumpkin. No telling what else they broke or damaged in him, that I couldn't see. I called you from the back of the ambulance as we headed to the hospital, but I got your voice mail."

Buddy was finished, both mentally and physically. I tried to get the Big Guy to go home, but he wouldn't hear of it. I called Lil and let her know what happened, and that we would be staying at the hospital overnight.

The grumpy nurse told us that Jason had been admitted, but since we weren't family, he couldn't have visitors after-hours. I asked to see the doctor, and she told me he was making his rounds. She said she would leave him the message, but there was no guarantee that he would have time for us.

We settled into the uncomfortable chairs for the long haul. Neither of us had eaten, but we didn't dare leave the waiting room and chance missing the doctor. Finally, around ten o'clock, the weary doctor came dragging up to the gatekeeper with the ugly white shoes. She motioned him in our direction.

We pulled ourselves out of our gray dread, and stood up. The doctor's name tag said McDougal, and he looked as if he were every bit of sixteen. He smiled tightly. I knew we looked like death warmed over.

He spoke, and his voice was much deeper than I expected, "You gentlemen relatives of Jason Bonnet?" He checked his chart.

"We're the closest thing he has in Florida," I countered, wary that he wasn't going to share his insight with us.

"We're his best friends," Buddy ventured.

Doctor McDougal looked skeptical and bit on the lead end of a well-chewed pencil leaving little graphite streaks along the side of his mouth.

We must have passed the test because he sighed and looked back down at his chart again.

"Mr. Bonnet is in stable condition. A compound fracture of the right arm is the worst of it. He might have a cracked rib or two. Another minute and it would have been much worse. They could have crushed his larynx with that rusty anchor chain. He looks pretty pathetic; lots of bruising on the neck and head, but there are no skull fractures, just multiple contusions. We've got the arm in a cast, so he should be fine, but we are going to keep him overnight for observation just to be on the safe side. You gentlemen should go home; there is nothing else you can do. We'll call you if anything changes."

We both looked at each other. "No way, Doc, we're staying here with Jason," I spoke for Buddy who affirmed enthusiastically.

McDougal grimaced, "Well, at least go down to the hospital cafeteria and get something to eat. It's open till midnight. You two look like hell."

With that, he dismissed us and went on his way to spread joy to all the other little people.

"What do you say, Buddy Bear?"

"Well, if nothing else, I could use a good strong cup of coffee." He gave a weak smile.

We walked down the antiseptic hallway together toward the cafeteria.

CHAPTER 18

▼

By the time we entered the hospital cafeteria, it was closing in on 11:00. The main fluorescent lights overhead had been retired for the night and only a few incandescent spotlights over a couple of random tables up front created islands of illumination. All the other tables had been stood on their edges and pushed to the far lonely corners of the large cafeteria.

An old black man wrung a gray mop into a bucket in the middle of the floor, preparing the circus rings for tomorrow's show. He gave us a slow glance through yellowed eyes as we entered.

"Cafeteria still open?" Buddy ventured.

I jumped at the sudden coarseness of his voice in the solitary room, as the sound echoed off the eggshell walls.

The old man pointed toward a buffet counter in the far corner, and kept slowly mopping the floor.

"The show must go on," I whispered to Buddy, who gave me a queer look.

We wandered over to the stainless steel buffet counter. Steam whispered from several covered industrial metal containers behind a thick glass window. A faded unlit signboard behind the grill listed sandwich specials and the never-changing soup of the day. Behind the counter everything looked deserted.

I don't know how long we stood there staring at that sandwich board. We didn't speak, lost in thoughts of "what if," "could I," and "why him." A big institutional clock behind a wire cage ticked on the wall. Each stroke sounded like a little man inside with a chisel was vainly trying to dig his way out of his prison.

When the large woman with Coke-bottle glasses and a hairnet walked in from the cafeteria storeroom, she let out a squeal that broke our trance. We both jumped and our hearts paused for a second on the edge of the abyss. Behind me, I heard the mop handle drop with a clatter to the floor and felt the wary jaundiced eyes of the janitor burning into our backs, appraising the situation, determining if action was required.

"Good Gawd," the pasty cafeteria lady guffawed through a heavy Mississippi accent. "You boys like to scare me half to death!"

I heard a gruff grumble behind me followed by the swishing of the mop once again.

"Sorry, ma'am," Buddy turned on his Savannah manners.

"What the heck you boys doing out here just staring at the signboard? Don't you see that little bell there with the note that says ring for service? Only reason I came out was to let Rufus know that they just had a woman on Jerry Springer who was being done the same way my Larry is doing me."

She paused to suck in a deep breath that rattled through her unfiltered Camel lungs all the way down to her orthopedic shoes. "But that's none of yer business anyway. What can I get you?"

Neither of us had much of an appetite, but we ordered cold-cut sandwiches and bad coffee anyway.

As we carried our bounty to the nearest table, the cafeteria lady wandered back into the storeroom and her five-inch, portable black-and-white TV. Janitor Rufus gave us a wide berth and focused his attention on those hard-to-get corners on the other side of the cafeteria.

"He's going to be okay, Buddy," I soothed. "You did everything you could."

He just scowled at his coffee.

"Let's get our minds off it," I ventured. "Tell me what happened with the Window Jenkins."

"I don't feel like it right now, Kris."

"Come on, Big Guy, talking about anything you may have found out will make us feel like we have control of this crazy deal. Jason would want us to keep trying to figure out what happened to Rhodes."

He wasn't thrilled with the idea, but he sighed audibly and began the tale of his sordid affair with the Widow Jenkins.

CHAPTER 19

▼

Buddy mused, "I decided that the best way to get in to see Biddy Jenkins was to hand-deliver her an invitation to one of The Season's benefits at the Celestion. There isn't a single damn socialite on Jupiter Island who could pass that up."

"The Season," I smirked. To anyone outside of Palm Beach County that means a change in the weather, but we all know that *The Season* is the time when all the wealthy trust fund babies and old money come down from the Hamptons to South Florida for the winter. "It is nothing but a nonstop party for the well-to-do from September till May."

Buddy gestured in the general direction of Jupiter Island, "Yes, between Jupiter Island and Palm Beach, almost every night of The Season is a party. The Have Mores all have their favorite charities, and they throw a hell of a fundraiser. They have these unreal theme benefits where they try to outdo each other. The later The Season gets, the wilder and crazier the parties grow."

I shook my head, "No ball gown or costume is ever worn twice, and the Worth Avenue jewelry stores have to import more exotic and ostentatious jewels and diamonds as women with limitless platinum cards compete in the high-stakes game of one-upmanship."

"And many of those parties are hosted at the Celestion," Buddy commented. "Especially later in The Season when the bashes have grown so monstrous that only a couple of the resorts are large enough to hold them. Biddy Jenkins used to run in those circles before she was left out in the cold by that son-of-a-bitch crook of a husband of hers."

I hummed nasally. "Yas, The ladies of The Season are very unforgiving. Gilded invitations are only delivered to white Anglo-Saxon Protestants with old money and uncheckered pasts."

Buddy chuckled, "Yeah, until Jones Jenkins high-tailed out of the country with wads of dirty moola, Biddy swam with those sharks. She's been hiding in her mansion on Jupiter Island ever since Jonesy disappeared. I knew that an invite to a Celestion benefit would get her drooling.

"So I gave her a buzz from my office phone. I knew her house staff would be on a short leash, and would screen all her calls. The Celestion coming over the caller-ID would get their panties in a wad for sure. The housekeeper answered on the second ring. I told her the Celestion had a personal invitation to a gala benefit for Ms. Jenkins. I told her that part of the theme for the benefit required the invitation to be delivered in person. The housekeeper put me on hold to "relay this to Ms. Jenkins." Sixty seconds later I was told to have the courier drop by in an hour. I was in!"

"Pretty sneaky, Buddy Bear," I grinned. "But what the heck did you propose to do when you got there with no invitation and no theme?"

"Hey, who says I didn't have a theme?" He beamed. "And besides the invitation part was easy, all that took was a little Celestion letterhead and a word processor.

"So anyway, I scrounged around and found my old leather jacket and a black T-shirt. I borrowed some chains from Hank in maintenance. My mirrored sunglasses completed the picture. With my theme down cold, I jumped on the Harley and headed up to the Jenkins'."

Entranced, I sipped bad coffee as his tale unfolded.

✳   ✳   ✳   ✳

I stopped at the gate entrance to the driveway. You know how Jupiter Island is, twelve-foot hedges broken only by ugly-ass gates down that one long single road. I pushed the button and told the little silver box that I was from the Celestion.

I could almost see the superior sour puss of the housekeeper before her Latin-accented voice stated flatly, "Do you have any identification?" I looked up at the camera on the top of the gatepost. I felt her down-turned eyes, as she sneered at the image of the Hell's Angel's biker on her little black-and-white TV. I pulled out my Celestion director of Security ID with my picture on it and held it up to the camera. I could hear the flat hum as the lens focused on the ID.

"The outfit is part of the party theme," I tried to sound encouraging.

Finally, after what seemed like five minutes, the voice came back on.

"Go down to the next gate; that is the service entrance. I will buzz you in there."

I burbled another hundred yards down Jupiter Island Road to the second gate. As promised, it swung open for me and I rumbled through.

The palms and ferns were thick and the Spanish moss hung from live oak trees above the curving drive. I couldn't even see the house until the drive made a turn around one of those huge goldfish ponds, and then the house burst into view. It was one of the modern chrome, marble, and glass block monsters; a two-story bunker with weird angles and jutting corners that must have compensated for the architect's little cock by inflating his checkbook. I know I don't have shit for taste, but this piece of crap was like a cold dead fish. It sprawled across two hundred yards of water frontage. A huge boatlift in front cradled a forty-foot Wellcraft scarab.

I walked up to the front door, which opened before I could even get my hand on the oversize knocker. A mean-ass lookin' maid in a flat black dress, strict gray hair bunched on top of her head, and a brown Latino face looked me up and down.

"May I have a closer look at that ID?" She asked.

I handed it to her. She examined it slowly, looking frequently from the picture to my face.

"And the invitation," she held out her hand.

I handed her the heavy envelope with the Celestion's wax seal securing the flap. She didn't even blink as she tore the seal and opened the letter.

She scanned it. I hoped that she had heard careless whispers about the wild themes of The Season's parties before; otherwise I was about to get a one-way ticket out the gate.

"A bikers and bitches party?" She questioned.

I grinned and shrugged, "Yeah, it's for the South Florida Hurricane Relief Fund." I crossed my fingers at the fictitious charity.

She stared at the letter another thirty seconds. "I will give this to Ms. Jenkins." She started to close the door.

I put my foot in the jam. "No, ma'am, I'm very sorry," I stated helplessly. "The theme rules are particular. I have to deliver the invitation personally." I tried to look sheepish, "There is a silly little speech I have to give as part of this."

"I'm afraid that will not be possible." She tried to close the door again.

I knew that I had to go balls to the wall. I grabbed the invitation from her hand and turned tail to leave, stating over my shoulder. "Your call, lady. As the party rules say, the invitation is withdrawn. Have a good one." I started down the steps full tilt.

I knew she was debating what kind of trouble she'd be in with the Widow Jenkins if she blew her boss's chance of getting back into The Season's social circle.

"Wait!"

I stopped, my back still turned to her as I tried to suppress my grin. I turned slowly. "Ma'am?"

"Wait here," she sighed. "I must go let Ms. Jenkins know what is required." She clicked the door closed and was gone.

Five minutes later, she was back.

"Ms. Jenkins requests you deliver the invitation to her by the pool, where she currently resides."

I stepped toward the door.

She blocked the doorway with her ancient tree stump of a body. "That will not be necessary. You may walk around the side of the house to get to the pool area."

I gave her a sideways grin. It was her little power play to show me who was still the boss.

"Thank you kindly, ma'am," I beamed at her and marched myself around the corner of the house.

The place was huge; it felt like it took twenty minutes to get to the damn pool area. The thing was more like a hidden tropical water park; several large fake lava-stone waterfalls dumped a small flood into three weirdly shaped connected pools. Doesn't anybody know how to do square pools anymore?

Ferns, dwarf palms, and huge boulders made me feel like I was on a Disney rejected rip-off ride. The edge of the pools that faced the wide expanse of the Intracoastal made it hard to tell where the pools ended and the waterway began. A hell of a layout, in a plastic tropical Barbie kind of way.

There was so much shit in the whole scene that it took me a second to spot her. There she was in a redwood deck chair over by the second pool. She wiggled her fingers at me without raising her head, and left me to figure out which cutesy Japanese bridge would lead me to her.

As I got close, I got my first good look at her. She was laid back on the lounge chair, lost in some Jupiter Island social rag. She was seriously rockin' in a banana yellow string bikini that was heavy on string, light on bikini.

Her skin was deep brown, not just from tan but from Cuban roots. Her golden hair made me think of Barbie again, and I busted my brain trying to remember if Barbie had a Latin friend named Rosa or some such. The hair came out of a very expensive bottle for sure.

Her boobs were huge and probably caused several silicon mines to be used up during their construction. She was lying down, but they sat up high and firm as if they had a life of their own.

From a stone's throw away, I would have guessed her at mid-thirties, but on closer look I changed that to late forties. I noticed all the things that her army of Palm Beach surgeons hadn't been able to hide with scalpels and fat-sucking machines.

Her face was tight, and she looked perpetually surprised from one too many face-lifts. They can stretch the face to hell and back, but they can't do much with the neck. The creases and valleys gave her away. You could also tell by her hands, and the interstate of veins and lines they held. I could also see the white edges of a tummy tuck scar barely peaking above her bikini bottom.

Yep, she was a damn package all right, and it had taken lots of bucks to wrap her.

I finally made it to her throne, and she sat up and removed her Versace sunglasses revealing huge, round, velvet brown eyes with long dark lashes.

I hate to admit it. I was stunned, definitely not what I was expecting of a grieving widow.

"Well?" She pursed her lips and tilted her head at me.

"Ma'am?" I stammered.

"Well, what is it you are supposed to tell me for the stupid party theme?"

She had benefited from years with a speech coach, but I could still pick up the steady undertow of her well-hidden Cuban accent.

I remembered she came from a seriously loaded Cuban family from Miami, with deep roots in the old country. Her grandfather had been Miguel Batista, cousin to Fulgencio Batista, the last president of Cuba before the revolution.

Her great uncle had controlled the political landscape of Cuba; Miguel Batista had controlled the business side. Gambling, hookers, and vice were his specialties.

Pre-Castro, Cuba, was the United States' party land. If you were a Cuban who owned a casino or if you were involved in other forms of vice, it was damn easy to make fast money.

Common Cuban citizens thought their country shouldn't be party central for foreigners. The Cubans saw the riches of these people who ran the country, but they couldn't afford bread for the table.

Along comes Castro, who bills himself as the voice of the common people, and starts the "popular rebellion." It wasn't the military trying to overthrow the government, but regular people who thought they were fighting for their families.

Fulgencio tipped off Miguel that the end was near, and he was able to escape to Miami with his family. Since things had started to get hot in Cuba, Miguel had been moving his riches to offshore accounts. When the Castro hammer finally fell, Miguel Batista was able to start a new life in Miami, living just as large as he had in Cuba.

Miguel quickly restarted many of his shady business deals in Miami. Underground gambling and drug smuggling were his specialties.

Miguel sent his only granddaughter, Esperanza, or Biddy as everyone called her, to the best tight-ass schools up north. When she graduated, Miguel was more than happy to take his granddaughter under his wing. Biddy was deep in the family business within a year.

Miguel decided to expand his operations north to tap into the lucrative Palm Beach County market. The tight-assed Jupiter Islanders had proven a harder nut to crack than he had expected. They barred Miguel's ass from their WASP nest. They weren't about to allow any Cubano, no matter how loaded, to get his greasy foot into the door of their country clubs, golf courses, and business deals.

Miguel decided if he couldn't beat them, he would join them, and then beat them. He sent his right hand in to defeat them from the inside out. Biddy had taken one of her grandfather's Bentleys and gone prowling for a Jupiter Island husband.

She had only three requirements: he had to be filthy rich, he had to be a Jupiter Island insider, and he had to have the ethics of a snake. With that combo, she could work Miguel's deals for him from the inside.

She found exactly what she was looking for in Jones Jenkins. He was old money, trust fund from some food company that one of his ancient kin had owned. The gene pool had seriously watered down over the years. Jones sucked at business but was damn good at being a sleazy politician. As zoning board commissioner for Palm Beach County, his fingers were in everyone's pie. There wasn't a construction site in the county that hadn't had to contribute to his "Orphans" fund, if they wanted to see their property built. As nasty as his business deals were, he was a third-generation Jupiter Islander and was grandfathered into the highfalutin social circle.

There was serious tongue wagging when he got hitched to the twenty-five-year-old Cubano. The Have-Mores invited her to their parties because they had to, but they never really accepted her.

Daddy-dear was gunned down in the streets of Miami only a year after Biddy had married Jones. His dreams of expanding business into Palm Beach County disappeared. Without a son to take the reins of his crime ring, his illegal businesses soon faded into the pulsing night of Miami.

Biddy was left in a loveless marriage. Jonesy had several girl friends carefully chosen from the sluttier socialites. Biddy didn't care; she got caught up in the sexy flash of Jupiter Island society. She lived for it.

That all came crashing down when Jonesy disappeared with all that stolen cash. It had been the opportunity that the society bitches had been waiting for. They dropped Biddy from their invitation list like an ugly-ass pool boy. Biddy went into hiding at her Jupiter Island digs.

"Are you going to tell me about the goddamn party, or are just going to stand there gawking like some big ape?"

I gathered my wits, but I couldn't stop thinking about her comment. If I were a big ape, I would have to peel me a big yellow banana bikini.

"What's so fucking funny?" her eyes were flashing now. When she got angry, her accent sneaked out—"fockin fawne."

"Sorry, ma'am," I stammered, trying my best to kill my giggles.

I cleared my throat. "You are cordially invited to a benefit in support of the South Florida Hurricane Relief Fund. The party will be held in three weeks in the Celestion's grand ballroom. The theme of the party is Bikers and Bitches."

I swallowed a lump in my throat. "Since you are a bitch, I have been instructed to find out if you have a biker, or will you need us to supply you with one?"

I held my breath.

I saw the red creeping up her face. Oh shit, I thought, I am going to get it for calling her a bitch to her face.

She exploded in a stream of Spanish cussing that rolled out way too fast for me to catch. She caught herself about halfway through and switched to English.

"Those goddamn whores. Who do they think they are insinuating that I need an escort?"

It took me a second to realize that she was mad at my fake party organizers, not at me.

"It isn't right. I attended every party for the last twenty," she stopped staring at me, "ten years. "And then they snub me for years just because my darling husband has disappeared. Then they insult me like this. How dare they!"

"I'm sorry, ma'am. I didn't mean to disrespect a lovely lady such as yourself."

She softened noticeably. I must be starting to pick this shit up from Jason.

Her lips got a real heavy look, as she tilted her head to look me up and down.

"So, if I was to need an escort," she fairly growled, "who would it be?"

I suddenly felt like I was trapped in the corner of a tiger's cage, with the cat ready to jump my ass.

My brain said, Get the hell out of here. I wanted to run from this she-devil, but I knew I needed info from her.

I gulped, "Well, that," I paused, "would be me, ma'am."

"Oh really," she grinned stirring her bloody mary with her finger, then sucking the tip. "In that case, I better put you through your paces to make sure you are up to the job!" With a one-finger snap, she popped the bikini top free and it puddled to the ground.

✻   ✻   ✻   ✻

"Holy shit, Buddy Bear," I exclaimed so loudly that Janitor Rufus dropped his mop again, grumbling.

He turned crimson. In the dim cafeteria lights, he looked like some perverse Santa Claus mask.

"You plugged the Widow Jenkins," I grinned, slapping the table. "I can't believe you plugged the Widow Jenkins!"

He shrugged apologetically. "It wasn't what I'd planned to do, I swear, but things just kinda got out of hand from there."

"So what happened, man? Don't keep me in anticipation."

"Well," he grinned, "I'm not one to kiss and tell, but let's just say that in theory we worked our way from the lounge chair to the pool to the hot tub and to this big waterbed she has."

"Damn, Buddy," I exclaimed, "You got some stamina, don't you?"

He punched me in the arm. "Forget about that. Do you want to know what I learned or what?"

"Okay, okay." I gave him a lecherous grin. "You can give me all the dirty little details later."

He rolled his eyes, "So anyway, afterward, lying in her bed, I got her to open up and answer some of my questions.

"Apparently there was some kind of dirty little business deal between Jones Jenkins, Donnie Rhodes, and some red-haired chick.

"She didn't know the redhead's name. She'd only seen her once, but apparently she had a tattoo of a wandering white rose that ran up her spine.

"They were going on a trip to St. Barts to hunt for something, but she didn't know what."

"That matches up with the journal," I commented.

He agreed, "Yes, Rhodes was supplying the plane, and Jenkins was supplying the cash to fund the project. I don't know what job the lady with the white rose tattoo had."

I wrinkled my brow. "But didn't the journal say that Rhodes had Jenkins 'taken care of'?"

"Hey, I said that Rhodes needed Jenkins's money to make it happen. I didn't say Jenkins actually made it along for the ride."

I sighed, "Well, this dovetails with what I found out, too."

Buddy glanced up at the wire-caged clock. It sleepily reflected three o'clock. "Spill it," he grimaced. "We've got nothing but time to spare."

"You got it," I grinned, "but at least you got the girl in your story."

CHAPTER 20

▼

"I actually boarded the *Nefarious*," I grinned.

"You what?" Buddy's eyes widened. "How did you even find her, let alone board her?" His voice dropped to a fierce whisper, "And are you freakin' crazy? You could have been laid up in here right beside Jason."

He was mad as hell. His eyes were taking on that bloodshot look again.

"Come on, Big Guy, take it easy." I patted his shoulder.

He deflated a little. "You and Jason aren't trained for this kind of shit. I am. I'm the guard, Jason's the running back, and you're the quarterback. That's the way it has always been. You guys have to let me protect you; you have to let me do my job."

His head fell to his chest, "I can't afford to drop the ball again."

I felt like shit, but he was right. Buddy was the one to guard the cave at night, the one to defend the gate of the Alamo. It was his birthright, and we had no cause to take that away from him.

"Hey!" I snapped my fingers. "Cheer up, I promise I will not go charging alone into battle again."

He raised his head and one eyebrow at the same time.

"Don't worry," I grinned, "Next time around I'm going to paint a big red bull's-eye on your wide rear end and push you through the door first, back-ass-wards."

Buddy rolled his eyes, "So you going to tell me what the hell happened or not?"

"Well," I began, "With the help of an old friend, I was able to pinpoint exactly where the *Nefarious* was docked."

"Who and how?"

I could almost hear the wheels of his military mind spinning.

"I can't tell you who," I sighed. "I made a promise. As for the how, let's just say with a little info from the U.S. Customs Department's data warehouse and a secret government satellite, I was able to locate the *Nefarious* moored at the dock at Captain Harry's Last Resort."

"Captain Harry's huh? I haven't seen that old pirate in nearly two years."

"That's because you got both of us banned from the Last Resort two years ago when you and I got carried away with the tequila shots.

"As I recall"—I looked down my nose at Buddy—"you passed out right in the middle of our pool game, and did a belly flop on Harry's antique billiards table."

He gave a little harrumph. "Who would have ever thought that slate could shatter like that?"

"I couldn't see straight enough to drive us home. Harry took my keys and called Lil to come pick us up. We literally had to drag your ass to the car. Harry was so mad that he made Lil promise never to let us within ten nautical miles of his place again. I think it was at least two weeks before Lil spoke to either one of us."

"A good time was had by all," Buddy chortled.

"Damn straight." I grinned crookedly, touching fists with my friend.

"Anyway, once I knew they were at Harry's, I took the long way round and came up on the place's blind side away from the water. I parked the M3 in the shadows to the left side of the building. I could see the bow of that big forty-two-foot trawler yacht sticking out from the end of the dock. I peeked through one of the front windows.

"Captain Harry's Last Resort looked exactly as it had two years ago; well, minus the pool table. Same old dusty tin roof with exposed cypress rafters. Same old knotty pine floors with about six feet of dulled floor wax on them. Same old yellowed pictures of ships, long abandoned or sunk, sailing across the walls."

"They still have the tiki bar?"

"Yep, still takes up the whole right side of the building. The little stage is still right by the kitchen door with the porthole in it. Amazing as it might sound, when I looked through that window, there was Captain Harry still sitting on that stage stool picking his banjo, while his wife, Lulu, played that creaky old stand-up piano, singing their raunchy vaudeville tunes."

"I got news for you," Buddy smirked. "It wasn't the piano creaking; it was the poor piano stool. Lulu must weigh close to four hundred pounds."

"Yeah, and she is still wearing that same sweat-stained pink chiffon prom dress."

"I've known sausages with looser-fitting attire."

"Yes, and old Harry is the same one hundred twenty-five pound walking shadow he always was. The face has a few more cliffs and crevices, the hair on his head is now completely white like his beard, but he is the same old privateer he always was."

"I miss that old guy," Buddy mused.

"Yeah, once this is all over, we'll take him over a big bottle of rum around closing time, and make amends."

"They replace the pool table?"

"No, Harry has a foosball table in its place now."

"Damn, that's really going to hurt," Buddy chortled.

"Anyway, as my eyes adjusted to the light, I could make out the faces of the patrons at the tables and bar. Harry only has about ten tables. I recognized seven of the ten tables as late lunch-crowd faces from around Jupiter. The other three tables were no-goes. One was a couple with two kids."

"Who the hell would take kids to a place like the Last Resort?"

I shrugged, continuing, "One other table held an elderly couple, and the last table had two guys who were—well, let's just say they were very close friends. I scanned the bar. There they were; it had to be them. They were facing the water, but they occasionally turned to speak animatedly with the bartender."

"Picasso?"

"Yes, your old friend Picasso, the one-eared, deaf mute, illegal Haitian bartender."

"Damn, he could pour a mean tequila shot," Buddy moaned.

"That's all he could pour, 'cause he never understood a word you said," I chided. "You ask for beer, you get tequila; you ask for wine, you get tequila."

Buddy interrupted, "You ask for the bathroom, you get tequila."

I chuckled in agreement.

"Hey, do you think that could have had anything to do with us getting expelled from the Last Resort?"

I shook my head with a smirk, "No, I'm sure that had nothing to do with it at all."

"So I'm checking out these two at the bar. One was a ruddy looking dude with wavy black hair. His face wasn't red from sunburn though; it had that permanent scorched look that you get from combining too much alcohol with high blood pressure. He was average height and wore long sleeves and long pants, all black, despite the heat and humidity. Although his clothing seemed out of place, they were all designer threads. He wore a big diamond-studded presidential Rolex on the wrong arm, and a large flashy ring on the pinky of his left hand. I couldn't tell the color of his eyes from that distance, but he squinted and frowned a lot. He chomped on the end of one of those thin, too-sweet-smelling cigars with the plastic tips. He had no patience for Picasso, and even raised his arm to backhand him once. In two seconds flat, Harry was off the stage and had the guy by the wrist. Gruff words were exchanged. Harry translated the drink order to Picasso, and things seemed to calm down. Harry and Lulu went back to playing, but Harry kept his eye on him.

"The lady was the exact opposite. She was like a tall, cool Long Island iced tea compared to her mad dog counterpart. She stood at least six-one, on long slender muscular legs. She wore a tight little skirt and an old-fashioned hippie blouse that rode high up under her breast, revealing a magnificent deep-water brown, tapered landing strip of an abdomen. A large ruby shimmered in her sculpted belly button. Despite the puffiness of her blouse, her breasts were heavy and firm, and very much given to her by Mother Nature. Her hair was that creamy kind of blond that looks like it was just poured out of a bucket of golden honey. Her face was clear and bright, but she showed no emotion. She never cracked a smile, or even interacted with her red counterpart or the bartender. She just stared beyond the *Nefarious* toward the waterway. For some reason, she scared me much more than her partner did, especially when I remembered she was the one who killed the Dime-Store Cowboy."

Buddy's eyes were as big as pie pans. He motioned impatiently for me to continue.

"Then and there I decided that I had to prove what I learned through U.S. Customs. I had to get onboard the *Nefarious*, but there was no way I could go through the Last Resort without being spotted. Red may not have seen me at the Gator Tail, but Blondie most certainly had during her little wet suit-peeling escapade. Crouching below the front windows, I made my way over to the blind side of the Last Resort. There I found exactly what I was hoping for, Captain Harry's old skiff."

"Oh shit, you think Harry was mad at me for wrecking his pool table; if you screwed with his bone fishing skiff, he is going to be really pissed."

"Hush." I held a finger to my lips. "You wanna hear this or not?"

Buddy sneered but motioned for me to go on.

"So I slipped the skiff in the water. There were no oars, but thankfully the water wasn't too deep for Harry's flat boat pole. I pushed myself toward the stern of the yacht. I considered climbing up the transom ladder, but I could barely see Red and the Blondie at the bar still. If I could see them, then they could see me. This would have to be done the hard way. I poled the skiff around the starboard side of the trawler yacht. She had two decks plus a flying bridge, so there was no way they could see me from the bar. It was easy enough to make the skiff rope secure to the railing, and I gently pulled myself up onto her deck. I crouched there silent for several minutes, waiting for any telltale sign that would let me know that someone else was on board. It was silent as a tomb; nothing but the muffled banjo and clinking piano, and an occasional drunken guffaw from the tables across the way.

"I slunk down the stairs to the lower state rooms. The spear gun was cocked, leaning menacingly in one corner. I don't know why, but I pointed its lethal barrel down toward the deck, and then carefully leaned it back in its corner. I'm not sure what I was looking for, a boat title, mail with a name on it—like trained killers usually use real names on legal papers and get light bills from Florida Power and Light. As I rummaged through drawers and cabinets, I was aware that I was seriously overstaying my welcome. They could come back aboard at any time. I was about to give up, when I looked under the mattress in one of the berths. There was a yellowed Polaroid picture lying facedown under the pad. I picked it up and turned it over.

"With the info you just gave me, the story clicked together. The picture was of Donnie Rhodes, the red guy from the bar, and a darkly tanned redhead. She was smiling sweetly, the Red Guy looked like he had a bad stomachache, and Donnie was wearing a big shit-eating grin. They were all three standing in front of the Jaega Seaplane. I realized that the same camera that took the picture in the journal took this one as well. The names were written on the little white flap at the bottom of the Polaroid. It confirmed what the U.S. Customs data had told me."

I pulled the picture out of my shirt pocket and laid it on the table. The name under the Red Guy's grimacing face was Jones Jenkins.

"Well, fuck me," Buddy stammered.

"I think his wife already did, pal.

"I was turning to leave when the boat started rocking. At first I thought they were coming back onboard, but then I realized that the *Nefarious* was rolling too much for that, there was another large boat pulling up to the dock. I peered out an aft porthole and felt my stomach drop. Orin Lawson's boat, the *Sweet Revenge*, was bumping up against the dock.

"I was just thinking that Lawson couldn't steer worth shit, when one particularly strong roll bounced the *Nefarious* in her moorings. I heard a little scrape behind me. I turned just in time to see the spear gun go sliding down the wall, to clatter to the floor. I instinctively dove to the deck, and just in time. With a *schwiiittt* and a *twang*, the loaded spear gun went off. The shaft cut across my shoulder blade and ripped a hole in my shirt."

I turned around to show the horrified Buddy the long red blood-clotted scratch across my back.

"It arced up and lodged itself in a dropped ceiling tile, which instantly disintegrated. For a second I thought someone had poured a bag of marbles on my head, but then I realized they were rubies. They were everywhere. I stuck one in my shirt pocket to prove it to you."

I took out the shiny three-carat stone and laid it in his hand.

"Why didn't you take more?" he whispered.

"Hey, I already had illegal entry and destruction of property going against me. Did you think I wanted robbery, too?"

He rolled his eyes, "Yeah, like those guys got all those rubies by legal means."

"Anyway," I frowned, "I didn't have time. Lawson had finally gotten the *Sweet Revenge* in close enough for his trained gorilla to jump ashore and tie them off. I could see Jenkins and Blondie meandering toward the dock to meet them. That was way too close for me.

"I moved as quickly and quietly to the upper deck as I could and dropped down into Harry's skiff. It was then I realized I had made a very big mistake. I had failed to secure the flat boat pole, and it had rolled off the skiff's deck when the *Sweet Revenge* had docked."

"Shit," Buddy fairly squealed, "What did you do?"

"I untied the skiff and did some serious hand paddling. What choice did I have? As I rounded the stern, and moved into the shadows of the dock, I could hear them hurrying onto the deck of the *Nefarious*, and Lawson shrilly yelling about the skiff he had seen tied up alongside.

"As I pulled the skiff onshore, I could hear muffled shouting coming from below deck. I didn't wait around. I high-tailed it back to the car and got out of there as soon as possible. It was shortly after that that I got your voice mail message, and I came straight to the hospital."

"Damn, if Lawson and Jenkins are in on this together, then by now they will have discovered that Jason wasn't where they left him. And anybody in the marina will be able to tell them what happened and who rode with Jason to the hospital."

"You're right. Let's just hope they don't pick up the trail before we can get Jason out of this antiseptic death trap."

CHAPTER 21

▼

Buddy and I decided that we didn't care what the duty nurse thought; we were going to Jason's room. We knew that sooner or later Orin Lawson or one of his cronies would come back to finish the job. It was seven o'clock on a Monday morning.

We almost made it undetected, until we ran smack into Dr. McDougal on his way out of Jason's room.

"What the heck are you guys doing up here?" he said crossly, blocking the doorway with his wiry body. "This area is off-limits when it's not visiting hours."

"Sorry, Doc." Buddy put a firm, meaty hand on his scrawny shoulder. "But we had to find out how our friend was doing." He gave his white lab coat a firm squeeze. "You understand, right?"

McDougal gulped and gestured feebly toward the clock on the wall. "Well, visiting hours do start in another hour."

"Thank you," I replied.

We glanced at each other. "Doc, can we get him out of here?" Buddy asked. "The bad guys who did this to him might be coming back to finish the job."

McDougal shook his head. "I'm afraid we still have a few test results that need to come back. To be on the safe side, he'll probably be released this evening at the earliest. I'm hesitant to ask, but what exactly did happen to Jason Bonnet?"

"Trust me, Doc." I shook his hand. "You really don't want to know."

He gave us a thin little smile. We cautiously opened the door of Jason's room and entered, leaving the good Doctor McDougal to stare after us myopically.

*   *   *   *

The lights were dim and a number of different machines beside the bed blinked and beeped. A ghostly hand rose above the sheet and motioned us in.

I had braced myself for the worst and was therefore somewhat more prepared than Buddy who wore his heart on his sleeve.

"Oh, my Gawd," his voice wavered, "you look horrible."

A croaky voice from the eggplant face gave a contorted grin, "You don't look that damn good yourself, Buddy Bear."

The Big Guy lost it, slumping in a chair as his shoulders jerked spasmodically and the tears ran down his face.

I tried to pretend not to notice, as he hid his face in his hands. "I'm sorry, Jason."

"For what, you big baby?" The eggplant soothed. "Get your ass over here."

He struggled out of his chair and over to the bed, chin on chest.

"Look at me, Buddy Bear," he commanded. He slowly lifted his head. "This wasn't your fault. It was mine. If I had listened to you, this would have never happened in the first place."

"I gotta be the nose guard," Buddy murmured.

"What?" asked the eggplant.

"Never mind," I shook my head. "How do you feel?"

"Like I've been beaten with a tire iron; oh wait, I was beaten with a tire iron."

I grinned. He certainly hadn't lost his sense of humor.

"More important, these Nazis in white will not give me a mirror so I can see myself. Tell me the truth, Grantford, how bad do I look?"

"Well the doctor said—" I began.

"Screw Doctor Ronald McDonald. He was just in here. I know the diagnosis: broken arm, maybe a broke rib, lots of bruising on my face and neck. I know all that shit. I want you to tell me honestly how I look."

"Are you sure you want to know that?" I asked skeptically.

"Look, Grantford," he croaked, "I know what I'm all about. I don't have Buddy's strength or your smarts. What I do have is the Bonnet face, and it has opened more doors for me than I can count. It's my bread and butter. Don't bullshit the king of bullshitters. How do I look?"

I sighed, "You look like shit. Your entire face is swollen with so many bruises that it's hard for me to tell where one ends and another begins. If I had to compare your head to something, it would probably be a big, overripe, lumpy blackberry. Both of your eyes are black and puffy, and you have a deep cut down your right cheek that's been stitched together with about a dozen sutures. Your throat is the worst though. I guess that anchor chain bruised your entire neck a dark black."

He closed his eyes, "God in heaven, it's worse than I thought."

He lay there silently with his eyes closed for a solid minute. I gave an awkward look in Buddy's direction. I was starting to wonder if Jason had fallen asleep when his eyes creaked back open and he spoke.

"Last question, Grantford, from what you can tell, what will be permanent?"

I paused, feeling my lips tighten. "I think most of the swelling will go down eventually, but all those bruises are going to go through a number of different hues before they disappear. The worst of it's going to be that long one down the right side of your face. No matter how you figure it, that one is going to leave a scar."

"Hey, think of it this way," Buddy offered. "Now you can really look like a pirate."

I glared at him, "You're not helping." He backed off like a whipped dog.

"You're right in a way. I'll make the best of it because that's what we Bonnet's always do best."

"The doc says you will probably be out of here by the end of the day."

He attempted a smile, but it would be a while before that famous Bonnet smile would be at a hundred watts again. In the meantime it produced something that was truly scary. "Besides I want to give you guys all the gory details on how I got here, and what I found out."

I looked at our poor friend lying there looking like a big grouper that had been used for batting practice. "I'm not sure it's a good idea for you to get yourself worked up that much."

"Look," he stated flatly, "I don't want y'all to wind up in beds in this place beside me. I know stuff you fellas gotta know."

"Yeah, and we have got some pretty wild stories for you too," Buddy ventured.

"Goody," he wheezed happily, "I love a good story!"

His eyes closed again, and I saw him attempting to pull it together.

He opened his eyes, "Okay I'm ready." His speech was clearer and his eyes were brighter.

"I thought that I had really conned Orin Lawson with my pitch. I went in to sell him my fictitious product called Barnacle Acid; an all-natural combination of various citrus and pepper extracts that was guaranteed to make barnacles simply fall of dry-docked salvaged boats without harming the environment. You spray it on with a paint sprayer; wait twenty-four hours, and all the barnacles just drop off."

"Cool," Buddy murmured.

I cocked an eye at him. "He just said he made it up."

"Oh right," he grinned sheepishly.

"And that," he stated, "is why I am good at what I do. If you make it believable enough, you can fool ninety-nine percent of the people all of the time. Unfortunately, little did I know that Orin Lawson fell into that other one percent.

"When I first arrived at Jupiter Marine Salvage, I was fairly impressed. I guess I was expecting some rusted-out hulk of a place, slowly expiring at water's edge. Instead the place was spotless and state-of-the-art, a huge, two-story warehouse with a monster door in back that led to a dock bristling with cranes. The whole warehouse sat out over the water, and a network of docks to the left and right of the warehouse was filled with boats in various states of repair. I watched as the workers used one of the cranes to pluck an old rusty fishing trawler from beside the dock, and deposit it onto a small, V-shaped flat car that sat on rails that led into the back of the warehouse. A little motorized tractor backed out on the rails to the flat car, linked up, and pulled it into the warehouse."

Buddy chimed in, "Yep, I have a couple of friends who do dock work for a marine salvage yard down toward Ft. Lauderdale. It's a multimillion-dollar high-tech business. My friends tell me there are at least a hundred thousand boats around the world that are either abandoned or sink every year."

I surmised. "The United States has gotten stricter in the last few years on marine salvage companies. It used to be if you found a wreck or derelict, it was yours to claim. Now the government retains all rights to everything found within three miles of the coast. That forced the Florida salvage companies to do their recoveries offshore, in the Bahamas or Caribbean."

"My friends hint that some salvage companies are doing so-called forced recoveries in international waters."

I raised my eyebrows. "Piracy?"

"For someone who hates the water, you sure seem to know a lot about the seedy business of marine salvage." Jason quipped.

He shrugged, "Hey, you got friends, you got beer, you get talk."

"So anyway," Jason drew us back in, "they have a slick little process going on there. I walked into the warehouse and they had half-dozen boats up on lifts being worked on by probably two-dozen workers who were scampering around the scaffolding like spiders in a huge web. The fishing trawler was still there on the flat bed, waiting its turn to be berthed. They were bringing a huge fully restored 1962 thirty-two-foot Chris Craft Roamer down so the fishing trawler could take its place."

"Wow!" I whistled, "That baby is a classic."

"So the second I walked in the door, I knew that I would have to bring an outfit like this something of major value to get their attention. So I came up with the idea of Barnacle Acid. The offices are in a small building inside the warehouse among the maze of rails and lifts. All the windows were one-way glass; they could see me, but I couldn't see them. I screwed up my courage to the sticking point, opened the door, and went in.

"I guess I was expecting cheap steel furniture, concrete floors, and a sallow secretary. I couldn't have been more wrong. Walking into the office was like entering the office of a Charleston divorce lawyer."

We listened intently as we fell into Jason's recollections.

✳ ✳ ✳ ✳

Deep burgundy carpeting, paneled walls, heavy large furniture made of dark wood, rare pictures of ancient ships and mariners graced the walls.

A gorgeous brown-haired woman in a formal business suit, with half glasses, sat behind a heavy antique desk. She appraised me, took her glasses off, and stuck one designer arm between her heavy lips.

"May I help you?" She hummed.

"Um, yes, I'm here to see Orin Lawson."

"And your name is?"

Before I knew it I had blurted out my real name.

"With?" she said it in such a way that the tip of her pink tongue flicked out and slowly retracted.

"Carolina Chemical Engineering," I thought quickly.

"Do you have an appointment?"

"Well, no." I gave her a wide Bonnet smile. "But I'm sure he would want to hear what I have to say."

She pursed her lips, and drummed her French-manicured nails on the desk.

Seconds passed, and I knew I was on trial.

Finally she gingerly picked up the phone. "One moment, please."

She talked into the handset in a muted tone, "Mr. Larson, I have a Mr. Bonnet here with Carolina Chemical Engineering. No sir. Yes sir."

She hung up the phone and turned to me. "Mr. Lawson will see you now, but he only has ten minutes before his next appointment."

She opened a door, and saw me in, closing it behind her. If I had thought that the outer office was plush, it was nothing compared to the inner sanctum. I felt as if I were sinking up to my knees in the carpet. Original nautical artwork was everywhere. Otis or Aunt E could have identified every artist; one for sure was a Winslow Homer. Nautical antiques stood tastefully on pedestals and stands. I felt like I was in the Charleston Yacht Club.

Lawson's desk was fashioned from the darkly stained teak of the bridge house of an ancient wooden steamship. Correction, it was the bridge house of the ship. Its wheel and controls were sealed in a large glass case whose top served as Lawson's workspace. The whole thing was unbelievable.

The only thing out of place was piggy Orin Lawson sitting above it all in a huge captain's chair. He motioned me to where several upright wooden deck chairs sat in front of the ship's bridge. I took a seat.

Sitting in the deck chair allowed Lawson to tower over me by a good three feet. I felt like I knew how my ancestor must have felt when he was on trial in front of Judge Trott in Charleston.

"So, what can I do for you Mr....Bonnet, is it?" The accent was Australian or New Zealand.

I knew you guys had described Orin Lawson as a swine, but that didn't come close to it. He was pasty and flabby with fat hanging from the arms of his Nautica shirt. Each of the buttons strained against the unnatural force that they were under to keep the seams together. I don't know that I have ever actually seen a human with jowls before, but Lawson had them. He had a pug nose and black button eyes with a deadly spark in them. He leered at me garishly, with a mouth full of overcrowded little yellow teeth. They didn't match the size of his head. It was almost as if he had never lost his baby teeth, and they had just stayed in their sockets to yellow and rot. To top it all off, he had a really bad toupee. I felt sorry for the humiliation that a poor rat was feeling somewhere in the world, knowing that a slime ball like Lawson was wearing its pelt.

I grinned as widely as I could and still look at that ghastly face. "Mr. Lawson, I am here to reduce your costs by half."

He gave a little laugh. "And how pray tell do you plan to do that, Mr. Bonnet?"

"Through the use of Charleston Chemical Engineering's new product called Barnacle Acid."

I wouldn't realize until later that I had just blown my cover.

I continued, "When I came into your beautiful facility, I noticed how technologically advanced you were, except for one thing. All your men are still scrapping barnacles off your salvage inventory by hand. We at Carolina Chemical Engineering have developed a chemical that can be applied to the hull of a ship with a high-speed paint sprayer, and in twenty-four hours, the hull will be completely clean of barnacles with no scraping."

Lawson singed me with his eyes, and whined with a curl of his blubbery lip, "We tried those damn chemical barnacle removers before. They only remove about half of the barnacles and you still have to scrape the rest. Besides, the meddling EPA took them all off the market a year ago because the residue left on the hulls was destroying the ecological system wherever the boats were docked for twelve months after treatment."

I was winging it, but I thought quickly. "Understood, Mr. Lawson, but that's why our new Barnacle Acid product is so exciting. First of all, it is guaranteed to remove all barnacles, or your money back. Second, we have developed a secret chemical formula that is based on citrus and pepper extracts that is completely environmentally friendly."

"Peppers and oranges?" he asked skeptically.

"Citrus extract," I corrected. "It creates a natural chemical rejection process that dissolves the barnacles."

He stared at me long and hard. "Barnacle Acid?"

"Yes, sir."

"From the Charleston Chemical Engineering Corporation?"

"Absolutely, sir, we have proven it in well over a hundred lab analysis cases."

His admin opened the door and pointed to her wrist at the watch that wasn't there.

Lawson leaned forward until he was looking down on top of my head. "I tell you what, Mr. Bonnet, I have another appointment right now, but I want an associate of mine to hear about your product. Can you come back in an hour?"

"Uh, sure," I smiled, standing. "I'll come back in an hour, and I will take you and your associate through it in more detail."

"Absolutely Mr. Bonnet, I'm sure my friend will want to give it a very thorough once-over."

I left the office and the warehouse, and then made my way to the pay phone where I called Buddy.

So I thought I had this guy right where I wanted him. I should have known something was up when the pretty brunette met me at the office door and led me to meet Lawson and his associate on the *Sweet Desperation*, which was docked out back. The *Sweet Revenge* was Lawson's private salvage yacht, only about thirty-two feet. The *Sweet Desperation* was its daddy by a factor of twelve.

Lawson was sitting at a little umbrella table on the dock in front of the gangway, sipping a short drink with a twist. "Patty, can you get our friend here one of the same?" He motioned at his glass, while nodding for me to have a seat.

"Yes, sir," she almost saluted as she turned tail and headed back for the warehouse.

"So what do you think of my baby here?" He motioned toward the *Sweet Desperation.*

"Kind of big to do local salvage work, isn't she?"

Lawson chuckled. "That she is. The *Sweet Revenge* does the smaller stuff; I use the *Desperation* for special missions in and around the islands. She was built by Peterson Builders for the U.S. Navy. She's a Safeguard Class salvage vessel. They are still new enough that none have been decommissioned. I have a knack for getting ex-military equipment before it hits the open market. This girl here was sold to Iraq, back when the U.S. and Saddam Hussein were best buddies. After the first Gulf war was over, Saddam needed cash, and through some shadowy channels I was able to pick her up for a song."

"Didn't the government have a problem with you doing business with Iraq?" I questioned incredulously.

"Well, number one, I didn't buy it from Saddam directly, and number two the U.S. government was just happy to have her out of that bastard's hands and back in U.S. waters before the second Gulf war started. They are more than cheerful to turn a blind eye to my acquisition."

Patty returned with my drink, which I realized was scotch on the rocks, with a twist.

"Come along, I'll give you the grand tour," Lawson waddled up the gangway. I followed reluctantly.

"She's a real beauty," he stated as we wound our way around the massive forward dock crane. "She has a length of two hundred and twenty-five feet and a beam of fifty-one, yet she only drafts sixteen. She has a range of eight thousand miles and a cruising speed of nine knots and can make fourteen when she has to."

He stopped below her forward crane and pointed up toward it. "That son-of-a whore right there can haul seven and a half tons. Its big brother on the stern can do forty tons. For wreck raising, her winches can pull up a hundred and fifty tons."

He paused for my expected look of admiration, which I provided, although I could have cared less.

"She is totally computerized and automated. As a Navy ship, it took six officers to run her. I can do it with two. Her state rooms have been customized to the level of sophistication to which I have become accustomed."

"Nice." I sipped my drink nonchalantly. "But why have you brought me here? I thought I was going to be discussing Barnacle Acid with your business associate."

Lawson grinned sardonically, and I suddenly knew I had stepped into a trap. "Oh, you are going to meet Uilleam alright, and the reason I brought you up here on the bow, is that it's a lot harder for my workers to hear you scream way up here."

"Uilleam," he called out, "at your leisure."

A tall, curly redhead with rippling muscles stepped out of the shadows. He wore a tight black T-shirt with the words "World Champion Muff Diver" on the front. Khaki shorts over huge calves and deck shoes completed his attire. He would have looked completely menacing, except his skin was a pale milky white with a universe of freckles. I automatically thought of Alfred E. Neuman on steroids.

"How you be doing today, Mr. Lawson?" he spoke with a distinct Irish brogue.

"I'm fine, thank you, Uilleam," he motioned toward me. "Allow me to introduce the two of you, Jason Bonnet, Leod Uilleam Urbay."

I felt hot coals in my stomach as I remembered the name of the man who killed Jones Jenkins from Donnie Rhodes's journal.

That big shamrock hugger was on me like white on low-country rice.

I was pinned to the deck, tasting the industrial deck cleaner and salt residue. My lip was busted and I could taste blood too.

"So," Lawson began, "tell me more about this Carolina Chemical Engineering, or was it Charleston Chemical Engineering, hmm?"

Shit, I thought as I instantly realized my mistake. "We changed names. We were the Charleston Chemical Engineering Company until we were bought out by Carolina Chemical Engineering."

"Oh, really?" He smiled in that ugly yellow baby-toothed way. "Well, I had Patty do a little Internet searching while you were gone for that hour, and guess what? There is no company listed by either name. Neither is there a product called Barnacle Acid. Now isn't that peculiar?"

I tried to glare up at him, but Urbay had his foot on my head.

"On a hunch, I checked with some friends who had recently had a little run-in with some guys near that old trash heap of a hotel, The Gator Tail."

My blood ran cold.

"Uilleam, where are your manners? Help our friend up so that he can look us in the eye. Tie him to the crane base."

Urbay decided to try some field goal practice on my ribs, before he scooped me off the deck.

"That should take any fight out that ye might have had."

He dragged me to the crane as I clenched my teeth against the pain of my every movement. My hands were lashed behind me with deck rope.

"So as I was saying," Lawson continued, "you and your buddies had a run-in with my friends. Seems they were very close to getting something very important from that blasted Kath Rose, but you came along and fucked it all up, and poor Kath got used for spear-fishing practice."

He glared at me, "Are you working with that damnable Rose family?"

I gulped, "I don't know what you are talking about."

Lawson gave the hi-sign to Urbay who gave me a vicious thrust punch to the ribs. The lights went out for a second and sparkles swam before my eyes.

Lawson hissed at me, "You know damn well who I am talking about, Rowland Rose and all his freaks at the Church of the White Rose."

My eyes rolled uncontrollably, but I muttered, "Never heard of him, but if I had I wouldn't tell a cesspool like you."

Lawson clenched his little yellow teeth. "Let's try a little stronger motivation, shall we, Uilleam?"

"With pleasure," he grinned, materializing a tire iron out of nowhere.

The pain was unbearable when the tire iron broke my arm. I looked down to see the jagged bone ends poking out. I looked back at my persecutor's face, and for some reason, said, "What, me worry?"

This seemed to infuriate Urbay even more; he slashed upward with the sharp end of the tire iron cutting a hole in my cheek.

Blood poured over my shirt.

"Last chance, Mr. Bonnet. Tell us where that journal is and we will let you go."

I couldn't hold my head up long enough to look him in the eye. I knew I was done for, and no matter what I told them, they were never going to let me go. "Go to hell," I muttered through a mouth full of blood.

Uilleam Urbay began to enjoy himself even more.

As everything faded to black, I heard him say, "Based on the account from my friends, I think I know two local boys who match the descriptions of your buddies. If you will not give us what we want, they will."

*   *   *   *

"Next thing I remember, I was feeling something cutting into my neck and not being able to breathe. For a second, I remember Buddy standing on a dock with a distraught look on his face. Then nothing until I got to the hospital."

"You are lucky to be alive." Buddy patted his shoulder.

"You saved me, Buddy Bear," he grinned. "If you hadn't shown up, I would have been a goner."

"He's right. If you hadn't come along when you did, he wouldn't be getting out of here."

Buddy shrugged sheepishly, "Oh, by the way, he's not dead."

"Who?" Jason looked confused.

"Jones Jenkins—he's back in town. He's the friend that Orin Lawson was referring to."

Buddy shook his head, "Sounds like we have another piece of the puzzle."

I grimaced, "Yeah, this Rowland Rose and the Church of the White Rose or whatever it's called."

"We should check it out," Jason ventured.

"I agree, but McDougal isn't letting you go anywhere today." I looked blearily at my watch. "We didn't sleep a wink last night, and we are both supposed to be at work by nine, which is in about thirty minutes."

Buddy shook his head, "I'm not leaving Jason, in case those bastards come back. I'll call into the Celestion and take the day off."

I agreed, "We need to do this thing in shifts if we don't want to get burned out. I'll go home and take a shower and try to drag my ass into work. With any luck I can get off at five, and then I'll go back to the ranch and sleep till eight. I'll come back up and we can check Jason out around nine. I'll take a personal day tomorrow, and we can look into this Church of the White Rose."

Buddy yawned and stretched.

"In the meantime," I grimaced, "try to catch some winks in the chair over there."

"I'll call you on the cell if anything changes. You may want to give Aunt Edna and Otis a call to let them know."

"Agreed," I slipped toward the door. "Take good care of him, Big Guy."

"No worries. The nose guard is on the line and ready to rumble."

CHAPTER 22

▼

I dropped into the M3 with a sigh of relief, which was quickly replaced with repulsion as the rain-soaked seats quickly drenched my ass.

I started to get pissed, but realized I was just too damned relieved at this point to get uptight. I turned the key and rolled out of the parking lot.

Once on the road, my conscience starting bothering me; I hadn't yet called Aunt Edna and Otis. I probably should have given them a ring last night while we were waiting, but at least now I could call them with good news. It was after nine, no danger of waking anyone up.

Even so, I was a little apprehensive. Aunt Edna was no spring chicken, and I was fearful of the effect the news might have on the old lady's heart. I had to call; I couldn't leave them in the dark any longer.

I unclipped my cell phone and dialed the number that was burned into my brain years ago.

She answered on the second ring, "Edna Bonnet's residence, Edna speaking."

"Um, hi, Aunt Edna…uh Ms. Bonnet, I don't know if you remember me but…"

"Saint Kristopher Grant, of course I remember you. Otis was just telling me what a handsome man you have grown into."

Her voice was warm and crackling, "And if you call me Ms. Bonnet again, I'm going to personally come down to Florida and take you to the woodshed or whatever passes for one down there in the swamps. I've always been Aunt Edna to all you boys, whether you were mine by blood or by function. I expect you to call me that."

"Yes, ma'am," I grinned. She was still as feisty as ever.

"My Otis has been telling me what a big help you and Anthony have been to Jason and his search. How is young Anthony doing? It's been years since I saw him. Is he eating right?"

"Yes, ma'am, Buddy's fine, but I'm afraid I have some bad news about Jason; there's been an accident."

"Oh my," she was quiet for a moment, the effervescence in her voice fizzling away. "Do you mind if I put you on speaker phone so that Otis can hear? He is right here."

It saddened me to hear her sound like a fragile old lady again. "Not at all, Aunt Edna."

There was a clatter and a click as shaking hands hit the speaker button and retired the receiver to its resting place.

"Master Saint Kristopher, you there?" It was Otis's voice, hollow and apprehensive.

"I'm here, Otis. I don't want to scare the two of you, but a bad man named Orin Lawson worked him over pretty good; he came very close to killing him."

"Damn it," Otis cursed, and I heard Aunt Edna wince in the background. My guess is that she had probably only heard Otis curse once or twice in the many years of his employment. It just wasn't proper to do that in front of one of Charleston's ladies.

"I knew we shouldn't have let him go off by himself to investigate that salvage yard," Otis hissed.

I thought the line sounded garbled, until I realized it was Otis's muffled sobs. "It's my fault. I should have stayed down there to watch over him, to make sure he was safe."

I heard Aunt Edna making comforting sounds to Otis in the background. Go figure. Otis and Jason have fought like cats and dogs as long as I have known them. Now that something has happened to the thorn in his side, he's inconsolable.

Aunt Edna's steady voice came back on the line as she picked up the receiver again. "I think I better do the talking from here on," she stated matter-of-factly.

"Yes, ma'am," I agreed. "I didn't know he was going to take it so hard."

"Sometimes you hurt the ones you love the most. Neither Jason nor Otis would admit it, but Jason has filled Otis's need for a son, and Otis has filled Jason's need for a father. All together, we are about the most dysfunctional family in Charleston, but we are still a family."

"You are very much a family," I agreed, "I miss those lazy Sunday afternoons on your piazza drinking tea when I was too poor to visit my family upstate. Y'all helped me keep my home sickness at bay."

"We miss you too, Saint Kristopher," I could feel her warm smile through the phone. "Otis has gone into the other room for tissues; please fill me in on his condition."

"Well, I'll spare you how he got in the condition he is in, but he has a broken arm, his ribs are only bruised, and he has lots of swelling and bruising from being beaten with a tire iron."

"Oh my," her voice wavered slightly.

"They also tried to hang him with an old rusty chain. He's one big bruise, but it could have been a lot worse."

"Is he, is he going to be all right?" She asked timidly.

"Well, the doctor hasn't released him yet, but I think he is over the worst of it."

"I should come down. Otis, Otis," she called into the other room, "we have to go to Florida right away!"

I heard Otis's subdued voice in the background, "Ms. Edna, you know that Doc Ravenell has forbidden you to travel. He says your heart couldn't take the strain."

"To hell with Doctor Ravenell," she fumed. "My nephew is on death's door and I am going to him."

I couldn't help but grin to myself as I imagined the shocked look on Otis's face.

I gently intervened, "Aunt Edna, I would advise against it. As I mentioned, I think he's over the worst of it. They are going to keep him today to run tests and observe him, but I think he is going to be out later tonight. Having visitors, especially ones he is going to worry about, will not help his condition any. He is in a private room this afternoon; you could call him there. That's the best thing you could do."

She sighed a long dry sigh, "Very well, Saint Kristopher, but I expect Anthony and yourself to take good care of him."

"We will, ma'am, I promise. Would you mind if I spoke to Otis for a second?"

"Of course," her voice was warm again. "You and Anthony take good care of yourselves. I don't want either of you running into those same bad men."

"Yes, ma'am, we will," I tried to sound genuine.

There was a click, and Otis's scratchy voice was on the phone.

"So," I ribbed, "I'll be sure to relay the depth of your concern to Jason."

"Not amusing, Saint Kristopher," he grumped.

"Sorry, Otis," I grinned, "I couldn't resist. What I really wanted to do was check with you to see how you had progressed with the journal so far?"

"I was starting to get really frustrated," Otis admitted. "I had been through the entire journal four or five times, and while it's quite a colorful chronology of criminal dealings, none of it really gave me the answer I was looking for. I left it alone for a few hours, and then went back and examined it from a format perspective, rather than for its content. I realized that each entry was very formal and similar in format, maybe too similar."

"I don't think I'm following you, Dr. Otis."

"Have you ever heard of equidistant-letter sequencing?"

"Uh, no, I don't think so." I wrinkled my brow.

"There was this book published a few years ago called *The Bible Code*. In this book, the author, a man by the name of Drosnin, claimed that he had broken a secret code in the Hebrew text of the Old Testament that contained predictions of events such as the Kennedy assassinations and the Oklahoma bombing.

"Drosnin says this code hadn't been broken earlier, because the computer hadn't been invented. The author makes the statement that 'what Moses actually received on Mount Sinai was an interactive data base, which until now we couldn't fully access.'"

"Okay," I clucked, "sounds like a bunch of baloney to me. What does that have to do with the journal?"

Otis ignored me and continued, "These supposed secret messages are written in skip codes, also called equidistant-letter sequencing. With the computer arranging the Bible into a continuous string of three-hundred thousand Hebrew letters, a computer program is devised to skip every tenth, hundredth, or thousandth letter. Drosnin claimed that the resulting grid examined up and down, diagonally, forward or backward, came up with hidden messages."

"Please tell me you aren't saying the journal has these kinds of secret messages in it?" I asked skeptically.

"I know it sounds far-fetched, but I scanned the journal into the system and then used optical character recognition to convert it to plain ASCII text. So far I have only run one simple equidistant-letter sequencing algorithm on it, but the result of the crossword grid was startling."

"I'm afraid to ask. What did it say?"

"The words 'Fear of the Church of The White Rose' were intersected with 'I burned the map.'"

I almost ran into the bumper of the car in front of me, as the big brakes of the M3 screamed. The phone went tumbling to the floor.

"Are you okay? Are you okay?" Otis was repeating incessantly as I fished around the floorboard for the cell phone.

"Yeah, I'm fine, I just dropped the phone."

"Well, I don't know what this Church of the White Rose is, but I was wondering if it had something to do with that tattoo the cowboy had and the girl he was talking about before he died."

"It has everything to do with it," I grimaced. I quickly filled Otis in on the high points of what the three of us had discovered.

"This is no coincidence," Otis stated flatly. "There is no way this kind of message could just appear."

I agreed.

"But if Rhodes really did burn the map, he may have encoded its contents further in the journal," Otis commented. "What perplexes me, however, is that this journal was written years before everyone had a computer in their home. Even now, it's going to take all my lab servers days to run through every deciphering scenario. To do this kind of encrypting would have taken some heavy-duty computing power that was just not accessible to the general public back then. Rhodes was a two-bit criminal and a con man. Where could he have gotten that kind of black-market processing power in South Florida in the early eighties?"

I pulled into the driveway of La Vie Dansante. "Back then there was only one place and one man," I growled, "and I know exactly which bunker to find him in."

"What?" Otis questioned.

"Never mind, I'll take care of that on my end. Run all your algorithms and give me a call back as soon as you have more info."

"Absolutely, Kris, take care of Jason and Buddy," he paused, "and yourself as well, my friend."

"Will do." I hung up the phone absently.

Across the pasture from La Vie Dansante, a stall door was banging loudly in the wind. That's odd, I thought. Lil would never leave a stall door open like that. Suddenly, in dawning realization, an icy fist gripped my heart.

CHAPTER 23

▼

I jumped over the door of the M3 and hit the ground at a sprint. I covered the distance between the driveway and the barn in half the normal time. The horses were stomping and snorting nervously around the open stall door. I could taste the bitter copper of fear in my mouth. I secured the flapping stall door to the catch made to hold it open, delaying the inevitable, if for only a few seconds.

I stepped into the musty stall. The hay was slick with blood. The smell of fresh death was in the air, and the black flies were already gathering.

There in the corner lay the crooked crumpled body of Jazmine. The poor horse's throat had been cut, and she had been left to bleed to death. Her eyes were rolled back in her head, and her mouth was full of white foam. She hadn't died easily or quickly.

I bent down on one knee in front of her to stroke her chestnut muzzle one last time. "I wish I had one last carrot to give you, old girl," I whispered softly, feeling the tears well up.

"My God," I said angrily, "who would have done this?" The other horses had gathered back at the stall door to mourn. They started at the shock of my voice and bolted around the corner of the barn.

She had been the kind and gentle one of the bunch, sensitive and loving to any man, woman or child who rode her, played with her, or just brushed her.

I had asked myself the question, but I already knew the answer. Bastards like Jenkins and Lawson, who would leave a man hanging to die, wouldn't hesitate to murder a poor helpless beast. I hoped there was an especially hot place in Hell for the both of them.

I got up and threw a horse blanket that had been hanging over the stall wall over Jazmine. Some people say that animals don't have a soul and that they don't go to heaven when they die, but anyone who had known this peaceful animal couldn't think that she hadn't now gone to a better place.

Lil and the kids were going to be heartbroken. Jesus, how could I ever explain this to Lil?

As I turned to leave the stall, I saw the blood-stained note tacked to the inner doorpost.

With shaking hands, I pulled it down and opened it up. The handwriting was stark and garish.

"We told you to give it back, but you wouldn't listen. Maybe a little death and sorrow will get your attention. It sure got the attention of your pretty blonde wife. She hasn't stopped wailing since her little ringside show ended. If you don't want her shed tears to turn into shed blood, you will bring the journal to St. Barts on Friday. Don't be late, or we will be sending your horsy her rider in short order."

"No, oh no," I bellowed. "They can't have taken my Lil." I bolted for the house, throwing open every door, screaming her name over and over again. Hoping beyond hope that it was a lie; that she had been at the store when they came, that they were just trying to scare me. There was no sign of her, but the kids' breakfast bowls were in the sink; the last thing they did each day before they left for school. At least they were safe.

Her car was in the garage. My God, what had I done? What had I gotten my Lil into? She can't be gone. Oh please, God, don't let her be gone. I stumbled erratically from point to point not knowing where I was going, not knowing where I had been.

I found the beagle Spooner locked in the downstairs half-bath. Lil would never have locked the dog up like that. When I opened the door, the poor dog was whimpering in the corner, as if it had been beaten.

I half walked, half fell out the front door, scanning the horizon for some thread of reality that I could grasp on to. The tears rolled down my face and soaked my shirt. I didn't even notice.

I suddenly remembered Lil's cell phone. With the tiniest glimmer of hope, I tried to dial the number. It took me three times to dial it right. In my state, I had completely forgotten about my speed dial option.

As the electronic tone buzzed in my ear, I realized I could faintly hear Lil's cell playing that silly ringer tune "You Light Up My Life," which was her special ring for me. I strained to hear where it was coming from, but it stopped and went to voice mail. Cursing I hung up and called again.

It was coming from the direction of the barn. I followed the sound like a bloodhound. I found the phone about halfway to the barn. It was mashed down into the soft earth by the tire tracks of a large truck or van. I fell to my knees and dug it out of the muck. I held it to my heart as if it were Lil herself.

What do I do now? How can I get my Lil back?

Buddy Bear. Buddy would know what to do.

I could barely control the spasms of fear and anguish rolling through my body long enough to dial his cell.

He answered in that quiet tone that people use when they are using a cell phone in the hospital, when they know they aren't supposed to.

I exploded in jerking sobs and screams. "Gone, Buddy! I, I don't know what to do! They took her! They killed Jazz and they're going to kill her too! Help me, Buddy, please. I can't lose her and Skylar too!"

"Kris, slow down. What are you talking about? Who's gone? Who's killed?"

I took a deep heaving breath and tried to pull it together. "Jenkins and Lawson. When I got back to the house they had slit Jazmine's throat. I found a note. They kidnapped Lil. If I don't deliver the journal to them in St. Barts on Friday, they are going to kill her, too."

I heard him puffing in the background, fighting to remain in control for my sake. If there was anyone in the world that even came close to loving Lil as much as I did, it was Buddy.

His voice was measured and mechanical. "Have you called the police yet, Kris?"

"No, I called you first."

"How about the kids? Are they okay?"

"I think so, Jess and the twins should be in school right now, but I don't know for sure. Oh Jesus, I can't take it if they are caught up in this too."

"Don't jump to conclusions, Kris. I'm sure they are all in school just like they are supposed to be. You just sit tight. You are in no shape to be doing anything. I'm going to call the schools and check on the kids. Then I'll call the Jupiter Police and have them come out to see if they can find any leads. After that, I'm coming over to La Vie Dansante. Jason will be okay by himself for a few hours."

"I won't be here," I stated flatly.

"What?" I heard the fear creeping back into his voice again.

"I won't be here. I'm going to take care of the problem where it started in the first place."

"What are you talking about, Kris? You're not thinking clearly!"

"Oh, I'm thinking clearly all right, Buddy Bear, old pal. I'm going to go fucking kill a backstabbing asshole by the name of Shrimper Dan."

"Who...?" He began. But I had already hit the end button. The phone rang to voice mail twice more before I finally turned it off. I went back inside La Vie Dansante to my library. I pulled a dog-eared copy of *Islands in the Stream* from a high shelf and opened the book. Inside the books hollowed-out interior were my old military-issue side arm and three full clips. I jammed one of the clips into the magazine and stuck the pistol in the back of my belt. I left the front door standing wide open as I stomped with bitter determination to the M3. I tore a great half-circle rip in the lawn as I lashed the car out onto the road, in the direction of Peanut Island.

CHAPTER 24

▼

I was in no mood to wait on the ferry to Peanut Island. I threw money at a dockside rental place and grabbed the nearest personal watercraft. As it happened, I lucked out and wound up with a souped-up 2001 SeaDoo RXX. In no time, I was roaring down the Intracoastal at nearly seventy miles per hour.

Almost all of the Intracoastal in that area is a no-wake zone. I ignored the signs and hoped that the marine patrol was nowhere around. It took no time to beach the SeaDoo on the north end of Peanut Island. I didn't bother with the docks or pathways; I cut straight across the island as the wild palms and underbrush tore at my bare arms, legs, and face.

I probably would have been wiser to hit the docks. It wound up taking me longer to barge through the underbrush, but in my blind rage I didn't care.

If you have never lost someone close to you, it may be hard to fathom the all-encompassing anger, fear, and sorrow that swallows you whole.

When my only son, Skylar, passed from this world, it was in the worst way. It wasn't peaceful or restful for him. He wrestled with the overwhelming pain as if he were fighting the devil himself. In many ways he was. He was a strong boy, and I was a helpless weak father. He fought the disease with every ounce of his being until the bitter end. I have never before or since witnessed such strength, but in the end the bastard killed him.

I refused to believe he was gone. I kept expecting him to open his twinkling eyes and grin at his mother, letting her know he was only kidding. Even after the funeral, I'd inadvertently go by his room in the morning to wake him for school. I attended his little league games, even though he was no longer a part of the team. I can still remember the pitying looks from the other parents. But I always held my breath when they got to his old spot in the lineup, "Next up to bat, Skylar Grant, the shortstop for the Jupiter Junior Hammerheads." He never made it to bat.

It wasn't fair. I was so angry then. I feel guilty now for all the times I had yelled at Lil and the kids. What kind of a husband and father was I to take it out on them? What kind of a father was I to let him die? Lil had been afraid that I was going to hurt someone or myself.

She had been very blunt with me. Find a constructive outlet for my anger, or she and the girls would be moving back to Charleston. The next day I had gone over to the Jupiter Kempo Karate Academy and signed up. I built my own dojo and workout area above the garage at La Vie Dansante to hone my skills and release my wrath.

I had failed. I let them take Lil, and now I had lost both her and Skylar. Shrimper Dan cooperated with that dirt bag Donnie Rhodes. He created the code in the fucking journal that caused me to lose my Lil. I wasn't going to let him get away with it unpunished.

There it was, the pipe; the entrance to the bunker. I tore the bushes camouflaging the entrance away by their roots. I stormed down the drainpipe, not caring whether Dan saw me coming or not. Down in the chamber, I went straight to where I knew the secret door was and starting pounding on it with the butt of the gun.

"Let me in you son of a bitch," I screamed. "You goddamn back-stabbing turncoat."

"Let me in or I am going to start shooting! These walls may be concrete, but they are meant to protect from the outside not the inside. I bet if I start shooting, I can take out enough of your ventilation and telecom infrastructure to send your god-forsaken mole-ass scurrying for the surface! Let me in, you bastard!"

The door creaked open.

I stormed in, thrusting the pistol in front of me. Shrimper Dan was sitting at his computer desk with a sad, drawn look on his face. "I'm sorry, Kris. You left me no other choice."

It was at that moment I felt the fishing line trip wire snag my ankle. I looked down just in time to see the powder explosion from the barrel of the booby trap. I felt a burning sting in my chest, and everything went black.

CHAPTER 25

▼

Slowly, ever so slowly I floated to the surface. It was like rising out of a deep blue diving hole. The waters around me sparkled with pretty colors and images that I couldn't quite make out. I struggled to reach out and touch them, but I couldn't seem to move my arms. All I could do was float toward the sunlight, the wavering rays just beyond the surface.

Suddenly it dawned on me that the light wasn't the sun, but a yellow bulb in a protective wire cage. It was attached to a concrete ceiling with rust-red water streaks. I tried to move my arms again but they were held firmly to my sides by the tight, rough, olive green blanket wrapped around me.

"So you finally decided to wake up, Sleepyhead?" A blurry voice walked toward me, and slowly assumed the features of Shrimper Dan.

It all came flooding back to me. "You shot me, you bastard," I hissed through clenched teeth. I could still feel the burning sensation in my chest.

"I'm sorry, Kris, you left me no choice. You were completely out of your mind. It's an old trick that I learned from the North Vietnamese. They'd nail a mousetrap to a wooden stake. Then they'd weld a firing pin to a pipe armed with a shotgun shell and tie it to a stake. The trip line is tied to the mousetrap. When the line is tripped, it triggers the mousetrap, which hits the firing pin, and you become Swiss cheese. You should be thankful that I load mine with tranquilizer darts instead of buckshot."

I fought to get my arms free.

"There is no point in struggling, Kris. You were down for the count. I put you in the bunk and seriously short-sheeted the bed. There is no way you are going to get out of there."

"How long was I out?" I snarled.

Dan looked at his watch. "Almost twenty hours. It's around six on Tuesday morning."

"Oh God," I whimpered, "they are long gone by now. You've got to let me out. I've got to get my shit together so I can get to St. Barts by Friday."

"You talked a lot in your sleep, Kris. I know the whole story and I know why you came here to take me out. But I am not going to let you go till you hear my side of the story. Then, if you still want to kill me—Well, I'll let you go and we can have at it. But you need to know that I don't die easy."

"Doesn't seem like I have much friggin' choice, does it?"

"No, I guess you don't." He pulled up a stool.

"I helped Donnie Rhodes encode his precious map. I fully admit it, but there was nothing shady about it. The son of a gun found out about me through the Coast Guard station night guard's kid; I used to pay him to do grocery runs for me. He came to me with a business proposition. He never came out and said that he would blow my secret if I didn't cooperate, but he danced all around it.

"He told me about this crazy guy named Rowland Rose and his family. Seems they claim to be descended from a guy who served on this pirate ship in the seventeen hundreds. They believe that the pirate found a book that had tremendous powers. They actually believed in it so much that it was a religious thing for them. They'd do anything to get their hands on that book. They even have a church; it's called the Church of the White Rose. They have a tent revival that goes all over the South. The thing is half carnival, half evangelical nightmare. I've heard they handle snakes and all kinds of crazy crap.

"Rhodes was sure as shit scared of this church. He thought that Rowland Rose was hot on his heels, and that if he didn't get rid of the map, they would kill him for it.

"He didn't believe the kooky story about the book, though. He believed that the map held the secret to three great treasures, rather than a road map to some mystical book.

"I thought the whole thing was hogwash; that is, until you showed up ranting and raving yesterday. I consider you one of my few friends, Kris. If you think these people are that dangerous, then I believe you."

I glared at him.

"Anyway, you have to believe me. I just thought Rhodes was a nut, but a fairly harmless one. I had caught wind of some of his shady dealings around Jupiter, but they seemed fairly innocuous. Besides, he had built that strip bar and had pissed off all of the tight-asses on Jupiter Island. Anybody who does that can't be all bad, huh?

"I'll be straight with you, Kris. I needed the money. This was back in the early days of my time down here. I had a good enough setup to do what Rhodes wanted, but not good enough for me to do my worldwide electronic search for Jill. I needed the bucks to upgrade, that's when I still hoped to find her and my child.

"Hate me if you want to, Saint Kristopher, but just like you I had lost the one I loved. I would have, and still would do anything to get her back. Encoding the map for Rhodes seemed innocent enough. At the time it didn't seem as if it would hurt anyone, and Donnie Rhodes paid me fifty grand to do it. That was a lot of money back then. All I wanted was to get Jill back."

I let out a long sigh. "So why didn't you tell me the other day when I was here?"

"I was ashamed. I have done enough killing. When you told me about that guy getting murdered at the Gator Tail, I felt like I had more blood on my hands. I figured it wouldn't hurt anything not to tell you, as long as I helped you as much as possible. I never imagined they would try to hurt anyone in your family. I'm truly sorry I didn't tell you the truth then and there."

I felt my guard dropping. This really wasn't his fault. It was Jenkins, Lawson, and that Blakely woman. It suddenly dawned on me that I'd never got the results of the search on Frances Blakely that Dan had been doing the other day.

"Let me out of these blankets, you asshole." I gave him a half smile. "I have to find my wife and I need your help."

Shrimper Dan helped me struggle out of the bunk. "Thanks, Kris, I promise to help you any way I can."

"Well, first of all did you keep any details of what you encoded into the journal?" I questioned.

"No, unfortunately everything I had was in electronic format. It didn't seem important after nearly twenty years. I dumped it long ago."

"Okay, then tell me about the universal search you were doing on Frances Blakely."

"She's a pretty interesting lady. She is actually Doctor Frances Blakely, Fran to her friends, of which she has few. She's a cold-blooded anthropologist from the University of South Carolina, specializing in ancient artifacts.

"She comes from fairly new money, made by a father who rode the Carolina textile boom in the seventies, opening up forty different mills in North and South Carolina. Then he sold them all to the international conglomerates that now own them and retired to his hometown of Charleston. He died mysteriously in his sleep two years later, and was survived by his darling daughter who inherited nearly three hundred million dollars.

"From what my research showed me, she is a real bitch. She has a ruthless reputation for doing whatever it takes to get her hands on the artifacts she wants for her private collection. This doesn't preclude theft or murder. She's been linked to several artifact disappearances around the globe."

"So she steals artifacts. What has this got to do with her association with Jenkins?"

"My point is she isn't after the three treasures that Donnie Rhodes sought. She has more money than she knows what to do with. She is after that pirate book, and she will do whatever she has to, to get it."

I blew out a fearful breath. "Okay, then we need to find the *Nefarious* again."

Dan shook his head sadly. "I already thought of that. I ran the satellite searches while you were out of it. I watched the *Nefarious* pull out of the Last Resort and head out to sea. About twenty miles out, she rendezvoused with a huge ship with stern and bow cranes."

"The *Sweet Desperation*," I ground my teeth.

"Yeah, how did you know?" He pondered.

"Anyway, the ship was so large that it actually used its cranes to lift the *Nefarious* out of the water and planted her in a special scaffold on deck. I swear to God, scooped her up like that forty-two footer was nothing but a dingy. After that, they turned tail and headed out into the open sea. There's nothing out there for thousands of miles till you get to Easter Island. So the spy birds don't even cover it. It's like she disappeared into the abyss."

"There is no way you can track them?"

"I'm afraid not, at least not until they come back within range of one of the satellites."

"My guess is that what they are doing is giving the shipping lanes a wide berth on their way down to St. Barts."

"That seems logical, and probably makes sense as to why they didn't want me to meet them till Friday. At top speed, it will take the *Sweet Desperation* at least that long to steam down there."

I slammed my fist down on the bunk. "Goddamn it, I can't just sit here until it's time to go to St. Barts."

"May I suggest that it might be worth your time to look into the Church of the White Rose? I don't know what they had on Donnie Rhodes, but they sure had him running scared. Maybe our friend Dr. Blakely would be afraid of the same thing?"

"It's worth a shot. Any idea where they are?"

Shrimper Dan beamed, "It just so happens I also did a little research on the location of that band of traveling religious zealots. You'll be happy to learn that that they are currently camped just outside Pahokee, on the shores of Lake Okeechobee."

"Hot damn," I commented. "That's just a couple of hours from here."

"Yep, I couldn't find much else out about them, but it certainly makes sense to pay them a visit."

"Thanks, Dan." I stood up. "I'm sorry I went postal on you."

"Not a problem," he sighed as I marched up the tunnel, "Come back and buy me a beer when this is all over. I could use the company."

CHAPTER 26

▼

Miraculously the SeaDoo was still up in the bushes at the edge of the water where I had dragged her. As I idled back up the Intracoastal, I was careful this time to obey the no-wake signs. The last thing I needed right now was to lose more time because the marine patrol had thrown me into the pokey.

So I played it careful. As I slipped by the waterfront mansions on my left and right, with their monster docks and multimillion-dollar yachts, I tried to switch off the chaotic thoughts swarming in my head and push myself into analytical mode by planning my agenda for the next few days.

First thing I had to do was check on the kids. Buddy had said that he was going to confirm that they were all right. I was certain that Jessica had kept an eye on the twins while I was gone. I would pull over and call them right now, but in my haste yesterday I had left my cell in the M3. The kids were priority one as soon as I got to the car.

Second was Buddy, he probably had the army out looking for me by now. I had to get hold of him to have him call off the hounds. I also wanted to find out from him if the Jupiter Police had found any clues at La Vie Dansante. I wasn't holding out any hope, but it wouldn't hurt to check.

Next I needed to check on Jason, and make sure those bastards hadn't taken a parting shot at him before they headed out to sea.

Last I needed to call Otis and get him to overnight the journal to me. Others might argue that I should get crafty with my plan, but I wasn't going to play with my Lil's life. If they wanted the journal, they were going to get the journal. Screw everything else.

I figured all that would take up most of the rest of today. Despite being out of it for the last twenty hours, I was totally exhausted. If I was going to make it through this for the long haul, I had to get some rest. I had to stay sharp, and that meant metering my energy and not turning into a crazy insomniac for the next four days. Tonight I would sleep and recharge my batteries.

I needed to visit the Church of the White Rose, but there was something more important I had to do first. I had to visit Jack Mason at Calypso to see if the Lady Orleans was flyable. I cringed at the idea of taking a commercial flight down to St. Barts. If I had to, I would, but as a dedicated pilot, I wanted the flexibility of flying my own plane. Besides, we were dealing with dangerous people here. You never knew when we would have to beat a hasty exit.

I figured arguing with Jack Mason would take most of Wednesday, which left me Thursday to go visit Rowland Rose and the Church of the White Rose.

On Friday, I would have to start out in the wee hours of the morning to get to St. Barts by noon. Thankfully, the Lady Orleans had the range to make it without any stops.

I pulled up to the dock, and a very cross rental agent. I paid him double the overdue rental fee just to shut him up and headed for the M3. Thankfully, this time it hadn't rained, since I had inadvertently left her out overnight again with the top down.

I fished my cell phone from between the seats where it had fallen and dialed La Vie Dansante, as I pulled away from the docks. To my surprise and relief, a frantic Buddy Bear answered the phone.

"Hey, I thought you would be at work?" I said nonchalantly.

"At work, at work!" A steady stream of expletives followed for a good thirty seconds. I held the phone away from my ear until the wave subsided.

"How could I possibly work? Lil disappears, you disappear, I have to guard Jason, and I have to make sure nothing happens to your kids. How the hell could I possibly have time to work? You scared the hell out of me, you son of a bitch!"

"I take it from that the kids are okay?"

"Yeah," he simmered down, "the kids are fine. They were pretty upset that both their parents had gone missing, but I kept as many of the details from them as possible. Jessica has been a big help. She's been watching the twins while I kept an eye on Jason and searched for your ass."

"I'm sorry, Buddy, I really didn't mean to put you through all of this; I just kind of went off the deep end for a while."

He grumped half-heartedly on the other end of the phone. "It's okay, I guess, just clue me in as to what you were doing. You didn't actually kill that shrimp guy you mentioned, did you?"

"No, I had every intention of doing so, but Shrimper Dan took me out with a tranquilizer dart booby trap. I slept for twenty hours straight."

"Must be nice to get some sleep," he mumbled. "So who is this Shrimper Dan guy anyway?"

"Well, he swore me to secrecy in the past, but I guess the cat's kind of out of the bag with you now. He's an old Seabee turned computer hacker who went underground on Peanut Island. He helped me find the *Nefarious* at Captain Harry's, and unfortunately he is the one who encoded the map into Donnie Rhodes's journal."

"Yeah," he commented, "Otis told me all about the journal being encoded when I called to tell him about what happened to you and Lil. He and Aunt E are both real sorry about the misery that has occurred. They feel responsible for everything that has happened."

I sighed, "Well, it certainly has been a world of trouble, but they couldn't have known that all this was going to happen. That reminds me, I need Otis to over-night the journal down here to me so I can take it to St. Barts."

"So *we* can take it to St. Barts," Buddy corrected, "I'm not about to let you go down there without me. And I'm way ahead of you. I had Otis send it out yesterday. It should be here this morning sometime."

"Thanks man, but aren't you going to get in trouble with the Celestion for being out of work so much during The Season?"

"Not a problem. I already called both of our places of employment and explained the situation to them. They both understood and said to take as much time as we needed. They are good people. They know the value that we bring to their companies and are willing to support us in whatever way is necessary."

"That's good to hear. At least that's one less thing to worry about. Speaking of worry; how's Jason? Did Jenkins, Lawson, and Blakely take another swipe at him?"

"No, I guess they figured they had done enough damage there. He's getting better pretty quickly. I brought him back to La Vie Dansante last night. He has the strength to teach bar songs to the twins, and to complain about my cooking, so I guess he is going to be all right."

"Sounds like he is becoming his old self again. I'm going to have to kick his ass myself if he is teaching the twins the same bar songs that we used to sing."

Buddy chortled, "Yeah, I think he is getting pretty tired of sitting around doing nothing. In fact, when I told him about having to take the journal to St. Barts, he insisted on going with us."

I groaned, "There is no way that he should be doing something like that by Friday."

"That's what I told him, but he is insisting. He feels responsible for everything that's happened, and wants to help fix the situation."

"That's great and good, but his broken arm will just slow us down, and I can't afford that, not for Lil's sake."

I could almost see him shrugging through the phone. "Hey, I tried to talk him out of it. Give it your best shot; maybe you will have more luck than I did."

I pulled into La Vie Dansante's drive behind Buddy's Harley. "I just pulled up, Buddy. I'll be inside in a second."

"Good," he stated flatly, "because the Jupiter Police did find one thing: a message from Dr. Frances Blakely to you."

CHAPTER 27

▼

I tried to catch up on my sleep that night, so I would be fresh to fight the creeping evil that had penetrated our lives, but I wound up turning and tossing in that big bed without Lil. I held her pillow close to me and inhaled her beautiful scent, and sometime around 2:00 I finally fell asleep. I awoke suppressing a scream at 6:00 and made my way to the kitchen. I found Buddy there nursing a cup of coffee. He looked worse for the wear than I did.

I sat down and poured myself another strong one.

"I've been thinking about the message on the answering machine," he began, "trying to figure out if there is more than meets the eye."

He was referring to the one clue the Jupiter Police had found; a message on my answering machine from Frances Blakely left mere seconds before I had arrived to witness the grisly site at the barn.

Buddy materialized a small tape recorder.

"Hey, I thought the cops took the tape as evidence?"

He grinned, "A good security guy always keeps backup copies." He pressed play, and the little hairs stood up on my arm again at the sound of that icy voice.

"Saint Kristopher Grant, by now I'm sure you know who I am. My colleagues took care of your friend, Mr. Bonnet, and they took care of your horse as well. We have your wife, Mr. Grant, and we will not hesitate to extinguish her life if you don't meet our demands. You will bring the journal to St. Barts on Friday. Meet me at the Tapas Bar in the Eden Rock hotel at sunset. Don't be late, Mr. Grant, or my friends will take great pleasure in filleting your wife."

"I wouldn't want to be trapped in a dark alley with that bitch," I grimaced.

Buddy frowned knowingly. I could tell that that military mind of his was still turning the problem in a million different ways like a Rubik's Cube, trying to figure out how to make this piece fit to our advantage.

I looked outside the bay window. The early-morning grayness was starting to fade to day, and the palms were rustling in a gentle breeze.

"Hey, why don't we run your Harley over to Jupiter Salvage and pick up Rocky Rhodes before we start out for the day? We'll come back by here and drop the Harley off, and then try to take the Vette down to Calypso's without waking Jason up. He needs to be resting right now, not tagging along with us."

"Works for me," he grinned. "But I don't think we have to worry about him till we get back. I called Dr. McDougal and had him prescribe a sleeping pill. I slipped it in with the rest of his meds when I gave them to him last night. He should easily sleep till noon."

"Buddy Bear," I chided, "I didn't realize Jason was having trouble sleeping."

"He's not," he growled. "But if he rang that goddamned bell one more time for me to bring him something, I might have had to throttle him!"

"We gotta go. We have a plane to see about."

He nodded, and we headed for the door.

CHAPTER 28

▼

Jack Mason wasn't a happy man. In fact, he was thoroughly pissed off.

"Saint Kristopher, please be reasonable," He begged. "You can't really be wanting to take this old girl into the air by Friday."

He gestured at the Lady Orleans sitting on her flat tires and broken front landing gear in the Calypso hanger. She looked as though she were hanging her head.

"That's exactly what I want, Jack. I need a seaplane to get to St. Barts on Friday, unless you want to cough up one of Calypso's Albatrosses, I need the Lady Orleans."

"You know I don't have the authority to pull one of Calypso's planes off their regular schedule. And we don't have anything in maintenance right now. That's the only reason I've been able to devote myself and the Betancur brothers to her full time." He pointed to the two Guatemalans who were on the Lady Orleans's port wing securing the final rivets of one of her new engines.

Buddy shook his head in amazement. "I'm surprised you have her this far. Last time I saw her, she didn't even have her wing attached. Now she not only has her wing back, but two brand-new shiny engines as well."

"You and the Betancurs have done a great job, Jack, her engines look great, but this is a matter of life or death. I have to be able to fly her out of here early Friday morning."

"Are you sure that's safe, Kris?" Buddy asked. "I mean those two shiny blue engines look great, but she still looks like crap. No offense."

"I know," I sighed. "It's not my ideal scenario either, but I did her avionics and hydraulics, I think they are ready. Her engines are new. If Jack can fix her front landing gear and put new tires on her, I think she'll make it there and back.

Then she can go back into the shop for as long as Jack wants to get her one hundred percent shipshape."

"It's a dangerous thing you are doing, Kris. The tires are a breeze, but the landing gear is going to take me right up to flight time to repair. There will be no burn-in time for the engines, no time for test flights, no second chances. You'll have to fly low, there's hardly a single piece of window glass intact on her. I can probably scrounge around the shop and get enough to do the pilot's windscreen, but the wind is going to whistle and howl through the rest of her like a banshee."

Buddy was walking around the Lady Orleans giving her a detailed once-over. "You're not actually going to try to land her in the water, are you, Kris? Not even counting all the broken glass, her sheet metal is so thin in places that the only thing holding her together is dried swamp muck and rust."

"She'll hold together," I stated flatly.

"God help us?" Buddy lifted his head skyward.

"You will not," Jack scowled, "I repeat, not try to land this old girl in the water. She cannot take that kind of punishment. She'll literally disintegrate. Promise me, Saint Kristopher."

I sighed, "All right, I promise, but believe me the alternative may be even less appealing."

"What the hell does that mean?" Buddy yelled from the tail section at the back of the hanger.

"Never mind," I mumbled. "You'll find out soon enough."

Jack stared me down. "I don't want you taking any risks. This isn't some easy-to-fly, forgiving Cessna on floats. She is old, unstable, and cantankerous. You treat her right or she will be the death of you; that I can promise."

"Don't worry. I swear we are just going to fly down there, get Lil, and fly back the next morning. When I come back, I will taxi her straight over here to you."

"All right," Jack grumbled through clenched teeth, "I don't like it, but the Betancurs and I will work around the clock between now and then to make her as airworthy as possible. Exactly when do you need her?"

I quickly calculated, "Well, a commercial flight down there takes about five hours. So with our reduced cruising speed and need to fly low, I would tack another three hours on to that. Probably about an eight-hour flight total. To give us a little extra window of time, we probably need to leave about 4:00 A.M."

"Friday morning?" Jack spat, "that's not Friday morning that's Thursday night! Have you by any chance noticed that it's now almost noon on Wednesday? God bless America, Kris, what are you trying to do to me?"

"I'm sorry, Jack," I groaned. "If I had any other choice, I would be taking it."

"You, big boy," Jack motioned at Buddy. Buddy got a 'who me?' expression on his face. "Yeah you, get your ass out of my hangar so I can get to work."

Jack marched into the hangar and started yelling in Spanish. The Betancurs began scurrying all over the Lady Orleans like fire ants.

Buddy came shuffling out. "Who does he think he is anyway?"

I squared my jaw. "He is the one and only person who can possibly get us to St. Barts in time to save Lil."

CHAPTER 29

▼

Thursday morning Buddy finally agreed to back off the sleeping pills so Jason could have breakfast with us. I was totally surprised to find he had no problem sitting at the table; chatting it up with the kids before they headed off to school.

"You look like you lost a fight with a pit bull," Buddy shook his head as the kids filed out the door, "And you still make the women swoon."

"You better keep your ass away from my women folk, Mr. Bonnet." I warned over my coffee cup.

"Grantford," he grinned. "Just a few more years on 'em and I could be calling you Dad!"

I smirked, "Not in my lifetime, and not in your life expectancy!"

He looked far better than I expected. The lumpy blackberry head had shrunk and faded to a kind of bruised tomato look. The eggplant-colored neck had now paled to a mottled green and yellow. I could actually see the outline of the anchor chain where it had constricted his neck. He had a nice cast with his arm in a sling. It looked as if every nurse for a hundred miles had signed it for him; lots of *is* dotted with little flowers and hearts.

"How do you feel?" I queried.

"Good enough to go help y'all with the Church of the White Rose today." He gave me that bright white Bonnet smile.

"No way, Jason," I frowned. "I know you are feeling a lot better, but there is no way you are going with us to Pahokee or to St. Barts."

"Aw, come on, Grantford," he whined, "I'm fine now, even Dr. Ronald McDonald says that as long as the swelling has gone down, and I'm careful with my arm cast, that I am fine, I swear. I just wish I wasn't so sleepy all the time."

"Jason, you don't understand. We aren't going to Disney World, we are going to deliver the journal to these killers, get my wife, and get out. It's going to be very dangerous, and I can't have you slowing us down."

Jason appealed to the Big Guy, "You think I should go, right, Buddy? Besides, you aren't really going to just hand the journal over to them, are you?"

Buddy shrugged helplessly.

"You're damn straight we are going to give the journal to them," I fumed. "We aren't going to do anything to endanger my wife. If they want the journal, they can have the journal."

Jason soothed, "I don't want to do anything to hurt Lil either, Grantford. I'm just saying we could have our cake and eat it too. With the three of us working together, we can save your wife and keep the journal."

"I'm not going to do anything that will put Lil in danger," I hissed through clenched teeth.

"Besides," Buddy added, "Otis has all the details in his computers, and is working to break the code. If he does that then we don't need the journal."

"Yes," I added, "I emailed Shrimper Dan last night and asked him to contact Otis. With his help, Otis should be able to crack the code in half the time."

"Shrimper who?" Jason queried.

"Never mind," I stated flatly. "It's a long story. You are staying here today and that is all there is to it. We can talk about St. Barts later."

I grabbed Buddy and we headed for the door. I whispered, "You still got plenty of those sleeping pills left, right, Buddy?"

He winked carefully.

"Just think about it guys, okay?" He echoed as we slipped away. "With the Krewe of Jupiter working together, we can save the girl and slay the dragon."

CHAPTER 30

▼

Buddy and I were headed toward Pahokee. You basically head west out of Jupiter Farms till you hit Lake Okeechobee, hang a left, and before long you're driving through the seven miles of towering palms that line Main Street, which hugs the shores of Lake Okeechobee.

Pahokee is the only town located directly on the shoreline of the lake. The locals call it Palm Beach County's "Other Coast." It's the coast without the crowds and the sticky sand. The lake is so big that songwriter and Pahokee native Mel Tillis once sang a tune he wrote called "The Okeechobee Ocean."

We had decided to take Rocky Rhodes, figuring that after all those years hidden away in the dark, she needed to stretch her legs as much as possible.

I shook my head, "We sure have some strange names in Florida. I mean Pahokee, where in the world did that come from?"

"It means 'grassy waters' in Seminole."

"Remind me not to challenge you on that kind of shit anymore," I shook my head.

We burbled through the small downtown of Pahokee. The balmy breezes from Lake Okeechobee felt great blowing across our faces. It's somewhat disconcerting to see a body of water to your west with no land horizon, instead of to the east as we are used to. Pahokee is definitely off the beaten path. It's kept the place small, quaint, and rural, and very old Florida.

As we moved farther out of town, I could see the top of a big circus like tent in the distance, little red flag fluttering in the breeze. We rounded a curve and the encroaching Florida jungle to our left opened up into a large grassy field. The field had a dozen or so dilapidated travel trailers parked haphazardly around a large stained tent.

"Looks like we found it," Buddy mumbled as I pulled to a stop. I put it in reverse and backed around the curve before anyone could spot us.

"What'cha do that for?" He asked.

"Look, Buddy," I whispered conspiratorially, although there was no way anyone could possibly hear me. "We don't know what we are walking into here. We know that these guys are neck deep in whatever is going on. Do you think they are just going to come out and tell us what they know about Donnie Rhodes and his mysterious book? Let's nose around a little first, and see what we can find out, instead of barging in like a bull in a china shop."

"I think you are going to get our ass shot; that's what I think."

I gritted my teeth, "If you want to sit here and twiddle your thumbs, go for it. If I can find out anything that will help us find Lil, I'm going to do it."

"Calm down. You know I want to find Lil, too." he placed his hand on my shoulder. "We just have to be careful." He reached underneath his seat and pulled out Donnie Rhodes's ugly little pistol. He pulled three bullets from his shirt pocket, dropped them into the chamber, and stuck the gun in the back of his pants.

"All right, let's do this then. We'll head through the brush and come up behind the tent where it backs up to those scrub palms. That way if anyone is watching from those trailers, they will not see us coming."

"I sure hope this place has a back door," he grunted as we slipped into the thick Florida landscape.

CHAPTER 31

▼

There was no back door, but there was a rip in the old canvas tent big enough for us to squeeze through. The tent was much bigger than it looked. The peak was centered a good fifty feet above the wood shaving-covered floor. The place was dimly lit, but I could make out a rickety looking stage with a makeshift pulpit in the center of the tent. At least a hundred metal folding chairs were set up in a big semicircle around the small stage. The smell of the place was sawdust, creeping mildew, and animals.

Buddy started elbowing me in the ribs. I tried to focus where he was silently frantically pointing. Several men and a woman were standing around a bunch of wooden crates. We tried to blend into the shadows.

The men varied in age; the youngest was probably twenty and the eldest had to be at least seventy. All but the eldest were dressed in old faded jeans and T-shirts. The old guy was dressed in a priest's black frock.

The girl was quite young, probably no more than fifteen. She had a blaze of copper red hair and wore a black leotard that flattered her blossoming figure.

As we watched, one of the younger men reached into one of the crates and pulled out a thick, ugly brown snake. I almost lost control of my bladder when I heard the all-too-familiar rattle; it was just like in the movies. I felt Buddy squeezing my forearm.

The guy held the snake behind the head, while its body whipped and beat at the air viciously. The old guy put his palms on the young girl's head and began to recite a prayer that was in a language I didn't understand. He nodded at the younger man and I realized far too late what he was going to do.

The younger man loosed his hold on the head of the snake, and it wrapped its ugly jaws around the young girl's wrist. I barely had time to hear a wince and a slow moan from her, and then Buddy was charging past me yelling at the top of his lungs.

"Stop, stop! Are you fucking crazy?" He screamed as he ran toward the surprised group. The girl had collapsed to the sawdust floor by the time he got to them. I was hot on his heels.

The snake let go and with a deadly shake of its tail began slipping among us, looking for its next target. Buddy pulled out the pistol and began firing in the general direction of the snake. The men scattered in every direction, except for the elder who stood his ground and gave a stern look to the younger men cowering in the corners.

I had just enough time to yell, "Buddy, look out!"

My friend turned right into the metal folding chair that made a disturbing *thwank* as it made hard contact with his face. Buddy slumped to the floor.

The other guy was on me like a charging linebacker, meaning to drive me into the ground. Thankfully, my hours in the karate ring paid off. As he barreled toward me, I did a quick *L* step to get out of his way and drove the heel of my palm into his chin; the move combined the power of my punch with his rocket-like forward momentum. It lifted him clean off the ground, and when he landed on his back, he was out cold.

I planted myself in a fighting stance in preparation for the chair wielder who had taken out Buddy. He was quickly approaching on my flank.

"That will be enough!" The old man was right behind me, and worse yet, I realized that he had the rattler by the head, and had it precariously close to the back of my neck.

I froze at the blood curdling sound of the angry snake.

Chair Wielder dropped his chair, which clattered to the ground making me jump.

"Turn around slowly," the old man hissed.

I did as I was told. He was older than I had thought, closer to eighty, with faint traces of red hair fading to silver like dying embers. His face had layers of wrinkles, but his eyes were sharp and intelligent amber.

"Take care of your sister first, then your moronic brother," he directed the ex-Chair Wielder. I noticed the white rose tattoo running up her exposed back as Chair Wielder picked her up and carried her out of the tent.

"Who are you and what are you doing here?" he commanded me.

"Maybe I should ask you the same thing," I snarled. "I just saw you murder that poor girl in cold blood."

He looked confused momentarily, and then understanding flowed into his eyes. "We aren't killing her. I was making her stronger. That is her third fang exposure; soon she will not even lose consciousness. Eventually it will be nothing more than a bee sting to her."

"I don't suppose you asked her about that in advance of throwing that slimy monster on her, did you?"

"It is her birthright, now that her brother is dead; it was her honor to take his place. And they aren't slimy; they are scaly. Over time she will become a skilled handler of my friend here, just as her brother Kath was. She will eventually perform for the flock in our ceremonies."

"Kath Rose?" I questioned.

The look of surprise on his face was genuine. "You knew my son?"

"I was there when that bitch killed him. We tried to save him, but there was nothing that could be done."

Buddy moaned.

"Look, I mean you no harm; the snake stuff just caught us by surprise. Can I check on my friend?"

He grunted an affirmative.

I bent down and leaned over Buddy. He looked to have a broken nose, and a big goose egg was rising on his forehead, but other than that, he'd survive. I helped him to a sitting position.

"Oh shit, what freight train hit me?" he murmured. I helped him to one of the folding metal chairs where he slumped dazedly. "Geez, does anyone have an aspirin?"

I looked back at the old guy who was grinning crookedly. He had put the snake back in its crate. At first it kind of bugged me that he thought it was funny, but the more I thought about it the funnier it seemed. Before long, we were both laughing heartily.

He stuck out his hand, "I'm Reverend Rowland Rose."

I slowly shook his hand in recognition, "Saint Kristopher Grant, just call me Kris."

"Saint Kristopher, huh," he smiled broadly. "The Patron Saint of Travelers— well, that's appropriate.

"I need to know what you know about the death of my son, and then I will share with you anything you like."

I looked at him, this traveling snake-handling priest, who used his daughter as a pincushion for vipers. I was apprehensive, but I looked into his eyes. Those amber eyes held the pain of a grieving parent. I could relate.

I told him what happened up to the point of Kath Rose's mysterious dying words, "You have to stop my Rose, the lady with the white rose tattoo."

Rowland Rose sighed. The other brother had come back into the tent to carry out what I now realized was his twin. "Lawrence, show Mr. Grant your tattoo."

The man named Lawrence turned and raised the back of his shirt to show a tanned muscled back. The intricate vines of a wandering rose climbed his spine, ending in the full blossom of a white rose between his shoulder blades. He carried his waking brother out of the tent.

"It is the mark of our religious sect, Mr. Grant, the Church of the White Rose. We are a splinter band of the Irish Travelers. Do you know who they are?"

"I remember seeing something on one of those news shows a few years ago," I recollected. "They are like modern-day gypsies, right? If I recall, the show wasn't very flattering, marking you all as con men and thieves."

He sighed, "That is the way it has been for centuries; even before we emigrated from Ireland. The show you referred to was an undercover exposé on the Irish Travelers who call Murphy's Village, South Carolina, home. The show made us out to be shady shysters in a secret clan who spoke a clandestine language. It's true that a lot of Irish Travelers live in Murphy's Village, but there are ten thousand of us in the United States. We consider ourselves a nomadic ethnic group, and we do continue to speak Shelta on occasion, which is the ethnic language we brought over from Ireland, It includes elements of Irish Gaelic, English, Greek, and Hebrew.

"Many people do call us 'White Gypsies,' but that is considered an ethnic slur by my people. We are descended from a race of pre-Celtic minstrels. My people use to travel from town to town performing tinsmithing, putting on shows with trained animals, doing odd jobs, and telling fortunes. Things are very different now. Now we have homes in places like Murphy's Village where we raise our children until they are old enough to go on the road with us. We still like our little shows; many go out on the road and do odd jobs in carpentry, roofing, and such as it comes along. Some, like the Church of the White Rose, spread the gospel, too."

"I'm sorry," I apologized "I didn't realize the word *gypsy* was a racial slur."

He waved my apology away, "Most don't realize it, but think of it this way, the source of the term 'to gyp' comes from the word *gypsy*. It's basically the same as calling us a thief."

"We are still widely stereotyped as troublemakers. New laws that criminalize trespassing keep springing up, thus making it easier for police to shut down our camps. We feel it's an attempt to destroy our very culture.

"Irish Travelers are generally devout Roman Catholics. The Church of the White Rose is an exception to this rule. We believe in the Holy Catholic Church, but we believe in something more as well."

"What do you believe?" I sat on the edge of my chair in rapt attention.

"The first Rose to migrate to this country was a man named Kath Rose. To honor his legacy, my poor son was given his name. The original Kath Rose was a fine seaman. He wanted to bring his pregnant wife from Ireland to the colonies. In her condition, there was no way she could make the trip. At his wife's insistence, in 1717 he went before her to get their household set up in the new land. To pay for his trip from Ireland to the colonies, he signed on as second officer on a ship called the *Eagle*. The *Eagle* was taken over by pirates. The pirate captain was an evil man named Stede Bonnet."

I felt the hairs on my arm stand at attention.

"Bonnet had a black ship that could defy the winds. The ship was called the *Nefarious*. It was rumored that the entire ship was carved from the dark wood of a single magical tree. The full crew of the *Eagle*, save Kath and the first mate, were killed in the attack. Bonnet took a liking to the first mate, a man by the name of DeUmbra, and made him the first mate of the *Nefarious*. Kath would have been killed, but DeUmbra refused to join the *Nefarious*'s crew unless Kath could come on board as the second officer. Bonnet relented.

"They marauded up and down the eastern seaboard. It was obvious to DeUmbra and Kath that there was black magic at work. Over time they were able to realize that Bonnet had a tome of spells called the book of Legacy and Destiny. It was the source of all of his power. Carefully, Kath was able to sneak letters ashore to be sent back to his wife, which told of his adventures. Eventually DeUmbra and Kath were able to help overthrow and capture Bonnet, but when the dust had settled, Kath Rose had perished."

I drew a deep breath. "Wow! I've heard parts of that story before."

"What do you mean?" The old man's brow wrinkled.

I quickly shared everything that had happened after Kath Rose's death, including Jason's history and his fateful encounter with Lawson and Leod Uilleam Urbay.

Buddy had regained his senses by now and helped me through a few spots as well. In between, the Big Guy took a deep breath and reset his own nose with a loud crack. "Jesus, Buddy!"

"Ad to be don," he shrugged nasally.

Rowland Rose's face was clouded and his amber eyes sparked, "Please tell me that you didn't say that Luu was involved."

"Lou?" I questioned.

The old man grimaced, "The initials *LUU* for Leod Uilleam Urbay. The kids in the camp stuck him with the nickname Lou. He is my stepson, my eldest child. His mother died giving birth to him. He was always bitter and mean growing up. We tried to make him feel part of our family, but he was always a brooding loner. He ran away from the church when he was fifteen. It sounds like he hasn't improved with age."

"Based on what he did to Jason, he is more than just mean. Jason said the man enjoyed tearing him to pieces. A man like that has a few circuits that aren't complete."

The old man looked down for a long time. "Mr. Grant, we don't believe that the book of Legacy and Destiny is evil. We believe that it is good, and that it was once protected by an ancient priestess of our faith. We have been looking for it for centuries. Stede Bonnet stole the book and used it for evil.

"If you truly have insight on how to find the book, you must make sure that it's brought back here to be protected by us. I don't know your friend, but if the blood of Stede Bonnet courses through his veins, I wouldn't trust him. You can't let him get his hands on that book. The results could be disastrous."

"My son Kath had a lead on how to find the book, and it cost him his life. My Rose is Kath's sister Mirasel. That was his pet name for his big sister. She was determined to find the book, so determined that she went away to college to study archeology and history, trying to piece together the clues.

"She thought she had figured it out. She said that with the help of a man from Charleston, she had found a hidden map. The map showed three great stores of hidden treasure. One was of rubies, one was of emeralds, and the last was diamonds. The book of Legacy and Destiny was said to reside with the diamonds. She took off in a plane with two men in search of the book almost twenty years ago. She never returned."

"Dommy Rodes," Buddy stated flatly through his broken nose.

"Yes, it has to be, Donnie Rhodes and your daughter Mirasel and Jones Jenkins. They flew down to St. Barts looking for the treasure. Rhodes and Jenkins wanted the jewels, and Mirasel was along to find the book."

"Or thu hep them transate the map," Buddy offered.

Rowland Rose agreed. "That makes sense. I would love to see my darling Mirasel again. Like Kath before her, she endured the fangs. She was a bright and strong girl. Kath always liked to make a show of the snake handling with his rodeo act, but Mirasel was always by the book. She took our religion seriously; she believed in the book of Legacy and Destiny."

"Mr. Rose, I appreciate your faith in us, but I have to tell you up front. I don't believe in magic books, hocus pocus, or any religion at this point."

"He dun't beleve in nut'un anymoe," Buddy mumbled sadly.

I gave him a stern sideways glance, "What I do know, Mr. Rose, is that a friend of mine said that Donnie Rhodes was very afraid of you and the Church of the White Rose. Do you know why that is?"

Rowland Rose's eyes twinkled. "Oh, I know all right. He is afraid because we know how to defeat the evil. It's all about the fangs. Stede Bonnet was defeated by the striking of the fangs of a panther. We don't have the luxury of keeping panthers around, but we have found over the centuries that the fangs of any creature will protect you, hence the presence of the snakes in our ceremonies. If you can build up a tolerance to the fangs, you can ward off the evil that hides between the bindings of the book."

I gave Buddy a grin, "I think old Buddy Bear here would like to get inoculated first!"

"I doan tink so," Buddy gurgled.

"It isn't a laughing matter, Saint Kristopher."

The old man pulled a small black statue from under his robes. It was a horrid anthropomorphic mixture of a panther and a crouching man, all big eyes, fangs, and exaggerated genitals. He handed it to me. It was made of a heavy black wood that seemed warm to the touch.

"This is a *zemís*, a sacred representation of our guardian protector Yucahu. His name means 'measure and movement'; he is the measure of the soul and the movement of the energy, which is spirit. Mirasel mailed it to Kath from St. Martin, when she was close to finding the book. It was the last contact we ever had with her."

"If you are truly the Patron Saint of the Travelers, prove it. Take this *zemís* and find that book, before it falls back into the hands of those who would use it for evil!"

CHAPTER 32

▼

I hated like hell waking Buddy up. The poor guy had probably not slept more than five or six hours in the past three days. He was snoring noisily through his bandaged and taped nose. Jason was out cold on the cot in the corner, generously dosed up with Dr. McDougal's sleeping pills.

We had gotten back from Pahokee at about eight, but Buddy's nose was a mess and we had had to make a pit stop at the Jupiter Regional Medical Center emergency room. The place was starting to feel like home.

When we got back to La Vie Dansante, we had to listen to Jason beg and plead to join us on the trip to St. Barts again. I had to admit he was looking a hell of a lot better. I still didn't want him going with us. I kept trying to tell myself that it was because of the risk to his recovery, but a nagging little voice in the back of my head that sounded a lot like Rowland Rose kept repeating, "If the blood of Stede Bonnet courses through his veins, I wouldn't trust him." For whatever reason, I refused to give in.

Buddy had handed Jason his regular meds with a secret side of sleeping pills, had fallen into his bed in the little efficiency apartment above my garage, and was asleep before his head hit the pillow.

I had forced myself to lie down in my big empty bed and had commanded myself to sleep. I did, but I kept waking up every hour, staring at the clock, willing it to read 3:00 A.M.

When the time changed to 2:59, I had already smacked the alarm shut-off. I hit the shower and then dressed quickly. I checked on the kids; they were sound asleep. Jessica was going to keep an eye on them and Jason while we were gone. Spooner, our beagle, padded around the house behind me, trying to figure out what the hell I was doing up at this hour. I made my way over to the apartment, with Spooner in tow.

I shook Buddy. "Hey, hey, wake up, Big Guy." He suddenly sat straight up with a wild-eyed yell, drawing back his fist to knock me a good one.

Spooner started barking hysterically.

"It's me, Buddy, it's me!" I squeaked, holding my hand up in front of my face.

His eyes cleared in recognition. We both turned to Spooner simultaneously and yelled, "Shut up, Spooner!"

The dog stopped barking and wagged his tail, a big sheepish grin on his face.

I glanced over at Jason. There was no need to worry; he hadn't even flinched under his mountain of blankets and medication cloud.

"It's time to go already?" Buddy groaned.

I shook my head, "Yeah, it's going on 3:30. We have to be down at Calypso's no later than 4:30."

"Give me five minutes." He dragged himself into the shower.

In ten minutes, we were climbing into the M3. Spooner jumped into the backseat as well.

"Spooner, get out," I pointed at the driveway. "You aren't going with us."

"Aw, let him come," Buddy scratched the beagle on the head. "You never know when we may need a good watchdog."

I rolled my eyes, "If Spooner had a minute and an hour hand, he wouldn't be a good watchdog."

Buddy and Spooner both tilted their heads and gave me the same sad look.

I sighed, "All right, all right, I give up!"

Spooner barked in appreciation and Buddy gave me a big grin as I slipped behind the wheel.

I squinted at him by the dashboard light. "Did you know that you have two black eyes?"

He pulled the rearview mirror around to look at himself and groaned. "Between the eyes and the nose bandages, I look like a raccoon with a surgical mask on."

He ripped off the nose bandage and threw it on the floorboard.

"Oh yeah, that's a big help," I smirked. "Plus Dr. McDougal is going to have your ass for taking that thing off this soon."

"Dr. McDougal can bite my ass," he huffed. "My nose needs to breathe."

"No duh?" I quipped.

Buddy realized his pun, and chuckled as we pulled out of La Vie Dansante and headed toward Ft. Lauderdale and Calypso's, in the wee morning hours.

CHAPTER 33

▼

We pulled up to the big Calypso maintenance hanger. I was thrilled to see the Lady Orleans sitting out on the tarmac. Buddy gulped.

The Betancur brothers were still crawling all over her, making last-minute adjustments. We got out of the car and walked over. Jack Mason stuck his head out of the missing pilot side window and gave us a wave. "I'll be down in just a second, boys."

Thirty seconds later, Mason was climbing down the rope ladder that led to the Lady Orleans's front entry hatch. "So what do you think, Kris?" He joined us on the tarmac.

I looked her up and down. Jack had gotten the front gear in place and she wore new tires all the way around. He had patched together the windscreens from several junk planes and had welded them across the front of the cockpit.

"She looks great, Jack," I whispered in awe.

"I hated having to jury-rig your windscreen, but with the limited amount of time, that was all I could do. It isn't pretty, but it's functional. Her gear is in good working shape now; you shouldn't have any problems with terra firma landings."

He shot me a "don't go near the water or I'll kick yer ass" look.

"She's missing pretty much all the rest of her glass on both the port and starboard sides. You should have no need for air conditioning. In fact, I would keep her as low as possible; no telling what the pressure change would do to this old girl at higher levels. She'll burn more fuel that way, but the PBYs had tremendous range, so you should have plenty to get you there and back. I did get a chance to do a little ground-only break-in on those new engines, and to check out her hydraulics. She's held together with bubble gum, spit, and a hefty dose of Southern Baptist prayer on my part. Be gentle with her, Kris, and bring her back so I can finish the job."

"You're a good man, Jack," I shook his hand.

He grinned crookedly at me. "You hold onto that thought, Saint Kristopher, you haven't seen my bill yet!"

Jack started yelling to the Betancurs' who came sliding off the plane as if it were a water slide.

We walked over to the entry hatch in front of the port wing. Buddy scooped up Spooner and tossed him through the open hatch that was above his head and six feet off the ground. The dog let out a startled yelp followed by a thump.

I cocked an eyebrow at him.

Buddy started up the rope ladder, "Hey, if he is going to join the Krewe, he has to take his lumps, too."

As Buddy's head rose above the bottom edge of the hatch, Spooner appeared and gave him a huge lick from the bottom of his chin to between his eyes.

"Yuck!" He spit and cursed.

Jack chuckled, "Like you said to be part of the crew you gotta take your licks...er, lumps."

Buddy grumbled the rest of the way into the plane.

Jack Mason looked me in the eye. "I always believe in being prepared, Kris. I know you plan to be back tomorrow, but I packed you a week's provisions, and the Betancurs loaded a crate in back that has a Zodiac rigid inflatable boat and a twenty-five horsepower outboard, just in case."

"Damn, that must have been expensive, Jack."

"Bring it back in one piece, Kris; it was shipped here by mistake on the midnight delivery last night."

"You worked a miracle here, Jack. I'm really indebted to you."

"I want you to focus on getting your pretty wife back safe and sound, and this pretty plane back to me in one piece." Jack squeezed my shoulder as I climbed the ladder.

"You got it, Jack," I gave him a thumb's up as I closed and secured the door to the Lady Orleans.

CHAPTER 34

▼

It felt good to be standing in the Lady Orleans. I took a second to soak it in. I was in her forward passenger compartment, I eventually wanted to get real seats in here, but right now she only had a four fold down military jump seats.

I glanced into the cockpit at my friend awkwardly trying to wedge himself into the co-pilot seat. "Don't touch anything up there, Buddy," I cautioned.

"You don't have to worry about that," he responded hesitantly, fastening the thick seat harness over his girth.

I turned from the cockpit to inspect the rear of the plane before we took off. Jack had told me he had personally done a preflight check, but the pilot in me made me want to see for myself.

Moving to the rear, there are four open compartments. The first is the forward passenger area where we boarded. Next is the area below the pylon onto which the wing is mounted. Farther back is the second passenger compartment, and finally the waist area with the blister windows.

The rear passenger compartment can accommodate seating for eight, but Coast Guard aircraft have provisions for casualty bunks. The empty bunk frames were folded flat to the floor. The huge glassless blisters allowed a slight morning breeze to pass through. That would quickly change to a roar once we were airborne. The blisters on the PBY-5As, like the nose turret, were used for machine gunners during World War II. The blisters can be opened and closed as needed, but with no glass in the frames there wouldn't be much point.

The rear bulkhead of the waist compartment is exclusively for storage. I could see the lashed-down cases of provisions and the big weathered crate that held the Zodiac, through the open hatch.

I crossed my fingers and headed back up front. The cockpit of the Lady Orleans is larger than it first appears. The control panel, yokes, and rudder are standard military issue.

Looking forward past the rudder pedals shows the area inside the bow. This is the entrance to the nose turret. I noticed that Spooner had already claimed the turret as his official home.

I slipped into the seat beside Buddy. "How you doing, Big Guy?"

"Just get this rust bucket rolling before I change my mind," he stated flatly through clenched teeth.

I noticed that Jack had taped a takeoff and landing checklist to my yolk. "That was nice of him," I commented.

"What?" He stared forward.

"Jack put me together a takeoff checklist."

Buddy's head slowly swiveled toward me like a tank turret. "Are you telling me you've never flown a seaplane before?"

"Don't be silly, of course I have. I've had my pilot's license for years now, and my dual engine and seaplane certification for at least two years. Of course, my certification was in a Grumman Widgeon, which is a much smaller plane. But hey, how much different can it be?"

"God save us," Buddy covered his eyes.

I shook my head, "You big goof, we are going to be fine."

I worked my way through the checklist and soon the port engine burst into life, and after a little reluctance, the starboard engine soon followed. I got clearance to roll from the Ft. Lauderdale tower, and we taxied out to the runway. This time of night I had the runway all to myself, and was given an immediate clearance for takeoff.

At the western end of the runway, I turned and ran the engines up. The Lady Orleans began to move forward, and I was quite surprised by the level of her acceleration. I hadn't expected it to be so strong. I pulled back on the yoke, and she lifted off the ground quickly and easily. As I climbed, the airframe vibration and wind noise through the broken glass turned into a roar. I climbed to about fifteen hundred feet, then experimented before leveling off at a thousand feet, and turning to run down the coast toward Miami. This height and speed seemed ideal for making headway, while minimizing the roar and vibration.

I looked over at a slightly green Buddy, a weird effect with his raccoon eyes. "How they hanging, Buddy Bear?"

"They feel like they are floating in my throat right now."

I chuckled.

I always approached the first takeoff in any new airplane cautiously. Nothing I have ever flown prepared me for the Lady Orleans. To say you fly her is a bit of a misnomer; it's more like you herd her. The ailerons are manageable, but the elevator is extremely heavy.

I started trying some stalls, single engine performance, and steep turns. I saw that if I didn't stop that Buddy was going to grab Spooner and bail out, so I backed off.

Suddenly there was a loud crash and bang from aft of us. Buddy let out a whimper.

"What the fuck was that?" I felt an icy chill run down my spine.

"Buddy, go find out what broke!"

"I'm not going," he cringed. "You go."

"I've got to fly the plane, dumb ass. Do you really want me to leave my seat?"

He shook his head vigorously, "No, no, of course not." He began fumbling to unfasten his harness.

Suddenly Spooner started barking like crazy and went charging from the nose turret into the back cabin as if he were rabid. Buddy gave chase.

I heard a howl, a scream, and frenzied thrashing about, then a familiar voice. "Get this crazy-ass animal off me, Buddy Bear."

The ruckus subsided. "What the hell is going on back there, Buddy?" I yelled hoarsely.

I could tell from Buddy's voice that he was pissed. "Looks like we have ourselves a stowaway. Jason decided to hide in the zodiac crate."

CHAPTER 35

▼

"Come on, guys, don't be mad at me," Jason pleaded. "I only wanted the Krewe to be back together."

Buddy grumped, "How in the hell did you manage to pull this off in the first place?"

He grinned, "Easy as jumping out of a plane. Hey Buddy, do you know you look like a big raccoon? What happened to your face?"

"You're a fine one to talk," I hissed flatly.

"Aw, come on, Grantford." He mussed my hair from his standing position behind the pilot seat. "You know you can't be mad at me!"

"Stop messing with me, Jason, unless you are fond of swan dives into the Atlantic. And trust me; I have no problem being mad at you."

Spooner growled in Jason's direction, from the safety of the nose turret, as if in agreement.

"If you ever want us to speak to you again," Buddy chided, "you better fess up as to how you got in that crate."

He sighed, "It wasn't that hard. When you told me at the beginning of the week about this trip, I immediately called Otis and laid on the guilt trip. I told him that he needed to make sure you guys at least had a life raft in case this bucket of bolts had to crash-land in the water."

"Jesus, Jason," Buddy hissed. "What you are telling us is that you guilted Otis and Aunt E into buying the Zodiac? You are a man of little conscious."

"I'm a man who likes to have a Plan B if Plan A doesn't work out. Anyway I told Otis that he had to make sure it didn't arrive before tonight, because the plane wouldn't be ready and there would be nowhere to store it. Getting out from under the watchful eyes of you guys was a breeze. Did you really think I didn't know you were slipping me those sleeping pills? After this big genius gave me the meds last night, his ass was snoring in five minutes. I piled blankets on my cot in a nice me-sized lump, then walked out and took Rocky Rhodes down to Calypso's in time to arrive before the delivery guy. I bribed him into opening up the crate and resealing it with me inside. Everything was fine until I started hearing the wind whistle and roar through those blister window things. In my mind I convinced myself that the sound was an open bomb-bay door, and that you guys were going to dump my crate into the ocean from ten thousand feet up!"

"You dumb ass." Buddy rolled his eyes. "Why would we dump the Zodiac into the Atlantic?"

"Besides," I said. "The Lady Orleans doesn't have any bomb-bay doors, and we were only a thousand feet up. That said it's still not too late to toss your ass out the cargo door. All in favor, say, Aye. Buddy?"

"Works for me," he started unfastening his seat belt.

Jason's eyes widened. "Come on, guys, that's not funny."

Buddy gave Jason a smack where his ribs were bruised. "That's for scaring the shit out of Kris."

"Out of me?" I queried. "I seem to recall someone else screaming like a girl and refusing to go see what the problem was."

"I didn't scream like a girl, that was Spooner."

Spooner wagged his tail at the mention of his name.

"Whatever you say, Buddy Bear." My anger at Jason melted away. "According to my calculations, at this airspeed, we still have about six and a half hours before we get to St. Barts. Let's make the best use of our time by comparing notes."

"Good idea, Kris," Buddy commented. "Well, we know that Donnie Rhodes, Jones Jenkins, and Mirasel Rose all went to St. Barts, presumably to look for the first treasure horde, which was the rubies."

"Yeah," I added, "and based on what I found on the Nefarious, they must have found them."

Jason chimed in, "But only Jones Jenkins comes back, almost twenty years later, with that super-rich scientist Dr. Frances Blakely in tow."

"We know that they are willing to kill to get the journal, which presumably has the secrets of Stede Bonnet's map encoded into it," I surmised. "Rhodes and Jenkins were willing to have Mirasel Rose along to help them find their treasure, but they are deathly afraid of Rowland Rose and his family."

"I get you, Kris. If they were so afraid of the Church of the White Rose, why would they risk bringing Mirasel along?"

Jason furrowed his brow, "It's the con man's last resort. You trust no one but yourself unless you have to. Uncle Donnie and Jenkins weren't bringing Mirasel along to be nice; they were bringing her along because they couldn't find the treasure without her."

"Right," I tapped the Lady Orleans's yolk. "And Mirasel wanted something equally as bad, the book of Legacy and Destiny."

Buddy snapped his fingers, "The answer is clear. The three of them went down together. All three had a piece of the puzzle to find the treasure and the book. They found the first one, then Jenkins got greedy, and either disposed of the other two, or ditched them somewhere. He thought he had all the pieces and could find it without Rhodes and Mirasel. He was wrong. He needed help. Then he found someone equally as desperate for the book as Mirasel—Doctor Blakely. He needed the map. Rhodes either burned it like he said or hid it. He caught wind of the journal, and he and Blakely came after it as a substitute for the map."

Jason hummed absently to himself. "One wild card, is Lawson and that bastard thug of his. If you remember from the journal, Uncle Donnie hired Luu to take out Jenkins. Obviously that didn't happen, and now Lawson, Luu, Jenkins, and Blakely all seem to be best buddies. How did that happen?"

I shrugged, "Maybe Jenkins gave Luu a better offer than Donnie Rhodes."

"Could be," Buddy interjected. "If that's the case, then Luu and Lawson may have enough dirt on Jenkins to squeeze him into giving them a piece of the pie."

I sighed heavily, "You guys know that so much of this is conjecture. The truth probably lies somewhere in the middle."

We fell silent for a moment, spinning our own conspiracy theories. As hard as I tried, I was having a hard time keeping Jason out of mine.

"Guys, we still have a few hours to go. I need one of you to stay up and keep me awake, but the other should try to catch a few winks. You could switch off midway if you wanted."

I looked over at a visibly exhausted Buddy. "Jason, do you mind taking first watch?"

"No problem, Grantford," he grinned. "Get your raccoon ass out of my chair, Buddy Bear."

He was too tired to even bother with a comeback. He dragged himself to some comfortable corner in the back of the plane and was snoring five minutes later. Spooner warily crept past Jason with a defiant snort and went back to join Buddy.

I kept up the constant minor corrections that are part of the pilot experience, and stole an occasional glance at the lightening gray horizon and slowly retreating stars. Jason talked constantly, more to hear himself speak than to carry on a conversation. I tuned him out, and focused on what I would do to Jenkins and his pals if they harmed one hair on my sweet Lil's head.

CHAPTER 36

With less than an hour and a half to go, Jason went back to wake Buddy, so that he could take his turn keeping me awake. There was a short fierce growl as Spooner tried to take a couple of fingers from Jason's good hand. Buddy handed the old Coast Guard blanket he'd found to Jason and scooped the posturing Spooner under one arm and walked toward the cockpit.

"Stupid dog," I heard Jason muttering over my shoulder.

Buddy sat the dog back in his nose turret, and he settled down with a disgruntled harrumph. Buddy dropped into the copilot seat with a big yawn and fastened his belt. I glanced over at him; his hair was going in a thousand different directions. He looked like a big kewpie doll; make that a big raccoon kewpie doll. I chuckled, shaking my head.

"What?" He gave me a wry grin.

"You ever meet a comb you didn't like?"

"Ha, ha, you try sleeping on a paper-thin blanket on top of a vibrating, wind-blown rusty griddle, and see how you look."

"Hey, at least you got to sleep on the griddle, I had to stay up and keep the flapjacks flappin'!"

After a few minutes, I could hear Jason's deep breathing from the back of the plane.

I looked over at my friend, not sure if I should mention it. "Buddy, what do you think about what Rowland Rose said about Jason?"

"What?" He raised his eyebrows. "You mean the blood of Stede Bonnet coursing through his veins and all that horse shit?"

"Exactly."

"Look, Kris," he paused, "we have known Jason a long time, and even though he just recently popped back into our lives, I still feel like we know him better than anyone."

"But you know as well as I do that he runs every scam in the book. If there is an angle, he plays it."

"True," Buddy agreed begrudgingly, "but we are his best friends; he would never scam or stab us in the back."

I shrugged my shoulders. "I hope you're right. I hope you're right."

We flew on for the next and final hour of the flight in silence. He would never admit it, but I knew he was taking what I said, digesting it, and trying to determine if it sat well with him or not.

Soon we could see St. Barts in the distance. I touched base with the small airport to confirm my landing clearance, and soon was in their traffic pattern, what little there was of it. There were two planes ahead of me. I watched as the first small commuter plane, three hundred yards ahead, flew between two mountains and disappeared.

"Uh, Buddy, you might want to go wake Jason."

He yawned, "He'll wake up when we land."

"Buddy, remember when I told Jack Mason that in regard to a water landing, the alternative may be even less appealing?"

His eyes widened. "Yeah, so?"

"We're coming up on the unpleasant alternative I was referring to."

"Oh shit." He jumped out of his seat bellowing for Jason.

Jason came dragging groggily to the cockpit, just in time to see the second commuter plane, in front of us by one hundred and fifty yards, slip through the mountain pass, and disappear like a dropped stone.

"Holy crap, Grantford, we're not going to do that, are we?"

"Strap yourselves in, guys; you are in for one hell of a roller coaster ride."

I had heard that landings at the airport, *La Tourmente,* were traumatic, but I had no idea. The airport has an extremely short runway that ends in the ocean. You have to fly through the mountain pass and do a controlled stall to drop straight down, so that you get every inch possible out of the stunted runway.

Dropping the landing gear, I held my breath and followed the commuter's flight pattern. I flew between the two hills, not more than twenty feet from the ground. Then immediately took a nose dive down the sheer cliff on the opposite side. I heard poor Spooner roll to the nose of the gun turret. I could feel my hair standing on end and my mouth going dry. I saw my predecessor hitting the brakes on the runway far below.

The nosedive was the only way to hit the airstrip with enough distance left to stop the Lady Orleans before she ran off onto the beach. I tried to execute a controlled stall as I'd been taught, floating somewhere between minimal control and maximum terror. The plane fought me every step of the way; the airframe shaking and screaming violently. I wrestled with the controls as the ground swooped up to meet me, but these old PBY-5As weren't made for maneuverability. At the last second, I pulled the nose up enough to get the big radials screeching on the tarmac.

I had landed at an angle, and I heard a sickening crack as my right float flipped down, then the support snapped as it hit the tarmac. I saw the float cart wheeling down the runway behind me. That float flipping down from where it was moored on the wingtip was the only thing that kept my wingtip from hitting the ground and us from rolling.

Buddy's hands were frozen in a death grip on the control panel. Jason was actually praying aloud. Spooner was too busy playing bumper pool with himself to make much more than a whimper. I couldn't worry about that right now. I was half-rolling, half-sliding down the runway with the end quickly approaching. The noise was awful, like some huge ancient bird being torn limb from limb. Worse yet, my commuter plane friend hadn't yet taxied from the end of the strip.

I had no choice. There was no way I could stop in time, and no way for the commuter plane to clear out of my way. I veered the Lady Orleans off the right side of the runway. I came so close to the commuter plane, I can still see the pilot's fear-soaked eyes.

I slid across the dunes and the sea grass, got turned around backward somehow, and wound up sitting about twenty feet offshore like a big wounded osprey.

"Well, we made it," I sighed faintly. Buddy and Jason were silent. Spooner promptly threw up about twice his body weight in the nose turret.

CHAPTER 37

▼

As we sat there catching our breath, I watched an older black gentleman in his seventies jump out of the pilot's seat of the commuter plane, climb feverishly over the dunes, and run splashing toward us. I stuck my head out the missing pilot's window and gave a feeble wave.

"Are you all right, young fella?" he asked me.

"Well, it's not exactly how I pictured my first landing in St. Barts," I grinned crookedly. Buddy, Jason, and Spooner had finally regained their senses and were making their way toward the exit hatch. "Hold on," I told the stranger. "We'll be down in a second."

With shaking hands, Buddy finally was able to get the hatch open. "Are you guys okay?" I had paused to throw an old blanket over the mess Spooner had made.

Buddy looked at me with wild eyes. "I am never setting foot in an airplane with you again."

"Aw come on, Buddy Bear, it wasn't that bad. Besides it wasn't my fault that the commuter plane was still on the end of the runway, right, Jason?" I appealed to my other friend for help. Jason just stared at me from a pale face with hollow eyes.

We climbed down the front hatch's exit ladder, Buddy carrying Spooner. The old man extended his hand and gave us a big grin and laughed, "My name is Remy de Haviland, and I was the first man to land a plane on this island. I gotta admit, my first landing when this airstrip was an open beach was smoother than that."

"Yeah," I splashed over to shake his hand. "But you only had to avoid goats. I had to avoid your commuter plane."

"Yes the tower"—he gestured toward a shack to one side of the runway—"usually spaces us out more than that. They must be hitting the rum and starting the weekend early."

"My name's Saint Kristopher Grant." We shook hands. "These are my friends Buddy and Jason, and that's Spooner."

De Haviland shook their hands and ruffled the fur on Spooner's head. "What say we get out of the surf, get you through customs, and then get you boys a drink? You look like you could use one."

"Y'all go ahead," I commented. "I want to check the Lady Orleans for damage, retrieve her busted float, and try to taxi her out of harm's way."

Buddy grunted absently. They followed de Haviland toward the tower.

I walked around the outside of the Lady Orleans; she had popped a few rivets on her right wing where she had lost the float. The wing hung at a strange angle. She definitely wasn't flyable until that was fixed. The life-saving float had sheared just as cleanly as if someone had taken an ax to it. She was leaking hydraulic fluid where the actuator arms had been ripped from their sockets. I grabbed my toolbox and tried to stem the flow as much as possible. I gave her a thorough all points preflight check on her exterior, and found nothing else amiss there.

I went inside and took a close look at the bottom of her hull. She was taking on a little water, but not as bad as Jack had predicted. Of course, she was just sitting in the water and hadn't actually suffered the impact of landing there. I went to the cockpit and flipped on the bilge pump, which began happily taking care of the matter.

The smell of regurgitated beagle chow was overpowering, plus I noted with amusement, apparently Buddy had sneaked Spooner a few Twinkies on the way down. That had probably contributed to his bad tummy. I took a few minutes to clean up that disgusting mess. I was so caught up in my quest to clean up the revolting puddle that I totally forgot to turn the manual bilge pump off.

I gave her interior the once over, and she seemed no worse for the wear. I slipped into the pilot seat, and tentatively attempted to turnover the left Wright Cyclone R-2600. She popped to life with no problem. I tried the right and she hummed to life as well. I played with the engines a bit, watching my gauges to make sure they had suffered no damage. Everything seemed fine there. I radioed the tower for clearance to taxi across the beach, over the dunes, and across the runway to park. They were for some reason highly amused by this; I was not. The last thing I wanted to do was to get t-boned crossing the runway as I had almost done to Remy de Haviland.

I eased forward on the throttles and began inching the Lady Orleans out of the surf. Getting her onto the dry beach wasn't a problem. Getting her over the dunes was a pain in the ass. I couldn't go back through the gap I had plowed on my way in; the sand was too loose and she couldn't get a grip. I wound up having to crab my way back and forth over the dunes until my wheels finally hit the tarmac again. I eased her over beside a short line of other planes by the tower and shut her down. I made her fast to several eyehooks protruding from the concrete. I also put her wheel stops in place as an extra precaution.

Now I had to find her float. I kept an eye on the mountain pass for any visitors as I hastily ran across the runway to the sea grape-covered strip of sand that separated the tarmac from the dunes of the beach. I had to walk all the way down to the very beginning of the strip. There it was, banged up to hell and back, but still in one piece. It was tangled up in the sea grapes and palm scrub at that end of the runway. There was no telling if the float was still airtight.

The float of a Catalina isn't a small thing. It's a good six feet long and nearly as high when you include the solid strut. It also weighs about three hundred pounds, way more than I could possibly carry back to the tower alone. It was out of harm's way, and wasn't obstructing any planes coming into the airport, so I was happy to leave it where it was until I could get some help.

I made my way back to the so-called tower, and my friends. Just as Remy had predicted, there was a bottle of rum and a shot glass sitting between two customs agents in rumpled uniforms. Two old black-iron fans with nodding caged faces pushed the stale air back and forth around the whitewashed tin walls and the gray concrete floor. A radio base station sat on the table in front of one of the agents. With a start, I realized he was the tower controller, and that there was no way he could even see the runway from his chair. It was no wonder we had almost creamed Remy de Haviland's commuter plane.

Buddy and Jason had cleared customs without a problem, but Buddy was arguing with one rummy agent about letting Spooner through. I could tell that he was back to himself because his blood was really boiling as he yelled animatedly at the cross civil servant. Jason was nodding enthusiastically beside him.

Remy de Haviland finally stepped in and said a few stern words in French to the agents, who immediately, if begrudgingly, backed down. "How did you do that?" I cocked my head at him while handing my passport to the agents.

The old guy grinned at me. His skin was ebony black and his hair was silver and cut close to his head. "Let's just say that I pull some weight on this island. I opened the first resort here, the Eden Rock, and am kind of looked at as the father of tourism here on the island."

"The Eden Rock?" My ears perked up. "I'm supposed to meet some uh acquaintances there at sunset today."

"That is very convenient then"—his eyes sparkled—"because that is exactly where I planned to take you for those drinks!"

CHAPTER 38

▼

We all piled into Remy de Haviland's Mini-Moke. It's kind of a miniature underpowered Jeep. It was quite a feat squeezing all of us into the vehicle.

Fortunately I called shotgun, and as we headed toward the Eden Rock, de Haviland filled me in on his history on the island.

In 1945 Remy was the first person to land a plane on St. Barts.

"Boy, I bet that was exciting," I commented.

"Well," he grinned, "you have already experienced La Tourmente, but beyond that, why would it be? I didn't know I was making history. I was just checking on my boats.

"My business at that time involved boats and transport and I came here just to check on deliveries."

"Come on, Mr. de Haviland, you must have felt like the first man on the moon!"

"Please, call me Remy," he continued. "Once I saw St. Barts, I decided to make it my home. Fifty years ago I built my house on a small peninsula made of lava rock on the La Plage St. Jean. I named it Eden Rock. Eventually I turned Eden Rock into a resort. She only has thirteen rooms, a small restaurant, and a bar."

"The Tapas," I commented.

"Yes, how did you know?"

"That's where I am supposed to meet my 'acquaintances' at sunset," I stated flatly.

"A few years ago, I sold it to some expatriates from England. I moved to Santo Domingo to be close to my granddaughter and great-granddaughter, but I do so miss St. Barts and the Eden Rock. I fly back to visit as often as I can, and the kindly folks that I sold the Eden Rock to are always gracious enough to let me stay in my old home once more. My wife died a few years ago, and there are so many memories locked inside those walls."

I could tell he was choking back the tears. I had to bite my lip in silence myself, trying not to think about my Lil, and what it would be like to lose her.

Remy cleared his throat and changed the subject. "Isle de St. Barthélemy is small, a little more than eight square miles. We have steep hills that divide the island into several valleys that open to the sea. Each valley is very different from its sisters, with different plants, people, and architecture. It makes our little island feel like a much larger place."

"I've heard this place has tons of beaches," Jason chimed in.

"Yes, we have fourteen beaches, each with gleaming white sand. Our year-round temperatures average seventy-eight degrees."

"Any of them nude beaches?" Jason grinned mischievously.

I gave him a look.

Remy didn't seem to notice, "Total nudism is illegal, but our custom in the French West Indies is that all beaches are topless."

"Hot dog!" Jason started scanning the water's edge.

"Don't seem to be many people on the roads," Buddy commented.

Remy explained, "There is only one town, Gustavia, and a dozen villages in the various valleys. Also it's the heat of the day; most folks take a break during this time and hide from the sun. They will be back out after three."

I looked at my watch, two o'clock, still four hours until sunset.

"We are coming up on St. Jean Beach. The Eden Rock isn't far now."

He sighed, "Unfortunately, since I opened the place to air traffic, the island has transformed itself to cater to the visiting tourists. Restaurants, boutiques, and gift shops now line streets that were once busy with merchant seamen and adventurers."

I don't know what I was expecting of the Eden Rock, based on Remy de Haviland's modest description, maybe a shack on a cliff. But when we rounded the corner, and the Eden Rock unfolded before us, my jaw hit the floor.

It was spectacular. I heard both Jason and Buddy gasp behind me. It sat out on a rock peninsula that jutted out into the sea. It was a wandering jumble of red tile-roofed villas and buildings that seemed to grow out of the towering volcanic rock on which it was built.

"That's your home?" I spoke in awe.

"Well, it used to be," he grinned shyly.

We met the cordial new owners, and we helped Remy get his baggage to his private room. He graciously asked us to use his room to freshen up before we all went down to the bar.

We made our way down to the Tapas and were seated at a table overlooking the cliff. Remy explained that at night, lights shined up from the blue waters, illuminating the rocks beneath the tables. Remy gestured fondly, "Back in my days running the Eden Rock, it was a hideaway for the likes of Greta Garbo and Robert Mitchum."

I shook my head at my friends who were obviously star-struck. Much to his disdain, Spooner was forced to stay in Remy's suite.

"So," Remy looked at me frankly, "Why don't you tell me about these so-called acquaintances of yours?"

I stumbled, "They're, uh, just business associates, nothing special."

De Haviland's eyes narrowed. "Saint Kristopher, I've been playing the hero and chasing the villains for too many years to buy that. Come clean with me, Kris. I can help you. There isn't much that happens on this island that I don't know about. I may be seventy-eight years old, but if anyone on this island can pull your ass out of a bind, it's Remy de Haviland."

I shook my head, grinning. "You saw right through me, didn't you, Remy?"

"Like glass, my boy, like glass."

I looked at Buddy and Jason, and they looked at me. "Where do we start, guys?"

"From the beginning," Jason commented, "from the beginning."

And we did.

*   *   *   *

Remy let out a long sigh as we finished our sordid tale. "I remember them."

"Are you sure, Remy, that was nearly twenty years ago?" Jason asked.

"I'm old, boy, but not senile," Remy bristled. "I remember them, and I remember what they did."

"What they did?" I queried.

"To understand what happened, you have to understand the history of my people."

Remy's eyes misted over, "The parents of my parents passed down to me the story of the first people. In the beginning the ancient ancestors of the Caribes, the Patwah, and the Arawak people were one, and lived in the bright land of the moon. The native name for the one family of our people is the Taino.

"The Taino looked down upon the dark earth; they determined to descend and clean it and make it like their moon country. Coming down on the clouds, they paddled mightily, but when they thought to return, behold, the clouds that had borne them had disappeared from their sight. Vainly they called upon Yucahu-Bagua-Marocoti, the ancient trilogy of holy ones on high, but there was no answer to their prayers."

"Hey," Buddy interjected, "Isn't that the name that...?"

"Shhh," I cautioned him with a wary look.

Remy continued, "As they wandered, they became faint with hunger. However, the Ancient Ones hadn't forsaken them, for they saw the birds eating of the fruits of the trees, and on eating these, they found them pleasant to the taste and good for food.

"And after many days, their souls loathed these wild fruits, and they said one to another, 'Would that we hadn't left our homes in the land of the moon.'

"Yucahu, Bagua, and Marocoti heard their complaint, and created a great tree, such as hadn't been seen before. Each branch bore a different fruit, while on the ground beneath the shadow grew plantains, bananas, maize, cassava, yam, potato, and all fruits of the earth that men now cultivate.

"The Taino were grateful and sang praises to Yucahu, Bagua, and Marocoti, who gave them such precious food. Then a voice from heaven was heard to say, 'Cut it down.' In wonderment, they took their stone axes and hewed down the tree. Ten months they labored, and at the end of the tenth month the great tree crashed to the ground. Three priestesses went to three separate islands, taking a portion of the Taino people with them. Each of these tribes eventually developed into the Caribes, the Patwah, and the Arawak people. Each priestess also took cuttings from the branches, trunk, and roots of the great fallen tree. From the branches and trunks, they made canoes that were swifter than night. From the roots, they made idols, which were representations of Yucahu, Bagua, and Marocoti. They each took an idol to their perspective island, and there they picked a hidden spot and they planted the idol as the source of the great tree again. Each idol once again sprang up into a full replication of the original tree and bore fruit, and the priestesses were able to provide food for each island in this manner.

"But alas the tribes of the Taino were now mortal, and like all mortal men, they thirsted for power and glory. They rose up against their priestesses and tried to kill them. The Caribe and the Arawak succeeded, and their trees immediately turned black and withered away. The third priestess was only able to protect and hide her tree because she possessed a magical book, a book that contained everything that had ever happened and everything that had yet to come. Unfortunately, her tree still turned black after the battle with the Patwah, and no longer bore fruit after the deaths of its sisters. The Patwah people were virtually exterminated in the battle, with only a few fleeing into the mountains. The Patwah tree survived, for as long as the priestess and the book was there to protect it."

"Wow!" Buddy shook his head. "That's quite a story."

"It's not a story," Jason grimaced. "It's true."

"Oh and how do you know that?" Remy raised an eyebrow.

Jason shook his head guiltily, "Because my great-great-great-grandfather is the one who killed the third priestess and destroyed the Patwah tree to build his infamous ship, the *Nefarious.*"

We all sat in stunned silence for a second.

Buddy finally cleared the air, "Aw, come on Jason, you can't possibly believe that your family legend is tied to this ancient myth, can you?"

"It makes sense. Think about it. The *Nefarious* was made from the black wood of an ancient tree. My ancestor killed an old woman and stole her book. They have to be related."

Remy shook his head as if to clear the cobwebs away. He looked at Jason. "Are you saying you are the great-great-great-grandson of the pirate Stede Bonnet?"

Jason affirmed, wide-eyed.

Remy cleared his throat audibly. "This all ties back to what happened when Donnie Rhodes and his friends came here twenty years ago. Rhodes, Mr. Jenkins, and Ms. Rose all stayed right here at the Eden Rock. Jenkins was nothing but mean trouble. I could tell that from the beginning. I steered clear of him."

"You can say that again," I commented.

"Ms. Rose stayed in her room much of the time. However, I did glimpse her sitting on the beach one night. She only wore a whisper of clothing around her waist. Her beautiful long auburn hair seemed to caress the wandering white rose tattoo that ran up her tanned bare back. She was quite beautiful, but all I can remember thinking about was how sad she looked as she stared out at the sea. Rhodes, on the other hand, was the life of the party."

"That sounds like Uncle Donnie," Jason grinned.

"We shared many a bottle of French wine here at this very bar. One night, after several bottles of my finest, he shared a secret with me. He told me they were here looking for the first of three treasures. He explained about that pirate killing the Patwah priestess, cutting down the tree, and stealing the book."

"See I told you," Jason commented. Buddy waved him off in rapt attention to Remy.

"But he said that Bonnet felt the priestess had cursed him before she died, and that misery had followed him even as his wealth from piracy grew. He said the pirate had decided to try to make amends. That he went to each of the Taino's islands, and offered up rubies, then emeralds, and lastly diamonds, but he refused to offer up the book. In the end the book was ripped from his hands when he revisited the place where the Patwah tree had stood. He had lost both the book and his three great treasures. In the matter of a few days, he was caught and hanged for piracy."

"So what happened to Rhodes, Jenkins, and Mirasel?" I questioned.

"Rhodes was being cautious and had burned the pirate's ancient map, after hiding its secrets away. He didn't trust Jenkins, and only carried the clues to the treasure here on St. Barts in his head."

Jason grinned widely, "So there was a treasure here. So tell us how they got it."

Remy looked out toward the sun, which was but a sliver in the sky. "That is a story for another day, my friend, and one that is easier to show you than to tell. But I believe I must now stop, for Saint Kristopher's 'business acquaintances' will be here at any moment."

"I'm supposed to be here alone. You guys better vamoose."

Buddy and Jason stood up.

Remy's eyes narrowed, "I've told you much, Kris, and you have told me little. If you don't want me to wait around to see for myself, you best tell me who these 'business acquaintances' are."

I sighed in defeat. "An old friend of yours named Jones Jenkins and a whole entourage of nasties he has brought with him."

Remy's eyes widened. "Why the hell is he back here? They already have the pirate's rubies."

Buddy cocked an eyebrow, "Were you going to tell us that part anytime soon, Remy?"

I could tell the old man was flustered. "As I said, tomorrow, I will show you everything."

I glanced at my friends, and they shrugged. I reached into my jacket for the journal. It wasn't there. My heart turned icy with fear as I searched my other pockets. "The journal, I could have sworn I put it in my jacket."

Jason pulled the battered journal out of his jacket, and laid it on the table. "You'd lose your head if it wasn't glued on, Grantford."

"What is that?" Remy questioned.

I frowned. "That is Donnie Rhodes encoded directions to all three treasure sites."

Remy began looking over his shoulder nervously, "And what do you propose to do with it?"

I set my jaw. "I'm going to give it to Jones Jenkins."

Remy made a frantic grab for the journal. Buddy had the old man tackled and on the ground before he touched the cover. Sobs of sorrow and regret wailed from the great adventurer, like a ship's horn in the night.

CHAPTER 39

▼

Jason helped the devastated Remy back to his room. Apparently the old man had assisted Rhodes on his treasure hunt twenty years ago. He was too broken up for us to get the whole story, but apparently something very bad had happened, something for which the old adventurer felt tremendous guilt. Through his sobbing, he murmured that he couldn't bear the idea of the secrets of the other two treasures falling back into Jenkins's hands. He said he couldn't live with himself if history repeated itself.

I shook my head at a worried looking Buddy as Jason walked off, arm around Remy's shoulder, supporting the old guy. "Don't worry, Buddy. Jason will talk him down. He's good at that."

"Yeah, you're right, Kris. I just wonder what it is the old man knows."

"Me too, I'm sure we will find out once he calms down. In the meantime, Jenkins and his crew will be here at any time. Do you mind hiding in the bar shadows? I may need you, Big Guy."

"No problem, Kris, but I know an even better place to hide. Don't worry, I'll be near."

He disappeared through the bar doorway, leaving me to wonder what he was talking about.

*   *   *   *

I dropped back into my seat, as the last glimmer of sunlight disappeared and the muted bar lights crept on. I was totally alone in the bar. I patted my jacket pocket; the journal was still there.

I smelled them coming before they walked through the door. That thin, sweet-smelling cigar of Jenkins's made me want to gag. The ruddy-looking face soon followed. He squinted in the doorway for a second, scanning the deck, then his eyes rested on me. He gave me a nasty little wink, and headed in my direction. I don't know that I have ever felt so violated.

Two steps behind him was the long cool presence of Dr. Frances Blakely, stunning in a monochrome white business suit, her creamy vanilla hair melting down her low-cut, silky white blouse. She was a knockout, but despite her virginal attire, I felt like I was looking into the depths of an ancient black hole.

Scurrying behind them came pig-boy Orin Lawson; his mouth full of sharp yellow baby teeth in a leering grin as he imagined what it would be like to take a bite out of Dr. Blakely's tight ass.

I stared Jenkins down. I figured in this kind of public place, he was the most dangerous of the three.

Jenkins held out his hand to me, giving me a tortured smile. "I'm Jones Jenkins. I don't think we've formally met?"

I stared at his hand as if it were a piece of dog shit. "I know who you are. Where the hell is my wife?"

Jenkins slipped into a chair across the table from me. Lawson plopped into a chair to my right and gave me a big baby-toothed grin. "Saint Krissy de Pissy, how's it going, mate?"

I ignored Lawson.

Dr. Blakely pulled up a chair to my left, and sat way closer to me than I was comfortable with. She gave me a slow blink. In a voice far deeper than expected, she spoke like melting ice, "Dr. Frances Blakely. How do you do?"

I nervously pulled my eyes back to Jenkins. "So, where is my goddamn wife?" I hissed.

Jenkins tapped the ashes of his foul-smelling cigar on the table, where they made a little smoldering mound and an ugly little yellow circle on the tablecloth. He measured his words, "She is safe…for now. Where is the journal?"

"I've got your damn journal," I growled. "Where is my wife?"

Lawson snickered, "She's being entertained by Luu right now."

"Shut up, you stubby little bastard," Jenkins's eyes flashed at Lawson.

"Hey, you can't talk to me like that. We are all equals in this deal, right, Dr. Fran?"

"Shut your stupid trap, Lawson," the lady stated flatly.

I could feel my face flushing; I stood. "If you ever want to see that journal, Lawson, you better produce my wife right now."

There was an audible click from under the tablecloth on Jenkins's side of the table. "Sit down now, Mr. Grant, unless you want me to blow your right leg off at the knee."

I settled slowly back into my seat.

Jenkins forced another grin, and looked at his Rolex. "Very well, you win. Look behind you."

I slowly turned and looked in the direction Jenkins was pointing. There, a hundred yards from the Eden Rock was a big yacht trawler—the *Nefarious*.

Jenkins pulled a two-way radio from his jacket. "Luu would you mind bringing our guest up for viewing?"

In horror I watched as the flame-headed nightmare named Luu dragged my sweet Lil kicking and screaming onto the deck. Her hands were bound, but she was fighting with every ounce of her being. Luu subdued her enough to lay a big wet kiss on the side of her face. He grinned and gave a big thumb's-up. The staticky Celtic accent came over Jenkins' radio, "Teste jus lik honey."

"Lil, Lil," I screamed to her, but there was no way she could hear me over the surf.

I felt my upper lip peeling away from my gums. "Okay, Jenkins, you've made your point." I stuck my hand in my jacket.

"Not so fast, Krissy." Lawson waved his hands frantically in the air. "He may have a gun or knife or something in there, Jonesy."

Jenkins bore a hole in Lawson with his eyes. "If you call me Jonesy again, I will personally take Dr. Blakely's spear gun, and discharge it up your ass." He turned to me. "Slowly, Mr. Grant, if you please."

I eased the journal out of my jacket pocket and carefully pushed it across the table to Jenkins. "Now give me my wife, asshole."

Jenkins grinned his first true smile of the night; it was enough to give a British dentist nightmares. Out of the corner of my eye, I caught the tiny pink tip of Dr. Blakely's tongue escape her stony face.

Jenkins turned to Blakely, "I assume you'll be able to use the university's computers to get this translated tonight, Dr. Blakely?"

Her liquid eyes were flashing whitecaps, "Yes, with the models I have already created, I should be able to make quick work of it."

I swear I could see her frosty breath, despite the eighty-degree temperature.

"Excellent," Jenkins cracked the journal open. His face turned into a quickly changing mix of confusion, fear, and then rage. Jenkins jumped to his feet, the barrel of the ugly little .45 pointing right between my eyes. "What are you trying to pull, you son of a bitch? Do you not value your wife's life?"

Lawson grabbed the journal and started flipping through it. "Blank, blank, the whole fucking thing is blank!" He tossed the journal in Blakely's direction.

She ignored it, instead leaning in even closer to me. I suddenly realized why she was sitting so near, when I felt the small derringer barrel thrust into my crotch. She whispered into my ear, "That was a very, very bad decision, Mr. Grant."

Lawson was spitting and cursing. Suddenly he stood up and grabbed the two-way radio lying on the table. "Kill her, Luu, kill her!"

"No, goddamn it," Jenkins slammed the butt of his gun into the bridge of Lawson's piggy nose. "We kill her now and we will never get the journal!"

Lawson screamed like a little girl.

Frances Blakely picked up the bloodied radio from the table and hissed for Luu to disregard his master's voice. In the effort to use the radio, she inadvertently directed the derringer at the deck and a few inches away from my crotch.

Lawson was still bellowing and holding his nose. He staggered backward toward the railing.

Buddy and I both realized our fleeting opportunities at the same time.

Big meaty hands came up over the edge of the deck from below, and grabbed both of Lawson's ankles. With a one-two jerk, Buddy belly-flopped Lawson to the floor, and yanked him over the edge of the deck. Thankfully, Lawson's balls took out most of the railing on the way down. He didn't know what had hit him. I don't think I have ever seen a more terrified look on anyone's face in my life. I could hear Buddy pummeling Lawson under the deck.

I put my shoulder under the edge of the table and upended it on top of Jenkins. His nasty little gun let off a wild shot. Dr. Blakely's shot was closer. I felt it graze my inner thigh before it hit the deck, the small caliber slug passing easily between two boards.

Jenkins was flat on his back, blinking dazedly with the tabletop on his chest. I crouched to spring onto the table to pin him to the deck before he could regain his wits.

Before I could jump, a small caliber barrel was forced rudely into the back of my neck. A cold hand and sharp nails massaged my chest, as a long tall body pressed against my back.

What is it with this chick and invading people's personal space? I thought insanely.

The alto voice ran like melting snow into my ear; I could feel that pink tongue tip flicking me with each word. "I wouldn't do that if I were you, Mr. Grant, you earned the opportunity for the championship round tomorrow. We will be back."

She stepped slightly back away from me. "Get up, Jonesy, let's get that idiot Lawson and go."

"But what about the journal?" Jenkins got up groggily.

"We'll let Luu loose on his wife tonight to make up for his trickery. He can sleep with that thought when his head hits the pillow."

"Yeah, we'll be back in touch tomorrow, and you better have that damn journal. You will not get another chance."

"Lawson," Jenkins bellowed. "Get your ass up here."

Orin Lawson came moaning and dragging himself over the side of the deck. He looked like someone had been beating him with an ugly stick.

"What happened to the guy who pulled you over the side?" Blakely muttered.

Lawson grinned a horrid grin that showed he had lost several baby teeth. "That tub of lard Buddy Phillips was beating the shit outta me, but you took care of that, Dr. Fran. That bullet you shot through the deck killed him."

"Buddy!" I yelled frantically. No response.

I heard worried voices and running footsteps coming toward the bar. Jenkins threw me his two-way radio. "I would keep that on if I were you. We'll be in touch tomorrow."

Jenkins and Lawson ducked out of the bar at a dead run, as the voices approached even closer. Dr. Frances Blakely blew me a frozen kiss, backed out, and was gone.

I quickly flipped on the radio. "Lil, Lil, are you there?" Nothing but white noise. I looked out into the bay, but the *Nefarious* was nowhere to be seen.

With prayers for both my wife and my best friend, I ran to the edge of the deck and dropped down into the darkness, hoping like hell not to find the body of one Anthony Phillips, aka Buddy Bear.

CHAPTER 40

▼

It took a second to adjust my eyes to the blue spotlights that were illuminating the steep rock wall beneath the deck. The lava rock angled sharply down to the angry crashing sea at the base of the Eden Rock.

I was on a small ledge no more than five feet wide and ten feet long that had been carved out of the nearly sheer rock face to support the deck pillars.

Buddy lay face-down in a pool of blood; splinters of wood covered him. I glanced up at the bullet's path. It had passed cleanly through the gap between two deck boards, but had the luck to obliterate a sea-rotted support strut on this side. The four-by-four beam that the strut had been precariously holding up had collapsed in the process. Another week and some unlucky tourist would have probably had the same effect on the rotted support.

As I looked at my friend closely, I realized that the small caliber bullet had indeed gouged an ugly little gash in the side of his cheek after shredding the rotten support, causing him to bleed like a stuck pig, but the beam had caught him solidly on the back of the head and knocked him out cold. I felt the strong pulse in his neck and breathed a sigh of relief.

Just at that time, the upside-down head of Jason Bonnet appeared over the edge of the deck. "You guys okay, Grantford?" The anxiety in his voice reduced it to a strained whistle.

Buddy moaned and raised himself up to a kneeling position, rubbing the back of his head. "Damn it, I'm tired of getting hit by shit."

I turned to Jason, snarling, "You son of a bitch, you switched journals on me!"

Jason's eyes got as large as deviled eggs.

I picked up the broken beam and swung it at his head. Jason squeaked and disappeared back above the lip of the deck just in time to keep his head from becoming a piñata.

I started to charge after him, but a moan from Buddy caused me to pause and go back to help my friend. I intended, however, to beat the crap out of Jason Bonnet when I was back up on deck. Once I was sure Buddy was up to it, I helped him to stand, then to crawl over the lip of the deck.

Jason was hiding behind Remy, cautiously watching to see if I needed help with Buddy. The Eden Rock's owners were talking to the local constables in an animated way.

"What the hell happened here?" Jason ventured.

I helped Buddy to a chair, and turned to Remy. "Can you get a doctor to look at Buddy? I think he is going to be okay, but he is going to need a butterfly where that bullet ripped his cheek, and he may have a concussion."

Remy nodded and dashed toward the bar phone.

I turned to Jason who was now standing there unprotected like a deer in the headlights. I spoke not a word; I just dived on him.

We rolled around the deck a couple of times before I pinned him solidly and started to throttle the life out of him.

"Stop, Grantford, stop!" He gargled, turning red and then blue.

I felt the heavy hands of the constables dragging me off him.

"You filthy bastard!" I screamed. "You may have just gotten my wife killed!"

Jason's eyes were red and watery. "I'm sorry, Grantford. I thought they would bring your wife here. I took Remy back to the room and was waiting just outside to grab her from them, while they were distracted by the journal."

"You idiot, what did you think they were going to do to me when they saw the journal was blank, give me an award?"

I attempted to break free for another tackle, but the strong arms of the St. Barts law held me tightly.

Jason pulled the real journal from inside his shirt and handed it to Buddy, "You had Buddy to protect you. We're the Krewe of Jupiter. Nothing can stop us."

I snarled, "There is no Krewe of Jupiter, you loser. Only two people who have made something of their lives and another who has never amounted to anything. You're an immature, selfish juvenile, Jason, and as crooked and untrustworthy as your godforsaken great-great-great-grandfather."

Jason's face was crimson, and I detected a small tremble in his lower lip, as the silent tears rolled down his face.

He turned stiffly and slunk toward the bar entrance. He turned, "I'm sorry, Grantford, I never meant to hurt anyone."

The pangs of guilt were hammering to free themselves from my chest, but the rage crammed them deeper. "Don't call me Grantford, Jason. You don't have the right. In fact, I don't ever want to talk to you again."

Jason Bonnet hung his head and disappeared into the night.

I wrestled my way out of the constable's grip, feeling the tears stinging my eyes.

Buddy groaned and shook his head slowly and handed me the journal, "Little hard on him, weren't you, Kris?"

"You've got to be kidding, Buddy, that bastard almost got you, me, and Lil killed! There's no telling what that monster Luu is doing to Lil right now, and you want to go easy on him?"

He held onto his eye sockets to support his head. "I know, Kris, I know. He made some very foolish poor choices, but he did it with the best intentions."

"How do you know that? Maybe he just used us to get this far. Otis will be finished translating the journal at anytime, and it will be easy enough to go after the treasure or the book or whatever he is in this for. Face it, Buddy, he is in this for himself. He didn't need us anymore, and this was an easy way to get rid of us."

"That's total bullshit, Kris!"

"Is it? Think about it."

Remy arrived with the doctor and started looking Buddy over.

I excused myself, and borrowed Remy's Mini-Moke. I began searching each harbor and marina sequentially around the island, looking for some sign of the *Nefarious* and my Lil.

The battle raged on inside of me. Did I really believe that Jason had done this on purpose? Rowland Rose's warning kept coming back to me from a thousand different angles as I traced the hills and valleys surrounding the coastline. God, I had known Jason for twenty years. He was irresponsible, and cocksure, but was he truly capable of this kind of evil? I just didn't know anymore.

At four in the morning, I finally gave up and made my way back to the hotel. There had been no sign of the *Nefarious*. Luu had obviously picked up Jenkins and the others and they had made their way back out to the *Sweet Desperation* anchored somewhere offshore. I could only pray to God for the safe return of my Lil.

Jenkins and his bastard crew were mobile, and at present I was not. It was a handicap that my Lil couldn't afford. When I got back, I used the house phone to make a collect person-to-person call back to the United States.

A scratchy, half-awake voice answered, "Hell-hello?"

"International Operator, is this Mr. Jack Mason?"

"Yeah"—a yawn—"yeah, who the hell is this at"—a pause—"four o'clock in the morning?"

"This is the International Operator, sir; I have a collect call from a Mr. Saint Kristopher Grant. Will you accept the charges?"

I heard Jack snap to attention, "Yes, yes of course."

There was an audible click.

"Jack, Jack, you there?"

"I'm here, Kris, what's the problem?"

"I'm sorry, Jack; I have to beg you for a favor one last time."

CHAPTER 41

▼

Dr. Frances Blakely was right; all I could think of after my head hit the pillow was what that warthog Luu was doing to my sweet Lil. I tossed and turned until seven, then finally got up. Buddy and Remy were down in the restaurant murmuring over breakfast.

"How you feeling, Buddy Bear?" I dropped into an empty chair.

He gave me a weak grin, "Like a Buddy Bear slamwich; I've been chaired from the front and beamed from behind."

"How's the face?" I gestured at the butterfly bandage.

"Not too, bad. The doctor says I might not have a scar."

Looking at the jagged streak down his face, I was skeptical, but I kept my mouth shut.

Buddy looked at me evenly, "Jason's gone. He never even went back to the room, just disappeared."

I grimaced. "Knowing that snake in the grass, he probably joined forces with Jenkins and his band of thieves."

He harrumphed in my direction but didn't push it.

I changed the subject. "I talked to Jack Mason about the Lady Orleans last night. He wasn't thrilled at our predicament. He chewed my ear off for fifteen minutes before I could get a word in edgewise. He's going to try to get a plane to bring him and the Betancur brothers down here as soon as possible to make repairs, but he was less than positive that he could get here in the next twenty-four hours."

Remy bit his lip tentatively. "You will stay here on my tab. It's the least I can do to make up for the way I acted last night."

Buddy patted Remy on the back. "Remy's been filling me in on what happened all those years ago with Donnie Rhodes, Kris. I think you will be interested in hearing about it."

"I'm sorry, Buddy, but right now all I can think about is getting Lil back." I sat the little two-way radio on the table. "I've been trying to get them to respond all morning, but they have it turned off on their end."

"But my point is that based on what happened back then, I think we have a fairly good guess as to where they are, or at least where they may be going."

I raised my eyebrows at the nodding Remy. "Okay, you got my attention. Tell me what you know."

Remy frowned inwardly. "When they first got to the Eden Rock, they kept to themselves. It was obvious that Rhodes and Jenkins didn't like each other. They squabbled amongst themselves constantly. Ms. Rose often sat at a completely different table from the arguing men, during mealtimes.

"Over the course of a few weeks, Rhodes and I became friendly. As I mentioned before, I provided the best French wines for him. After a while, he confided that they were down here looking for a huge stash of rubies. Mirasel Rose had been able to translate the map, which Rhodes swore he burned, but the island had changed dramatically since the early seventeen hundreds. They were having a hard time finding the landmarks that would guide them to the site of the lost Caribe tree and the ruby horde.

"When he mentioned the Caribe tree, my ears perked up. I had heard of it from ancient island lore. It was high up in the mountains in the middle of the island, and was considered a holy place by the elders who still followed the old religion.

"What you need, I had told him, was a local guide, and for one fourth of the treasure, I would help him find it."

"And you found the Caribe tree and the rubies?" Buddy queried.

"Yes, well, there isn't much left of the tree, but we did find the ruby horde. Unfortunately, both Rhodes and I underestimated Jones Jenkins. He double-crossed us, stole a faux map that Rhodes had created to fool him, and left Rhodes, Mirasel, and myself in a trap to die. Luckily I knew the layout of the holy site better than Jenkins and was able to get us out. Unfortunately, Jenkins got away with the rubies and totally desecrated the holy site.

"I was shunned by the island clerics after that. Our desecration of the holy site caused me to become a hermit in my own home. Eventually I sold the Eden Rock and moved away."

"So what happened to Donnie Rhodes and Rose Mirasel?" I asked.

"I overheard Rhodes calling back to the States. He called an Orin Lawson, and asked him to bring the journal to St. Martin, where he would pick it up. At that time, that was the closest island that had commercial airline service. Donnie Rhodes and Mirasel flew in that little parrot-looking seaplane of his to pick up the journal. That was the last that I ever saw of them."

Buddy looked perplexed. "But if Lawson brought the journal to Donnie Rhodes twenty years ago, what was it still doing hidden in the Gator Tail?"

I furrowed my brow, "The one we have must have been a second copy that Rhodes was keeping, just in case the first one fell into the wrong hands."

"So did Donnie Rhodes make it to the second island and the Arawak tree?"

"Who knows?" I shook my head. "But based on the company that Lawson is keeping now, he double-crossed Rhodes during some part of the game. Lawson probably also found out from Rhodes about the possibility of a second journal."

Buddy sniffed, "Yeah, the little rodent probably spent the better part of the last twenty years looking for it himself, and only brought Jenkins back into the picture when he had given up finding the second journal, or had gotten desperate."

Remy added, "Yes, once we escaped, all the locals were gossiping about the horde of rubies, and how Jenkins was boasting that he had the map to the second and third treasures. Jenkins wasn't a pilot, so he took the next boat out to St. Martin, where he could connect to whatever wild goose chase that fake map was sending him on. Until recently, he too hadn't been seen back in St. Barts, but I always knew that they would be back."

"How do you know that, Remy?" Buddy looked at me to make sure I was paying attention.

"Because Jenkins may have gotten the ruby horde, but what he didn't know is that the ancient priestess of each tree held the key to the next one in the chain. The priestess who once guarded the Caribe tree held the key to unlock the Arawak tree, and the Arawak priestess held the key to unlocking the mighty Patwah tree. Without the key to the Arawak tree, no map or journal in the world will ever get them to the second treasure."

"You think Jenkins knows this?" Buddy wondered aloud.

The old man grimaced. "Jenkins wouldn't know, but Dr. Frances Blakely would."

I stood up abruptly. "Remy, please lead us to the Caribe tree. We find that tree, and I bet a dime to a doughnut we will find Jones Jenkins!"

CHAPTER 42

▼

As we walked out of the Eden Rock into the bright Caribbean sunshine, we were just in time to see a white Grumman Albatross with the Calypso's markings drop between the two hills of La Tourmente, and do an expert controlled stall down toward the runway.

I looked at Buddy, "That could only be Jack Mason and the Betancur brothers. They're at least fifteen hours ahead of when I expected them."

"Good ol' Jack," Buddy beamed, "Always ahead of the game!"

I snapped my fingers. "I almost forgot about Spooner. Remy, do you mind if Spooner joins us for the ride to the airstrip? I feel bad about keeping him locked up in the hotel room."

Remy agreed.

"I'll go get him," Buddy volunteered. "I bet he is about to pop!"

Remy bounced down the highway toward the airport. By the time we got there, the big Albatross had already unloaded its passengers and taxied down to the back of the runway and turned to make its takeoff run.

Jack Mason and the Betancurs were just coming out of the tower, stamped passports in hand.

"Jack!" I jumped out of the Mini-Moke and ran over to him. The greeting was drowned out as the Albatross ramped up her engines, and let loose the brake.

She came roaring down the runway, and performed a perfect takeoff with yards to spare. She turned to the west and headed out to sea on a lazy bank that would turn her back toward Florida.

"Jack!" I tried again, running up to my friend and shaking his hand. "Boys," I nodded to the Betancurs.

Jack grinned crookedly.

I introduced Jack to Remy. Jack was in awe. Apparently Remy had quite the reputation among bush pilots and adventurers.

We walked over to the Lady Orleans, and I thought Jack was going to cry. "Look at that poor broken wing. What have you done to this old girl? I told you she couldn't take that kind of stress. Where the hell is her float?"

I pointed to the splash of orange down in the weeds at the far end of the runway.

Jack spoke in Spanish to the Betancurs and they hurried off in a trot in the direction of the float.

I heard the screen door of the tower twang open on its spring behind me. "Oh yeah." Jack stopped wringing his hands for a second, "I brought a friend of yours with me who needed to hitch a ride."

I turned and there was a beaming Otis walking toward us.

"Otis!" Buddy ran over and grabbed him in a big bear hug.

Arms pinned to his side, feet dangling off the ground, Otis looked up worriedly at his face. "What happened to your face, Master Buddy?"

He dropped his old friend back onto the tarmac, and ran a finger along the bandage on his cheek, and his crooked nose. "Oh nothing, I just got banged up a little here and there."

I looked at Otis, "Does this mean you decoded the journal?"

Otis's whole face lit up. "Down to the minutest detail, Kris."

I quickly introduced Otis and Remy.

"And who is this?" Otis questioned, scratching Spooner on the head.

"Oh I forgot that you hadn't met Spooner when you were in Jupiter," I commented.

Spooner wagged his tail at all of the attention.

Between the two of them, the Betancurs were carrying the Lady Orleans float on their shoulders as they made their way back down the runway. The two brothers were amazingly strong, for being so wiry.

I turned to Jack. "I'm sorry, Jack, I don't mean to be rude, but my wife's life depends on us getting to an ancient temple site hidden in this island's interior. If we can get in, get her away from the thugs holding her, and get out, we may need to make a quick getaway. How soon can you have her ready?"

Jack looked at me crossly, and then softened. "The only thing you need is the wing straightened out and the float reattached?"

"Yeah, I checked her out thoroughly after our landing and everything else seems sound."

Jack rubbed his chin, "Best-case scenario is six hours. It's a good thing I brought all my tools along."

"Thanks, Jack." I patted him on the shoulder.

Mason turned to give orders to the sweating Betancurs.

I turned to Buddy, Remy, and Otis. "You guys ready to go?"

Otis looked around, "Where's Jason?"

I felt the red rising up in my face. "You've been right about Jason all these years, Otis. He is good for nothing."

"I never said that, Saint Kristopher. I've always said that Jason has never lived up to his potential; that's why I always push him so hard. The man has the ability to do great things."

I sneered, "Well, he certainly has the ability to be a double-crossing coward. After he almost got Buddy, Lil, and me killed last night, he slunk off with his tail between his legs and hasn't been seen since."

Otis said nothing, but his brow was furrowed with worry.

I repeated, "So are we all ready to go?"

Buddy and Remy nodded.

Otis cleared his throat, "If you don't mind, Kris, I would like to stay behind and collate some of the decoded data from my algorithms?"

I raised an eyebrow. "Suit yourself, Otis. If you are going to stay here, do you mind keeping an eye on Spooner?"

Otis answered by patting the dog's head.

"Jack, we'll be back by three o'clock. I'm counting on you, old friend."

Jack stuck the stub of a cigar in his mouth, "Don't worry, Kris, she'll be as good as before in no time, but that ain't saying shit."

CHAPTER 43

▼

As the Mini-Moke bounced farther up the mountain roads, they began looking less and less like roads and more like trails. There were no guardrails protecting us from the drops that were sometimes hundreds of feet down. Sitting to the outside, I could hear the dirt break away under our tires and tumble down the cliff sides as we passed by. We were eye to eye with the clouds, and soon they were a veiled mist that surrounded us. We hadn't passed as much as a donkey cart in the last forty-five minutes. I felt as if we were ascending the road to Mt. Olympus, and Zeus was going to come out to greet us at anytime.

The trail finally petered out completely. Remy got out and motioned us to follow. His voice was a conspiratorial whisper, even though I would have been surprised if there were another human being within a ten-mile radius. Remy motioned up through the low hanging clouds at a flat-topped mountain in the near distance. "That is where we must go. It's still a good three-mile hike to get to the Mother-Daughter Falls. From there, we will follow the river to the temple of the Caribe tree."

We followed the old man as we fought our way through the underbrush. Machetes would have been great, but we hadn't considered this luxury before we started our climb. The land got steeper as we went, and at times we had only a couple of feet to walk on between the side of the mountain, and a five-hundred-foot drop straight down. Far below I could hear a river thundering. "Is that the river we are going to be following?" I asked.

Remy grunted weakly, "Yes, the river below is fed by the Mother-Daughter Falls. It's the fall's headwaters we will follow to the temple."

The old adventurer was panting heavily. I glanced back at Buddy worriedly; he had noticed it too. Remy had been a far younger man twenty years ago when he had made this journey. Just at that time, my worst fears were realized. In his exhaustion, Remy lost his footing. It was as if we were watching in slow motion. The old man went down on one hand, trying to catch himself. I heard the brittle bones snap. With no support, he did a half head roll and went over the five-hundred-foot drop, without even a whimper.

"Remy!" I screamed. Time finally started moving at its normal pace again. We rushed over to the edge of the drop-off.

"Oh, thank God, he didn't go all the way!" Buddy stammered. Remy had flipped on his way over the cliff and was now hanging caught by some vines, looking back up at us from about ten feet down the side of the cliff.

"Remy, are you okay?" I yelled.

"Yes." He shifted and the vines loosed a little and dropped him another two feet. "But I think my wrist is broken."

Buddy looked over my shoulder as Remy dangled precariously over the drop to the river five hundred feet below.

"Hold on, Remy, don't move a muscle. If you slip anymore, Kris and I will not able to reach you!"

I looked knowingly at my big wide-eyed friend. If Remy slipped anymore, it wouldn't matter if we could reach him. I glanced around us. How could we have taken on a task this dangerous, with none of the tools needed to get the job done? We had no rope, no saw for branches, nothing but the clothes on our back.

"There is only one thing to do, Buddy. You are going to have to lower me down to him headfirst."

"Are you crazy, Kris? The ground here is nothing but mush. What if I lose my footing? Both Remy and you could fall to your deaths."

"We don't have a choice. Those vines aren't going to hold him much longer. Brace yourself as much as possible, and lower me down."

He let out a big sigh and fearful grin. I lay down on my stomach and Buddy dug in his heels and held on to my ankles.

I looked over my shoulder. "If anything happens to me, Buddy, you save Lil no matter what."

He swallowed hard. "You know I will, Kris."

I lowered myself over the edge of the cliff.

I was careful of the vines. They all supported each other in a great entangled maze. Put pressure on the wrong one and Remy would fall to the rocks and roaring waters far below. I tried to stay lucid as the blood rushed to my head.

The old man was wide-eyed but still as I approached him like a huge spider stalking a fly. I could feel Buddy straining behind me with his death grip on my ankles. Finally I was within reaching distance. I grabbed Remy's arm and he cried out painfully.

I felt guilty. "I'm sorry, Remy. Pulling you out of here by your arms is definitely not going to work."

I tried to turn my head far enough to look back at Buddy but couldn't. "You need to lower me another two to three feet. I'm going to have to get low enough so that I can get him underneath his armpits."

Buddy's voice wavered from above. "There's no way, Kris. I can't brace myself and lower you any farther. You are at your maximum stretch."

I sighed thoughtfully. "Buddy, you're going to have to lie down on your stomach and inch over the side. It's the only way you can go the extra distance."

"Okay, Kris," Buddy stated quietly.

"And be careful, if you put too much of your body weight over the overhang, then all three of us will fall."

"I know."

I felt shifting around from above, but his grip on my ankles never lightened. Ever so slowly he edged himself out over the abyss, and I inched closer to Remy.

I finally got my arms under the old man's armpits. "Okay, Buddy, I've got him! Pull us up."

It was probably better that I couldn't see behind me, but I could tell from the abject terror in Remy's eyes that Buddy had seriously overextended himself over the cliff for me to be able to reach him.

Buddy said not a word, but ever so slowly he started to wriggle and inch himself back over the top of the cliff using nothing but his lower body. The minutes were agonizing, as I listened to my oldest friend grunt and strain behind me to save us. It took minutes, but it felt like hours. At one point I thought it was raining, but then I realized it was the drops of perspiration falling from my big friends' brow as he agonized above me.

At last enough of my torso was over the ledge that I could help pull too. Shortly thereafter the old man was lying on the ledge between us. I grinned crookedly at Buddy, and he gave me an exhausted thumb's-up.

Remy groaned and worked himself to a sitting position. "I owe the two of you my life," he smiled weakly.

"All in a day's work," Buddy beamed.

I sighed out loud, and then I frowned. "We have to get you back. Your wrist is definitely broken."

Remy set his jaw, "Nonsense, after saving my life like that, do you actually think I would put your wife in further danger by delaying our journey?"

I looked at Buddy skeptically and he looked at me.

Buddy started ripping the sleeve from his shirt. "Then we have to at least try to set the bone and immobilize it."

As an MP, Buddy had to be trained in basic first aid to treat the victims of the many bar fights that broke out around his base. He made short work of Remy's arm, setting the bone expertly, bracing it with branches and lashing it down, and finally putting it in a makeshift sling.

We helped the old man to his feet.

Remy attempted to shake our hands with his undamaged left arm. "I am eternally grateful to you boys for what you did today. Now let's be off. The falls are very near now."

And they were. We rounded a bend and I could hear the roar. After another hundred yards, we were standing at the top of a spectacular twin waterfall that fell to the river five hundred feet below. The main waterfall was a good forty feet across. The second waterfall started about a hundred feet down and was probably half as wide.

"I see why they call it the Mother-Daughter Falls," Buddy laughed as the spray soaked our faces.

Remy spoke loudly above the roar of the falls, "We need to follow the head river for about a mile before we get to the temple."

The going was easier by the river's edge, and soon the sound of the falls faded behind us. "I must warn you," Remy stated flatly. "There are many who still follow the old religion on this island. This is a sacred place to them. There is one who lives in this forest who believes it's his birthright to protect the temple. He is called the Guarao."

"One who lives in these forests," Buddy stammered. "You mean like a monster?"

I rolled my eyes.

"No, he is a man, but many think he is insane. He guards these holy lands from outsiders, and defends the temple with a sharp machete."

"Great," Buddy grumbled, "What next, swarms of locusts?"

We plodded along in silence, until we rounded a turn in the river. We had almost reached the top of the flat peak we had seen in the distance. A mere hundred feet more rose up in front of us, but the last hundred feet were a sheer thimble of solid rock, flat on the very top. Great boulders lay strewn around the base of the cone as if the child of a giant had carelessly left its playthings behind. A ramshackle shack sat beside one of the largest boulders.

I looked at Remy. "Where is the temple?"

Remy gestured toward the top of the mountain, "You're looking at it."

"That shack?"

"No," Remy laughed, "that is the Guarao's house."

"The guy with the machete?" Buddy's eyes widened.

"Yes, and he has been known to throw large stones too."

I took a closer look at the dilapidated shack. There were scraggly handwritten signs and messages all over the outside of it.

I read some of them aloud, "I seek justice, let justice be my plea. Too much injustice in this land. The government is an infestation. Keep off this." There were another two dozen in the same vein.

Buddy grunted, "He sounds more like a social protestor than a temple guard."

"On this island there isn't much difference between the two."

"Well," I surmised, "whatever he is, he doesn't appear to be at home right now."

"Yes," Remy gestured toward the river. "It is a good time for us to enter the temple undetected. Please get into the river."

"Do what?" Buddy sputtered.

Remy sighed, "Please trust me, my friends. We have to follow the river into the temple. The temple is inside the rock cap on this mountain. The great Caribe tree once grew from the top of this very peak. The temple sits beneath where the roots once grew."

We glanced at each other nervously, but we rolled up our pants legs and followed Remy into the icy water. It was only about two feet deep.

"One thing puzzles me." Buddy's logical mind was at work. "You said that this temple contains a key to the Arawak Temple, and the Arawak Temple contains the key to the Patwah Temple. It seems to me that a key should be required to get into this temple as well?"

"Very astute," Remy replied. "A key is indeed tied to this temple, but it disappeared with Donnie Rhodes and Mirasel twenty years ago. I know of a passage that will allow us to bypass the temple gate by slipping through the guardian's nesting area."

"Umm, nesting area?" Buddy swallowed hard.

"The temple's ancient guardian." Remy frowned grimly.

"That machete guy?" I quizzed.

Remy shook his head. "No, the Guarao is simply a deranged follower of the old religion. The ancient guardians are legendary beasts that were the last line of defense of the priestesses when their followers attacked."

"Great," Buddy sighed. "Now we're back to the monsters again."

I changed the subject back to the temple gate. "Exactly what kind of key are we talking about?"

"The priestess called them *zemís*," Remy replied. "It's a small idol carved out of the root wood of the temple's tree. There is one for each tree. Each one represents one of the gods of the old religion's ancient trilogy. The one for the Caribe tree Temple is a figure of Yucahu."

"You mean like this one?" I pulled the dark wooden figure that Rowland Rose had given me from my inner jacket pocket.

Remy stopped cold in the freezing water, his face turning pale. "Where did you get that?" he whispered coarsely.

"Mirasel Rose's father gave it to me. Apparently she shipped it back to him years ago."

Buddy spoke up, "If I get a vote, I say we use the key. I have no urge to disturb some monster's nesting ground."

"No disrespect, Remy"—I rolled my eyes at Buddy—"but there are no such things as monsters or magic books for that matter. It's probably just a tale to keep the curious away from here."

Remy turned and looked at me evenly. "An old college friend of mine once said, 'There are only two ways to live your life. One is as though nothing is a miracle. The other is as though everything is a miracle.' From what I can tell, Saint Kristopher, you could use a few more miracles in your life."

I tried to outstare the old man but finally had to drop my eyes. I wanted to believe that he had a point, but I just couldn't open that door anymore.

"Who did you say said that?" Buddy quizzed as we started trudging through the icy water once more.

"My college roommate when I was schooled in Switzerland. You may have heard of him, guy by the name of Albert, funny hair, went on to be a physicist."

We followed the river behind the large boulder that sat next to the Guarao's shack.

We both caught our breath as we rounded the bend. There the river flowed out of the mountain, from a cave whose entrance was ornately carved into the shape of a large serpent's head.

"The entrance to the temple of the Caribe tree," Buddy murmured.

Remy motioned us to enter the snake's maw, "Yes, we must hurry before the ancient guardian senses we are here. You can swim, can't you?"

"I can," I raised an eyebrow, "but why, the water is only two feet deep?"

Buddy walked through the snake's mouth, "I hate the wa…" He immediately sank from view.

Remy looked at me, "Because it drops off to about twenty feet when you cross the threshold."

He bobbed to the surface sputtering and cursing. I suppressed a laugh.

Remy and I joined Buddy in the mouth of the serpent.

CHAPTER 44

▼

"Keep together, and keep the *zemis* close," Remy instructed. "Perhaps the presence of the key will keep the beast at bay."

I took point, paddling the best I could with the *zemis* in my hand. Buddy helped Remy the best he could. The cave narrowed substantially once we were inside. While we still couldn't touch bottom, we could push off from one sloped side of the cave to the other, which made the going a little easier. A strange fluorescence illuminated the winding passage with a green radiance.

About fifty yards into the switchbacks and curves of the cave, I was completely disoriented.

Suddenly there was a grinding sound of rock on rock.

"What the hell was that?" Buddy's teeth chattered.

We didn't get a chance to respond. Coming directly toward me was a huge V wake in the water. Whatever was making it was coming fast.

"Hold the *zemis* out in front of you!" Remy commanded.

I did what I was told and added a little prayer, without realizing it; it was something I swore I'd never do again.

When the wake got to the *zemis*, it suddenly disappeared as the guardian dived. I felt thousands of small brushes against my legs as something slipped rapidly beneath me. It seemed like it took five minutes before the sensation stopped.

"What the heck was that?" I tried to control my shaking.

"That was the ancient guardian," he responded flatly. "But we must hurry. The *zemis* diverted it in its frontal attack, but once it gets its collective wits about it, it will turn around and attack from the rear."

We didn't have to be told twice. We doubled our pace, and soon around the bend the passage opened up into a huge cathedral-like cavern. We felt rock under our feet again, and we were able to pull ourselves up onto the cavern floor where once again the water was only two feet deep.

The cavern was spectacular. It was at least five hundred feet across. Sunlight and water were spilling in from a hole fifty-feet up at the apex of the cavern. I followed the pillar of light down to the center of the cavern, where it illuminated the jagged remains of an ancient black tree stump.

I sucked in my breath. "The Caribe tree!"

Remy walked up beside me. "Yes or what's left of her anyway. The islanders made pretty quick work of her during their battle with the priestess, a millennium ago."

Buddy scooted away from the passage entrance. "So you said that the temple is under the roots of the tree?"

"Yes, the *zemís* is the key to opening the temple doors." He shook his head. "It was ingenious how Mirasel managed to hold onto the key twenty years ago. I guess it was Rhodes and her insurance that Jenkins would never get the second treasure."

I sighed, "I can't say that I am not intrigued by all this Remy, but we didn't come here to get the second key. We came here to find Jenkins and his crew, so that we could save my wife. Where the hell are they?"

"Right here!" A female voice echoed from above.

We all looked up in time to see Dr. Frances Blakely, rappelling from the hole at the apex of the cavern, on a self-tensioning mountain rope.

She hit the stop when she floated just over our heads, resplendent in a white Lycra body suit. It was quite obvious what the long white holster attached to her belt held, for she was pointing her infamous spear gun directly at my head.

"Dr. Blakely, I presume?" Buddy smirked.

Two more rappelling lines dropped behind Blakely, and Jenkins and Lawson came sliding down, but not nearly as gracefully.

"Who else would it be, you tub of lard?" Lawson commented. "I thought we killed your ass back at the Eden Rock?"

"It'll take a lot more of a man than you Lawson, to take me out," Buddy sneered.

Blakely, Jenkins, and Lawson dropped to the cavern floor, with the clumsy Lawson doing a tremendous belly flop and drenching his partners in crime.

"Goddamn it, Lawson!" Jenkins hissed. "Can you at least attempt to not be a total moron?"

"Sorry, Jonesy," Lawson pulled himself out of the water.

Jenkins's eyes narrowed, but he thought better and turned to us. "So, Remy, I see that you have played tour guide once more. Apparently I didn't succeed in drowning you and Rhodes twenty years ago."

"As Buddy said," Remy growled, "it'll take a lot more of a man than you to kill me, Jenkins."

"Perhaps that is true," Jenkins surmised. "Maybe this time we will let a woman take a shot at it." He motioned to Dr. Blakely.

"With pleasure," she grinned. She pointed the spear gun at Remy and pulled the trigger.

There was a sharp twang, and Remy was cart wheeling backward with the ugly shaft of the spear protruding from his belly. He fell backward into the water with a mighty splash.

"No, you bitch!" I howled. We ran over to Remy. Buddy supported the old man's head above the water.

"You're going to be okay, Remy. We'll get you to the hospital."

The old man smiled gently through his pain. "Not this time, Saint Kristopher. This was the last adventure for Remy de Haviland."

"No way," Buddy's voice cracked. "You're going to make it, Remy."

The old man grimaced, "Whatever you do, don't let those bastards get their hands on the second *zemís*. It is the key to the Arawak Temple."

"Saint Kristopher," he waved me closer to whisper something to me. He slipped his last words to me softly, and then he closed his eyes, as his body went slack.

I looked at Buddy and he looked at me. At first, I thought that the Big Guy was going to burst into tears; then I saw the fire in his eyes. Buddy stood slowly.

I glanced over at Blakely, who had reloaded the spear gun. Jenkins was brandishing his .45. Lawson was the only one unarmed, and unfortunately he was the one standing closest to Buddy.

I turned to my friend. "Buddy, don't do anything…"

That was as much as I got out before he charged Lawson and caught him in the gut with his head. Buddy must have driven the piggy little marine salvager back a good twenty feet. They rolled and tumbled in the water, with Lawson trying to escape and Buddy trying to beat him senseless.

I made a move to intervene, but Jenkins motioned me back with his gun. I could tell by the stupid grin on his ruddy face that he was getting great enjoyment out of the life-and-death struggle that Lawson and Buddy were in.

Lawson was tiring, and it was becoming more of a one-sided fight, with Buddy winning. They had rolled over toward the entrance to the cavern.

Jenkins turned to Blakely, "Let's see if we can even this up a bit; shoot the big one, preferably somewhere that isn't life threatening so our little wrestling match can proceed a bit further."

Without a word, Blakely raised the spear gun and fired again.

"Buddy, watch out!" I screamed.

Buddy had worked his way back up to standing with Lawson, and had the blubbering fool by the shoulder, getting ready to give him another round to the face. He had but a split second to react to my warning. He spun in the direction of my voice, still holding onto Orin Lawson.

Unfortunately for Lawson, that put him directly in the line of fire. The spear caught him in the back, just under the shoulder blade. It entered at an angle, went between two ribs, missed his heart by an inch, and reemerged out of his chest, just below the collarbone.

Lawson's eyes rolled, and from the echoing screams he was making, I knew exactly what it was like to stand in the middle of a pork slaughterhouse.

He grabbed the sharp end of the spear sticking out of his chest, and stumbled backward into the deep-water entrance to the cavern.

He came up blubbering and screaming for help, but he didn't have long to suffer. There was a strange sound like the overlapping clicks of thousands of crickets, but played at a high rate of speed. The water all around Lawson lit up with a yellowish phosphorescence, and boiled and shifted as if it were alive. There was an overwhelming stench of vanilla in the air.

Suddenly the water seemed to envelope him like some bizarre Jell-O mold. I couldn't tell what they were, but there were thousands of small glowing animals swarming all over him. It was like a high-speed camera view of maggots devouring road kill. In seconds his screaming flesh melted from his bones, like a pig being devoured by tiny piranha. And then he was gone.

"Holy shit!" Buddy exclaimed. "Did you see that?"

Jenkins remarked nonchalantly, "Well, Dr. Blakely, I would be guessing that you and I will be leaving the same way that we came in."

"You bastard!" I hissed. "Lawson was your friend, and Remy was mine. Have you no compassion?"

Jenkins sneered, "The last thing that Orin Lawson was, was my friend. I needed the little bastard to lead me to the journal; he did that very nicely. His boat also came in handy as well. Beyond that, he was a reckless liability. I would have cancelled our arrangement soon anyway, but the killer sea lice or whatever they have in this godforsaken place just saved me the trouble."

"Why did you have to kill Remy?" Buddy splashed up beside me. "That old man never hurt anyone."

"That nice old man, and Donnie Rhodes conspired to send me off on a wild goose chase with a fake map twenty years ago; payback's a bitch."

Buddy moved to charge Jenkins, but I held him back. "Steady, Buddy."

"I see"—Jenkins motioned toward the *zemís* in my hand—"that you have that stupid idol key. Please insert it into the tree lock so that we can get the key to the next tree."

I wondered over to the black burned-out stump of the Caribe tree. I wasn't exactly sure how this was supposed to work. As I got closer to the tree, I saw a small alcove carved into the side that was the exact size of the *zemís*. Holding the *zemís* by the middle, I inserted it into its alcove. Immediately the black wood of the tree, closed in around my wrist, immobilizing me as if there had never been an alcove there.

There was a great rumbling of ancient machinery from beneath the floor of the chamber. The center of the chamber around the tree began to rise. I realized that the entire floor was tilting upward around the tree like a big inverted funnel. The water rushed off in all directions to the low sides of the cavern, and then drained out the entranceway, leaving the floor dry for the first time. I gasped in awe at the runes and ancient pictures on the floor of the great chamber. It was a great spiral story that went round and round, till it ended at the tree. It was immediately obvious that it was the history of the Taino people and the three great trees that were carved upon the stone floor.

Buddy, Jenkins, and Blakely fought to keep their footing as the floor tilted and the water drained away; Buddy especially had a hard time, as he didn't expect it to happen. Jenkins had been through all this before and had surely shared the experience with Dr. Blakely.

I had a queasy feeling as I suddenly felt the floor dropping away under my feet. Not only was the floor tilting, but also as the water drained away, it was retracting into the cavern walls by a good ten feet all the way around the base of the tree.

I tried to hold onto the tree as best as I could with my one free arm, but it was hopeless. I felt my stomach drop as I fell, but thankfully I only went down about two feet, before my feet landed on the first of a series of spiral steps that wound around the tree stump, and down into the darkness.

All the machinery finally ground to a stop. An eerie silence followed, the tree alcove opened back up and set my hand free. I realized that this was simply a safety measure to keep the key bearer from rolling into the mouth of the ancient guardian, when the floors tilted.

Jenkins and Blakely herded Buddy over to the stairs with their weapons.

"The mistake we made twenty years ago," Jenkins offered, "was in not taking time to have Mirasel Rose translate these runes." He gestured at the floor. "This contains the secret to where the next key is hidden in the temple."

He continued, "Rhodes and I were so intent on being the first ones to get our hands on the rubies, and preventing the others from getting them, that we almost killed ourselves getting down these stairs to the temple. I lucked out, and was able to trick Rhodes out of the ruby horde. I then trapped Rhodes, Remy, and Mirasel in the temple, and then I reversed the process you just saw, and refilled the chamber with water. Apparently that damnable Remy knew of another way out."

I looked over at poor Remy's corpse lying on the tilted floor. We wouldn't have old Remy to save us this time around.

Jenkins gestured to Dr. Blakely. "I will not make the same error twice. Dr. Blakely, if you will, please translate the runes before we enter the temple?"

Blakely started at the far end of the cavern, at the beginning of the spiral, and slowly traced her way round and round until she was back at the head of the stairs again.

"Well?" Jenkins demanded impatiently.

She gave him an icy smile, "Piece of cake. For each tree there is a *zemís*, an idol key. Each key is a representation of one of the three gods that make up the Taino's religious trinity: Yucahu, Bagua, and Marocoti. The key that we just used was the Yucahu *zemís*. Yucahu is the fertility god. The one we need for the Arawak tree is the Bagua *zemís*. It is the god of war. The great and final Patwah tree will require the Marocoti *zemís*. The Marocoti is the god of the harvest."

"Thanks for the history lesson, Fran, but where is the Bagua *zemís*?" Jenkins sneered.

She gave him a frigid stare that made him look away, "I was getting to that. Each *zemís* is actually the source root for each tree. The Yucahu *zemís*, which we have here, was the original source root for the Patwah tree. Because the Patwah has the book of *Legacy and Destiny* within its base, it no longer needs the *zemís* to survive. All the others are still attached as the very base root, the original seed from which its tree grew. To find the Bagua *zemís*, we have to travel to the lowest part of this temple. To unlock the next temple, we have to have the base root, the Bagua *zemís* from this tree."

Buddy furrowed his brow. "But if this *zemís* is from the Patwah tree, how did Rhodes originally get it?"

"He couldn't have gotten it from the tree himself," I surmised. "It must have been with the map when Rhodes found it."

Blakely affirmed, "Based on my research, Stede Bonnet stole it. When Bonnet took the diamond horde to the Patwah tree, to make amends, the temple took the book back from him. The *zemís* and his life were all that he escaped with."

"Nicely done, professor!" Jenkins clapped.

"Gentlemen, after you." He motioned us down the stairs and into the darkness.

CHAPTER 45

▼

The stairs spiraled down around and around the remains of the great Caribe tree for what seemed like eons. We passed through floor after floor of broken statues and shattered altars for worshiping, of storage bins and cubbyholes used to stores food that had now turned to dust, until we reached a floor that was obviously the living quarters for the long-deceased priest.

"So where exactly were the rubies hidden when you found them?" Buddy queried.

Jenkins grumbled, "That was a total pain in the ass. Rhodes and I figured the rubies would be in one of those altars or statues on the worship level. We busted the shit out of those things and didn't find a single ruby."

"It's called desecration, you bastard," I sneered.

"Whatever, the jokers associated with this temple haven't cared about that for a very long time.

"Anyway," he continued, "we finally figured out that that crazy pirate Stede Bonnet had put a single ruby in every storage bin on the warehouse floors. I guess the priestess considered the food this tree produced holy. So Bonnet had hoped that distributing the rubies throughout the food bins would make up for his thievery and treachery. It took us forever to go through every one of those damn bins."

The roots of the tree had been branching out in a thousand different directions all the way down the stairs. Now they were getting smaller and smaller, until we were down to one main feeder.

"We should be getting close now," Blakely stated flatly.

Abruptly the stairs ended. We found ourselves in a small chamber, no more than ten feet around. There in the center of the chamber was a small wooden *zemís* statue. This one was as dark as its brother, but it depicted a warrior god with spears and clubs in its many hands. Growing out of the *zemís'* crown was the source root that flowed upward to the remains of the great tree.

"The Bagua *zemís*," Frances Blakely whispered reverently.

"That's what we're here for," Jenkins announced boldly. "Keep that spear gun trained on our friends here while I cut this ugly monstrosity loose, Blakely."

Jenkins pulled a knife from his pocket and started sawing the fragile source root from the *zemís'* head.

"I don't know if I would do that if I were you," I said, looking up at the root structure above us.

"Shut up!" Jenkins snarled. "Your opinion means nothing to me. You and your fat friend are going to be sealed in this watery hell forever."

With a snap, the source root broke free. There was a distant rumble that sounded like thunder. The entire structure shook violently as bits and pieces of the roof began to fall to the floor.

"See, I told you!" I yelled above the din.

"Look at that!" Buddy motioned frantically toward the severed source root.

The source root was shrinking, as was the entire feeder root system above it. The remains of the ancient Caribe tree were disappearing before our very eyes.

"The entire temple structure is tied to the ancient root system!" Blakely yelled. "If the root collapses so will the temple!"

All pretenses were dropped as we scrambled up the stairs as quickly as we could.

We made it to the top of the stairs, just before the ancient structure collapsed in a great roar. The vibration had caused the cavern itself to become unstable, and great chunks of rock began to fall from the ceiling.

Jenkins and Blakely held us at gunpoint as they scrambled up the rappelling ropes. Jenkins looked down, "I was hoping to trap the two of you in the temple, but I guess leaving you under a hundred tons of rock for eternity is just as good an option."

Blakely blew me a silver kiss as she hit the automatic release that would pull her to the top. "You can always take your chances with the sea lice, if you feel frisky!"

"I don't think so," Buddy grimaced. "They can leave us to die, but I'll be damned if I will let Remy down by allowing them to desecrate another temple."

He picked up a large stone and with a heave hit Jenkins in the small of his back just before his rappelling rope pulled him over the lip of the opening high above.

With a roar, Jenkins grabbed at his back, and momentarily lost his grip on his rope. For several seconds, he fought to maintain his hold. In the end he succeeded, but in his effort to save his own skin, he dropped the Bagua *zemís*.

I made a beautiful dive and caught the *zemís* before it hit the floor.

"Nooooo!" Jenkins screamed, but Blakely was pulling him back from the opening as edges of it broke away and fell to the floor of the cavern, under their very shoes.

I pulled myself to my feet, holding my prize to my chest. Buddy side-stepped over, dodging big chunks of ceiling as they fell.

"Looks like this may be it, Buddy Bear. See you in the happy-ever-after, old friend."

We looked up, as the cavern came down around our ears.

CHAPTER 46

▼

As Buddy and I gazed up at the ever-widening hole in the cavern ceiling, a black face appeared over the rim of the hole.

"*Nous sommes des amis des vieilles manières!*" I yelled aloud at the face hovering above us.

The face disappeared.

"What the heck was that?"

"Just a little last advice from Remy, let's just hope to hell it works."

"You can say that again," he yelled above the din, barely dodging another huge chunk of rock.

Seconds later, a rough hemp rope came rolling down from the hole in the cavern ceiling.

The black face reappeared. "Come, climb quickly, we don't have much time."

"You first, Big Guy."

"No way, Kris, you need to take the lead."

"Get your ass up that rope, Buddy, we don't have much time." I crossed my arms.

He sighed. "Okay, okay." He began climbing.

"Besides," I smirked, "I just want to make sure it will hold your weight before I give it a try."

Buddy gave it his all, and clambered through the hole. I watched as my friend disappeared. He was safe, and that had been my goal. The cavern ceiling was falling at such a tremendous rate now, that I didn't have a prayer of climbing the rope before the whole cavern caved in on me. At least Buddy was safe, and I knew he would give his life if necessary to save Lil.

Above the roar of the rock fall, I could hear him screaming for me to climb up, even though I could no longer see his face through the dust.

What the hell, I thought. I tucked the *zemís* into my pants, and took hold of the rope as the stones rained down upon me.

The second that I put tension on the rope, I felt myself being jerked upward through the darkness. Large stones bounced off my shoulders and arms, but one caught me in the side of the head and all went dark and silent.

Slowly, ever so slowly the night turned to dawn, and I opened my eyes. I tried to sit up, but my head swam wildly, and I fell back down.

"Easy, easy," Buddy commanded. "You took a pretty good lick on the head."

I groaned. "Yeah, you're the one who's supposed to get hit in the head with stuff."

He chuckled, and helped me to a sitting position. It took me a second to realize I was lying in the Guarao's shack. In fact, the Guarao was sitting cross-legged on a grass mat beside me.

"You okay now, mon?" he asked.

"You speak English?"

"Of course, I do. I may protect this holy area from intruders, but I still have a life. I got a generator and a satellite dish out back of the shack."

Buddy grinned. "The Guarao helped me pull you out of there just as the whole place was collapsing. We barely got you out and down the hill before the entire mountaintop imploded."

"Thank you, friend," I nodded to the Guarao. "I am deeply indebted to you."

"Your thanks is appreciated, but not required. All I wish is that you stop those evil men before they desecrate our other holy temples."

I struggled to my feet. "Trust me. I plan to do everything in my power to stop Jenkins and his gang."

"Are you sure you are ready to travel?"

"We have to go, Buddy. If I'm guessing correctly, since Jenkins and Blakely didn't get the *zemís*, they are going to go after the journal back at the Eden Rock."

Buddy helped me hobble out of the shack. We bid our farewells to and started down the trail as quickly as possible.

"So, what exactly did Remy tell you before he died?"

"He said that if all looked lost, to call on the Guarao and he would help us. He said to say *'Nous sommes des amis des vieilles manières'*"

"Which means…?"

"We are friends of the old ways," I stated flatly.

"So does that mean that you believe in those miracles Remy was talking about now?"

"I-I have to believe there is a reasonable scientific explanation for all of this," I murmured. "I'll give you this. These ancient people were advanced and built mechanical wonders into their temples."

He shook his head, dismayed. "That radioactive sea lice wasn't some Disney special effect, Kris, and you saw what happened when the *zemís* was cut away from the Caribe tree with your own eyes."

I shook my head, square jawed, as we walked along in silence.

Buddy broke through my wall of obstinacy. "Did you mean what you said to the Guarao about stopping Jenkins from desecrating the other temples?"

I simmered to myself, "My first priority is saving Lil. But if I can take that bastard out in the process, you bet your ass I will do it."

Buddy started to mutter an agreement, when we were both thrown to the ground by the rolling repercussions of a giant explosion.

"Holy crap!" He commented. "Was that an explosion from the temple?"

We pulled ourselves back to our feet. "No way, that came from the opposite direction, out in the bay."

Buddy scrambled up a nearby boulder, and threw a salute to hide his eyes from the sun's glare.

"What do you see?" I called impatiently from the ground.

He lowered his hand and looked down at my anxious face. "Unless I am mistaken, I think the *Sweet Desperation* just blew up out in the bay."

"Oh God," I exclaimed, "I hope that Lil was still on the *Nefarious*."

"And that the *Nefarious wasn't* in dry dock on the *Sweet Desperation*," he added.

We tore through the dense foliage as quickly as possible, back in the direction of La Tourmente.

CHAPTER 47

▼

It took far too long to get back to the airport. Otis was sitting on an old wooden bench outside the tower, dripping wet, his face in his hands. A soggy Spooner was by his side.

"Otis, did you hear that explosion...?" I began, then stopped.

Aunt Edna's faithful servant raised his head, his eyes were red rimmed and swimmy.

"What's wrong, Otis? What happened?" Buddy's face betrayed his concern.

"Jason," Otis stammered, tears running down his face. "Jason is dead."

Buddy stopped frozen in his tracks.

I ran the last few steps to Otis, and began shaking him violently. "What are you talking about, Otis? Jason can't be dead!"

Buddy came and put a hand on my shoulder to calm me down.

"It's true, Master Kristopher," Otis cried openly, "I saw it with my own eyes! How am I ever going to break the news to Ms. Edna?"

"Take a deep breath, Otis," Buddy encouraged, "and tell us what happened."

He forced me down on the bench beside Otis, and then sat down on the other side of our old friend and mentor.

Otis let out a deep staggered sigh. "I stayed behind to look for Jason, when you guys went to the temple. Ms. Edna expects me to take care of him, and I figured you boys had everything under control on your end."

"After you left, I sat on this very bench, thinking about Jason, and what he would do based on the argument that he had with you, Kris."

I started to object to Otis's terminology, but Buddy quieted me with a stern look.

Otis continued, "Jason would want to fix what he felt he had screwed up. He would have tried to save your wife, Kris. I remembered you telling me that you had checked all the marinas and hadn't found the *Nefarious* tied up anywhere, and had assumed that it was anchored out in the bay. Jason probably went through the same search, and came to the same conclusion. Based on that, he would have tried to get out to the *Nefarious*."

"That sounds like Jason, always trying to save the world on his own."

"So, on a hunch I check the cargo hold of the plane."

I snapped my fingers, "The Zodiac!"

"Yes, when I checked the hold of the Lady Orleans, the inflatable boat and motor were gone. I grabbed Spooner and rented a small boat from a nearby marina. It took me a while to find the *Sweet Desperation*'s anchorage, but when I got there they were already in a terrible predicament. Apparently, that goon Luu had been in the process of dry-docking the *Nefarious* on the *Sweet Desperation*. The *Nefarious* was twenty feet off the water, dangling from that huge crane on the back of the ship. The Zodiac was floating near a rope ladder that was hanging near the bow. With his broken arm, Jason was in no shape for taking on this kind of mission."

I grunted, "It must have taken him forever to climb that rope ladder with his arm."

"But by the time I got my boat near, Jason was already on board, and had made his way to the stern crane. I was just in time to see him sneak up on Luu and take a swing at him with a piece of pipe he had found. Unfortunately, with only one good arm, his swing was inadequate to have much effect on that brick wall. He and Luu were rolling and fighting in the crane's control room. The crane was thrashing back and forth every time one of them fell on one of the controls. The *Nefarious* was being shaken back and forth like an alley cat in the maw of a junkyard dog. The yacht trawler came close to creaming the *Sweet Desperation* several times. Finally the unbearable torque and g-force was too much for the crane cable. One particularly violent shake sent the *Nefarious* flying a good hundred yards away from the big salvage ship. She hit with a tremendous splash. I just knew she was going to break in half on impact, but she didn't. She listed to one side for the next half hour until her automatic bilge pumps could clear her of the excess water she took on, but she survived.

"Jason was putting up quite a fight for someone in his shape. Without the weight of the *Nefarious* to hold the crane down, it was swinging in huge arcs and loops. At long last, that bastard Luu finally had Jason pinned down. I saw that he was mere moments away from Luu's taking him out with the same pipe that he had used. I-I guess he saw that too. He used his free arm to jam the crane controls to full max stops."

My mouth dropped open, "Are you saying that Jason destroyed the *Sweet Desperation*?"

Otis's shoulders sagged. "The huge crane swung around at a tremendous speed and cleanly took out the entire superstructure of the *Sweet Desperation*. There was a small explosion, which I guess set off a chain reaction. Four more explosions followed, each increasing in power until the fifth one that was surely the salvage ship's fuel tanks. She blew with a tremendous fireball that capsized and sank the small boat that Spooner and I were in. The charred remains of the ship broke in half and sank in less than five minutes after the explosions. I tried to make my way to the listing *Nefarious*, but the tide was working against me. I finally gave up and focused on dragging Spooner and myself to shore."

"My God," I whispered, "I was such a bastard to him, and he died trying to save my Lil."

Otis gritted his teeth. "Yes and unfortunately his death was for nothing. I couldn't make it to the *Nefarious*, but that son of a bitch Luu did. He was battered and burned, but he was alive, and I watched him drag himself aboard the ship."

"I can't believe he's gone," Buddy squeaked.

I fought to breathe as I suffocated under my own tears, sinking deeper and deeper into the darkness, drowning under the responsibility of another life lost.

CHAPTER 48

▼

"God, I can't believe that Jason is gone," Buddy moaned again as we bounced toward the Eden Rock in Remy's Mini-Moke.

"I know," I grimaced, "I feel like the biggest piece of shit on the face of the planet."

I looked back at Otis, who was totally distraught in the back of the car. Otis and Jason had been at each other's throats for years, but I had always known that Aunt Edna's loyal assistant had always felt like a surrogate father to Jason.

"And poor Remy too," Buddy screwed up his face. "I even hated to see Lawson go like that. There is too much death here. I guess we need to send a message to his granddaughter to let her know he's not coming back."

I agreed as we pulled up to the Eden Rock, "But first we have to see if Jenkins went for the journal after he left us to die in the temple."

We scrambled out of the Mini-Moke and went straight for Remy's room.

The door was hanging from one hinge. "Not a good sign, Buddy Bear."

We pushed it aside and entered. Remy's beautiful room had been ripped to pieces. All of the old antiques were destroyed. Canvases were ripped from their frames, backs were pried off chests and vanities, drawers were broken into kindling in an effort to find hidden compartments.

In reality, I had been nowhere near that sophisticated in squirreling away the journal the night before. I walked over to the glass case that held the antique snuffbox collection. The case was shattered and the boxes were strewn about the room. I gently picked the broken pieces of the case away from the cherry-wood base it had been sitting on. I had taped the journal to the hollow underside of the base.

I held my breath and picked the base up and gazed underneath; nothing, but the remains of the tape that I had secured it with.

I hung my head. "It's gone."

Otis trailed in behind us. "You don't need the journal anymore. I have all the coordinates translated for the other two temples."

"That's not the point, Otis," I murmured quietly. "Jenkins thinks the Bagua *zemís* is lost to him. The only thing he has to go on now is the journal. He is going to be high-tailing it to the second temple."

"Yeah," Buddy commented, "You can bet that by now Luu has picked up Jenkins and Blakely in the *Nefarious*, and they are on their way."

My face dropped. "Yes, and I pray to God that Lil was on the *Nefarious*, and not on the *Sweet Desperation* when she blew."

I felt tears of anger well in my eyes. "The worst thing is that now that Jenkins has the journal, and he thinks there is no hope of getting the Bagua *zemís*, there is absolutely no incentive for him to keep my Lil alive."

CHAPTER 49

▼

Thankfully, Jack Mason had come through for me again. The Lady Orleans was roaring over the ocean toward the site of the second temple.

"Hey, look what I found in the Zodiac's crate." Otis handed the small electronic instrument to Buddy.

"Oh yeah," he grinned, "I've used one of these before. It's a handheld Global Positioning System. Type in the coordinates of where you want to go, and it will lead you there. What are the coordinates where we are going to, Kris?"

I paused to glance over from the Lady Orleans's controls. "Twelve thirty North, Sixty-Nine Fifty-Eight West, just off the coast of Venezuela."

He dutifully plugged the numbers into the little machine. "Aruba?"

"That's where Otis says the journal's translations say, and not just Aruba, but a place on Aruba called the Hooiberg."

"What the hell is a Hooiberg?" Buddy commented.

"It's a mountain, shaped like a haystack. In Dutch *Hooiberg* means haystack. The mountain sticks out of the middle of the island like a big old thumb. It's one of the strangest natural phenomena around. You ever seen *Close Encounters of the Third Kind*?"

Buddy grunted an affirmation.

"That's what the damn thing looks like. It just kind of rises out of the middle of the island, and according to Otis, that's where we will find the temple of the Arawak tree."

Otis agreed. "Yes and you can bet that is where Jenkins and the *Nefarious* are headed as well. By plane, we can head them off at the pass."

I shook my head in agreement. "Yeah, my hope is to get there first, and set up a base of operations. Then have a message waiting for them when they set foot in Aruba. 'You want the Bagua *zemís*, hand over Lil.'"

Buddy's eyes narrowed. "And if we get Lil back safely, then what?"

I squeezed the yolk till my knuckles turned white, "Then we give Jenkins and his crew a dose of the same medicine that those bastards gave Remy."

Buddy mused, "Isn't Barbados just off the coast of South America, too, Otis?"

Otis beamed. "Yes, but Aruba is farther north than my home. However, I was fortunate enough to go there often when I was a small boy. My father couldn't make enough money to support us raising sugar cane in Barbados, so he took a job at the oil refinery in Aruba. My mother and I would go visit him there once a month. It's very different from most of the other lush tropical islands in the Caribbean."

"What's so different about it?" Buddy questioned.

"Aruba is one big desert, much like the American Southwest. It almost never rains," Otis shared wistfully.

"A strong, steady wind from north to south produces lopsided divi-divi trees all over the island."

"And eliminates the need for hair dryers," Buddy grinned.

"It was probably a good haunt for Jason's great-great-great-grandfather. In the seventeen hundreds, the island became a hideaway for pirates who preyed on ships transporting Indian treasures back to the Old World. There are actually ruins of an old pirate castle at a place called Bushiribana on the northeast coast."

We all grew quiet for a while at the mention of our lost friend's name.

To break the silence, I finally ventured, "Wasn't there a big gold rush there at one time, too, Otis?"

"Yes, during the year 1824, gold was discovered near Bushiribana. It lasted until 1916 when the mines went dry. There are small natural caves all over Aruba. Many of the old gold-mining tunnels crisscross and attach to these caves, making the whole of Aruba one big underground maze."

I looked at my watch; we had been in the air for several hours now. "We should be coming up on Aruba soon."

Buddy looked down at the little GPS, and then out the makeshift windshield of the Lady Orleans. "Yes, according to my little magic box here, we should be able to see the coastal capital city of Oranjestad any second now."

And there it was, shimmering on the horizon. I took her down as low as I dared, as we flew over the city. Oranjestad is located on the southern coast of Aruba.

We flew over the Dutch colonial architecture in pastel colors. At the marina, merchants were selling fresh fish and produce right off the boats. Everyone stopped to wave at the flying boat as we passed overhead.

We burbled over the city and went heading out into what Otis called the Cunucu, which is the local word for countryside. It's the rugged, rambling, generally flat interior of the island, but as we neared the center of the island a five-hundred-foot mountain appeared out of nowhere. It was the Hooiberg, and it looked as out of place in the desolate interior of this island as a hooker at a church banquet.

"So that's where the temple is supposed to be? It does look like something out of the mind of Steven Spielberg."

"Yes," I said, cutting a wide turn around the mountain and then heading back toward the airport at Oranjestad. "I'm surprised that some enterprising archaeologist hasn't tried to excavate there before."

"They have," Otis commented. "There have been more than a hundred digs in and around the Hooiberg over the years, and none of them have found anything."

Buddy turned to Otis. "So how, pray tell, do you think we are going to find the temple?"

"You forget, Master Buddy, we have the journal translations and we have the *zemís*. We will find our way in."

I growled in both of their directions. "Don't you guys forget: We save Lil first, and then we worry about Jenkins and the temple."

I sighed; I hoped it would be that easy to separate the two. I made out the lights of the Oranjestad Airport, and took the Lady Orleans down for a soft and safe landing, much to the relief of Buddy, Otis, and Spooner.

C H A P T E R 50

▼

Buddy and I sat at De Olde Molen's bar sulking in our Balashi beer. Brewed locally from a secret island recipe, Balashi quickly became our favorite island inebriation. De Olde Molen's also became our favorite watering hole; it's an old windmill that was first built in 1804 in Holland and then shipped to Aruba, piece by piece and reconstructed in 1960. It has a tiny cheap restaurant and bar in its base, and a laid-back Dutch atmosphere, with actual wooden shoes hanging on the wall. The place is so small that the grill and cook stove sit right behind the bar.

We had spent the last three days scouting the Oranjestad marina, watching for the *Nefarious*. Jenkins thought we were no longer of this earth, so he would have no reason not to take the easy route and dock in the marina. At least that was our rationale. There had been no sign of him.

Thinking that he had docked the ship somewhere else, we even went out to the Hooiberg and traipsed all around it, and even climbed to the top. Nothing. We were pretty disheartened that there was no visible means of getting inside the haystack mountain either.

Otis's translations gave us the location of the temple, but there was no mention of how to get in the damn thing. Otis had locked himself in his hotel room with Spooner and was using a laptop and a high-speed Internet connection to access his lab back in Charleston. He was working twenty-four hours a day, rerunning his models, hoping to find some clue he had overlooked.

About the only thing Otis's research revealed was the so-called ancient guardian that had taken out Lawson in the Caribe temple. Jenkins had called it radioactive sea lice, which was wrong, but not too far off.

My twins could tell them all something about sea lice, which are the larva stage of thimble jellyfish. During certain months of the year, the kids are covered with itching, stinging whelps from going in the ocean.

Otis discovered that our temple guardian was made up of thousands of larva of the chaetognaths or arrow worm.

When they mature, they leave the water and live a life much like any other caterpillar or silkworm. The adults grow to no more than three or four inches and are characterized by a slender, semi-transparent body, with sharp spines on either side of the mouth.

The adults, as well as the larva, are voracious meat-eaters and are capable of attacking and consuming prey larger then themselves. The large spines around their mouths help them grab and restrain their prey, which they attract with the vanilla scent secreted from their glands.

I, for one, was extremely relieved to have a scientific explanation for what had happened. Buddy, as usual, wasn't so easily convinced, and I had quit trying to reason with him.

$$*\qquad*\qquad*\qquad*$$

Twilight was falling, and we had given up on our third day of searching for the *Nefarious*. We finally broke poor Spooner free. We'd argued with the bartender/cook, a tough-looking lady named Ruby Casibari, to allow us to bring him into De Olde Molen's with us. The poor dog had been going stir crazy locked up with Otis all day.

Ruby Casibari had short straw-colored hair and a deep-water tanned face with a constant struggle going on between the smile and frown lines. She wore wool plaid shirts, despite the temperature, and jeans that looked as though they had originally been sewn by Levi Straus himself.

She was pretty standoffish with us at first, chalking us up as just another group of tourists blowing through. Buddy teased his way into getting his fingers smashed with a heavy beer mug. When he squealed and sucked them like a baby, she couldn't help but laugh.

Buddy slowly got under her skin, and eventually we found out that she and her life partner had come down here to escape their prior lives as investment bankers. They'd pooled their resources and bought De Olde Molen's. During tourist season, her partner ran jeep tours into the Cunucu, so tourists could gawk at the divi-divi trees and huge blue lizards.

Once we had her stamp of approval, all the other locals ho frequented the bar and restaurant started to warm up to us as well. We were starting to feel like locals. It was well past closing time for most businesses on the island and all the regulars were in various stages of drunkenness.

We had downed around six frosty mugs of Balashi each at this point. Buddy kept sneaking and pouring a little into a bowl for Spooner. I kept telling him he was going to turn the dog mean by feeding it beer. He was arguing that it was gunpowder that made dogs mean if they ate it.

We were so caught up in our blurry argument that it actually took a good thirty seconds for us to react when a battered and torn Jason Bonnet stumbled through the swinging doors of De Olde Molen.

Buddy and I looked at each other dumbly. For some strange reason, I kept thinking that Jason had eaten too much gunpowder, and that was why he looked so straggly.

His eyes opened wide, he mouthed our names, and then promptly collapsed onto the hard-wood floor.

We I finally shook ourselves out of our stupor, and hurried over to drag him to a nearby table. He looked like hell.

He was battered and bruised again, and had cuts and lacerations on his arms and chest. His clothes were nothing but dirty ribbons of fabric, vainly trying to cover up his wounds. Worst of all his entire body was covered in horrendous sunburn that had gone well beyond red, and was almost black. Huge water blisters had risen up all over his scorched body.

"Ruby!" I yelled, "Please bring me some water."

Buddy patted our friend's hollow face gently until he gained some degree of consciousness. I carefully poured a trickle of water down his throat.

"More," he croaked.

I gave him a little at a time. "You can't go too fast, Jason, or it will make you sick."

He grinned weakly.

We spent the next hour nursing him back halfway to human. Slowly, ever so slowly, he began sitting on his own and drinking the water while holding the glass himself. He went through four pitchers of water in that hour.

I studied the pattern on the tablecloth intently. "Jason…Jason, I just want to apologize for what I said to you. I had no right."

He shook his head. "You had every right, Grantford. I almost got Lil, Buddy, and you killed. I tried to make it up. I found the *Nefarious* and the *Sweet Desper-*

ation, and tried to rescue Lil, but that bastard Luu kept getting in my way at every turn."

Buddy grinned from ear to ear at having Jason back, "Yeah, Otis saw the whole thing, including how you blew up the *Sweet Desperation* in the end!"

Jason turned on that infamous Bonnet smile. "Otis was there? You bet. That was cool. Unfortunately, Luu gave me another good beating before we got to that part. When the *Sweet Desperation* exploded, the concussion blew Luu and me through the glass windshield of the crane cockpit. I got scratched up a good bit, but Luu was in front of me and took the brunt of it. I'm surprised he made it out alive."

Buddy grunted, "Otis said he looked liked burnt toast."

"I managed to grab a piece of floating debris, but I was too stunned to do anything but drift. Luu landed closer than me to the *Nefarious* and was able to drag himself aboard. When my fog lifted, I realized that Luu and the *Nefarious weren't* going to be sticking around long, and if I didn't make a move then, any hope of rescuing Lil would be gone."

I shook my head. "Otis's boat capsized in the explosion too; it's ironic to think that he and Spooner were probably floating just a few feet away from you."

His face clouded. "Otis was caught in the explosion? Is he okay?"

"Pretty upset at the thought that he had lost you, but other than that he is fine. He's at the hotel room playing with his translation models as we speak."

Jason grinned, "The Big O will have to try a lot harder than that to get rid of me!"

I cringed, recalling Remy's last words to Jenkins.

"So how did you get here?" Buddy queried.

He sighed, "I made it to the *Nefarious* just in time, before Luu went speeding off. As you can imagine, I was in pretty sorry shape at that point. I was able to drag myself into the lifeboat, and under its cover. I passed out, I don't know how long I was out of it, but when I woke up it was dark outside. Jenkins and Blakely were on the boat by then, on the aft deck. I guess Luu was on the fly bridge. Jenkins was screaming and cursing you, Buddy. I don't know what you did to him, but you sure pissed him off."

"How about Lil?" I questioned hesitantly. "Did you see her?"

He shook his head, "I never actually saw her, but she was onboard. I think those Grand Banks trawler yachts have a front and an aft stateroom. Blakely stayed in front, and from what I heard, that's where they kept Lil tied up."

I let out a long sigh of relief; Lil was still alive.

He continued, "I kept listening, trying to hear where they were going, but I could never pick it up. In fact I don't know now! Where are we exactly?"

Buddy raised his eyebrows, "You don't know you are in Aruba?"

He shook his head, "From the bits and pieces I overheard, they were going to be looking for some kind of pirate castle when they got here. Apparently there is an entrance to some old gold-mine tunnels in the castle that Blakely believes will intersect with caves that have access to the temple."

I snapped my fingers. "That's how they plan to get into the temple without the Bagua *zemís*!"

"They don't have the *zemís*?"

"That's what Jenkins is pissed off about!"

"Ah," Jason sighed. "Well, anyway, I was trying to figure out how I could sneak out of my hiding place, to try to rescue Lil. I finally decided that I would disable their engines after dark when they anchored for the night, create a distraction, and then try to get Lil to the lifeboat for our escape."

"Pretty lofty goal to do all that with four other people on board a forty-two foot boat, without being caught," Buddy commented.

"Unfortunately, damn near impossible," He grimaced. "I had managed to lower the lifeboat, and to tow it out behind the *Nefarious*, where it would be less noticeable. I figured if Lil and I had to make a hasty escape, we'd drop overboard anywhere, drift back to the lifeboat, and I could cut our tether loose and we would be free.

"After setting up the lifeboat, I went to crap on Luu's engines. Anything that was removable, I ripped loose."

The light bulb went off. "That explains why the *Nefarious* hasn't shown up yet."

Jason continued, "Then I needed a distraction; nothing like a little pyro for that. I took a spare gas can I found. It didn't have much fuel in it, but it was enough to get their attention. I stuck a rag in the can's opening and made a big old Molotov cocktail out of it. I edged along the outer railing and placed the can on the bow, just in front of the fly bridge. I lit the rag and tried to hide in the shadows."

"You're lucky you didn't turn yourself into a crispy critter like Luu!" Buddy mused.

Jason rolled his eyes. "It took less than ten seconds for my little bomb to go off. It caused no great damage, but it sure made a huge boom. Luu came hobbling down from the fly bridge, obviously fearful of any more burns. Jenkins came running out from the main stateroom dragging a huge fire extinguisher behind him.

"I waited to see if Blakely would follow. She didn't. It wasn't going to take them long to put out my little light show. If I was going to make my move, it had to be then. I opened the door to the saloon, and missed being shish-kebab by one of Blakely's spears by about two inches. It stuck in the door frame right by my head!"

"She was just waiting for you?"

"I think the bitch is clairvoyant. She wasted no time yelling for Jenkins and Luu, and at the same time she was reloading that damn spear gun. She was blocking my way to Lil, and Jenkins and Luu were going to be there any second!"

He hung his head. "I'm sorry, Kris, I gave it my best shot, but it was impossible. I ran for the stern. I almost made it clear, but that son of a bitch Luu dove for my legs. He tripped me up and I fell hard on the railing on my broken arm. I swear I thought my lights were going to dim then and there; the pain was so bad. I was fortunate that Luu was so badly burned. The dive he made at my legs hurt him as much as it hurt me. He was moaning and writhing on the deck, in no shape to follow.

"I dragged myself over the side, and somehow managed to cut the lifeboat's tow rope. I held on to the rope as best I could and slowly paddled out as far away from the ship and the lifeboat as I could bear to go. I kept low and still in the water. They were soon scanning the water with a portable spotlight. They spotted the lifeboat and Jenkins fired a few shots in that general direction.

"After a few minutes they gave up. They probably figured I was done for after my fall. I waited for what felt like hours before I finally used the towrope to pull myself to the lifeboat. It had no motor, and there was no land in either direction. I fell asleep in my exhaustion, and when I awoke, the sun was up and the *Nefarious* was just a speck far out on the horizon. I didn't know it then, but I would drift for another whole day and night before I beached on these shores."

$$*\qquad*\qquad*\qquad*$$

Jason continued his tale, cognizant that the rest of the bar was listening, exaggerating as he went along. When the lifeboat landed on the shores of Aruba, he hadn't known where he was. He wandered around in circles for most of the next twenty-four hours in the deserts of the Cunucu, encountering all manner of rattlesnakes, tarantulas, and scorpions. He swore that all the fauna of the island was ten feet high. Normally I would take his tall tales with a grain of salt, but after what I had seen in St. Barts, I wasn't too sure anymore.

He had finally stumbled onto a road, faint with delirium and sunburn. He had followed the road until it had ended at De Olde Molen's. When he had seen the big Dutch windmill turning in the breeze, he had thought he was having a Don Quixote hallucination. When he stumbled in and saw us, he had been sure of it.

I watched Ruby Casibari stirring a big pot on the stove behind the bar. I wondered what she thought of Jason's wild stories. Buddy must have been reading my mind, because he spoke aloud what I was thinking.

"Ms. Casibari, what do you think of Jason's crazy adventures on your island?"

She turned slowly, "First of all, I'll beat your ass if you call me Ms. Casibari again, Buddy. My name's Ruby, unless you were one of my kids, of which I have none. Second, I've heard that tale before."

She turned her back and went back to stirring the pot. The warm smell drifted back to us.

Jason rubbed his stomach. "I haven't eaten in two days Ruby, what you got cooking?"

She turned again, scowling at Jason, "You and I haven't been properly introduced. I'm still Ms. Casibari to you, mister. This is sopi mondongo, but you wouldn't like it; it's an old island favorite."

I turned from Ruby and whispered to Buddy out of the corner of my mouth, "Did she just say she had heard crazy shit like Jason was spouting before?"

He nodded.

Jason grinned and managed to pull himself up to a standing position, so that he could stagger over to the bar, "Now how would you know that? I'm starving to death; I could eat sand at this point. What is sloppy mondago?"

The locals around the bar chortled.

She tilted her head with a little frown and shook a big wooden spoon at him. "It's sopi mondongo."

Bastiaan, a local fisherman spouted from the end of the bar, "It's hot, mister, kind of like Aruban gumbo."

Jason balanced himself cautiously on a barstool, "Hey I love good Louisiana gumbo; serve me up a bowl."

"I really don't think that's a good idea," Ruby shook her head.

Jason was feeling more like his old cocky self. "Well, I've been known to put some gumbo away in my time, but I'm very particular about it. Maybe you don't think yours can make the grade?"

I looked at Buddy, and mouthed, "Here comes trouble."

"Go ahead, give him the sopi, Ruby, he likes gumbo," Bastiaan and the other locals goaded and snickered.

Ruby grinned slyly, "Oh, I would put my sopi up against just about anyone else's on the island, because I put a very special ingredient in mine. You like the Scotch?"

"Well, sure"—Jason smiled self-assuredly—"if it's aged properly."

Ruby turned to the huge pot bubbling behind her and dragged something through it. "Are you sure you like the Scotch? I can take it out."

"Take it out! Heck, I don't mind if you add half a bottle," Jason stated heroically. The entire bar teetered.

"Your choice, mister," Ruby says dropping something in the pot. She stirred, and then poured Jason a huge steaming mug full of sopi mondongo.

He turned self-consciously to us; we were making "cease and desist" hand motions. "Who do these snickering yokels thing they are? I'll show them. A little Scotch added to the brew won't hurt me."

Unexpectedly, he grabbed the mug and drained it half empty with one huge guzzle.

I looked around the bar. Bastiaan and the others were wide-eyed with surprise. Ruby had a shocked look on her face.

Jason grinned at us while he chewed, "Gee, this gumbo has some really huge chunks in it."

Suddenly his face fell, and his eyes bulged. I didn't think it was possible for him to turn redder than the sunburn he already had; but he did.

He let out a scream that sounded like someone had jammed a flamethrower up a cat's ass! He jumped up and began running around the bar chugging everyone's beer as the locals rolled.

I tried to hold it in, but it was impossible. I was soon beating the table with my fist as the tears of laughter rolled down my face. Buddy was already rolling on the floor.

Spooner had been keeping a suspicious distance from Jason up to this point, but now decided that he was a menace. He jumped up and chased Jason around the bar, leaping and tearing at the seat of his pants. Jason kept trying to chug beer backwash with one hand and fight off Spooner with the other as his eyes and nose ran like Niagara Falls from the heat coming out of every orifice of his body.

Finally Jason began running out of steam, as he finished gulping the last of the patron's beers. We were all laughing so hard that I know for sure that more than one person wet their pants. Buddy managed to disengage Spooner, who growled viciously in Jason's direction.

At last, Jason was able to catch his breath. "What kind of Scotch was that, Ms. Casibari?" he bellowed.

Ruby wiped the tears from her eyes, "That my friend was the Scotch bonnet pepper. I merely drag it through the sopi mondongo to make it hot, leaving it in like that is like death from eating hot coals."

"You truly have some nerve, my friend. What is your name?"

"My name is Jason Bonnet." He grinned, shaking her hand. At this, the bar erupted into laughter once more.

"What's so funny?" He questioned.

"Now you can call me Ruby, and from now on your name will be Scotch Bonnet."

Buddy gave a hoot, "Scotch Bonnet, I never thought of that before. That's a perfect name for Jason!"

Buddy smacked our old friend on the back vigorously, and handed him a new frosty Balashi.

I pulled Ruby over to the side, as the bar gathered around Jason to hear more of his sordid tales.

I spoke in a hoarse whisper, "What did you mean Ruby when you said you had heard stories like Jason's before?"

She shrugged conspiratorially, "They just stories. When my Sally is out doing her jeep tours, sometimes she hears stuff from the locals at the various tourist traps; crazy stories about desert monsters. It's just stuff to scare the tourists around the campfires. I wouldn't put much stock into it."

I looked her in the eye. "Ruby, in the past few days, I've seen a lot of things that I wouldn't have believed before. Some very bad people have my wife. If there is something, anything you aren't telling me, please spill it. My wife's life may depend on it."

Ruby shifted awkwardly from one foot to another, and she dropped her voice down another level. She leaned into me. "Look if you say I told you this, I'll call you a liar to your face. If Bastiaan and the boys thought I believed this shit, I'd never hear the end of it."

I grimaced. "I believe you, Ruby, go ahead."

She sighed deeply. "Sally used to do sunset tours out into the Cunucu. She'd take the tourist to climb up the Hooiberg, so they could watch the sunset. The view is breathtaking at twilight: the desert shadows, the golden sea, the Caribbean stars twinkling on overhead. Anyway, it would be quite interesting for Sally to get the tourist back down the mountain in the darkness, even with the steps they've now carved in the side. She always had to take it slow, to ensure some octogenarian didn't fall and break a leg on the way down."

"I can't believe she would even try to do a tour like that," I commented. "I've climbed that thing during the day, and it's no cake walk."

"Yeah, but you should see the sunset from there, nothing like it in the whole world. Anyway, Sally had just gotten this one group of tourist down the mountain, and they were heading back for the Jeeps. This little old lady came tearing up, frantic and screaming. When Sally got her calmed down enough for her to tell her what happened, the old woman explained that her husband had an incontinence problem, and had excused himself to drain his shriveled old weasel on a bush off the side of the trail. The little old lady stayed behind on the trail to wait on her husband, while the rest of the group went ahead. She heard him give a little urgent squeak, and she went to check on him."

"Was he okay?" I stammered tensely.

Ruby shook her head forlornly. "They looked for him all night, and even called in the police to scour the area all around the Hooiberg, but he was never found. They made Sally stop doing the sunset tours after that."

"What happened?" I felt the burning realization climbing my esophagus.

Sally gritted her teeth. "Well, Sally believes, because she saw the woman's face, that what the old lady said was true. She said when she rounded the bush where her husband was taking a piss, she saw him all tangled up in some kind of webbing, and he was being dragged kicking and screaming into the darkness."

I felt the burn in my throat turn into a gorge, and I had to chug my own beer to wash it back down.

"Hey, Ruby!" Buddy yelled from the other side of the bar. "Old Scotch here says except for the hellacious fire of your gumbo, that the taste wasn't half bad. Why don't you enlighten him on the ingredients of sopi mondongo?"

Jason was beaming in our direction.

Ruby shook off the story and gave a big smile right back, "Well, Mr. Scotch, that would be one pound of cow's stomach, cut into chunks, one pound of cow's heel, the jelly adds flavor, and one pound of cow's white-bone."

The color that Jason turned when the green was overlaid over the red sunburn was quite ghastly. He jumped up and ran from the bar to wretch into the goldfish pond outside the front door.

Laughter could be heard for miles around, echoing from the warm golden windows of De Olde Molen's.

CHAPTER 51

▼

Otis was overjoyed that Jason was alive, then immediately pissed off that he had scared him so. I hated to break up the happy reunion, but time wasn't on our side if we were to rescue Lil. I quickly brought them up to speed on my plan, and what Ruby's companion Sally had seen.

Buddy frowned. "That old lady must have seen the ancient guardian for the temple that's inside the Hooiberg."

Jason shook his head. "But how is that possible, I thought you guys said those things stayed near the hidden entrance of the temples, instead of wandering around the countryside?"

Otis grimaced. "I think I can explain that. In my research to find an entrance to the caves, I poured over miles of maps of the old gold mines under the island. The mine tunnels run very close to the Hooiberg. The ancient guardian must have broken through where a mine shaft and a temple wall passed close."

Jason snapped his fingers. "Yes, Jenkins was thinking that he could enter the temple from the mines."

"And that's exactly why my plan calls for Otis to go to the old pirate castle where the mines begin, and the rest of us to go back to the Hooiberg."

Otis wrinkled his brow. "Explain how you think this is going to work again, Master Kristopher?"

"Simple, Jenkins may have figured out how to get inside the Hooiberg, but he still needs the Bagua *zemís*. I'm betting that he will be willing to trade Lil for it. I need you Otis, to go to the ruins of the pirate castle and deliver this message to Jenkins; if he wants the *zemís*, he will have to bring us Lil unharmed!"

Jason's face clouded. "You can't send the Big O in to deal directly with those monsters; they are just as likely to slit his throat as look at him."

"Hush, boy!" Otis commanded. "I've carried out worse duties than this before."

I let out a long tense sigh. "I have no intention of sending Otis into a death trap. They never need to see him. He just needs to leave a message for Jenkins and his crew. A message that tells him we are already in the temple via the mines, and that we will wait for him there to exchange Lil for the *zemís*."

Jason looked relieved.

"But," Buddy began, "we still don't know how to get into the temple, other than via the mines. Otis has been running his models day and night and still hasn't found the entrance."

"My best speculation is that a rock slide covered the entrance eons ago. There is no telling how much stone it's buried under now."

I grunted flatly. "Yes, but the ancient guardian that made a snack of that old man got out somehow; and how he got out, we are going to get in."

"So you are saying you believe in the ancient guardians now, Kris?" Buddy grinned slyly.

I wrinkled my nose. "Hey, science finds new species every day."

Jason blinked. "That's crazy, Grantford. It's starting to get dark already. How are we going to find some kind of hole or cave in the dark?"

I shook my head slowly. "We aren't going to look for a hole; we are going to look for the ancient guardian."

Buddy's jaw dropped. "How the hell are we going to catch magic sea monkeys, or whatever these thing happens to be?"

I dropped my eyes to the floor. "With the proper bait, Buddy Bear, with the proper bait."

CHAPTER 52

▼

Otis headed out to the ruins of the pirate castle on the far side of the island, carrying a sheet from the hotel and a can of spray paint to deliver his message. The rest of us bounced and dipped in our rental car over the rutted dirt roads of the Cunucu toward the Hooiberg. The night closed in around us.

Buddy was pissed about the details of my plan. "Goddamn it, this isn't right. I don't like this one bit!"

"He'll be fine, Buddy Bear," I tried tentatively to soothe. "You've got a strong grip on his leash."

Spooner trailed ahead of us by ten feet on a long piece of rope, pausing occasionally to pee on an interesting weed or rock. The beagle's nose was to the ground as he absorbed the myriad of scents in the island desert.

The Hooiberg loomed above us like some huge monolith, blocking out the rising moon and leaving us to stumble around the base of the mountain in almost total blindness. We had flashlights, but I had everyone turn them off so we wouldn't scare the guardian.

"Fat chance of that," Buddy grumbled, but he complied.

We were definitely a ragtag lot to be hunting an ancient killer. We had scrambled to borrow whatever makeshift protection we could from Ruby and Sally. The only real weapon we had was Donnie Rhodes's .38, which Buddy still carried. I had a rusty old machete, and somehow Jason had scavenged an aluminum baseball bat.

I planned to walk Spooner myself and have the others follow, but Buddy had become really attached to Spooner and insisted on walking the dog. I agreed, but only if he also carried the Bagua *zemís*. I figured if the ancient guardian skipped the appetizer and went straight for the entrée; at least Buddy would have the *zemís* to help defend him. After Buddy, I trailed next, straining my ears and eyes for any foreign sound. Jason came last, spinning like a top at the back of the line, and making way too much noise as he kept looking behind himself to see if anything was sneaking up on him.

The night was cloudless and enormous; I don't think I have ever felt the stars were farther away than they seemed to be. What little light they provided only fueled grotesque shadows dripping from every scrub brush, divi-divi tree, and looming boulder.

Suddenly Spooner froze ahead of us. I could see the hair on his back standing up in the gloom. A low guttural growl escaped his lips.

"Spooner, let's pull you back…" Buddy began, but it was too late.

Out of the darkness silvery strands seemed to fly from every direction at once, cocooning the pup almost instantly! The lead line snapped as if it were a thread! A terrified scream escaped the poor dog. I fumbled and somehow managed to get my flashlight turned on.

In those few fractions of a second when my flashlight illuminated the desert floor, I saw something that would haunt my dreams forever. Hundreds of silvery eyes stared at me from every corner and crevice! The entire desert floor was a living moving patchwork of tiny animals. Their small translucent bodies absorbed the beam of the flashlight and reflected it back dully. But the worst part was the needlelike mandibles opening and closing around each and every tiny razor-sharp mouth.

"Holy shit!" I heard Jason squeal behind me.

In the split second after they had leapt upon the poor dog, the little monsters had already wound a silky bond around his struggling body. Dragging their prey with them, the legion of tiny beasts turned as one, almost like a school of fish, and flooded into a dark maw of a hole in the desert floor.

"Oh my God, oh my God!" Jason was stammering behind me.

Buddy didn't pause. He was running at full blast toward the monster's hole before the dust even settled around it. Without a moment's hesitation, he jumped into the thing's lair with a roar of vengeance.

I shook myself out of my stupor. "Come on, Jason, let's go; we have to help!"

Less than two seconds later I was preparing to drop into the pit as I had seen my friend do. I paused for Jason.

"Jason, go. I'm right behind you!"

Jason hesitated, shaking with fear.

"Goddamn it, Jason, this is Buddy we are talking about!"

He nodded grimly and dropped into the hole. I found my lost faith, said a little prayer, and dropped in behind him, as the darkness closed in around me.

CHAPTER 53

▼

I frantically played my flashlight around the hollow searching for Buddy. The fragile shaft of light flashed onto old wooden roof and support beams. We were in one of the ancient mine shafts. It trailed out behind us, and forward around a bend. We could hear Buddy yelling just ahead.

Jason and I rounded the bend to find he had backed the swarm of arrow worms into a corner. He had the Bagua *zemís* thrust out in front of him and had reversed the carnivorous caterpillars slowly away from their struggling prey. It was strange how the arrow worms were reacting to the *zemís*. They were like moths to a flame. They were obviously attracted to the ugly little statue, but when they got close, they withdrew squealing and clicking in pain. Spooner lay at his feet fighting to get free of the sticky webbing.

The guardians furiously hissed and clicked! Venom dripped from their horrid mandibles as they jumped and dodged at Buddy and Spooner in one undulating curtain of death. Buddy had done a good job up to this point, but this monster was too fast and had a thousand heads; it wasn't going to stay cornered very long.

I leaned down and grabbed Spooner, and with a low toss threw the brave little dog behind us and out of harm's way.

This infuriated the guardians. I could see them crouching as one, preparing to spring on Buddy and devour him. Jason and I saw this at the same time. There was no way we were going to let this monster take out our Buddy Bear!

Jason and I both sprang first! Hitting every slimy worm within reach with everything we had from both the right and the left. It was easy to smash the individuals to goo, but there were so many of them it was like playing a twisted game of whack-a-mole with a never-ending supply of moles.

We had blind fury on our side. I swung the machete in large arcs, hacking ten of the beasts at a time. Jason focused on their ugly little heads, and repeatedly slammed the bat into everything that moved.

The monster howled as one in fury and the rolling carpet of teeth rose up to cover the roof of the mineshaft. I immediately knew that the dull groupthink that seemed to guide them had deduced that if they couldn't reach us from the floor, they should attack via the ceiling out of our reach. If they did, we were goners.

"Buddy!" I screamed above the din. "Look behind the swarm, do you see a crack or something where they entered from the temple?"

He squinted through the horde, careful to dodge their deadly fangs, as they sought the *zemís* and retracted in screams.

"Yeah, I see it!" he yelled. "A five-foot hole right behind them!"

"Throw the *zemís* through the opening!"

"I can't do that," he panted. "If I do we have no bargaining power with Jenkins."

Jason chimed in grimly, "If you don't do it, there will be no one left to bargain."

Buddy narrowed his eyes deliberately, and with one clean hard throw, the *zemís* went zooming through the temple entrance. The swarm instantly followed in a continuous evil flood, until there was nothing left but a few squirming half-dead bodies on the floor, and a thick, heavy odor of vanilla hanging in the air.

CHAPTER 54

▼

The sudden silence in the mineshaft was almost as disturbing as the vile ancient guardians. Then I realized all wasn't silent. There was a little horrific mewing sound from one of the dying arrow worms that Jason had smashed mid-thorax with the ball bat. The yellow puss that was its life's blood ran in rivers from its wound.

I shivered. For all the world, this little dying monster sounded like a wounded kitten. We took two steps back involuntarily. I suddenly felt sorry for this beast; although I knew that it would have ripped the flesh from my bones in a second. I looked at Jason, and his look of utter pity summed up the exact way I felt.

I turned to Buddy, and once again my old friend had read my mind.

"We have to put the poor thing out of its misery," he stated flatly. He raised his foot and put his full weight on the creature's skull. The beast let out one long last squeal that seemed to echo for an hour in the mineshaft before it faded away. There was a sickening squish, and the then those silvery eyes went dark.

My chest felt heavy, and I quickly moved the beam of the flashlight so that it didn't illuminate my face.

Jason and Buddy now stowed their weapons and added the light of their flashlights to mine. It was enough to illuminate the small area. The shaft was only about ten feet wide by eight feet high. Arrow worm silk was everywhere. It was like being inside a huge feathery bubble. Dried-out husks of the worm's prey were entombed along the walls.

The swarm's means of survival looked to have been waiting till nightfall, leaping from the hole leading to the mine, grabbing whatever prey wandered by, and then wrapping it in a cocoon and securing it on the lair's walls with silk. Then they could take their leisure coming back to devour the life from their victims with those terrible jaws.

There were all manner of animal and fowl husks secured to the wall; everything from desert foxes to wild goats. There must have been hundreds.

Jason let out a squeak as he pointed to the mummified husk of Sally's tourist hanging on the wall. The look of pain and fear on his petrified old face was more than I could stand.

"He never even had time to pull up his pants," Jason noted flatly.

There was a whining behind us, and we all gratefully turned away from the horrific tapestry. Spooner was rolling on the ground, struggling to get free of the silk that held him tight. Buddy knelt down and ripped the pup's bonds free. Spooner barked happily and gave the Big Guy a lick from his chin to the tip of his nose.

"You're welcome, old boy!" He grinned.

"So what now?" Jason questioned.

I looked up and down the shaft and pointed away from the carnage. "If my bearings are straight, that's the way that leads toward the beginning of the mineshaft near the pirate's castle."

"So this bend here is where the shaft probably passes closest to the temple?"

"Yes, which means the corner that you backed the swarm into, is probably the only entrance to the temple."

We made our way over the scattered carcasses and sticky puss, and tried to gaze past the darkness of the temple entrance to the shadows behind.

Buddy carried the thankful Spooner, who didn't want to get any closer to his prospective diners than he had to. The ragged black hole in the side of the shaft seemed to have evolved naturally from the shifting sticky, Aruba sand. A foul wind was whistling through it.

"Well, that explains why the swarm only started appearing outside recently," I surmised. "This hole has probably only existed for a few months"

"Some of the swarm must have come through when it first opened up and then, for some reason, couldn't get back to the rest of their hive. They basically got trapped outside the temple."

Jason gulped audibly. "Are you saying that there are more of those things than what we just fought off?"

Buddy finished, "Yeah, probably thousands."

I frowned. "And the rest of the hive is still in there somewhere."

We all stared apprehensively into the dark hole.

"Hey, can we throw the dog in first again?" Jason queried.

Buddy squeezed Spooner tightly. "How about we throw your ass in first instead?"

"I'll go," I grimaced, shining my flashlight into the hole. "After all, how many more of those things can there actually be?"

CHAPTER 55

▼

I could see practically nothing when I stuck my head through the fissure; it looked like just one big, low-ceilinged cavern. The smooth rock roof was no more than two feet above my head, and the sand-covered floor was about ten feet below. I could see the ugly-ass *zemis* sticking out of the sand about fifteen yards in. There was no sign of the arrow worms. The place looked completely empty.

I was about to pull my body the rest of the way through when a familiar voice from behind me made me freeze in my crouch.

"What's the matter, Saint Kristopher, the sea chiggers getting to you?"

Jones Jenkins and his absurdly red face were leering at us from beyond the carcasses of the dead arrow worms.

I grabbed my machete, and looked over at Buddy and Jason to grab their weapons, but they were furiously shaking their heads.

As I pulled myself up to a standing position where I could see better, I understood why. Five paces behind Jenkins were Dr. Blakely and Luu. Blakely had her spear gun pointed at my sweet Lil's head, and Luu had a knife to Otis's throat. Jenkins was brandishing his pistol at us.

"I'm sorry, Master Kris," Otis choked out the words. "I had the message sheet up on the wall of the castle ruins when they came up. I thought I was well hidden, but this ruffian sneaked around behind me and surprised me."

Buddy and I hadn't seen Luu since the explosion of the *Sweet Desperation*, and we were both repulsed that the monster on the outside now matched the monster within.

Most of his red hair had been singed off, and his skin was blackened, cracked, and peeling. The layer beneath was a bloody mess that would scar horribly. It would all peel eventually like leprosy. His right ear was totally melted away, and part of his mouth was permanently atrophied, causing a creepy half-grin.

I shook away my shock over Luu and focused on Lil. "Are you okay, Lil?"

She grimaced in Blakely's direction. "I'm peachy, but I'd be doing a lot better if this bitch would point her stick someplace else."

Jenkins smiled broadly, "It appears as if I have the upper hand once again."

"Don't bet on it," I sneered. "Buddy, hand me the *zemís*."

He momentarily looked confused, then immediately caught on. He faked a handoff to me by pulling his flashlight quickly from his belt and handing it to me. I held it low and at an angle out of Jenkins's sight.

"I still have the *zemís*, and you need it to get into the temple."

Jenkins clucked, "My dear boy, we are going to have to send you back to kindergarten. I have your wife, and your friend. That makes two. You have the Bagua *zemís*; that's one. Two doesn't equal one in any equation."

I quickly poked the flashlight into the hole from where I had just had my head. "Not this time, Jenkins, on the other side of this wall is a bottomless pit that you are going to have to rappel down to get to the temple. If I drop the Bagua *zemís*, it will shatter on the stone floor of the pit a thousand feet below!"

"You're full of shit!" Jenkins muttered apprehensively.

It was a bluff, a bold-faced lie, but it was the only card I had. I looked at the pale faces of my friends and gave them a knowing look.

Buddy missed it, but Jason locked onto what I wanted him to do immediately.

"Are you fucking insane, Grantford?" He bellowed. "We worked too damn hard getting this far to throw it all away! Hand over the *zemís*; I'm sure we can cut a deal with these guys. Working together, we could find the treasure and split it fifty-fifty."

Buddy looked at Jason as if he had lost his mind, until he kicked him in the calf, sight unseen; then it dawned on him what we were doing.

"Um yeah, right, Kris," he muttered. "I'm tired of killer worms and sea lice, and getting hit in the head all the time. Let's join forces with these guys and split everything up equal."

Jenkins grunted, "Listen to your friends, Saint Kristopher, you drop that *zemís* and no matter what you do, either your wife or your friend will die, if not both."

My eyes narrowed. "You want to join forces, so be it, but you have to let Lil and Otis go free."

"Don't do it, Kris!" Lil screamed. "This asshole will slaughter you the first opportunity he gets."

My heart went out to her, but my first priority was her and Otis's safety. The Krewe of Jupiter could take care of itself.

Jenkins rubbed his red chin. "Very well, but just as a little insurance, I'm going to have Dr. Blakely take them at spear point back to the ruins of the pirate castle. If for some reason, I don't return in an hour. She will make a shish kebab of your pretty wife and the old man."

Blakely spoke up harshly, "But, Jones, there are bound to be runes that need translating in there. You need me!"

He smirked, "We have the Bagua *zemís*; it will get us into the Arawak temple, and therefore I will not require your services until we are ready to tackle the third temple."

"You bastard!" she growled, "You better not try to double-cross me."

"My dear Dr. Blakely, do you really think I would walk away from the third temple and its horde of diamonds, for the stash of emeralds hidden here? No, my dear, I will not be happy until I—we have the last *zemís* and all three treasures."

Jenkins turned back to me. "The ball is in your court, Mr. Grant."

I hung my head; I had no choice. "Let them go, and let's go get this goddamned treasure so we can get out of here."

"Here take Spooner, too," Buddy handed the beagle off to Lil.

Blakely gave Jenkins a long sideways glance and hustled Lil and Otis back down the mineshaft in the direction they had come.

I looked over at Luu who was still grinning stupidly. I suddenly realized that with his deformed mouth, it was the only way he could look.

Jason couldn't pass up the opportunity to berate the man who had already tried to kill him three times. "Hey Luu, why so happy, man? I hope you're not too burned up over what happened, you bastard! Let's let bygones be bygones; why don't you give me some skin? Oops I forgot; you don't have any left!"

With a garbled roar, Luu came clamoring over the arrow worm carcasses toward him, squirting soft putrid goo all over his legs as he groped for Jason.

Jason leaned into me and whispered, "I hope to hell you were really bluffing about that bottomless pit." Then he grabbed the flashlight, and dove through just in time before Luu got his hands on him. Luu never even paused as he clambered through the crevice after him.

I looked down at Jenkins, who'd picked up Luu's dropped supply pack. Jenkins motioned at us with his pistol, "Gentlemen, once again, after you."

I grabbed my machete and stuck it in my belt. I ducked through the crack before Jenkins could yell for me to leave it behind. Buddy shrugged at Jenkins and jumped through the hole behind me.

CHAPTER 56

▼

It was an easy drop to the sand floor ten feet below. The sand was actually much deeper than I had expected, a good three feet deep at least. It was like trudging through snow. I quickly retrieved the *zemis* before Jenkins realized that I hadn't been holding it all along.

Now that I was inside the huge cavern, I could get a better look. The room appeared to be round, at least several hundred yards across. The rock ceiling twelve feet above my head was perfectly smooth, without a blemish. It reminded me of the shiny finish of those rocks I used to get from the rock-polisher machines when I was a kid. Other than the sand and the ceiling and the walls, there appeared to be nothing else in the enormous room. Well, except Luu trudging through the silica after Jason about halfway across the chamber.

"Geronimo!" Buddy did a huge cannonball into the sand behind me, causing it to fly up and sting my eyes. I put my hand over my face until it cleared.

When it did, I looked up into the furious face of Jones Jenkins staring through the hole. "You son of a bitch, you lied to me. That's no bottomless pit!"

I smirked waving the *zemis* up at him, "Hey, we're down here, the Bagua *zemis* is down here, and somewhere down here is the entrance to the Arawak temple. Are you going to bitch, or are you going to get your sorry ass down here so we can find this thing before Blakely's time limit runs out?"

Jenkins grumbled but leaped down to the cavern floor, being careful to keep the pistol pointed in my direction.

I heard Jason's panting voice from across the cavern, "Hey, a little help here, guys. Mr. Night of the Living Dead is catching up to me!"

We went trudging across the cavern floor as fast as we could in the deep sand.

He was in the middle of the cavern backing slowly away from the wheezing Luu, who was brandishing the knife he had used on Otis. He had a good ten feet between him and Luu, as we approached. Luu was about done for, with the severity of his wounds, the last thing he had needed was the total exhaustion of chasing Jason through the deep sand. We slowed, as it appeared that Jason wasn't in any immediate danger.

Then he tripped over something in the sand and fell backward onto his ass.

Luu summoned the last of his energy and with a roar jumped at Jason across the last few feet!

Jason squeaked and tried to crab away. I made it to Luu just as he started swinging the knife wildly at him. I swung my machete and cleanly took off Luu's knife hand at the wrist!

He screamed and grabbed his spurting stump of an arm. You change a man's perspective real quick when you cut something off. Luu lost all interest in pursuing Jason, and curled into a fetal position nursing his stump.

Jenkins came panting up behind us. "Oh quit yowling, you big cry baby, and put pressure on it!"

Jenkins turned to Jason. "What did you trip over?"

He shrugged, scooting as far away from Luu's severed hand as possible, "I dunno, but it was hard, whatever it was."

We helped Jason to his feet and we retraced his steps to where he originally fell. There was a small black tip of wood poking out of the sand.

Jenkins waved his pistol at us. "What are you waiting for, dig!"

Between us, it didn't take very long to uncover the burned-out remains of the stump of the huge Arawak tree. Just like the first tree, there was a cubbyhole key slot for the *zemís*. There were also runes all across the face of the stump.

I sneered in Jenkins's direction. "Too bad you sent Dr. Blakely away, since she is the only one who could have translated this. There is no telling what kind of Pandora's Box will open when I insert the Bagua *zemís*."

"Just shut up and do it," Jenkins hissed.

I took a deep breath, and inserted the *zemís* into the opening. Once again, the black wood closed in around my hand. I scrambled up onto the stump, determined not to have a repeat of what happened last time. A rumbling and a dull whine commenced beneath our feet.

Suddenly Buddy, Jason, and Jenkins seemed to float to my right! I looked over at the fetal Luu, and he too seemed to be moving across the sand, even in his prone position. I realized what was happening. The entire room was spinning round and round the hub of the stump, and it was picking up speed!

We all looked at each other, but no one knew what to do. The centrifugal force was so strong that they were thrown to the ground. I screamed to them, but the roar of the hidden machinery and the generated wind tore my voice away and threw it to the far edge of the cavern.

They were flashing by so fast now that they were just blurs. Sand was being pushed out toward the edges of the giant wheel. Suddenly there was a new groaning sound. The floor closest to the stump dropped down and away and I realized that the entire room was turning into a big funnel, and the spinning sand was becoming a huge whirlpool!

My friends, Jenkins, and Luu were fighting to keep their heads above the shifting silica whirlpool as it pulled them closer to the center and downward with every orbit they made!

From my perch on the stump, I looked down over the edge and into the abyss that the sand whirlpool was feeding. My stomach sank as I realized that what I had told Jenkins was coming true; they were all being inexorably drawn into the center of the whirlpool, and into a bottomless pit!

CHAPTER 57

▼

I could only watch helplessly as my friends and enemies fell through the bottom of the vortex. I had no rope or anchor to toss, and the cursed stump of the Arawak tree still held my hand at the wrist. I screamed in vain as each of them disappeared down the dark drain hole.

Ever so slowly, the great machine wound down. All the sand was gone from the great stone funnel. More of the stone hieroglyphs were revealed on the floor, just as they were at the entrance to the Caribe temple.

As the funnel ground to a stop, the tree opened up once again and released my hand. I left the Bagua *zemís* in the cubbyhole in the side of tree. I dared not remove the key from the slot, for fear the funnel would close again and trap my friends forever.

I had somehow managed to hold onto my flashlight and shone it down into the great darkness below. "Buddy, Jason, can you hear me?"

No reply.

The flashlight revealed nothing but the remains of the narrow stone stairs leading round and round the stump of the tree down into the abyss.

I fought the wave of emotion that washed over me. I had lost too much in my life, to lose my two best friends as well. I had to go after them. I choked back my fear and began scrambling down the stairs.

The stairs were in much worse shape than the stairs at the Caribe temple had been. In fact, only about every third step was in place, and they were sometimes hanging by a thread over the dark pit. I tried to make my way as quickly as possible, but any single misstep and I would tumble in after my friends.

As I followed the shaky steps round and round and down the tree stump, I realized what had happened here. At the Caribe tree, the temple itself had pretty much survived the eons intact, at least until our visit anyway. Here at the Arawak temple, the original battle must have been much fiercer. The original temple would have been an exact replica of the Caribe temple, but the entire underground temple itself had been destroyed in the Arawak priestess's battle so long ago with her followers. The roots of the great tree itself were still intact, but the temple was nothing but dust and rubble on the floor hundreds of feet below. I was lucky the trembling remains of the steps were still here for me to follow.

As I moved farther down the stump in this great cavernous chamber, the ancient root structure of the tree branched out in a thousand different directions all around me. My eyes searched frantically for my friends, hoping that they had lucked out and caught one of the roots in their fall. There was no sign of them.

A dark dread came over me as the stairs left the great root ball and continued down around the taproot. The whole root structure of the tree was shaped like a giant mushroom floating in the abyss, and I had just left the cap behind.

I caught my breath and paused for just a moment at the unexpected beauty that suddenly surrounded me. Mineral deposits had seeped down over the thousands of years and formed beautiful sparkling stalactites that hung all over the base of the root ball. There were thousands of them, some no longer than a couple of feet, and many that must have weighed several tons. They sparkled with traces of gold deposits that had escaped from the veins the old mines tapped. It was truly gorgeous, like having a mouse's eye view from under the Christmas tree.

I hurried down the taproot as quickly as possible as its size slowly diminished. I had hoped that the taproot would end on the floor of this great empty chamber, but it did not. As the root shrank with every orbit I made around the stairs, I still couldn't make out the floor far below. It was like being in outer space, nothing but blackness in all directions.

Then I was at the end; the stairs merely crumbled into nothingness. Hanging from the very tip of the root was the Marocoti *zemís*. It was an ugly little bastard, a representation of the ancient religion's harvest god. It held a sickle in one black hand and a bundle of grain of some kind in the other. It just dangled there in the darkness, the root of all evil.

I looked forlornly into the darkness below. I picked up a small fragment of one of the stone steps and dropped it over the edge. A good twenty seconds passed before I heard it hit the floor of the cavern far beneath me. There was no way that they could have survived that kind of fall.

Then I heard a hoarse whisper from out in the darkness. "Grantford, is that you?"

Startled I swung the light out into the darkness. It immediately reflected back a dazzling green flash that came from thousands of sparkling strands of web silk. It was a great arrow worm's web that was attached to the edges of the root ball and hung down below the taproot like a huge inverted parachute. Emeralds sparkled everywhere in the webbing.

"Turn off the light; turn off the light!" Jenkins squealed. He was closest to me, no more than ten feet out into the web. My flashlight beam also briefly lit on Buddy and Jason, about fifty feet out in the great web, and Luu, who appeared to be unconscious, was farthest out at about sixty. They were all stuck fast to the great safety net that had caught them and kept them from plunging to the floor of the cavern and their death.

At Jenkins's yell I impulsively flipped off the beam, but not before the light caught on something that would cause me to wake screaming in the night for years to come. The light reflected off thousands of translucent cocoons. Each held a single silver eyed arrow worm, hanging just feet above my friend's heads. They appeared dormant, unmoving, each dangling from the root ball far above.

I suddenly realized that this was a hatchling nest. The larva-stage arrow worms probably dropped from the root ball on silent silk, wove their opaque shells, and settled in for the long transformation process. I also understood the necessity of the web my friends were stuck in. It was meant to catch and hold food for the hungry adolescents when they emerged. From the brief glimpse I got, these looked ready to burst at anytime.

"Get me the fuck out of here!" Jenkins whispered.

Buddy hissed in the darkness, "They are definitely attracted to any struggling or sound. Jenkins was screaming like a girl when we first hit the web. Every yelp he made caused the little monsters in these cocoons to roll and wiggle.

"Yeah," Jason added carefully. "All their little silver eyes were turned toward Jenkins. We finally got him to hush before he brought the whole brood down on our heads."

"Luu's pack," Jenkins moaned, "It has a rope in it."

I strained my eyes in the darkness, until I spotted Luu's pack; thankfully, it was only a couple of feet out into the web.

"I can get the pack," I whispered, "but it's going to jiggle the web and probably wake the whole nest."

"Who gives a shit?" Jenkins cried, "You'll still have time to get me out before they get me!"

"Yes, but no one else, you selfish bastard," I sneered. "You'll be the last one I'll pull out of there."

As usual, Buddy had a plan.

"You need a distraction, Kris," he surmised. "Something that will take their attention away from our escape; you have to cut the Marocoti *zemís* free."

"But, Buddy," I cringed, "don't you remember what happened in the Caribe temple? The last remains of the Arawak tree will shrink and disappear."

"Exactly!" He whispered. "Their entire web is tied to the root structure. When the root shrinks, their nest will collapse. They'll be more concerned with saving themselves than coming after us."

Jason grunted, "But if the web falls, we fall too!"

Buddy sighed, "Not if Kris moves quickly. The web should fall in pieces, once he cuts the *zemís* free. He should have time to retrieve the rope, tie the end to the taproot, and throw the other end to us. We'll all have to try to hold on and scramble up the rope at the same time."

"What about Luu?" I hissed, "He's unconscious. How do we get him out of there?"

"Leave the poor son of a bitch!" Jenkins wailed. "Just save me!"

Just at that second my question was answered for me. Luu regained consciousness and let out a horrid series of screams! I had to risk it; I had no choice. I flipped on the flashlight in his direction.

The cocoons closest to Luu were gyrating wildly, and I could see them start to split as their hungry seeds were drawn to prey. We all whispered in desperation for Luu to shut up, but he was insane with pain and confusion. He continued to scream and thrash about wildly. The stench of vanilla was overpowering.

Hundreds of arrow worms were dropping from their shells onto the web and scurrying toward their first meal. The web vibrated like a plucked string, and it seemed to set off a chain reaction, sending multitudes wriggling out of their shells. The early hatchers started devouring the screaming Luu!

It was more than I could stand. I flicked the light off, stuck the flashlight in my pants, and hurriedly turned my attention to the Marocoti *zemís*. I used the machete that I had tucked into my belt to hack at the taproot above the *zemís*' head.

In less than thirty seconds the *zemís* was free, and as the echoes of Luu's dying screams faded away, they were replaced by a far more ominous rumble. The great Arawak tree had started to shrink away forever!

I didn't know where the ancient guardians were, I dared not stop to turn on the light. I hastily grabbed in the darkness for Luu's pack. Just as Jenkins had said, the rope was in there, and thank God it was at least a hundred-foot coil.

The taproot was quickly shrinking upward above me, and what was left of the stairs, with no support, were disintegrating under my feet! I stuck the *zemís* in my shirt and draped the coil of rope over my shoulder. I had to jump up to catch the very end of the taproot as the step I was on fell out from under me! I caught it with one hand and struggled to hang onto it as it flicked and whipped about in my hand like a snake as it shrank.

I somehow managed to get a second hand on the collapsing root structure, and with much effort was able to get a passable knot around the taproot above an offshoot that would hold it secure.

I held on with one hand and managed to turn the flashlight back on in the direction of my friends. My heart turned cold as I realized that the taproot had already shrunk upward enough to put me twenty feet above them! I had to make my throw now or I wouldn't have enough rope to reach them.

The web itself was falling apart like a massive suspension bridge. Great twangs echoed throughout the cavern as foundation web strands the size of a grown man's leg let loose their grip.

The stalactites from the root ball were falling and raining down on us like sparkling missiles!

I had only one opportunity to throw the rope to my friends, and I made it true. The end of the rope actually hit Buddy in the face! They both caught hold and were dragged free from their sticky bonds as the taproot continued to shrink upward.

The arrow worms finally turned their attention from Luu's dead husk, when they realized that their upcoming meals were getting away. With a tremendous surge, the swarm came bounding across the straggly remains of the web after us!

Jenkins was screaming, "Don't forget me, oh God, please don't forget me!"

Buddy was able to reach down with one hand and grab hold of Jenkins's belt as they dragged by.

The web was collapsing under the weight of a thousand ancient guardians! The tip of the swarm was within five feet of Jenkins when a huge two-ton stalactite fell from above and took out half of them! A huge gush of yellow goo exploded all over Jenkins's and Buddy's legs, as we continued to be dragged upward like a runaway freight elevator!

Hundreds of worms fell into the abyss as the web collapsed behind us, but others managed to get a web strand of their own in time to keep them dangling from the taproot. They begin climbing their lifelines toward the smell of the blood of their siblings.

"We can't just wait for the taproot to pull us up!" I yelled down to my friends. "Eventually the root is going to disappear completely, and we'll plummet like rocks!"

Jason looked down. "Before that happens, the killer maggots will catch up with us."

"We have to climb up into the roots, and get ahead of the shrinking taproot." I gritted my teeth. "Jason, I'll help you climb, since it's going to be tough for you with your bad arm. Buddy, Jenkins is going to have to climb the rope like the rest of us. You are going to need both hands to climb!"

Jenkins was squalling and wailing, "I can't, I can't. Please, I don't want to die!"

Buddy snarled at Jenkins, "You've got a choice, climb or I let you go and you can try to fly!"

Jenkins agreed hysterically through his streaming tears.

The taproot had us rising so fast now that my ears were popping! We began climbing slowly, hand over hand. I worked my way up a little, then grabbed onto Jason's collar to help him climb up to meet me. At first only I was beyond the rope, and up into the shrinking root structure. It was like trying to climb through a can of worms! The offshoots we held just vanished right in our hands. It was all a matter of timing; we had to be careful to grab the larger roots that still had a few seconds of life left in them.

Soon Jason and Buddy were in the root structure as well, and with a lot of coaxing, Jenkins. As an afterthought, I yelled down to Buddy to untie the rope and bring it along. We hurried as fast as we could. I could see the opening into the funnel cavern twenty feet above my head, but the remaining arrow worms were still hot on our tails!

I pulled myself through the opening at the bottom of the funnel and helped Jason, Buddy, and Jenkins through.

"Hurry, everyone, get up on the stump!" I screamed above the horrible sound of the retracting root structure. "Let's just hope this machinery still works or we are going to have company!"

With everyone on the stump, I reached down into the cubbyhole to remove the Bagua *zemís* from the stump. I was looking right into the silver soulless eyes of the first of the arrow worms no more than ten feet below. I pulled the *zemís* from the stump and the room began to spin again in the opposite direction, faster and faster! Just as the first of the arrow worms stuck their heads through the hole at the base of the stump, the great funnel snapped level again, once more making the big room one flat cavern. The worms were cleanly sliced in half!

Above us, there was an ominous sound that we hadn't heard before. The ceiling started spinning now, and with every spin, it dropped closer to the floor like a big corkscrew!

"Damn!" I yelled above the din, "Removing the *zemís* set off another mechanism!"

"We've got to get out of here!" Buddy bellowed.

Just as each of us jumped off the stump to trudge through the sand toward the hole between the mine and the temple, the taproot finally disappeared, taking the remains of the stump with it! This left a huge hole in the middle of the cavern, and my blood ran cold as the remaining arrow worms came scurrying over the side.

"Run!" I screamed. "Run for the crevice. The ceiling will close over it in no time!"

We all ran for our escape, with the arrow worms close behind! I quickly tied the rope to my machete to use as a grapple for the hole, ten feet above our heads.

"I go first!" Jenkins demanded.

"Not a goddamned chance!" Buddy sneered.

"Jason, you're the lightest, go!" I commanded.

Jason scurried up to rope and into the mine.

"Go, Buddy!" I demanded.

"Not this time, old friend," he grinned crookedly. "I will not fall for that again."

"Oh, for God's sake," Jenkins yelled and grabbed the rope. "We don't have time for this!"

He scurried up the rope and into the mine.

I looked at the advancing swarm; they were no more than twenty feet away.

"I've got the rear, Kris. This is what I do, now go!"

I squeezed my big friend on the shoulder and scurried up the rope. The advancing ceiling had already covered up the first foot of the hole.

"Come on, Buddy, come on!" I yelled down into the darkness. "The hole is almost closed!"

I dimly heard three shots from the .38 below. Didn't he know a gun would have no effect on hundreds of individual worms? The hole was now halfway closed by the spinning, dropping ceiling!

"Come on, old friend," I whispered.

Buddy's head popped through the hole, soon followed by the rest of him.

"Get back, everyone, get back!" he screamed. The hole was three-quarters closed, but the arrow worms were still trying to get through.

"Shoot them; shoot them!" Jenkins squealed.

Jason grabbed the aluminum bat he had left in the mine and beat at the stragglers rabidly trying to get through the crack.

We watched as the spinning roof descended, removing several heads from the struggling worms, and then the hole was completely closed. The machinery gave a great screech as the ceiling spun to the ground, with no support structure underneath from the Arawak tree roots, the great cavern floor fell away!

"We better get out of here," I mumbled. "This whole place is going to fall into the cavern!"

We ran for the guardian's entrance into the mine and kept running when we hit the desert floor. Behind us with a great roar, the entire Hooiberg sank from sight into the ground!

CHAPTER 58

▼

Buddy bounced us all over the road as he sped our rental car through the night toward Bushiribana on the northeast coast and the ruins of the old pirate castle. We were now two hours past the deadline that Jenkins had given Blakely. I could only pray that Frances Blakely hadn't done something stupid.

I rode shotgun, and poor Jason was stuck in the backseat with Jenkins. Buddy had managed to strong-arm Jenkins's pistol away from him, and without it he had turned into a blubbering wimp. He finally stopped sobbing about almost getting killed and started moaning about his lost fortune.

"All those beautiful fucking emeralds gone, gone. I can't believe it, buried under tons of stone, way too deep to ever excavate."

"Shut up, you big baby!" Jason snarled for about the twentieth time.

I turned in my seat and glared at Jenkins who shrank into the upholstery. "Doesn't it bother you one damn bit that we also buried another human being under all that rock, you bastard?"

Jenkins just sniffed, and tried to stay out of range of my fists if I decided to use them on him. He wasn't worth the effort.

"Yeah," Buddy glanced in the rearview mirror. "By the way, you're friggin welcome for us saving your sorry ass."

Jenkins ignored him and focused his attention on the countryside, whizzing past under the full moon that was now high in the sky.

I stared hard into the darkness ahead, willing Lil and Otis to be okay.

"Take a look at that!" Jason pointed from the backseat. "That must be it."

Around the curve ahead, huge stone ruins were outlined against the sky. We pulled up and parked. There was no sound except for the pounding surf behind us. No lights played in the ruins.

We got out of the car and moved closer to the castle shell. We could see Otis's message sheet flapping from the castle wall. In red spray paint on the white sheet was painted: We are in the temple. We have the *zemis*; bring Lil unharmed if you ever want to see your precious treasure. It seemed somewhat anti-climatic for everything we had gone through this night.

"I don't like this," Buddy mumbled as we entered the ruins.

"Yeah, something smells fishy around here," I commented.

"And I'm betting it's Dr. Blakely!" Jason commented with a crooked grin.

A shadow stepped out from behind a stone wall. "That wasn't very nice, Mr. Bonnet," Blakely said. "Maybe I should give you a personal tour, and you may change your mind about that."

"Not on your life, sister," he muttered.

The shadow moved closer and the stark moon backlit the perfect glacial figure of Dr. Frances Blakely.

I sent a severe look in Jason's direction, and then turned my attention back to Blakely. "Where're my wife and Otis, Blakely?"

"Awwww," she patronized, "don't you remember what Jonesy said? If I'm not back in an hour, kill them!"

"That was," she faked looking at a nonexistent watch, "nearly three and a half hours ago. They are swimming with the little fishes now."

"You bitch!" I yelled and roared toward her.

Buddy held me back just in time as Blakely raised the spear gun in front of her. Another two inches and I would have run myself through on its tip.

She smirked, "Do you really think I would be stupid enough to use my only bargaining chip? I figured Jenkins would screw this up somehow, and now he has. Your wife and friend are bound and gagged nearby. You play nice and I may even let them live."

Jenkins piped up, "The big guy has a gun, Blakely, and Grant has the one they took from me."

"You pathetic piece of shit!" she sneered at Jenkins. "I'm betting that you also let them take the emeralds and the Marocoti *zemis*, too?"

Jenkins stuttered, "Now just wait a minute, I'm in charge here. The emeralds were a lost cause, and Grant has the *zemis*."

"Not anymore, you arrogant asshole; I'm tired of taking orders from you. From now on, you listen to me! If you disagree, I'll be happy to help you get the point," She motioned with the spear gun.

"No problem, no problem," Jenkins simpered.

"Good, then get the guns and the *zemís* from them."

Jenkins moved in our direction.

"Not so fast, Blakely!" I grated. "I don't give a flying fuck about the treasures or your godforsaken book. You can have them. But if you think I'm going to let you walk away with the key to everything you want, without even knowing if Lil and Otis are alive; you're crazy!"

"I don't think you have much of a position to bargain from," she hissed.

"Don't I?" I paused. "There are three of us, and you only have your damn spear gun. You may shoot one of us, but I can guarantee that the other two will take you out before you get a chance to reload!"

She paused, "Very well. I'll take you to your wife and friend. Once you see that they are well, you hand over the guns and the *zemís*."

"Agreed."

"Please, you first," She pointed us around the stone wall.

We walked fewer than twenty paces, and there on the ground, bound and gagged, were Lil and Otis. Spooner was sitting between them protectively, and let out a happy bark when he saw us.

I bent down and removed Lil's gag. I held my sweet wife's face in my hands once again, and kissed her tender lips soft and long.

I reached over and removed Otis's gag, too. "Are the two of you okay?"

"We are a little bruised up, and Lil took a slip in the mine and sprained her ankle, but other than that we are fine."

I went to remove their other bonds.

"Not so fast, Mr. Grant," Blakely berated. "We had a deal, give Jonesy your guns, and I'll take the *zemís*."

Jenkins looked at her crossly, "I can get the guns and the *zemís*, too."

"Not a chance, you weasel," she sneered.

I stood and carefully removed the *zemís* from my shirt and handed it to her.

"Now give Jonesy back his pop gun."

I slowly removed Jones's nasty little pistol from my belt, but instead of handing it to him, I tossed it to him.

"Goddamn it!" He squeaked, butter-fingering the gun from hand to hand until he dropped it.

When he bent to pick it up, Spooner took his chance! The brave little dog was all over Jenkins like white on rice, sinking his teeth into the meat of Jenkins's arm.

"Get it off; get it off!" he squealed, spinning in circles like a madman. Spooner had a death grip on the red man's arm. He had the pistol in the same hand as the arm Spooner had hold of. Thankfully, Jenkins never got his wits about him enough to switch the gun to his left hand, or Spooner would have been a goner.

"Oh, for God's sake!" Blakely sighed. "Hold still you idiot." She raised the spear gun and tried to focus on the little dog, as Jenkins slung him this way and that in a mad attempt to dislodge him.

She took aim and fired.

"No!" Jason yelled, and pushed Jenkins from behind, who stumbled to his knees.

The spear literally left a burn trail across Spooner's fur where it grazed him, but it didn't break the skin. With a yelp, the beagle let go. Unfortunately, those who were still bound behind Spooner had no option to avoid the lethal spear. It hit Otis with a sickening thunk.

Otis let out a scream of anguish, and then was quiet.

"Oh God no!" Jason screamed, and rushed to his old friend's side.

Jenkins cursed, got to his feet, and pointed the pistol at Spooner to blow him away.

There was an audible *click* behind his right ear.

"Not so fast, Jenkins," Buddy poked the muzzle of the .38 into the back of Jenkins's skull.

Blakely was quickly loading another spear.

"Hold it there, Blakely," I cautioned, "or Buddy will give Jenkins another hole in his head."

"Like I give a goddamn!" she hissed, never stopping. "Blow his good-for-nothing brains all over the rocks for all I care."

Jenkins made a mewing sound.

"Look, let's use our heads here," I cautioned. "You want the *zemis* so you can get to the third temple. We just want to take care of our friend."

Blakely furrowed her brow in deliberation. "Fine, I have what I came for. Let's get out of here, Jenkins."

Blakely backed out of the ruins. Jenkins scampered after her on shaky legs.

Buddy and I rushed over to join Jason with Otis. I hastily untied Lil, holding her tightly, filled with ecstasy and anguish.

The spear had entered Otis's thigh at an angle. The shaft didn't seem to have hit any major arteries, but he was still losing a lot of blood. We had to get him to a hospital, and quick, or he would bleed to death.

"Buddy, help me get him to the car!" I went to grip our old friend under the armpits. It was just then that we heard the four shots. An engine started up down below the ruins, and headlights swept over us before a car sped away.

Jason was near hysterics, "Damn it, Buddy, why did you leave the keys in the car?"

"I didn't. Otis must have left the keys in the rental he drove out here earlier!"

"Why would they take the car?" Jason cried in anguish. "The *Nefarious* is anchored just offshore."

"Simple," I grimaced, hugging my Lil tightly. "They wanted to eliminate any hope of us following them."

Buddy shook his head grimly. "Yeah, and I'm guessing those four shots took care of the tires on our rental car."

Gathered in a circle around our fallen friend, we could only pray for a miracle now. I hoped like hell that my skepticism about miracles wouldn't turn out to be true.

CHAPTER 59

▼

It was well past dawn, and the Lady Orleans had been in the air for several hours now, speeding toward the home of the Patwah temple. I let my mind wander back to the events of the last few hours.

Buddy had done everything he could to stem Otis's bleeding while Otis drifted in and out of consciousness. Jason and Lil sat close by his side. I had climbed up high in the ruins of the pirate castle, looking for the lights of a nearby village, or a boat, or any sign of life. But on this desolate side of the island, there were none. The *Nefarious* was still anchored out beyond the breakers, but she showed no indication that Blakely and Jenkins were coming back for her. It didn't surprise me. Now that Blakely was in charge, all she cared about was getting that book.

We searched the beach and found the spare inflatable lifeboat that Jenkins had used to come ashore and the rigid lifeboat that Jason had beached here.

Our only hope was to get Otis to the *Nefarious*, and make our way to Oranjestad as quickly as possible. We carefully carried our old friend down to the beach, and gently laid him in the inflatable lifeboat, as Jason's rigid boat had no engine. Lil held Otis's head in her lap as Buddy started the engine. There was no way all of us were going to fit in the small inflatable.

We all knew that time was a precious commodity for Otis. We couldn't risk expending the minutes it would take to make a second trip in the inflatable. I insisted that Buddy take the helm and go with Lil and Otis to the *Nefarious*. He argued that I was the seaman, not him. I could see that old fear of the water in the back of his eyes. I wouldn't back down, however; he was the closest thing we had to a medic, and he needed to stay with Otis at all times.

I had looked to Lil; she had grown up in Charleston and had been around boats all her life, but she had never piloted one the size of the *Nefarious* before. There had been no hesitation in her voice; she would do what it took to get Otis safely back to Oranjestad and the hospital.

They puttered away from shore, trying to be as careful as possible over the breakers. Jason, Spooner, and I watched helplessly from the beach as Buddy and Lil struggled to get Otis aboard ship. We caught our breaths sharply as they almost dropped him once halfway up the side of the trawler yacht. Then, he was safe and sound on the deck. I saw Lil run to the pilothouse, and suddenly the *Nefarious* was ablaze in lights and the echo of her anchor chain rising clinked to us over the waves.

With a great rumble the twin engines grumbled to life, and we watched as Lil expertly turned the huge boat and sped off toward Oranjestad.

Jason, Spooner, and I were left alone with nothing but the crashing waves and endless Aruban wind whistling in our ears. I looked back toward the ruins of the ancient pirate castle. You could almost see the ghost of Stede Bonnet perched upon the great stone wall, watching his dark ship's namesake speeding off toward the lights of the capital city.

Lights! Jason pointed to the road, and then I could see it too. Headlights were coming our way and fast. I wondered if it was Blakely and Jenkins returning to finish the grizzly job they had started. I scooped up Spooner, and we slipped down to the road and attempted to merge with the shadows of the divi-divi trees.

As the lights got closer, I could tell from the engine song that it definitely wasn't our rental car; it sounded like a four-wheel drive.

A Jeep! Jason exclaimed, and so it was. As it got closer I could see the worried faces of Ruby and Sally in the front seat. We jumped from our hiding place and flagged them down.

They explained that the implosion of the Hooiberg had shaken the entire island. They had rushed there first hoping to find some sign of us. They said there was nothing there now but a giant sinkhole.

Knowing that Otis had headed to the ruins of the pirate castle, they had sped in our direction. We briefly explained what had happened, and of Buddy and Lil's rush to the hospital. Ruby and Sally confirmed what I had suspected; they would actually get there faster by boat than by car.

We piled into the back of the Jeep, and we sped in the direction of Oranjestad. When we got to the hospital, Otis was already checked in. Buddy and Lil were waiting in the hospital lounge. We rushed in with grim faces and dire questions.

All was well. They had removed the spear, and sealed the wound. They were giving him blood. He was going to be okay.

I turned to my sweet Lil, hugging her tight. Telling her how great she had done, and how much I loved her. She was safe; we had saved her. Buddy beamed from ear to ear.

I looked at her gravely, questioning if she could see that Otis made it back to the States safely. She nodded apprehensively.

I turned to the Krewe of Jupiter. "Boys, we have some unfinished business. I'm guessing that Blakely and Jenkins caught a commercial flight to their final destination. They will get there before us, but now that Lil is safe, we have to do everything we can to take those murdering bastards out of the game."

CHAPTER 60

▼

Jason leaned over my shoulder, breaking my trance. He sported a new cast on his arm that had been reset at the hospital. "So the Big O didn't look half bad when we left, huh?"

"Yep," I agreed, grinning. "He had his color back, and he felt well enough to chastise you for getting him shot."

He made a face, "I didn't get him shot. I was just trying to save friggin' Spooner. I don't know why, the damn dog hates my guts!"

At Jason's mention of his name, Spooner gave a low growl from the nose turret.

Buddy chuckled from the copilot seat, "Well, Jason, sounds like Spooner is a pretty good judge of character."

He popped Buddy on his big meaty shoulder. "You gotta call me Scotch now." Buddy rolled his eyes and tried to return the lick but was limited in his reach by his seat belt.

"One thing disappoints me," Jason stated wistfully, "we didn't see any sign that Uncle Donnie had been anywhere near the Arawak temple."

"We know he had the copy of the journal, he was probably like us and couldn't find a way in."

"Yeah, that hole between the mine and the temple probably only existed a few months. With the original entrance being covered hundreds of years ago, Rhodes would have had no means of getting into the Arawak temple."

"Yeah," I surmised, "he probably tried, gave up, and then made his way to the Patwah temple."

"So where exactly is the Patwah temple?" Jason questioned, being careful to stay out of Buddy's range.

I read the coordinates off to Buddy who plugged them into the GPS: 18 15 N, 77 30 W.

"Jamaica?" He looked up at me.

Jason grunted, "By the time we get there, and get through customs, they will have half a day on us."

Buddy snickered, "Not necessarily, I arranged a little bit of a surprise for them when they land in Kingston. Some old MP friends of mine are based there. They somehow have gotten the idea that Blakely and Jenkins are drug smugglers. That should hold them up for a little while. I specifically recommended a full body cavity search for Jenkins!"

Jason hooted, "Boy would I love to see their faces!"

"They can't detain them indefinitely, but they can sure as hell slow them down."

I grimaced, "Let's just hope that Otis's translation of the journal is more detailed than Blakely's."

"You sound like you have your doubts?"

"Well, Otis's translation for the Patwah temple wasn't exactly a wealth of knowledge. We know that the temple is located high up in the Blue Mountains, in the interior of the island at a place called Ascension Falls, near a natural hot tar pit called the Black Cauldron."

"Geez," Buddy commented, "that's not much to go on. Jamaica's almost the size of New York State."

"Yes and all the major cities are around the coast line. The Blue Mountains take up most of the interior."

"Why do they call them the Blue Mountains?" Jason asked.

"Cause they're blue, dumb ass," Buddy quipped.

"That's Mr. Dumb Ass to you, Buddy Boy," He returned sardonically.

"Actually," I ventured, "it's because they are almost always shrouded by mists that give them their bluish color. They rise steeply and quickly. It's possible to drive from the coast to an elevation of over seven thousand feet in less than an hour!"

"Wow!" Buddy commented. "What do you do, drive straight up?"

"Pretty much," I added. "More than eight-hundred species of plants live there, and two-hundred species of birds. The world's second largest butterfly makes the Blue Mountains its home."

Buddy grunted, "We couldn't get that lucky, that those damn arrow worms turn into butterflies."

"So we don't have much to go on from the translation," Jason stated wistfully. "But we do have my family history, and the legends that Remy shared with us, which Blakely and Jenkins may not have."

"That's all well and good, Scotch Tape," Buddy grunted, "But how does that help us find the temple before Blakely and Jenkins?"

"I'm not sure yet," Jason mumbled to himself, ignoring Buddy. "But I know there is a clue in there somewhere."

I sighed, "Well, regardless, we have a long day ahead of us and none of us have slept for over twenty-four hours. I suggest we get some shut-eye. Buddy, why, don't you take the wheel for the next hour or so while Jason, um, Scotch and I catch a cat nap."

"Me?" He squeaked. "I can't fly the Lady Orleans!"

"Why not?" I grinned. "You're sitting in the copilot's seat."

"I don't have a clue how to fly a plane," he stammered.

"Well, it's high time you learned. I'm not asking you to land her, you big boob. I rigged her with an auto pilot. All you have to do is hold her where she is, and make slight adjustments to the wheel if we start to wander off course from the GPS."

"But I, but I…"

"Good night Buddy Bear, wake me in an hour and a half," I pulled my hat down over my eyes. "We should be getting fairly close by then."

I closed my eyes, and immediately fell asleep.

CHAPTER 61

Buddy woke me up exactly an hour and a half later, all white knuckled and sweaty. He had done a fine job keeping the Lady Orleans on track, but he was a nervous wreck.

We were still about that much time again out of Kingston, and I suggested that he try to get a little sleep. Jason was snoring somewhere back in the first passenger compartment, and we let him be.

Buddy tried to sleep, but he was pretty keyed up. He finally dozed off a half hour later when Spooner crawled up and settled into his lap. I listened to my friends exchange snores for the next hour until I got into radio contact with Kingston's Norman Manley International Airport.

After some brief confusion with the tower, we got clearance to land. I roused Buddy and Spooner and had Buddy go back and wake Jason so he could get strapped in for landing.

The Lady Orleans made a perfect landing, and I taxied her over to a private hangar where the tower had directed me.

We deplaned, and I bargained with the attendant for the tie-up fee, and, I hoped, assistance in cutting through the red tape to get through customs a little quicker.

Except for having to put Spooner in a rented pet carrier, we whizzed through customs. The beagle wasn't pleased about the situation.

Buddy spotted his MP friends smoking in the airport bar. Jason and I grabbed a quick bite to go, while he went over to slap backs and find out what happened.

I introduced Jason to the Jamaican national dish of salt cod and akee. Salt cod is sautéed with akee, pork fat, onions, peppers, tomatoes, herbs, and garnished with crisp bacon and fresh tomatoes.

Buddy came walking back, "Boy, something smells good!"

Jason turned up his nose, handing his akee to Buddy. "Good you can have mine. I don't know how these people can eat fish for breakfast."

He shrugged and devoured the remainder.

"So what did you find out?" I queried impatiently.

"Well," Buddy talked with his mouth full, "Blakely and Jenkins were just released about thirty minutes ago. They caught a cab in front of the airport, and headed off toward the mountains."

"So did they enjoy their drug search?" Jason snickered evilly.

Buddy beamed, "My friends said Jenkins is going to be walking funny for at least a week. Somehow or another, the inspector seemed to have gotten jerk seasoning all over his rubber gloves before the rectal search."

I grinned and Jason fairly crowed. "Old Jonesy will be shitting fireballs for a month!"

"Did they give you any idea where this Ascension Falls place was at in the mountains?" I questioned.

"They had never heard of it." Buddy swallowed the final bite of the akee and salt fish. "But they said if anyone would know it would be the local cabbies. We need to catch one and get on the road as soon as possible to catch up with Blakely and Jenkins."

"Agreed.", and we made our way to the front of the airport.

The cabbies had their routes timed with the arriving commercial planes, so there was only one rusted-out cab waiting at the front of the airport. As we approached, the smell of ganja was extremely strong emanating from the open windows. The cabby was obviously napping off his buzz in the driver's seat, with a newspaper over his face.

I knocked on the windshield. "Hey you on duty, man?"

The cabbie sat up with a slightly glazed look in his eyes, "Ya mon, but it depends on where you be wanting to go?"

I looked over at my friends, who looked like they had no intention of getting into the car with our stoned friend.

"We need to go up into the Blue Mountains, to a place called Ascension Falls to find something called the Black Cauldron," I stated flatly.

The cabbies eyes got huge and white. "No way, mon, you don' wanna go dere, dat whole heap wicked, nuh? Besides it not a place, it a ting. How 'bout I takes you to da nice Blue Mountain bicycle tours?"

I shook my head, "No we have to go to Ascension Falls. In fact some 'friends' of ours just left here, for there, about thirty minutes ago."

"Would you know anything about that?" I asked, handing him a twenty-dollar bill.

He sighed heavily, "Ya mon, that be my friend Quao. He tek a red mon ana truly bashy woman up da mountain road. Ya nuh see it that you cannot find the Black Cauldron by wheels? I be taken ya as far as Nanny Town and the land of da Maroons. From dere who is to say, the Black Cauldron in da magic place dats only seen in da dreams of the Maroon mas."

"I understand. Can you take us as far as Nanny Town?"

He gestured toward the door. "Aright, mon, get in, but dis not gwine to be duh cheap trip."

We piled into the car, and I stuck my hand out to him. "My name is Saint Kristopher."

He shook my hand.

"This is Buddy, and this is…"

"Jah know," he clapped his hands laughing, looking at the battered Jason, "Ju musta be dat Scotch Bonnet!"

Jason grinned and raised his eyebrows in surprise. "Yeah, how did you know?"

He pumped Jason's hand. "Da word travel fass in da Caribbean. I got a bredda-in-law done some fishin ova in Aruba, his name be Bastiaan. He called da oder night rollin on da floor laughin tellin about dis crazy jake wid sunburn and da brokin arm who drunk da sopi all gone."

"That would be our Scotch, all right." Buddy elbowed Jason.

"Mah name be Cudjoe." our cabbie turned to his wheel. "From Kingston we gwin take da road ta Irish Town; from dere we make way to Nanny Town."

He pulled out onto the dusty road. "Is ah very pretty drive in the mountains. Waterfalls spring from da rock along the road and hills be covered wid farms and jungle, both barely holdin' on for da dear life. Da roads dey are in poor repair, and dey few guard rails on da tight mountain pass."

Before long we knew exactly what he meant as we watched the edges of the loose stone-and-mud road crumble from beneath our tires as we made an especially tight curve, around a drop-off that was at least three hundred feet down.

Buddy and Jason had jammed themselves against the far side of the car, and as far away from the cliff's edge as possible. In the passenger seat up front, I gulped and tried to take my mind off the sheer drop mere inches from my shoulder.

"So tell me about these Maroons and this Nanny Town we are going to?" I questioned.

He sighed, "Da Maroons ana Patwah be all dats left of Nanny's people. Nanny was a high nuf priestess of da old religion. She said to have da magical powers. The Patwah da original ones of dis island; da Maroons be all da former slaves who be brought by duh Spanish and duh British. Over years, da Patwah and da Maroon blood be mixed. Now dey all called Maroons, and dey live in da Nanny Town."

I glanced back at Buddy and Jason. "You say this Nanny was some kind of priestess?"

"Ya mon, some say dat Nanny was born in Africa and she be brought to da Jamaica as slave. But my great-grandfader remember her from when he da boy. He say she no look African, she too pale and had da hair da color of shiny copper. Mas elders told dat she been in dis land since da beginning of time, and only walked again cause da people suffered."

"What do you mean the people suffered?" Buddy asked.

"In 1655, da British captured Jamaica from da Spaniards. Spaniards fled da island. Dere slaves be escapen to da isolation of da Blue Mountains, and da Patwah be taen them in. Da British facing da great problem cause da former slaves boxing continuously against dem."

"Wow," Jason commented, "Sounds like a full-scale rebellion?"

"Da British tried to vank da Maroons but good, but it costing dem too much money and men. Dey wanted da peace, but wit da string attached. Da British make a treaty dat said Maroons free men, but in return dey not set free any more slaves."

"And the Maroons refused?" I guessed.

"Day refused, and da British a mind to wipe dem from da face of da earth. Da priestess Nanny come down from da temple to lead dem in dere fight. Nanny be not standin for any of da people not bein free. Da rebel town named da Nanny Town after dat.

"Da Nanny Town be protected well from da British attack. Da town located ona high ridge. Da town oversee da Stony River. There be a nine-hunred foot cliff tween da Stony River and Nanny Town. Along da cliff be a narrow trail leadin to da town. Dat be what we drivin on now.

"In da end, da British gave up and Nanny's people be free. Da Maroons want her to be nuf chieftain of all da people, but she say she priestess not da king. She disappear to her hidden temple in da Blue Mountains, and never seen since."

"Holy cow!" Jason stated unceremoniously. "So how does this Black Cauldron thing fit into this?"

"No Maroon never saw da great temple at Ascension Falls, where she came from, dat her gates. Day say dat Nanny keep a big old black cauldron at da entrance to her gates. Dis huge pot be kept boiling all da time, but don haf no fire under it. A true I heard was dat some British soldiers once follow da Nanny back to her gates. Dey was surprised, cha! At dat strange sight of obeah magic bubblin cauldron. Dey become sleepy and dey fall over in da pot and kyan neba seen again."

We pulled into a little village, as the road abruptly ran out. Chickens ran wild in the dusty paths, chased by screaming dirty-faced children. A dozen haphazard shacks lined both sides of the trail. Old men with rheumy eyes played dominoes on top of a wooden crate. Women carried baskets of washing down the street and to the Stony River, which could be heard roaring in the distance.

"Welcome to da Nanny Town," Cudjoe stated with a smile. "No promise you will find dat Black Cauldron, but you be askin for my cousin Cuffy, he take you down da Stony River by raft, in da direction of da Ascension Falls."

We got out of the car and I slipped Cudjoe a hundred-dollar bill.

"Ja Guide, my friens," he waved a hand, and was gone in a cloud of dust.

I looked around, and felt as though a thousand eyes were burning into us from every direction.

CHAPTER 62

▼

We somehow managed to find Cuffy; he was nowhere near as amenable as his cab-driving cousin. However, with some animated negotiations, we finally got him to agree to take us down the Stony River. He flat refused to take us all the way to Ascension Falls. That was Nanny's Gate, and a very obeah holy place to the Maroons. He would get us close, but then we would be on our own.

As we followed Cuffy down the switchback narrow trail, down the nine hundred-foot cliff face that separated Nanny Town from the Stony River, we caught our first glimpse of Blakely and Jenkins since we had gotten to Jamaica. Far below we could see them stealing a bamboo raft at gunpoint from several men on a small beach that seemed to be the drop-in point for the rafting villagers.

The rafts used by the residents of Nanny Town were little more than half a dozen bamboo sections tied together with hemp. The entire raft was just wide enough to sit on and about eight feet long. It was meant to be poled, rather than paddled, up and down the shallow river. Blakely had taken a seated position toward the front of their raft, and Jenkins was awkwardly trying to steer with the pole. It was obvious that with Jenkins's total ignorance of what he was doing, they would soon be at the mercy of the rapid currents. The deal we struck with Cuffy suddenly seemed like a bargain.

As we made it to the bottom of the cliff trail, and the small beach, we were once again struck by the beauty of this place. The Blue Mountain peaks rose all around us on both sides of the river and seemed almost close enough to touch. To set out without a guide through this wilderness would be a machete-wielding, trailblazing affair. I marveled at how Jason's ancestor and his men had done this so long ago.

We boarded two of the slim rafts. Cuffy stood in the middle of one and tried to counter-balance Buddy and Spooner. Jason and I manned our own raft, which was attached to Cuffy's lead raft by a six-foot hemp rope. The only choice for passengers on these narrow conveyances was to sit cross-legged, Indian style. The inexperienced who tried to stand would surely tip the raft over. Only Cuffy, as the pole man on the lead raft, stood.

We pushed out into the rough water of the Stony River. Cuffy expertly guided the rafts around hidden rocks, whirlpools, and small waterfalls. I could only imagine what kind of shape Blakely and Jenkins were in by now. There were too many curves and blind bends in the river for us to catch site of them. I kept scanning the rocks, expecting to see their beaten bodies and broken raft piled up around every corner.

The lush river jungle was a gorgeous site. Even at this time of the day, mist still floated over the water. The botanical richness of these mountains was amazing. Initially, the river passed through an elfin forest of stunted soapwood and rodwood trees, their low canopy resulting from the extreme climatic conditions. Gradually, the cloud forest replaced the stunted trees with their dense, shaded undergrowth of mosses, lichens, ferns, and lianas. Finally the riverbanks changed a third time, giving way to primeval tree ferns, bamboos, and shrubs.

It was right before we passed into this third phase that Cuffy called back to us. "You be makin your own way soon. I not be goin any closer dan dis to Ascension Falls and Nanny's Gate."

Before I could answer, I saw something ahead, piled up against a rock outcrop, in the middle of the river. At first I thought it was Blakely and Jenkins, getting their just deserts at last, but then I realized it was something bigger.

Buddy with his forward position, got the words out before I did, "Holy Shit, it's a wrecked plane!"

I glanced back at Jason who had gone pale. It wasn't just a wrecked plane; it was the same plane we had seen in a Polaroid, paper-clipped to a page of Donnie Rhodes's journal.

From appearances it looked like Rhodes had tried to make a water landing on the Stony River, and had misjudged the tricky currents. One wing was completely gone. He had probably dropped its tip into the water when landing. This would have caused him to cartwheel in the shallow water, ultimately slamming against the huge rock outcropping. The Jaegas's ass was in the water, and her parrot head was forever pointing forlornly toward the sky.

Jason's voice cracked behind me, as we floated closer to the wreck of the Jaega, "Cuffy, what do you know about that plane wreck ahead?"

"Na much to know, mon," Cuffy shrugged. "It been dare bedder dan ten year now."

"Do you know if there were any survivors?" Jason almost whispered.

"I don tink so, mon." Cuffy turned to our raft and gestured at the river. "Wha Nanny wan, she get, and we don mess wid it. We be passin nearest 'bout now. You see da pilot man still be in his seat, waitin for Nanny to let him fly once mo."

And at that second, we did pass within about thirty feet of the Jaega. With trepidation, all of our eyes scanned the cockpit.

There he sat; there was no doubt who the skeleton was. The rags he wore were the once fine clothes of a notorious Charleston businessman and con artist. The skull that was cocked half out of the missing pilot's window still wore the mirrored aviation sunglasses and the faded navy captain's hat. A bony arm extended out of the window frame as if trying to hitch a ride as we went past. It was the final landing place for Donnie Rhodes.

We floated past in silence, and rounded a bend. I looked back at Jason, but he was still staring back in the direction of the Jaega. Buddy and I shared a look of concern for our friend. Jason and Rhodes had never really been what you would call close, but he was still his uncle.

I started to try to form the words to tell Jason how sorry I was, but Cuffy abruptly pulled the two rafts upon a shallow sandbar midriver.

"Dis be as fa as I go, mon. Ascension Falls just round da nex corner, but I still tink it be bad idea for you be goin to Nanny's Gate!"

"We'll be okay, Cuffy." I waded out onto the sandbar. "We appreciate you bringing us this far." I shook his hand.

"No problem, mon, you tree and da doggie, be needin to all ride on da one raft. I take da oder back wid me."

Buddy grabbed Spooner and made his way back to our raft.

Cuffy turned and with muscular arms started poling the first raft back up the river. "Ja Guide, my friens, I be hopin you not be dead soon."

Buddy grinned crookedly at Jason and me. "I really hope that means good luck in Jamaican."

CHAPTER 63

▼

We all turned in the direction that Cuffy had motioned down the river. Beyond the sandbar the water took a noticeable slope downward, as it went round the next bend. There was an audible roar that drifted back to us around the corner.

"Sounds like rough water ahead," Jason ventured.

"The name of anything water related, with the word 'falls' in it scares the shit out of me," Buddy agreed.

"Look at the rocks ahead though," I pointed out. "The river doesn't appear to be anymore than two or three feet deep down there. Surely we can sit on the raft and pole ourselves slowly. If it starts getting too rough, we'll just stand up and wade out."

"Famous last words if I ever heard them," Jason grinned. "I'm game!"

"You guys are determined to friggin' drown my ass, aren't you?"

"Hey you gotta face your fears sometime, Big Guy," I smirked.

We all straddled the raft, our legs hanging over into the frigid water, just in case we had to make a hasty exit. Spooner sat in the front at point, then me, Buddy, and Jason last. We took the pole with us, but it was pretty useless in our inexperienced hands. We more or less floated down and around the bend, and into whatever was waiting for us there.

Around the corner was a sight that we would never have believed, if we hadn't seen it ourselves. The angle of the river grew progressively steeper downhill for the next five-hundred yards, and then there was a huge three hundred-foot waterfall where the roaring torrent flowed straight up.

"Jesus Christ!" Buddy yelled above the water's roar, "The damn waterfall is flowing backward!"

"Now we know why they call it Ascension Falls!" Jason barked up to Buddy. "Grantford, how the hell does it do that?"

"I'm guessing it's like Spook Hill!" I shouted.

"That place in Lake Wales, Florida, where the cars roll uphill?" Buddy questioned.

"Yeah!" I bellowed above the noise, "Spook Hill is actually an optical illusion. The lay of the land creates the illusion of a small dip that should cause cars to roll forward, but instead cars drift backward, seemingly uphill. It's not obvious that you are really on a down slope the whole time, even when you feel like you are going uphill. This is the same kind of thing, only on a much larger scale."

"Look there!" Jason pointed frantically.

Far below, just starting up the waterfall was Blakely and Jenkins's raft. They were both in the water up to their necks, and clinging to the raft for dear life.

I watched in horror, as they seemingly defied gravity and began floating up the waterfall. It was then I noticed that about halfway up the falls was a gaping hole. Water rushed into the hole, which I think was actually down, but the optical illusion screwed up your perceptions. The excess water that couldn't flow into the hole flowed around it and over the top of the falls.

We watched transfixed, as Blakely and Jenkins fought and kicked to keep from being sucked into that black hole. The battle was in vain; they were dragged up and into the void!

We had now floated to within a few hundred yards of the base of the falls ourselves. At this range, we were astonished to realize that the opening in the waterfall was actually the huge gaping maw of a stone panther's head carved into the solid rock wall of the falls.

We also realized that we had almost waited too late to stop ourselves from following in Blakely and Jenkins's footsteps. Unfortunately we all got the idea to wade ashore at the same time. We tried to swing off the side of the raft. The combined momentum of all of us getting off the raft, and stepping into the rushing white water, caused the nose of the raft to dip down, with only poor Spooner's weight on the front. The little dog immediately went into the drink, and despite frantically trying to swim back to us, he was quickly tiring and losing the race.

"Spooner!" Buddy yelled and went splashing after him. Jason and I were close behind, but suddenly the water level rose to four feet. We could barely hold ourselves upright in the raging torrent.

Buddy looked back at us, his abject fear of water on his face, and the total panic in his eyes for the dog. Spooner was now being pulled up the falls.

Jason and I looked at each other.

I raised my eyebrows. "What do you say, Scotch?"

"I say the Krewe of Jupiter stays together. Despite the fact that the beagle hates my guts, he's just as much a part of the Krewe as the rest of us!"

I grinned, "Grab the raft then, and let's go get Buddy and Spooner!"

Jason and I threw our chests over the raft, and kicked frantically in Buddy's direction. We picked Buddy up and added his motivation to our forward motion. Jason was paddling in the middle, with Buddy and me on each end of the raft. We reached the little dog about a quarter of the way up the falls, just as he was going down for the last time. Jason dragged his soaked body up onto the raft. The poor dog was exhausted, but had just enough strength to raise his head and lick him from the bottom of his chin to the tip of his nose. Jason beamed at Buddy and me.

Then we all turned our attention to the great stone panther's head that our raft was being drawn into. Like it or not, we were entering Nanny's Gate!

CHAPTER 64

▼

As we were swallowed by the great stone panther's jaws, the optical illusion of Ascension Falls was instantly broken. There was no doubt about which way was down because gravity pulled us there abruptly.

We literally fell through the mouth and straight down fifty feet into a large lagoon. Our raft was bashed to pieces on impact with the water.

We all came blubbering to the surface, coughing and spitting. Buddy started yelling and floundering madly. It was then that I realized that the Big Guy couldn't swim. I made my way over to him, got an arm around his neck, and got him to relax and calm down. I got him a handhold on a couple of the floating bamboo poles that remained of the raft.

Jason paddled over, still supporting the exhausted Spooner. "Why didn't you tell us you couldn't swim, Buddy?"

"Why the hell do you think I didn't join the Navy?" he grumbled.

I looked around, "Man, would you look at this place!"

We were in an enormous natural cave that ran behind Ascension Falls. The huge stalactite formations hanging from the rounded concave ceiling above us reminded me of what we had seen below the Hooiberg in Aruba. The water pouring in from the panther's mouth far above created a beautiful waterfall that fed the huge lagoon we were floating in. Even more spectacular, the entire end of the cave opposite the waterfall was totally open, and a huge sheet of roaring water covered it completely it. The lagoon also drained into this torrent.

It was then that I realized the paradox of Ascension Falls. The optical illusion gave you the feeling that you were going up the waterfall, when in reality you were still traveling downhill. If you didn't go through the panther's maw, and instead rode all the way to the top of the falls, you would have expected calm water at the top. Instead, you would have been confronted with the true falls, and a three hundred-foot drop to the rocks below. It was these falls that covered the rear opening of the cavern.

"Check out the island!" Buddy pointed toward the center of the lagoon.

Indeed, there was a small island in the middle of the lagoon, complete with palm trees, and some kind of structure on it, although we couldn't tell what at this distance. We also could see Blakely and Jenkins dragging their soggy asses up onto the shore.

I could feel the current pulling us toward the brink where the lagoon spilled its waters into the torrential sheet of the great falls. "We better move toward the island," I advised, "or we are going to get swept out into the real falls."

We all started paddling toward the small island a couple of hundred yards away. Thankfully, the current pulling us toward the brink wasn't overpowering yet. When we got closer, we could feel sand and rock under our feet. We trudged through the choppy water toward the beach.

Jason whistled. "Well, that's the last thing I would have expected to find in the middle of a cave in Jamaica!"

We agreed. Nestled among the palms in the middle of the tiny island was an old, white, two-story, clapboard-style farmhouse. Smoke curled out of the chimney. A winding path led from the beach to the huge front porch, complete with a porch swing. The path sported a hand-painted sign saying, Nanny's House and Travelers Rest.

I looked at Buddy and Jason as we dragged ourselves onshore. Spooner was finally able to stand on shaky legs.

"I've got a bad feeling about this," Buddy sighed heavily.

"Yeah, me, too, but you know that's where Blakely and Jenkins went."

Jason set his jaw stubbornly. "We can't let that bitch get hold of the book of Legacy and Destiny. We have to follow!"

We made our way up the winding path, past gardens of tropical flowers. The porch step creaked and groaned as we made our way to the front door. There was no wooden door, just a rusty screen door with white gingerbread trim. We all took a deep breath, opened the screen door on its protesting spring, and went inside.

There was a huge hole right near the entrance with a velvet rope hanging around it. Above the hole floated a black, bubbling pot. The hole was so near the door that we had to step around it to keep from falling in.

The acrid smell of burning tar, which emanated from the pot, made my head ache and throb, and my vision swim. Whatever gases were coming out of that pot were doing a number on my mind's eye.

"Damn," Jason commented. "It's like a bad acid trip."

Buddy grunted, although he had never touched anything harder than baby aspirin his entire life.

I kept trying to shake the cobwebs out of my head. It was like seeing double. When I concentrated hard, the floating black cauldron turned into a natural tar pool, and the house faded to jungle; but when my attention lapsed, I could see the floating cauldron again.

On one side of the hole sat half-dozen old women in rocking chairs; on the other side was a sign-in desk manned by a gorgeous woman with copper red hair in a black bellman's outfit. The desk had a huge guest registration book on it. The lady was smoking a cigarette from a long holder.

Buddy glanced back at us and spoke in a voice as slow as molasses, "Do you guys feel like we just fell down a rabbit hole?"

"It's got to be the gas from the tar pit playing tricks with our heads," I whispered.

We made our way around the huge gaping hole to the registration desk. Buddy paused to pick up Spooner, and I fell back to wait on him. Blakely and Jenkins were already there, eyes transfixed on the hole.

The whole place was dimly lit by what appeared to be lanterns. There were no other furnishings in the room—only the gaping abyss, which went straight down. Although it seemed bottomless, steps ran down its side for as far as we could see.

As we walked up, Blakely and Jenkins finally snapped out of their trance. Jenkins tried to pull his pistol, and Blakely pulled the spear gun from her leg holster. Instantly, Jenkins's pistol changed into a fist-sized hairy spider, and the spear gun turned into a two-foot snake. They both squealed and dropped their weapons, which scurried into the gaping hole. The old women in their chairs stopped their languid rocking, and mumbled and cackled.

The redhead removed her cigarette and purred, "Oh, you won't be needing those. You weary travelers here for a journey's rest, or to see our little roadside attraction?" She gestured toward the hole in the floor.

Jenkins glared at us and turned to the lady. "Look, you freak. I'm here for the diamonds. If that hole in the floor is the way to get to them, then that's what I'm here for!"

Blakely pushed Jenkins aside roughly and used a softer voice that belied the fire in her eyes, "What we are looking for is an ancient book called Legacy and Destiny. What can you tell us about that?"

The bellman's eyes twinkled; she ignored Blakely. "Right there is the entrance to our world-famous Patwah Caverns, but they're closed being that it's so late at night."

I glanced out the screen door, knowing it was no more than four in the afternoon. Indeed, the island had fallen into twilight, and if I didn't know better I would have sworn I saw thousand of fireflies winking in the garden.

The bellman offered Blakely and Jenkins a room to stay in and asked them to sign their name in the registration book.

Jenkins removed the Marocoti *zemís* from his shirt, and slammed it down on the registration desk. "Look, lady, I don't want no fucking room. I want those goddamn diamonds!"

The crones stopped rocking and leapt from their seats.

The lady put up her hand to halt them. "Ah, I see that you already have a room key! Why didn't you say so?"

The old women stood still but didn't return to their rockers. They merely stared at Jenkins and Blakely through thick silver spectacles.

The bellman picked up the huge registration book in one delicate hand and began flipping pages. "Yes, yes, here we go. That would be the Bonnet Room."

Jason raised his eyebrows at the mention of his family name.

The lady continued, "Quite sad what happened to that chap, made a mess of things for us here, killing Nanny as he did, and chopping down our beautiful old Patwah tree to build a boat of all things."

"Spare me the history lesson," Jenkins grumbled. "Just tell me where to find the diamonds."

"Well, I'm afraid it's not that easy, my friend." The bellman smiled at him, revealing sharp incisors. "You see, after that nasty episode with Mr. Bonnet, certain safety precautions were put in place to ensure that Nanny's property would never again be used for evil. Anyone can insert the key, but only one with pure intentions can open the door."

Jason spoke up from his position behind Jenkins, and slightly ahead of us, "But didn't Stede Bonnet make retribution? He brought the three treasures, one to each temple, to make amends."

"That he did," she turned her steely eyes to him. "His plan was to sacrifice the treasure but to keep the great book. The ancient guardians could never allow that to happen. True repentance was never attained."

Jenkins growled, "Enough of the bullshit just show me where the diamonds are!"

"Very well." The tip of her red tongue escaped her lips. She touched a spot in the registration book, and a wide dark board appeared that led from the floor to the lip of the boiling cauldron.

I noticed Blakely eyeing the cover of the registration book. I followed her line of sight. There were three initials on the cover of the great tome: L A D. I nudged Buddy, and pointed to the book. He squinted and then nodded at me.

"What the hell am I supposed to do with that?" Jenkins demanded.

The bellman closed the book and set it back on the registration desk, picking up her cigarette holder, "If you want to share Nanny's bounty, you have to unlock the gate. Enter Nanny's cauldron with the key. If you are worthy, what is Nanny's will be yours."

Jenkins turned toward the cauldron apprehensively.

"Don't be a fucking idiot, Jenkins!" Blakely cautioned, but Jenkins had already started up the board.

We all watched transfixed. Jenkins got to the end of the board and peered down into the bubbling pot. The cauldron was filled with hot tar that emitted a euphoric stench. The cauldron was a good twelve feet across. A tumultuous gaseous belch from its gullet sent bubbles into the air. The registration book glowed in the woman's hands as each bubble rose and carried an image from ancient times.

The original Patwah tree in all its grandeur, providing food for the followers of the priestess called Nanny. The three *zemís* that were the root and beginning of all three trees. The great battles for the trees, with the death of all but the Patwah, which turned black and no longer bore fruit. The arrival of Stede Bonnet, the murder of Nanny, and the destruction of the Patwah tree. Bonnet's attempt at penance, and its failure. The book's return to the Patwah temple, and Bonnet's escape with the Patwah *zemís*. And finally, the plane crash on the great river, and the sole survivor swimming to shore on the little island.

Jenkins turned back to the bellman from his perch on the lip of the cauldron. "Are you sure about this?"

"If you have the key, and you are worthy, what is Nanny's will be yours," she repeated.

Jenkins turned back to the bubbling pot, held the Marocoti *zemís* in front of him, and without another word stepped off the edge of the plank.

"No, you moron!" Blakely yelled. But it was too late.

Jenkins dropped from sight. The great black pot boiled with even greater fury. We held our breath, staring at the black storm.

There was a great belch that sloshed tar into the pit below. The floor of the house shook, and the old ones pawed, mewed, and held on to each other for comfort.

Suddenly a dark form bobbed to the surface of the pot. It was Jenkins, or what was left of him. The hot tar had boiled half the skin from his bones, and only the stark white of his eyes wasn't covered in tar. His mouth was frozen in an eternal scream.

Blakely gave voice to Jenkins's last silent scream!

He tilted to the side and sank back into the pot.

Blakely's horror changed from abject fear to rage. She turned to the bellman. "You murdered him in cold blood!"

"He went of his own will, and was judged not worthy by Nanny's cauldron." The lady frowned sympathetically. "According to the book of Legacy and Destiny, it is no less than what he has done to many before himself."

"I'm sick of this shit!" Blakely growled. She grabbed the book of Legacy and Destiny from the redhead's hands. "This is all I came for anyway!"

"That would be unwise." The bellman put a hand on Blakely's arm.

"Fuck off, sister!" Blakely pushed the bellman back against the wall, and turned to barrel through Jason, Buddy, and me to get to the door.

She never got the chance. Behind her, the six old women changed into their ancient guardian forms. Each old lady was composed of hundreds of moth-like, winged arrow worms.

They were all over Blakely before she was able to take a step in our direction. I turned my head at the carnage as the beasts tore her to pieces. She had time to scream once, and then the air was filled with the sounds of crunching bone and ripping and tearing flesh. Jason and Buddy had turned their heads as well, unable to watch.

It was over in less than a minute, and when we turned to look again, there wasn't even a stain on the floor. The book was back on the registration desk, and the six old women were humming and rocking contentedly in their chairs.

With great trepidation, we walked up to the desk. The bellman winked at us, and then she was no longer the bellman, but a beautiful red-haired goddess in a flowing white gown.

"Are...are you Nanny?" Buddy mumbled fearfully.

She laughed, a light sound like the tinkling of a wind chime, "No, the body of Nanny passed long ago at the hands of Stede Bonnet, but her spirit still lives in this place."

"Then who are you?" Jason asked.

"Maybe this will answer your question," she turned her back to us. The gown dipped low in the back, baring the beautiful curve of her body, and a white, wandering rose tattooed up her spine.

"Mirasel Rose!" I murmured in awe. "Your father asked me to try to find you and the book."

"Yes I know, and the book of Legacy and Destiny would be good in the hands of the Travelers. Here it's helping no one; out there in the world it can continue the destiny it once fulfilled."

"Then why don't you bring it back with us?" Buddy ventured.

"I am not looking to be rescued. My destiny is to continue Nanny's legacy on this island, and to help the Patwah and the Maroons flourish once more."

"But the book—" I said. "Will the ancient guardians let anyone else touch it?"

Mirasel shook her head. "After the book was retrieved from Bonnet, a powerful curse was put on it that prevents the guardians from ever letting it leave here again, until penance for the murder of Nanny is finally done."

I looked at Mirasel. "But how can that ever happen? Stede Bonnet has been dead for nearly three hundred years."

Mirasel Rose looked evenly at Jason. "It is his birthright."

"Me?" Jason squeaked.

She affirmed solemnly. "The red man put the key in the lock. The one who makes penance must turn the key and open the door."

"Hold on, lady," Buddy interrupted, "I hope you aren't saying what I think you are. Jason isn't going to take a swan dive into that black cauldron!"

She shook her head. "He should not, if his intentions are pure. If his penance isn't true and sincere, he will suffer the same fate as that of the red man."

"Jason, you can't really be thinking of doing this?"

"It would be good to get the book, for the Church of the White Rose, I mean. Plus I could finally clean up my family name."

I thought back to the words that Rowland Rhodes had said to me, "I don't know your friend, but if the blood of Stede Bonnet courses through his veins, I wouldn't trust him. You can't let him get his hands on that book. The results could be disastrous."

"Jason, this is nothing to screw around with," I insisted. "This is serious. What if you're really not sincere?"

Jason looked at me long and hard. "Grantford, all my life I've been running from ghosts. I've always played the con, worked the angles. I've always done whatever it took to get ahead. I never killed anybody or anything like that. But it was always the little sins, but little sins all add up in a big way. It's not that I wanted to be that way; it's like I always had my great-great-great-grandfather looking up from hell, goading me to do whatever it was that I was doing. He never learned his lesson, and he suffered for it. Maybe, just maybe this is my chance to learn mine. And by doing it, I can finally put the Gentleman Pirate's ghost to rest forever."

Buddy and I looked at each other apprehensively.

"It's your call, Scotch." Buddy patted his shoulder, using his new nickname.

"Whatever happens, Jason"—I looked him in the eye—"I just want you to know that I'm glad you are a part of my life again."

Jason's eyes started welling up with tears. He scratched Spooner between the ears and turned quickly to Mirasel Rose. "What do I have to do?"

She handed him a golden thimble, with an ornate panther head and roaring fangs on its tip. "Enter Nanny's Cauldron. Just as you do, draw blood with the fangs of the thimble. If your penance is true, all will be well."

He squared his jaw, taking the golden thimble. He walked slowly up the plank to the lip of the boiling cauldron. All of the little old ladies were sitting up and taking notice. Jason turned back to us and gave a little wave. He raked the fangs of the panther thimble across the palm of his hand, and fell face-first into the boiling tar.

I squeezed Buddy's shoulder as we held our breath. Suddenly the black cauldron began to spin. The black board fell into the pit below. The faster the pot spun, the larger it got. The wind roared. The crones metamorphosed once again, dancing and flying around the pot in jubilation.

"We've got to get out of here," I yelled above the din. "The cauldron is going to destroy the house!"

"Mirasel, come with us!" Buddy bellowed above the noise.

She smiled gently, and shook her head.

Buddy had a tight grip on Spooner, and I pulled both of them out of the front door and down the steps.

The entire house was breathing in and out as the spinning cauldron forced the air out of the place. There were creaks and groans as the wood frame started to give and buckle. We ran for the shore, and the house exploded in every direction. The cauldron was a massive spinning black blur, and I realized that as it spun, it was sinking into the ground. The wind generated by the rotation of the huge pot swayed the palm trees and gardens as if they were caught in a colossal hurricane.

Then the top of the cauldron was level with the ground, and the spinning ground to a stop. We ventured a look. The top of the pot looked like a small pond of bubbling tar now, a good fifty feet across. We moved toward it, and the ground started rumbling beneath our feet.

Buddy and I gave each other a "what now" look.

From the far edge of the tar pool, something was rising out of the murk. At first I thought it was a man, but then I saw that the upraised arms contained a sickle and a bundle of grain. It was a twelve-foot-high version of the Marocoti *zemts*. It fell into the middle of the tar pool with a mighty splash and sank from sight!

There was a brief period of silence, and then the rumbling started anew. This time the force was so strong that it knocked us off our feet. We scrambled to our knees to see what was happening!

From the middle of the tar pit, a huge tree was growing. It grew at an astonishing rate in both height and width, but this wasn't the blackened stumps and roots that I had seen in the other temples. This was a dynamic, living, glowing tree that spread in every direction and grew to the top of the cavern, burst through, and kept on growing!

Stalactites were falling everywhere, but we couldn't move; we were so fixated by its glory! Right before our eyes, the tree began bearing fruit! Every fruit, vegetable, and grain known, and some that are not, hung heavy from its branches.

The great Patwah tree was once again of this earth!

CHAPTER 65

▼

As we looked up at the tree, I was reminded of what Jason had told us that Stede Bonnet had first seen, "It would have taken thirty linked men to stretch around it. It flew so high into the island sky that it seemed to reach heaven."

We watched the growth of the tree slow and stop. As the last thirty feet rose from the tar pit, a doorway appeared in the shape of the maw of a roaring panther head. It sat up high, fifteen feet above the base of the tree.

Stunned, Buddy, Spooner, and I just stood there at the edge of the tar pool. The huge, glowing tree with all its fruit was miraculous. There was nothing left of the clapboard house. The tree had punched a massive hole in the cavern under Ascension Falls, through which a torrent of water now poured into the lagoon!

The gardens were still intact, and now the fireflies returned to wink on and off around the base of the tree as if nothing had happened.

A figure appeared in the doorway of the tree.

"It's Jason!" Buddy yelled.

We skirted the edge of the tar pit as quickly as we could to get to the tree.

Natural steps carved into the side of the trunk allowed us to climb up to him in quick order.

Buddy got there first and gave Jason a huge bear hug.

"Okay, okay, Big Guy," he laughed. "You're breaking my ribs!"

I came over and gave Jason a big hug, too. "We thought you were a goner there, Scotch!"

Spooner barked happily at our feet.

"So what happened?"

He laughed wistfully. "Well, from the second I fell into the Cauldron, I found myself sitting cross-legged in front of Nanny. She is really quite a cool old lady. She made me feel warm and loved, and she helped me to understand who I am and who I am going to be. I tried to tell her I was sorry for what my ancestor had done to her, but she just held a finger to my lips and told me to hush about that. She knew I was sorry, and that all was forgiven. The next thing I knew I was waking up inside the tree here."

We looked at each other skeptically, but with all the strangeness we had witnessed lately, nothing really surprised us.

"Your penance was well received, Jason Bonnet!" said a voice issuing from the dark of the tree.

We all turned to see Mirasel Rose walking toward us. She was beaming broadly. She carried the book of *Legacy and Destiny* under one arm, and held the hand of a very young child, wearing nothing but a loin cloth, in the other.

She handed the book to Jason. "Take this back to my father and the Church of the White Rose. Tell him to use it for all the good that it can bring."

She turned to me, "Saint Kristopher Grant, I have a special favor to ask of you. Before Donnie Rhodes and I came here, we had become lovers. When our plane crashed above the falls, Donnie didn't make it, but his unborn son and I survived. His name is Cameron Marley. I know that you love one who is lost to you forever. I know that you can never replace the loss, but perhaps you can share your love with my son. I must remain here, but he needs to be a part of your world. Will you take my son, Saint Kristopher, and raise him as your own?"

I bent down on one knee in front of Cameron Marley. He had curly red hair like his mother and dark snapping eyes like his father. "Hi, Cameron," I grinned. "I have twin girls who are going to love you very much!"

He turned and hugged his mother shyly, and I could see the wandering white rose tattoo on his back. He peeked back at me under his arm with a sly grin. I tousled his hair, and stood up with a nod to Mirasel.

"Buddy, Scotch," I beamed, "I think it's about time to head the Krewe of Jupiter back home!"

I took Cameron's hand and we walked toward the steps.

Buddy sighed, "It's too bad that we never found any of the treasure in this entire adventure."

Mirasel Rose grinned, "Thanks for reminding me!" She touched the book under Jason's arm and all of the fireflies seemed to land on the nearest leaf or branch at once. When each one touched down, it turned into a shimmering diamond.

"Please take them. I have no use for them here."

Jason, Buddy, Spooner, and I took Cameron out into the tropical garden to teach him the fine art of hunting diamond Easter eggs.

EPILOGUE

—————————— ▼ ——————————

We've been back in Jupiter now for almost six months. Cameron is adjusting well to life at La Vie Dansante. His adopted sisters were ecstatic to have a new baby brother. Lil was a little surprised, but she welcomed Cameron Marley with open arms.

As to be expected, Lil was pretty shaken up after the ordeal. At her insistence, we built a hedge around the entire perimeter of the property, which conceals an electric fence. I hated to isolate us like that, but I understand Lil's fear. We each hold each other a little tighter at night. We have survived worse in our lives. I know that Lil will survive this too.

We used part of the diamonds to salvage the Jaega, and to ship the remains of Donnie Rhodes back to Charleston for proper burial. We made the trek to Charleston to attend Rhodes's funeral with Aunt Edna and Otis. Otis and Jason, who everyone seems to now call Scotch, were good-naturedly back at each other's throats again.

We had to fly commercial to Charleston, as Jack Mason had the Lady Orleans sequestered for a full restoration, and wouldn't hear of an early release. We all went down to Calypso's yesterday for the grand unveiling. The old girl looked great! Jack had made her as good as new all the way around, and she had shed her rust and mud-bog apparel for a brand-new shiny blue coat of paint to match her engines. Jack was feeling pretty proud of himself, until I gave him his next project, the restoration of the Jaega, which had been sitting in a jungle river for over a decade. He cussed and blustered about, insisting that I thought he must be Jesus H. Christ and capable of miracles. When we left the Calypso hanger, Jack was happily yelling orders to the Betancur brothers as they scurried around the husk of the Jaega.

We delivered the book of Legacy and Destiny to a grateful Rowland Rose. Two days later his traveling snake-show circus had pulled up stakes and disappeared from the face of the earth.

Jason has decided to move down to Jupiter full-time. Aunt Edna gave him the Gator Tail, and we spent the rest of the diamonds on restoring the bar and hotel. He should be ready for the grand reopening in another couple of weeks. He even got the big neon sign working again, complete with the tail that moves. Unlike Donnie Rhodes's version, the new Gator Tail has a nice waterside restaurant and bar to accompany its restored hotel rooms, rather than a strip club. In honor of his great-great-great-grandfather, Jason is naming the bar part of The Gator Tail, The Gentleman Pirates.

Seems the Widow Biddy Jenkins came into quite a windfall of insurance money, upon our confirmation of Jones Jenkins's death. She showed her gratitude to Buddy in a multitude of ways, one of the public ones being to give him the pink slip of the *Nefarious*. It's kind of ironic that someone as deathly afraid of the water as our Buddy Bear is now living on a boat! Jason invited him to dock the *Nefarious* at the Gator Tail, so I once again have my dojo back above the garage. It took Buddy about a week before he was able to find the few remaining rubies that Jenkins had stashed aboard ship. He is using them to replace all the worldly possessions that his ex-wife stole from him.

I just got an email from Shrimper Dan. Apparently he got a mysterious message from someone who claims to be his long-lost daughter. Dan's ecstatic, as he assumed that the child died in childbirth with her mother. I'll have to pay him a call on Peanut Island tomorrow to find out what that's all about.

Me? I was just sitting here in my library in front of the computer, watching Cameron and the girls catching fireflies in the twilight outside my big bay window. Spooner is hopping around them like Tigger, snapping at the little winking beacons.

Then the phone on my desk rang, "Hello, Saint Kristopher, here."

"Saint Kristopher, this is Remy de Haviland."

"Remy, holy shit, we thought you were dead and buried under a hundred tons of rock!"

"Ah, as I told Mr. Jenkins, It will take a lot better man than him to take me out. The Guarao used the same secret passageway that I used years ago to get back into the chamber to rescue me. I'm an old man, and it took me months to recuperate, but here I am talking to you on the phone!"

I shook my head with a big smile. I'm not sure if Remy convinced me to lead my life as if everything is a miracle, but I'm definitely no longer living it as if nothing is.

THE END

0-595-32339-1

Printed in the United States
26948LVS00003B/49-255